Blue Like

Ian MacCabe

*To my beautiful Kochand.
All my love
Ian ♡ xxxy*

Copyright 2019 Ian MacCabe

All rights reserved

Cover Painting and design by

Ian MacCabe.

For Mary

Born under a bad sign, if it wasn't for bad luck,
I wouldn't have no luck at all.

William Bell

Prologue

Breathing heavily, the big man stepped back and looked impassively down at the figure lying at his feet. The figure, stretched out semi-conscious on the floor, was a short, stocky, middle-aged man known on the street as, Ari the Gun. His once sallow Greek face had been beaten to a bloody pulp.

Ari lay on his back, and his laboured breathing came in raspy, uneven gasps. The absurd comb-over hairstyle he normally sported had been knocked awry, and his bald head was now exposed and streaked with blood.

The nickname referred to his trade, although he himself never carried one, Ari the Gun supplied guns to anyone who had the cash to buy them. He bought replica weapons cheap on the Continent, and then had them re-bored and modified to fire live ammunition. And although he sold these weapons on at up to £500 a time, and was never short of clients, you would never have guessed by the way he lived and dressed.

It hadn't taken too long for the bulky figure, now towering over him, to find out all about Ari's business. The big man was well aware his method of extracting information from people wasn't unique, but it worked: he simply scared the shit out of them.

As he continued to look down at his handiwork, there was not a flicker of emotion in his eyes. He crouched down and went through the man's pockets, but could find nothing of worth except a crumpled five pound note, some small change, and a less than half-full pack of Marlboro reds. He lit one, and then slipping the pack into his jacket pocket, he looked round the grubby room, and his face creased in a frown.

"Listen you fucker," he said, not bothering to look at his victim. "I know you got a lotta money stashed away somewhere in this shit-hole. In London, I was given your name by a former associate of yours, who wasn't too fuckin happy with the way you shafted him in a deal. He owed me a big favour, and convinced me it would be more than worth my while coming up here and paying you a visit. So here I am."

He tossed his cigarette onto the grubby carpet and ground it into the pile with his boot. Squatting down he then began patting the man's body, frisking it down, and then, suddenly, his eyebrows arched when he felt something under the waistband of the cheap suit.

"Gotcha," he said, ripping open the man's shirt and trouser waistband to reveal a money belt. It took him a minute or so to find and undo the release; but when he did, he stood up and yanked on the belt so hard that Ari the gun was flung onto his side, where he lay groaning and helpless.

The belt had four narrow pouches, and every one held a neatly folded thick bundle of fifty-pound notes. The big man slowly nodded his head at the sight of the money, and then stuffed the contents of the belt into the two inside pockets of his leather coat.

As he did this, he noticed drops of blood fall onto his sleeve, and realised he had forgotten about his nose. This bloody reminder instantly made him aim a vicious kick to the fallen man's groin, causing Ari to emit a raw, wheezing gasp of air.

Ari the gun had not gone down without drawing blood, however. As all of his clients were gangsters, his instincts were well honed to sense when something bad was coming his way.

Earlier in the evening, when a large black man had approached him in his local pub, and placed a large Scotch in front of him, he was naturally suspicious; but then again, business was business, and the pub was, after all, his office. The man had intimated that he had heard from a reliable source, that Ari was the man to see if he wanted to get hold of a gun. Ari had replied that possibly this could be arranged, and so, after a few more large scotches, they had gone back to Ari's flat.

Unbeknown to his new client, however, the sole reason Ari had agreed to the big man accompanying him back to his dingy apartment, was that he had expected his usual backup to be there. This backup took the form of his hulking young brother, Demetrius, and his even more formidable cousin, Yannis, both of whom shared the flat with Ari, and were always present at these meetings.

On entering the flat, however, Ari had found it to be unoccupied, which had immediately made him a very anxious man. Once inside of course, he'd had no option but to proceed with the transaction. He had pointed to an armchair in the living room, and motioned for the big man to take a seat, saying it would take him a minute or so to fetch a sample of his goods from another room.

After closing the bedroom door, Ari had used his mobile phone in a desperate attempt to contact Demetrius, in order to get him and his cousin immediately back to the flat, but he got no answer. The best he could do was to leave an angry, whispered voicemail message, all the time cursing to himself for not phoning earlier from the pub, to make sure they were home.

Moments later, he had come back into the living room carrying a roughly wrapped greaseproof package. Unwrapping the package, he had laid the unloaded gun on the cluttered coffee table, and then sat in a chair opposite his client. Ari's unease had been further heightened when the big man hadn't even attempted to look at, or touch the gun, but had continued to stare directly and coldly back at him.

Ari gave it a moment, and then swallowing nervously, had asked to see his client's money. But when the big man gave a mirthless laugh, Ari had sensed immediately, that his initial suspicions were soon to be realised.

"Listen, ya greasy little fucker, I'm not ere to give you money," said the big man, in an icy business-like tone. "I'm ere to take yours."

Even though he had drunk a fair amount of whiskey, Ari had still been equipped with enough presence of mind to attempt to defend his hard-earned cash. He looked the big man straight in the eye, and the instant he saw him start to raise his bulky frame from the chair, he had grabbed a large chipped cut-glass ashtray from the coffee table, and brought it down hard on the bridge of the big man's nose; it was the only time he landed a blow.

For a few seconds the big man's eyes had stood out in his head; it was as if he was thinking: *how could this bald headed little fucker have the nerve to do something like that?*

Ari had instantly dropped the ashtray, and then leaping up, had tried to make a run for the door. But like lightning, the big man had lunged, and picking Ari up by the neck, had shaken him like a doll, causing the smaller man's glasses to fly into the air.

He had then pinned the defenceless Ari against the wall and began punching him repeatedly in the face, his multi ringed fist tearing the skin until it was a mass of blood and flesh. When Ari's legs had begun to buckle, the big man had let the now semi-comatose figure drop to the floor. The big man, however, liked to be thorough, and although it was bad news for Ari, he considered his task to be unfinished. With an icy diligence, he had then proceeded to lay into the fallen man with heavy booted kicks, and continued this work until his anger was spent.

Now, however, the big man's breathing had become calm and controlled. He lit another cigarette, inhaled deeply, and blew a column of smoke down onto the motionless figure on the floor. He gazed down at the man for a long minute, and then turned and went to the bathroom. He dropped his cigarette butt in the toilet, and then, after bathing his face, looked in the mirror.

Ari had done a good job; the big man saw that his nose was broken, and laid open in flaps of bloody flesh. He gathered a handful of toilet roll, and held it tentatively against his tattered nose, while he unzipped his pants, and urinated. There was a grimy cabinet fixed to the wall, and he opened it in the vain hope that it would contain some sort of adhesive plaster, but it was empty. There was however, a roll of silver duct tape sitting on top of the cistern. He could see it had recently been used to stem a leak in the shower pipe.

He removed the toilet paper and again looked in the mirror. It took him a few tender minutes to pick away the remaining few fragments of tissue, but he could see that the wound was already congealing. He picked up the duct tape, and tearing a two-inch strip from the roll, placed it gingerly over the bridge of his nose.

What do you fuckin look like? He thought, and gave his mirror image a grim tight-lipped smile.

On returning from the bathroom, he stopped at the threshold of the living room, and let his eyes wander over the interior. He just knew there had to be a big stash of money somewhere in the house, and how could he possibly leave without finding Ari's secret hoard.

"It's a matter of principal, shit-head," he said to the comatose figure on the floor, and lighting another cigarette, he entered the room.

Chapter 1 (Summer)

It was in the art section that she first became aware of him. She was flicking through a book on Surrealist painters, and had stopped at a Rene Magritte painting of little bowler-hatted men raining down through a bright blue sky. This image had so absorbed her that it took a few minutes before she realised that the woman, standing just a few feet from her, was sniggering. When she looked round the woman gave her a silly grin and then raised her eyes heavenward, as if to say: "tch, honestly". Laura was puzzled, and didn't quite know how to react, but then she heard it, the snoring. She wondered how she had failed to notice such a sound: *I mean snoring, in a library, it sort of stands out,* she thought.

Everyone seemed intent on ignoring it. Laura glanced over at the reception desk, and even the librarians appeared to have been struck deaf. *Librarians,* she thought, *they're sort of on their own, big softies, really.* She could never imagine them being aggressive, and, for example, angrily confronting a little old lady who was a few days late with her books:

"Okay, bitch, we've warned you, and warned you, but no, you have to push us to the limit" And then without warning, slamming the date stamp down on one of the fragile, bony little hands clinging to the counter. Anyway, they were ignoring the snoring.

Curious now, and drawn to the sound, Laura replaced the Surrealist book back on the shelf, and sidled round to biographies. She just had to get a look at this man. From the volume of the snoring, she had decided it had to be a man, even though she hadn't actually seen him yet. From biographies, she then slipped round to the end of the travel section and peeked over a book on China, and there he was.

He was sitting alone, hunched over a small table by one of the big bay windows. At first he appeared to be face down on an open book, but on closer inspection, Laura realised he was face down on a Big Mac: it was in a container, sandwiched between his forehead and the book. It looked as if exhaustion had beaten hunger to the punch.

Well, you don't see that everyday, thought Laura. *He doesn't look homeless or anything; so what is he doing there?*

Taking the large picture book on China as a prop, she sat at a nearby table and pretended to be engrossed in the colourful images. But every so often, she would slyly look up to see if there were any further developments. After something like ten minutes of this charade, however, she was beginning to feel a little bored, and decided it was probably time she got back to work.

She closed the book, and was just about to leave, when all of a sudden the man grunted, sat bolt upright, and looked around dazed and confused. She would later remember thinking that there had been something attractive about him, even with half a burger bun stuck to his forehead, but at that particular moment there was nothing she could do to stop herself from laughing.

The sound of a stranger laughing made the young man even more bewildered, and he gazed over in her direction, trying to figure out what she found so funny. On seeing this, Laura put her hand over her mouth to try and stem the flow. But unfortunately, at that exact moment the bun took it upon itself to fall from his head, and she was off again, tears streaming down her face.

As if released from some sort of anaesthetic, the young man appeared to become revived with the removal of the bun, and after looking briefly down at the table, he frowned with embarrassment. The look on his face instantly made Laura feel guilty, and she managed to stop herself from laughing long enough to bend down and search in her bag for some tissues; however, by the time she had wiped her eyes and looked up again, he had gone.

* * *

The sound was raw and beautiful, Ruler Of My Heart sang Irma Thomas, her voice flowing like honey out into the sun-filled yard. Mrs McIntyre, who was hanging out her washing, looked up at the blue-curtained window, gave a fleeting smile and shook her head.

Inside the room, a young man blew smoke from the side of his mouth, while nodding his head ever so slightly to the music. He stared ahead, trance-like, at the almost finished painting propped up on the easel. It portrayed a Blues musician, a guitar player, cradling his instrument in his arms, and gazing soulfully out from beneath the brim of his black fedora hat.

The young man continued to study his work until Irma had squeezed the last tender note out of the bittersweet song. As if coming out of a dream, he then crushed his cigarette out in the ashtray, rose from his chair, and went to the window.

He was just in time to see his landlady pick up her basket after finishing her laundry chores, and feeling the need of some sunshine and company, he decided to join her. Bounding down the stairs two at a time, he breezed into her kitchen, and called out to her from the open door:

"Hello Mrs McIntyre. Lovely day, eh?"

He sat down on her backdoor step, lit another cigarette, and looked up at the sky.

"Yuh lookin rough, bwoy."

He laughed and nodded his head.

"Aye well, Ah didnae get ma beauty sleep."

He got up to let her into the kitchen, stretched his arms above his head and yawned. He was thirty years old, tall and slim, with dark hair, and brown eyes that didn't miss much. His name was Mickie Lee.

"Don't ye dare put that kettle on," he said, sitting down again. Mrs McIntyre gave him a wry look, but then smiled. She filled the kettle, and then turned on the radio; it was tuned to a Jazz station.

"Why don't yuh sleep at night, like everybody else?" she asked, even though she knew the answer.

"Ah'm tryin to finish ma paintings," he answered, almost to himself.

The kind of blue tones of Miles Davis's, 'So What' coming from the radio made Lucy McIntyre smile and nod her head, as though at some secret memory. Lucy was a striking sixty-five year old Jamaican woman, who though having a big heart was no pushover. It could never be said of her, that she suffered fools gladly, but there was something about this pensive young Glasgow man she liked; he had a way about him. She put his tea down next to him on the step, and asked:

"And what yuh gonna do with them when yuh finish?"

He sighed, and answered, again almost to himself:

"Ah don't know."

* * *

Laura had been back in the office only a few minutes when she heard a familiar voice. She knew immediately by its irritating, mocking tone, that it just had to be Lewis.

"Well, Laura, did you get what you were looking for in the library?" he said, putting a sarcastic tone to the word library.

"No, well yes. Well, I mean, sort of." She was trying not to get annoyed but failing.

"Oh, right," said Lewis, making a face. "I don't know why you bother. Why don't you use the computer like everybody else?"

Oh, shut up! She thought, as she strode past his desk. She was well aware that Lewis had a big crush on her, but she, like everyone else in the office, thought that he was a smug little shit, that she couldn't even stand to talk to him most of the time.

Laura had been an assistant art director with the Martin & Maclean advertising agency for over a year now. She loved her job.

While hanging up her jacket, she accidentally dropped the file she was carrying, and bent down to pick it up.

"Ooh, nice!" said Lewis, smirking.

Laura turned and gave him a pitiful look, while thinking: *Don't you ever get tired of being a wanker?* She put the file on her desk, and went to get a coffee.

On entering the kitchen, her face immediately lit up when she saw John was there. All the girls loved John, but since she had come to work for Martin & MacLean, the two of them had become close. He listened to her, and looked out for her. She voiced her frustration:

"Why has Lewis got to be such a smart-arse?" she said through gritted teeth. "He's one of those people who just has to comment on every little thing."

"Oh, please!" said John, with a dismissive wave of his hand.

"Who gives a shit what little Dick thinks?"

Laura giggled, and started to feel better. John didn't appear gay, until he got angry, or tried to make you laugh.

"More importantly," he said. "Where are we going for lunch?"

Laura made a face.

"Don't do that dear, you'll curdle the milk."

"I'm sorry, John, but I've got to get these drawings done for the meeting on Monday. It's my first big chance to show my potential, and it took longer at the library than I expected, but I'll tell you about that later. We can go for a drink before I meet Toby in the Fox."

"Ooh that'll be nice," replied John, with an exaggerated grin.

* * *

The afternoon sun, shimmering through the partly closed curtains, threw abstract patterns on the wall, and a light breeze made them dance. Mickie watched them lazily, and then closed his eyes again.

He had told Mrs McIntyre he was going to catch up on some sleep for a few hours, but here he was, still staring at the back of his eyelids. He felt tired, but thoughts kept spinning around in his head: *What the hell was he doing working in a dead end job, and living from hand to mouth in a bed-sit? He was thirty years old for fucks sake, and now he was falling asleep in the library.*

"Aw fuck!"

He said it louder than he meant to, and his eyes popped open again. *And then there was Mona,* he thought, and said the name softly: "Mona."

The sound of the name made his heart sort of flutter in his chest.

* * *

"Two bottles of Leffe Blonde, darling?"

The barmaid didn't even look up from the pint she was pulling, so he tried a passing barman.

"Two bottles of Leffe Blonde please mate, when you're ready?"

The barman looked with distain at the tall skinny, City type, and giving the slightest lift of his chin, carried on.

"I think that was acknowledgement, it's hard to tell. Why do we drink in here again?" he asked over his shoulder. "I told Laura we'd meet her here," said Toby Sutton; he and Tom Paine worked together in the City.

The barman came back with two bottles and two glasses, took the money, and gave the change without saying a word. Tom Paine accepted the change, and with a phoney smile, said:

"Thank you ever so much."

They took their drinks and went outside to smoke.

"What's wrong with the staff in this place?" said Tom.

"You probably," replied Toby, accepting the offered cigarette.

"Moi, vraiment? Heaven forbid, old chap."

"Oh ho, yes old chap," replied Toby, hooting his irritating laugh.

"Last week, don't you remember? It was Harry Sachs birthday, and you were rat-arsed old chum. You sprayed champagne all over the barmaid, knocked three glasses over, and farted out loud. Oh, you were in fine form; of course, I wasn't much better. I think the landlord only let us stay because we were flashing the cash. I'm afraid it all got a bit dark side of the moon in the end."

"Aren't the common people funny?" Declared Tom, causing both of them to break into loud derisive laughter.

* * *

Lucy McIntyre couldn't believe her eyes, Sammie 'Toots' Turner was walking down Portobello Road towards her. She could see that he looked lost in thought, sauntering along with his head down, and his well-travelled old instrument case slung over his shoulder. Lucy stopped and waited for him to get closer, and just as he was about to walk past, she reached out and lightly touched his arm. When he looked round and saw her, his face broke into the biggest smile.

"Lucy girl, how yuh doin?" he said, embracing her warmly.

"Oh mi fine, Sammie. What about yuh, yuh bin playin some place?"

He closed his eyes and slowly nodded his head.

"Oh mi still get a gig from time to time."

"Cain't keep a good horn man down, huh?" said Lucy, smiling up at him.

Sammie grinned wide, and gave a deep-throated laugh like a Tuba playing a bass line. Lucy looked at this old man, and remembered good times. Sammie and her late husband, Harry, had been inseparable, and had played together all the time.

Harry had come down from Glasgow with his saxophone in'65, and almost immediately teamed up with the big, amiable West Indian. Tall, wiry and wild, that was how Sammie always referred to Harry, and when those two boys played together, they could really rip it up. It was through Sammie that she had met Harry for the first time; Sammy had introduced them to each other late one night at Ronnie Scott's club, and that was it: boom, she was in love.

Sammie was a trumpet player, and like Lucy he was from Jamaica. She had heard from a mutual friend that Sammie had recently come back from living in America, and that he had been ill, and down on his luck. Unlike Harry, he hadn't been fortunate enough to find a Lucy to take care of business, and any money he had made in the good times, had somehow melted away.

Lucy's heart went out to him, standing there with his old pork-pie hat pushed to the back of his head, and a soft smile on his big old face.

"Say, Sammie, yuh got time to look at someting? Mi got some old photographs, and only yuh could tell me where they were taken."

Lucy knew it was a thin line, but she wanted to feed him up. She was afraid, however, that if he got a whiff of charity, he would make some excuse, and say he had to be somewhere. So she was more than pleased when he just nodded, and said:

"Sure, Luce, sure."

* * *

On first opening his eyes, Mickie had felt uneasy, like some bad dream was still clinging to him, although he couldn't remember what it was. But he was grateful that at least he had managed to get some sleep, albeit it somewhat troubled.

A long hot bath and Muddy Waters slide guitar had eased him eased him back into life. And now he was out on the street, and it was a warm beautiful Friday evening.

Since he had been a teenager, he had always loved Friday nights; the people on the streets seemed more alive, happier, especially in summertime. The girls all dressed up, laughing and showing off; the old guys watching them going by, and remembering how it used to be. Music was booming from an open window, and Mickie walked along, sucking it all up. *Fuckin hell, steady on, Mickie,* He thought. *You'll nearly be approachin cheerful here, if you're not careful.*

The pub was busy, but he spotted Billy at the bar, and as usual, he was making someone laugh. Mickie smiled, and made his way over.

"Don't believe a word, Sally," he said, addressing the girl behind the bar, and then laying a friendly hand on Billy's shoulder.

"Well, well, if it's not the late Mister Lee," said Billy, turning to shake Mickie's hand.

"A pint of Guinness, please, Sal, and the same again for Mr Dunn."

Billy Dunn was short and stocky, with a tough looking face, and a grin like a headlamp; he and Mickie had been childhood friends in Glasgow. It was Billy who, after Mickie's divorce a year ago, had encouraged him to make a break and try his luck in London for a while.

As Mickie wanted to smoke, they took their freshly poured pints, and made their way outside. There were no free seats, but they found a place to stand, where they could place their drinks on a large barrel set against the wall.

"Sorry ah was late, Billy, but it's been a funny day."

"Och don't worry about that; ah was well happy talkin to Sally."

"Aye, ah noticed."

Billy grinned, took a long pull of his pint, and then putting it back on the barrel, he asked:

"So, how's the painting goin?"

* * *

"He was what?" said John, with a look of mock horror.

"He was sleeping face-down on a Big Mac," replied Laura. "And you could hear him snoring all over the library. It was ever so loud."

They had popped into a Wine Bar after work, to have a drink and a gossip before they went on to the Fox. Laura had persuaded John to come along with her to the Fox, as she suspected he didn't have any other plans.

"I feel a bit guilty now, you know, laughing. He must have felt really embarrassed," said Laura, looking thoughtful.

"He had a nice face," she added softly. "Well, he did after the bun fell off."

John exploded with laughter.

"Oh stop it, he was very good looking."

"Oh was he?" said John, grinning.

"Well, in a scruffy sort of way," said Laura, blushing slightly, and quickly changing the subject.

"Okay drink up, we better go."

* * *

Toby Sutton, after making his unsteady way back from the toilet, stood swaying in front of his friend, and then squinting his eyes to focus, he said:

"Don't look now, but here comes Laura, plus shirt lifter."

"Oh really," said Tom Paine, frowning, and then turning to look.

On catching sight of Toby, Laura smiled and waved, and then she and John made their way over to the table. Toby took the cigarette out of his mouth, and then standing up with some effort, gave Laura a wobbly kiss on the cheek.

"Hello, darling, what would you like to drink?"

"Oh no, allow me," said Tom Paine, with a sleazy grin. "It's my round. What would you like darling?"

"I'll have a spritzer," said Laura, starting to feel uneasy.

"Actually, I was talking to thingy," said Tom Paine, with a smirk.

Toby let go a stupid, stifled laugh, and then, biting his lip, looked away.

Laura was mortified; she couldn't even look at John. John, of course tried to rise above it, and camping it up, he replied:

"Thank you, darling, I'll have a gin and tonic."

Tom Paine, grinned, and then pursing his lips, turned and wobbled off to the bar.

Laura sat down opposite Toby, and John took the seat next to him. She reached over and took a cigarette from Toby's pack on the table, lit it, and then blew the smoke skywards. Toby sensed he should maybe say something to break the silence, and so, forcing a smile, he said:

"Oh don't mind old Tom, he doesn't mean anything; he's just having a laugh."

Laura looked away, sighed, and then, in a strained voice, said:

"He's an idiot. He's vile and an idiot. Every time I see him he's drunk. Why do you bring him along when you know I can't stand him?"

Toby looked petulant.

"He's my friend. And anyway you've brought thingy here."

John was starting to feel a little uncomfortable, but he just smiled, and raised his eyebrows.

"Thingy?" Laura crushed her cigarette out in the ashtray.

"Thingy? His name is John. What is the matter with you? I think you've been hanging about with that cretin for far too long."

"Oh Laura!"

"Oh fuck off!" cried Laura, loud enough to make a few heads turn. "I've had enough of this."

With that, she grabbed her bag, got up, and marched off, leaving Toby with a stunned, stupid open-mouthed expression on his face, as he watched her stride away.

John had to bite his lip to stop from laughing.

"Well, don't you think you should go after her?" he said, raising his eyebrows.

Toby looked blankly at John, and then at the rapidly disappearing Laura. It appeared to John, that a decision was trying to seep its way slowly through the beer. When it finally reached its destination, Toby's eyebrows shot up, and then leaping to his feet, he disappeared into the crowd.

John laughed out loud, and then helped himself to one of Toby's abandoned cigarettes. He leaned back in his chair, crossed his legs, and after lighting his cigarette, blew a column of smoke through pursed lips. When he saw Tom Paine re-appear with a laden tray of drinks, he smiled wickedly and thought: *Now for some fun with little Tommy.*

* * *

It was dark now, but still warm, and the tables outside the pub were thronged with Friday night revellers, laughing, talking, and drinking.

Billy, returning from the bar with two fresh pints, sat down and stole a quick glance at his friend. He could tell there was something bothering Mickie, and he had been waiting patiently for him to bring it up in conversation. But now, having eventually managed to get a table to themselves, and this being their fifth pint, Billy now felt that Mickie was ready to be primed into spilling the beans.

"Okay, what's up?"

Mickie took a long pull from his glass, and then looked down at his hands.

"Why has she got to be such a bitch?"

Billy had no need to ask to which bitch Mickie was referring. He had never liked Mickie's ex-wife, and the feeling was mutual.

"She really loves to stick it to me, and make me feel guilty. She knows how much ah love and miss Mona, but twists the knife every chance she gets. Ah mean, what the fuck ah'm ah supposed to do? Ah'm sendin as much money as ah can afford."

He toyed nervously with his Zippo lighter, repeatedly flicking the lid open and then closed, open and then closed.

"Gonny stop doin that?" said Billy, tilting his head, and making a funny, scowling face at the lighter.

Mickie looked up and laughed in spite of himself.

"Och, ah'm sorry Billy, but ye know what ah mean?"

"Look, ah know it's not easy bein away from Mona, and Sharon bein a manipulatin bitch doesn't make it any easier, but ye really needed to get away from that woman. Your painting again, and it's good, ye know it's good, and ye were doin fuck all in Glasgow."

"Ah know, ah know, but what am ah gonny do with them? Down here it's all about what school you went to."

"Look, if they can sell them, they don't give a fuck what school ye went to."

"That's the whole point, ah don't know any, they's"

Mickie started flicking his lighter again, and Billy grabbed it from him, and put it on the table.

"Listen, something good is gonny happen, ah can feel it. And anyway, ah thought ye told me Sharon was bringing Mona down to London for a couple of weeks?"

Mickie immediately brightened.

"That's right, she'll be here for her seventh birthday. They're staying with Sharon's auntie in Ealing."

"Well there you go. That'll be great, eh? Seein Mona again."

Mickie's face lit up.

"Aw man, tell me about it. Ah just hope her mother disnae fuck it up for me. Ah don't trust her Billy; she loves to play wee mind games."

He had just lit a cigarette, when a pretty girl at a nearby table, who suddenly threw her head back and laughed, grabbed his attention. A grin spread across his face.

"Oh aye! Ah forgot to tell ye, there was this girl."

"Girl, what girl?"

"In the library; she was nearly wettin herself laughin at me, when I woke up with the bun."

Billy scrunched his face up in confusion.

"Bun, what bun?"

"Ach, it disnae matter. Listen, what time is it? Ah want to get Mrs McIntyre a few bottles of Guinness; there's something ah want to ask her."

* * *

"Blue Monday, oh Blue Monday . . ."

Mickie had worked all weekend behind the bar of the Falcon, and now he had two full days to paint. He lay in his bed staring at the ceiling, and listening to the piano man from New Orleans. And when Fats Domino had finished his lament to the working week, Mickie closed his eyes. He loved to lie here on mornings like this, and listen to the sounds coming up from the street, knowing he didn't have to get up and join the masses. *Need to get up soon, though,* He thought. *I've got a lot to do,*

After daydreaming for a short while, he opened his eyes and looked at the painting of the Guitar Player, and pondered on his first task of the day.

I just have to finish the hands. Oh yeah, right, just, he thought. He disliked painting hands, and always left them till last. It wasn't that he was so bad at painting them, he just wished he had the effortless ability of someone like Rembrandt; when you looked closely at the detail in a Rembrandt painting, there was almost nothing there, just a few strokes of colour; it was like the man was a magician with a brush.

He heard the back door open, and knew it would be Mrs McIntyre putting her cat's food bowl on the step; he heard her talk softly to him:

"Come Dizzy, baby, eatin time."

Mickie smiled, closed his eyes, and thought of Sammie; Lucy had introduced him as an old musician friend of her late husband's. When they had shook hands, and Mickie had looked into the old man's eyes, he saw a tender strength, and quiet dignity. This is what he was trying to achieve in his series of four Blues Musicians waiting to play.

Arriving back from the pub on Friday night, Mickie had heard voices coming from the kitchen, and after knocking on the door, had looked in.

"Hello Mrs McIntyre, ah'm sorry to bother you when you've got company," he had said, cradling a bag of beer. "Ah just wanted to ask you somethin."

She looked up at him in that way she had.

"Sure, darlin, come in, come in."

Mickie had then shuffled into the room and laid the beer on the table.

"Ah was wonderin if ma daughter, Mona, could stay for a couple of days when she comes down from Glasgow?"

Lucy smiled one of her big smiles. "Tch, bwoy, sure your daughter can stay, and you don't even have to bribe me," she replied, looking at the four bottles of Guinness he had placed on the table.

Mickie had laughed, and looked embarrassed, but Lucy had instantly put him at his ease, telling him to sit down while she fetched him a glass. He had only stayed for one drink, however, as he didn't want to intrude. But he had been intrigued by all the old photographs spread across the table, and also by the way Lucy and Sammie had laughed and joked like a couple of teenagers.

"Oh man, was mi ever this good lookin?" said Sammie, holding a snapshot at arms length to bring it into focus.

"Oh, yuh still a brown eyed handsome man, Sammie Turner," replied Lucy, pouring some more rum into his glass, and winking at Mickie. It had given Mickie a good warm feeling to see them together like this, yet later that night, lying in bed, he had felt an acute sense of his own loneliness.

Dismissing these thoughts, he opened his eyes and gazed for a few minutes more at his painting. He then got up, stretched, wiped the sleep from his eyes, and went to run a bath.

Some hours later, he was siting on his painting chair, sipping coffee. Without taking his eyes off his work, he put his cup on the floor, and reaching for his cigarettes, lit one, and then exhaling slowly, watched as the smoke curled and billowed round the now finished Guitar Player.

* * *

It was a big room filled with radiant light, which glowed through the pale green, remote-control blinds attached to the steel and glass windows.

Seated around the long hardwood conference table were eight of the so-named, 'creatives' of Martin & MacLean. They were assembled for the customary Monday morning meeting, and all eyes were focused on the open door.

Through it, moments later, strode Andrew MacLean, a tall, immaculately dressed figure, who, taking his rightful place at the head of the table, immediately assumed complete control.

"Right, let's get to it; first on the agenda, the new client. This client is important, why?"

"Because they are new to us," said Dick Lewis eagerly, his eyes almost popping out of his shiny, polished little face.

"Ye-es," said Andrew MacLean, a little impatiently. "I think we've already established that. More importantly," he continued. "They are big, they have a surfeit of cash, and I want some of it. In fact I want a lot of it."

Dick Lewis cackled, and then went red when Andrew MacLean peered at him over his glasses. Andrew then turned his attention to Tim Farrell, the senior art director.

"Okay Tim, what have you got to show us?"

Tim blinked, and adjusted his glasses.

"Well, after the initial briefing, we ran with the Surrealist theme. Laura has produced a fine set of preliminary drawings, of which everyone has a copy on the table in front of them."

There was a rustling of pages being turned.

"I believe, working on these initial ideas, we can show the product in an exciting and innovative way. We have initially spoken to a Model making company, who will get back to us later today with their input, but have also given thought to CGI. It obviously comes down to costing, and what technique we think will ultimately achieve the best results."

Again all eyes were on Andrew MacLean, who pursed his lips and slowly nodded his head, while perusing the sketches. He was a distinguished looking man in his late forties, who clearly knew a thing or two about making money.

"Good," he said at last. "Good work, Laura, I like this, interesting concept."

"Thank you," said Laura, glancing at Tim Farrell, who smiled approvingly.

"Right," said Andrew MacLean. Let's get all the elements together as soon as possible; I would like to give them a ball-park figure before the end of the week."

* * *

"Well done, you," said John, giving Laura a hug. They were in the kitchen having a coffee after the meeting.

"Oh, thank you, John," she replied, looking delighted. "I think it was having that argument with Toby that worked in my favour. I was so furious, that I spent the whole weekend working on those drawings."

"Oh you little swot."

This made Laura laugh, and then giving John a wide-eyed look, she said:

"Talking about swots, what about Lewis?"

"I know!" replied John, equally wide-eyed. "How does he get his face like that? It looks like he boils it."

Laura laughed again, nearly choking on her coffee.

"Actually, I meant did you see his face when Andrew complimented my work. I almost felt sorry for him."

"What, don't feel sorry for that pink little toady. He deserves everything he gets." John then flicked his hand, as if dismissing a boring subject, and breezily declared:

"Now we're definitely having lunch today, and wine, I insist on lashings of wine." He looked puzzled for a minute. "Is it lashings, or is that just lemonade?" He shook his head. "Anyway loads."

"Oh yeah, that sounds lovely," agreed Laura. "But then I have to go and check something out at the library."

John raised his eyebrows and gave her a knowing look, but made no comment. Instead, he closed his eyes, and then lifting his nose in the air, in a faux, haughty fashion, turned and sauntered back to his office. Laura smiled to herself.

Chapter 2

Entering the library was a relief. It had been so hot in the taxi on the ride through the afternoon traffic, but now it was cool and quiet. Laura removed her sunglasses, and adjusting her eyes to the light, made her way to the art section.

Lunch had been a riot. John had really made her laugh, especially when he related how he had managed to wind Tom Paine up so much that he had left the pub furious and embarrassed; he had apparently almost fell over a table in his rush to get away. What was curious, though, was that Laura had sensed that behind all the hilarity, John had seemed genuinely sorry for him.

She was glad of this chance to sit down and browse through the beautiful colour plates in the book of Surrealist Art she had taken from the bookshelf. The wine had flowed a little too freely at lunch, and she was really quite tipsy. *I'll get some coffee in a minute,* she thought.

She got so engrossed in her studies that she forgot all about coffee. But after an hour or so, she decided she had garnered enough reference information for her needs, and gathering up her notes, put them in her folder. She replaced the book on the shelf, and then wandered slowly towards the coffee machine. She paused here and there to glance at something that caught her eye, and then something really caught her eye.

He was sitting hunched over a large picture book at one of the other study tables. This stopped her in her tracks, and she quickly stepped back behind a bookshelf, but then slowly, peeked round for a second look.

Well, she thought. *He certainly looks a lot cooler than the last time I saw him.* He was wearing a sparkling white t-shirt, black jeans, and white Converse boots.

From what she could make out, he appeared to be drawing something from the book into a sketchpad, and seemed completely absorbed in what he was doing.

What should I do, she thought, *speak to him or leave? What would I say? Not snoring today, then? Or, fancy a Big-Mac? Oh, get on with it, you know you want to,* said the wine sozzled little devil inside her.

She sighed, made a futile little gesture to fix an imaginary stray lock of hair, and then walked over to the table.

"Excuse me?" She said, and immediately, to her horror, thought it sounded more like: "excuzzze me?" She got no response, but clearing her throat, she decided to try again before her nerve went:

"Excuse me?"

He looked up, and for what seemed to Laura like a long time, took in this vision before him; but then a smile of recognition slowly lit up his face.

Laura smiled back sheepishly.

"I'm sorry, you probably don't remember me."

Still smiling, he tilted his head slightly, and replied softly:

"Oh aye, ah remember you all right; the laughing girl."

Laura gave an embarrassed little laugh, as if to prove she could still do it.

"I'm so sorry. I just wanted to apologise." She made a face, "You know, for before."

"Och, listen, don't worry about that," he responded graciously, and then looked down at his hands and smiled. And then raising his head again, he looked into her eyes, and said:

"So it was that funny, was it?"

"Oh yeah!" she replied, nodding her head vigorously. She was teasing him now; she trusted his eyes. He laughed out loud, and shook his head.

There was an awkward silence for a long few seconds, and then Laura said, as casually as she could:

"Listen, I was going to have a coffee, could I possibly buy you one, to, oh, I don't know, sort of make amends?"

He tried not to look too surprised.

"Eh, aye. . . Ah mean, yeah, that'd be great."

She smiled, and he thought she looked lovely.

He stood up, closed his sketchbook, and put it with his pencils in an old leather schoolbag. Walking behind her to the coffee machine only confirmed his first impression: she was lovely. She was wearing loosely tailored, dark blue linen trousers, and a matching Chinese style top. He loved the way her body moved within the soft confines of her clothes.

When settled at a table with their coffee, they faced each other, and almost simultaneously realised they hadn't been introduced.

"My name is Lau. . ."

"Ah'm Mic. . . Oh, ah'm sorry, you go first," he said, laughing.

"My name is Laura Taylor."

"Ah'm Mickie, Mickie Lee. Pleased to meet you," he said, extending his hand across the table.

She took his hand; it felt warm and strong, and she was struck by the sweet formal way he had introduced himself.

Mickie had fallen into a sort of dream, and held her hand a little too long; she gave him an enquiring look.

"Oh, ah'm sorry, ah'm . . . Ah'm a wee bit nervous," he said letting go of her hand.

"Oh, I know, me too; it's a little strange, but nice."

"Oh aye," he said.

Laura giggled, and said:

"You're Scottish, then?"

"Yes," he replied, grinning, and Laura felt somehow, more alive.

* * *

Lucy left the market and started making her way home. As she walked, her thoughts were with Sammie; she was thinking how good it had felt spending time with him after not seeing him for so long. She also felt, however, that it had exposed a sense of loneliness she had only been vaguely aware of, or perhaps was aware of, but hadn't wanted to acknowledge.

She was still pondering on these issues, when her thoughts were abruptly interrupted by a loud cacophony of voices. A group of kids, who congregated at the local burger bar everyday after school, appeared to be in the middle of an angry dispute. Two boys in particular were squaring up to each other like dogs being held back on invisible leads. But then, it suddenly kicked off, and she saw the taller boy snarl, and swiftly head-butt his rival hard in the face.

Lucy was shocked by the animal ferocity of what followed. The boy, who had been struck, was now on the ground, being savagely kicked and punched by the obviously older, stronger boy. It was then, as if from nowhere, that Lucy saw a tall, powerfully built figure, push his way through the baying crowd, and seize the older boy by the arm, and pull him off the cowering form lying on the pavement. Lucy couldn't believe her eyes, it was Sammie. She immediately crossed the street in time to hear him say, through gritted teeth:

"What's the matter with yuh, bwoy, cain't yuh see he's had enough? Yuh almost a grown man, yuh should know better. Yuh tink this make yuh a tough guy, beatin the shit out of schoolboys?"

The youth looked at Sammie with withering contempt, and then said with a sneer:

"Mind your business old man, this black bastard's gotta learn respect. The silly fucker knows the rules."

He then turned to grin and shake his head at the bystanders, as if to say: "Can you believe this old fool?"

Lucy saw a cold hard look cross Sammie's face, and she cried out:
"Sammie! Sammie leave it." She touched his arm, and felt him relax his grip on the boy.

"Come, Sammie, it's over."

Without taking his eyes off him, Sammie reluctantly released the sneering youth, who just kept staring defiantly at him. Friends of the victim, now stepped in and helped the fallen, bleeding boy to his feet, and led him away.

Lucy looked into the scowling face of the sneering youth, and saw nothing, no shame, no remorse, nothing; it brought a chill to her heart.

She took Sammie by the arm and guided him away, and then together they walked slowly towards Lucy's house, watched by the now silent, remaining group of kids. The still sneering youth, continued to stare after them, and then spat contemptuously in the gutter.

* * *

They had stayed talking in the library, with seemingly no perception of time passing. Mickie had eventually got round to telling Laura that he was divorced, and had a six-year old daughter whom he missed terribly. While relaying this tender information, he had studied her face for signs, signs of dread or disinterest, but she had listened with consideration and compassion, which made his words come easily. He didn't know exactly why, but he felt he had to be honest with this girl, even if she ran, and he never saw her again; it just had to be this way.

Laura in turn had told him how she had just broken up with her boyfriend of two years, but had no regrets, as she had recently become aware of how little they really had in common.

At one point, while telling Mickie how much she loved her job, Laura had suddenly stopped mid-sentence, and then standing up, had abruptly excused herself, saying she had to make a quick call to her office. Mickie, looking somewhat confused, watched her walk quickly towards the main door.

The sudden realisation that she was actually supposed to be in the process of doing that job, had led her to rush outside and phone Tim Farrell. When he answered her call, she cleverly explained how she thought it would be much more sensible if she worked from home for the rest of the day, rather than come all the way back to the office, and to her delight, Tim had readily agreed. Afterwards, she had felt a tinge of guilt, but not for long, and anyway, she thought: *I did work all weekend.*

They eventually left the library, and with no particular plan in mind, had strolled the sun filled streets for a while. When they came across a quiet pub with a garden, Mickie, not wanting to let her go, had asked if she would like to stop for a drink. Laura had smiled, and said, yes, that would be very nice.

Sitting in the dappled shade of the garden, sipping their drinks, they had eased into feeling so right in each others company, laughing and talking, and looking with longing into each others eyes. They decided to have a second drink, and then, still holding fast to an unspoken desire not to part, they had left the pub in search of a restaurant. A short time later, they were facing each other across the table of a local Pizzeria.

"So what are you going to do with your paintings when you finish them?" asked Laura.

"Aw, not you as well."

"What do you mean?"

"Well, that's the bit ah'm not very good at."

"What do you mean?" Asked Laura again, this time with a teasing look.

Mickie grinned, and shook his head.

"Persistent, eh?"

"I'm just interested, that's all. Perhaps I could help."

"Oh, ah don't know. Ah love painting; it's all ah've ever wanted to do, and ah think my paintings look good when ah'm workin on them in my wee garret, but then ah pass a gallery, and my confidence somehow drains away."

Laura took a sip of wine, and looked thoughtful.

"Why don't you photograph the ones you've finished, and then email them to me. I know people who buy art."

Mickie laughed.

"See, even that makes me nervous."

"Oh, don't be so silly."

For a few seconds he was taken aback by her reprimand, but then he smiled.

"Okay, okay ah will," he said, as if surprised at his own confidence.

"Ah'll have to borrow a digital camera from Mary, ma mate Billy's wife, and ah'm sure ah can also use her computer to mail them to you."

Laura looked at his smiling face, and was glad she had spurred him into action.

"Don't worry too much about the picture quality," she said, as if to further reassure him. "As long as they're in focus, and the colour is reasonably correct, I can, if you trust me, enhance them at work. I will of course let you see them before I show them to anyone else."

Mickie's gratitude had left him speechless for a moment, but then feeling he should respond, he gave a shy smile, and said, rather formally:

"That's very kind, ah really appreciate it." And then something struck him.

"Speaking of computers, how come ye use library books for reference? Ah would have thought ye could find any information ye needed with the touch of a keyboard."

Laura nearly said: " Oh, not you as well," but thought better of it.

"I like libraries, and I love books; it's a tactile thing. Sure, I use the computer to verify certain facts, but for creative inspiration, it has to be books. And anyway, you never know who you might meet."

"Oh yeah, right," replied Mickie, and they both laughed.

On leaving the restaurant, they walked slowly along the street, not really conscience of where they were going, nor even feeling the need to speak, just happy in the fact that they didn't need to.

After a while, Mickie stopped, and turned towards her, and when she looked up, he leaned in, and kissed her tenderly on the mouth.

"Ah've been wanting to do that all day." He said, softly.

In spite of herself, Laura blushed, but then smiled, and for some absurd reason, she said:

"Oh aye?"

She had attempted her best Scottish accent, but then realising how silly it had sounded, she giggled in embarrassment, and then covering her face with her hands, she thought: *This isn't like me at all.*

She then felt Mickie's arms embrace her, causing her to peep up through her fingers into his eyes, as if to gauge the truth of his emotions, but then instinctively slipped her hand around his neck, pulled him close, and lovingly returned his kiss.

* * *

"When did this happen?" asked Billy, placing his glass back on the bar.

"Monday, in the library," replied Mickie, a wide grin spreading across his face.

"For fucks sake," said Billy. "Ah canny turn my back for a minute."

He continued to look at his friend for a few seconds, and then scrunched up his face into a frown.

"Gonny stop grinnin like that? People are lookin."

Mickie pretended to switch off the grin, but seconds later brought it back wider than ever. And then, giving Billy a cheeky wink, he sauntered off to serve another customer.

It was early Wednesday evening, and Billy had dropped into the Falcon for a pint or two. Mickie had phoned him earlier, asking if he could borrow the camera, but there had been something in Mickie's manner that had instantly intrigued Billy; his friend had sounded. . . happy.

Mickie arrived back with his grin, and directing its full beam on Billy, said, in a very bad cockney accent:

"Anuvver beer, guv?"

Billy gave him a long pitiful look, and then deciding it was time for another wind-up, he pushed his empty glass towards Mickie, and said:

"Is yer face not getting sore yet?"

"Aw shut up," said Mickie, pouring him a fresh pint. "Yer only jealous."

Billy grinned; he knew he couldn't keep it up any longer.

"You're bloody right, ya jammy bastard," he said, lifting his new pint, and sinking a couple of inches of beer.

"Ye know ah'm only kidding," he added, wiping his mouth with the back of his hand. "Ah'm really happy for ye."

"Thanks Billy," said Mickie, genuinely touched.

"But does that mean we've got to suffer that fuckin grinnin all the time now?" asked Billy, not quite through teasing Mickie.

This just made Mickie laugh out loud.

"So, what time are ye comin round?" said Billy, finally changing the subject.

"Oh, around eight o-clock, if that's okay? Ah'm doin a couple of hours extra, and a double shift tomorrow, so ah can have Saturday off."

"Nae bother," said Billy, and then sinking another couple of inches of beer, he placed it back on the bar.

"Do ye want Mary to save ye some dinner?"

"Och no, ah'll get somethin here, and then ah want to go back and check on Mrs McIntyre. Ah think there's somethin troublin her; she's not been herself for the last couple of days."

"Oh aye, why is that?" asked Billy, with genuine concern. He was very fond of Mrs McIntyre. He too had lodged with Lucy and Harry when he had first come to London.

"Ah don't really know, but ah think it might have somethin to do with Sammie, ye know the old trumpet player, but ah don't like to ask."

Mickie then glanced at something over Billy's right shoulder.

"Ah'll be back in a minute, Billy," he said. "Ah just want to check somethin with Paddy." He then disappeared through the door that led to the back of the pub.

Billy had almost lifted his glass to his lips, when he became aware of someone standing a little too close to him for comfort. He glanced out the corner of his eye, just as the figure slipped onto the stool next to him. Billy took a sip of his drink, and then put it back on the bar. He recognised the figure as the little man who had been sitting alone at a corner table, when he had first entered the pub. As he had been one of the only two people in the whole place, Billy had nodded a vague hello; but now he wondered: *why the hell is he up here now, being creepy?*

Billy turned his head, and saw a sort of smile begin to creep across the face staring back at him. Such teeth as the face had left, were tobacco stained, yellow and black. The face then began to swivel slowly to the right, and then up slightly, until the eyes, which never left Billy, were now looking at him out of their corners, so to speak. A rogue draught from the overhead fan toyed with the few strands of oily hair that lay across the otherwise barren scalp. This made Billy inadvertently look up, and in the seconds it took him to return his gaze, the face had replaced the smile with a scowl, as if offended.

The face then spoke, and said, sourly:

"See that Marie Antoinette, she was a bastard."

"Eh?" asked Billy, confused.

"That Marie Antoinette," repeated the face, with emphasis. "She was a bastard!"

"Oh aye?" said Billy.

The face nodded, sage-like.

"And see that Sun King, Louis the thingy; he was actually three people ye know."

"Getaway," said Billy, and again the sage nodded.

Billy lifted his glass to his lips, and swallowed half its contents. He was just placing it back on the bar, when he caught sight of Mickie through the half-open door, obviously trying to stifle laughter. Billy now realised why his friend had vanished so quickly from the bar, and so, turning his attention again to the face, he nodded in the direction of the door, and said:

"See that barman, Mickie?" The face looked intrigued. "He's actually three people."

The face's eyebrows shot up.

"And, everyone of them, is a bastard!"

Billy watched with interest as the face considered this information. And then he saw the yellow smile creep slowly back, the eyes close, and the head start to bob up and down, as if on a spring, making the wispy strands of hair even more animated. As there was no sound, just this nodding, grimacing mask, it took Billy a few seconds to realise that the face was actually laughing.

Billy took advantage of this to finish his pint, and then said:

"Okay, laughin boy, take it easy."

He then got off his stool, but just before he turned to go, he saw Mickie, still hiding in the back, wipe tears of suppressed laughter from his eyes. Billy grinned, shook his head, and left the bar.

* * *

Mickie felt good walking home after finishing his shift, he hadn't felt like this in a long time. He still couldn't believe what had happened; it was almost as if somebody had flicked a switch, and suddenly, the grey was gone, and the sky was blue. Even his natural inclination to brood over things he had no power to change, had been replaced by a new feeling that anything was possible.

He was excited about photographing his paintings and emailing them to Laura; who knows, something could happen.

As he approached Mrs McIntyre's house, he noticed a hooded youth sitting on the low wall, in front of the house opposite. Mickie couldn't make out his face, but he sensed the boy was staring straight at him. The youth then blew a great stream of smoke up into the falling dusk, and Mickie guessed it wasn't a cigarette he was smoking. It wasn't an uncommon sight in this area, however, and so thinking no more about it, Mickie walked to the front door, and let himself in.

On entering the house, it struck him as unusually quiet: no music. He called out:

"Mrs McIntyre."

Getting no reply, he knocked on the sitting room door, which was slightly ajar, but again there was no answer. He pushed open the door, and saw that the room was empty, but the table-light next to Lucy's armchair, the one she used when reading, was lit. He then went through to the kitchen, and called out again:

"Mrs McIntyre."

And then he saw her through the window, walking back and forth in the yard, wringing her hands in an agitated manner. When he opened the back door, she jumped, and cried out in alarm, her patois thickened by fear:

"Wha yuh tink yuh tryin to do to mi bwoy, gimmi a heart attack?"

He was surprised at the venom in her voice, but then her face creased in sorrow.

"Oh Mickie, mi sorry it's . . . Mi cain't find Dizzy . . . Mi haven't seen him all day."

Mickie tried to reassure her.

"Och ye know what cat's are like, Mrs McIntyre; he'll be back when he's hungry."

He could tell she wasn't convinced, as she continued to look helplessly round the yard.

"Look, come inside and I'll put the kettle on and make ye nice cup of tea."

Mickie saw her look at him like he was the biggest fool she had ever come across in her life. He had never seen her like this; he thought he better try another approach.

"Look Mrs McIntyre, ah don't know about you, but ah could do with a proper drink. Why don't we go inside? Ah'm sure Dizzy will be back soon, and if we leave the door open, we can see him comin."

This seemed to placate her a little, and he managed to lead her in and sit her down at the kitchen table. And then, without asking permission, he went through to the sitting room, and was just taking a bottle of brandy from the cabinet, when he heard her cry out:

"Oh, Dizzy, baby. Where yuh been all this time?"

Mickie came into the kitchen carrying the brandy, in time to see the little cat being smothered with hugs and kisses, and its delighted owner wearing a beaming smile.

He put the bottle on the table, got glasses from the cupboard, and poured two generous measures. Mrs McIntyre released the little animal, and watched as it immediately went to feed hungrily from its bowl by the door. She continued to watch for a few minutes more, and then turned, and picked up her glass.

"Thank yuh, Mickie," she said, looking a little embarrassed.

"Och, no worries."

Mickie smiled; he was trying to make light of the incident, but he sensed there was more than a lost cat troubling his landlady.

They sipped their drinks in silence for a long minute, and then Mickie felt the need to speak:

"Is everythin okay, Mrs McIntyre?"

She responded, a little too eagerly.

"Sure, darlin. Mi just been feelin a lttle tired lately."

Mickie nodded thoughtfully, and Mrs McIntyre looked down at the table.

"Is Sammie comin round again anytime soon?" continued Mickie. "I'd like to get to know him a bit better, he seems like a interestin man."

She looked up, and Mickie saw, just for a second, a flicker of alarm in her eyes, but then she quickly looked down again, and said:

"No, he had to go away for a while . . . Visit some friends . . . In Bristol."

"Oh, right," said Mickie, and took another sip of brandy.

"Listen Mrs McIntyre, ah was goin to go round to Billy's tonight, for a couple of hours; ah want to borrow Mary's camera, but ah can put it off until tomorrow."

"Huh! Why yuh want to do that?" said Mrs McIntyre, sharply.

"Ah don't like leavin ye on your own; you've had a bit of a fright."

"What! Listen here bwoy, you go and take care of yuh bizness. Mi gonna be fine."

She at least sounded like her old self again, and although Mickie wasn't entirely convinced, he finished his drink, and stood up from the table.

"Okay, ah'll just pop up and get some money; ah want to buy Mary some of her favourite chocolates."

Before leaving, he put his head round the kitchen door, and saw her still sitting at the table, staring out the window, only now with Dizzy on her lap. Becoming aware of him, she turned and made a movement with her head, as if to say: "Go, go."

* * *

Mickie put his empty glass down on the coffee table, and lit Mary's cigarette. He then lit his own, and inhaling deeply, sat back in the sofa, and blew a smoke-filled sigh up to the ceiling.

"There's somethin not right," he said. "Ah don't know what it is, but there's somethin."

They were sitting in the living room of Billy and Mary's small flat in Ladbroke Grove.

"Och, she's probably just had a wee fallin out with yer man, Sammie," replied Mary; searching through the box of chocolates Mickie had bought her.

Mary was a striking-looking Irish girl, with green eyes and cropped auburn hair, and a no-nonsense, Dublin way about her.

"Ah don't think so," said Mickie, shaking his head. "Ah'm sure it's somethin more serious. She's not a silly woman, and she seemed genuinely scared."

Billy came in from the kitchen carrying two cans of beer, and a vodka and tonic for Mary, and continued the conversation:

"Look, Mickie, Mrs McIntyre's a tough wee woman," he said, setting the drinks down.

"She's seen life; when she came here in the fifties as a young girl, it wasn't easy; and then there was her man. As ye know, ma Da and Harry were friends from way back, and he said Harry was always a bit of a wild boy. So basically, what ah'm sayin is, if she went through all that, and managed to keep Harry in line, ah don't see her bein intimidated too easily . . . Och fuck!"

Billy, too busy talking, had poured his beer too quickly, and now watched helplessly as it foamed all over the table, and on to the floor.

Mary looked at Mickie, and rolled her eyes, and Mickie bit his lip, trying not to laugh. Mary then gave Billy a wry look, and said:

"Well, don't just look at it. Ye know where the cloth is."

"Yes dear, of course dear," replied Billy, feigning grovelling obedience, and scuttling into the kitchen in a parody of the

Hunchback of Notre Dame, which made Mickie and Mary laugh out loud.

"What is he like?" said Mary.

Mickie loved this: the craic. But in the past it had often been a somewhat bittersweet feeling, when he had to leave the laughter, and go home alone.

"Och ah know she's no fool," continued Mickie. "But she's older now. It's a wee bit different."

"Look ah'll have a quiet word with a couple of the local guys in the bookie's, and see if ah can suss out if anybody knows anythin," said Billy, coming back with a cloth, and mopping up the spilt beer.

"Well, that would be good. It's just that they seemed so happy together, her and Sammie. And ah know she gets lonely,
 and ah know how that feels."

"Not annymore, loverboy," said Mary, reaching out, and ruffling Mickie's hair.

Mickie blushed, and immediately wished he hadn't revealed his emotions.

Mary had been dying to turn the conversation round to Mickie's newfound romance all evening, and now grabbed her chance.

"So?" she said, with an exaggerated smile, and raised eyebrows.

"What?" replied Mickie, pretending he didn't know what was coming next.

So, what's she like, Laura?"

"Oh you better spill the beans, pal, or you'll be here all night," said Billy carefully pouring what remained of his beer.

"Och, she's lovely."

He felt the colour come to his face again. He hated being questioned, especially by Mary, she was so good at it; you found yourself unwittingly blurting out your innermost secrets.

"Awww!" said Mary, tilting her head to one side, and smiling her exaggerated smile.

"If your just gonny take the piss, ah'm not saying anythin," replied Mickie, reaching to crush out his cigarette. Mary bit her lip.

"I'm sorry, I'm only messin. I really do think it's grand to see you so happy for a change."

"Aye, well, it's early days. Ah've only really seen her twice, and the first time ah was face-down on a Big-Mac."

"Sounds so romantic," said Billy, mimicking Mary's beaming smile, and raised eyebrows.

"Fuck off you," replied Mickie, pouring his beer.

"So when are you seeing her again?" asked Mary.

"Saturday, and ah'm a bit nervous about it to be honest."

"Tch, why?"

"Och, it's that old confidence thing; she's in a high-powered job, and ah'm skint most of the time. Her ex-boyfriend works in the City; ah can't compete with that."

"Ex-boyfriend," cut in, Billy. "And anyway, ye told me she said he was a wanker, and she couldn't believe she'd wasted so much time on him."

"Ah know, ah know. Ah'm still nervous, though."

"Ah sure it'll be fine," said Mary. "And annyway, didn't she make the first move?"

"Aye, ah suppose so, but that was before she knew about . . ."

"Och, gimmie peace!" cried Billy, raising a hand, and stopping Mickie mid-sentence. "Just shut up, and drink yer beer, ya tosser."

Mickie looked at Billy's teasing grin, and tried to think of an appropriate response, but then, giving in to the mood, he laughed, and reached for his glass.

Chapter 3

Something was bothering Tom Paine, something had been bothering Tom Paine for quite some time. He stared blankly at his computer screen, and felt empty. He couldn't even summon up the will to do the simplest task his job required. *What is the point?* He couldn't help thinking. *Here it is, Friday once again, and once again, it was time to play the piss-head fool with Toby the bore.* He was sick of the whole charade. A slap on the back roused him from his gloomy thoughts.

"Cheer up old chum, it's Friday, time to get rat-arsed," bellowed the very bore.

Toby Sutton stood over him, with his hands stuffed into pinstripe trouser pockets, and a stupid grin spread over his face.

Oh, fuck! Thought Tom.

He looked up at the silly grinning face, and thought: *I just can't do this anymore.*

"I'm sorry, old chap, but I'm afraid I can't make it this evening, family commitments and all that."

"What?" replied Toby, doing his, too often repeated imitation of a gruff old army officer.

"Breaking ranks; that will never do."

Tom smiled wearily, and said:

"Yes, I'm sorry, but my sister is in London for the weekend, and I'm afraid I'm duty bound to entertain her."

"Well, bring her along, I'm sure the chaps would love to look over some new blood."

Oh, what a wanker, thought Tom. *How could I have been a part of this nonsense for so long?*

"Well, no, it's not really her thing, I'm afraid she doesn't drink. I'm just going to take her for a quiet meal."

"Oh," replied Toby, somewhat deflated, but then again switched on the grin.

"Well, there's always lunchtime; we can get a few down our necks, at least."

Tom frowned, and then tutted, as if bitterly disappointed.

"Actually, I'm going to have to work through, as I want to leave early, sorry."

"Oh," said Toby, again. "Fair enough . . . I'll . . . I'll see you Monday, then."

He remained standing there for a few awkward minutes, and then wandered off. Watching him leave, Tom Paine felt a vague sense of freedom.

* * *

The shaft of sunlight beaming through the office window, fell onto the three images Laura had laid out on the desk, making their rich dark colours glow. *They're wonderful,* thought, Laura. *All those beautiful blacks and browns. And the faces are so tender, tough, but tender.*

Mickie had explained to her, how he had always thought that the old Blues players had an iconic look, a quiet dignity; he said it shone out from the old photographs he had studied as reference. He had especially loved a photograph he had found of an old musician, named, Huddie Ledbetter, nicknamed, Leadbelly.

He had told her how the big man was portrayed sitting with his guitar flat across his knee, and his big hands resting on the instrument, while gazing straight at the camera. Mickie had immediately thought that he had the presence of a Buddha, or an Egyptian Pharaoh. That image had been the inspiration for this series of paintings, entitled: 'Blues Musicians Waiting to Play'.

She smiled, remembering his passion when describing the music. How powerful it felt to the musicians who played it, and also to the people who listened to it. How it could be hard like a weapon, or soft like a kiss, or as raw and joyful as sex. And he really believed it could soothe your soul; it was medicinal music.

"Oh, this is where you're hiding."

Laura turned to see John's smiling face peer round the door.

"Oh hi, John. Come and have a look, I've just printed out Mickie paintings."

He came over to the desk, and put his arm round her shoulder.

"Oh wow!" He exclaimed in genuine surprise. "Aren't they great? Ooh, I love the drummer," continued John, holding up the image. "Look at that beautiful mouth."

Laura laughed.

"Yes, I know, he's very handsome."

They continued to gaze silently at the images for a few minutes more, and then John took her by the hand.

"Okay, lovely, enough of that, it's time for lunch."

They left the Martin & MacLean building and walked the short distance to the local pub, where Laura sat down at a table outside, while John went in to order some food and drinks. On his return, he noticed Laura seemed lost in a daydream, but when he sat down opposite her, she looked up and smiled.

"So, the second date, huh?" he said, passing her drink over, and guessing her thoughts.

"I know," said Laura. "It still feels a bit unreal. To be honest, I'm a little nervous."

"Oh, phooey!" said John. "As soon as you look into each others eyes again, it'll be magic. Trust me, I'm a doctor."

"Phooey?" echoed Laura, wrinkling her nose in disbelief.

"I know, I know," replied John, shaking his head, and wrinkling his own nose. "I think I heard Bette Davis say it once. Anyway, you know what I mean."

"Yes, I do," said Laura, smiling. "And he is lovely; he really makes me laugh, he's very funny. But there's also this sadness in his eyes, especially when he talks about his little girl."

"What do you think about that, his little girl, I mean?"

"Oh, God, I haven't really had time to think about anything like that. Mona, that's the little girls name, is coming to London in two weeks time with her mother. They are apparently staying in Ealing most of the time, but then Mona is going to spend a few days with Mickie. I have a feeling he would like me to meet her, but he hasn't actually said so. I think he feels it may complicate things at present."

"And, would it?"

Laura thought for a few seconds, and then shrugged her shoulders.

"What can I say, she exists, she's real, and she's a huge part of his life. I can only take his lead, and deal with it, if and when it happens. At least he's been honest; he didn't have to tell me about Mona at all. I do, however, get the feeling he wants the two of us to get to know each other a little better, first."

"Well, it's obvious you like him very much. I can tell just by the way you talk about him. It was never like this with, thingy."

Laura laughed at the barbed reference to Toby.

"Oh yes, I do, very much. There's something tender about him; I just feel like hugging him all the time."

"Well, there you go, everything will fall into place," said John, in conclusion, as if no other evidence were needed.

Laura smiled tenderly at her friend.

"Oh John, you're such a romantic underneath all that cynicism."

John frowned, and reaching for his drink, said:

"And a fat lot of good it does me."

"It will, though," Laura said, trying to reassure him. "I'm sure of it."

"Yeah, right," he replied, looking away.

"It will. There's someone out there for you; I know it. Trust me."

John gave her a brief, sad smile, and they continued to sip their drinks for a few silent moments, until John, feeling the need to break the silence, asked:

"So, what have you got planned for tonight?"

"Oh, a long bath, a few glasses of wine, and a soppy film. I just want to relax on my own for a while."

"Sounds wonderful," said John, with a sigh.

"What about you?"

"Oh, the same old, same old, I suppose. I'll probably go to the Jolly Gardener, and see the same old faces. Nothing seems to change for me. I'm getting sick of it to be honest."

"Oh John, this isn't like you."

"Oh, I'm sorry, don't mind me. I just went into a bit of a whinge, there. Anyway, it's all your fault, bitch, falling in love indeed, tch."

Laura couldn't help laughing, as John made a face, and turned away, pretending to be annoyed. When the waitress then arrived with their food, and they ate, and talked of other things.

* * *

The Soho streets were bathed in a pale summer light; the kind of evening lemon-light that floods down through the buildings, illuminating windows like fire, and making everyone fixed in it's beam appear as if in a play; their pantomime gestures caught in a kind of celestial limelight.

Good God, thought John, frowning at his own fanciful prose. As a copywriter at Martin & MacLean, words were his tools, and he found that even when he wasn't trying, phrases like this would just pop into his head. In his better moments, normally after more than a few drinks, he could convince himself that he had the makings of a novelist, but it never came to anything. *Too much like bloody hard work,* he thought, dismissing the idea, yet again.

Without being conscious of exactly where he was going, he had been wandering through Soho's Friday evening throng for over an hour, and was now strolling down Dean Street.

Outside the bars and restaurants, people were laughing, talking, or simply watching the passing parade. Forgetting his rejection of the form only a few minutes before, John again found his thoughts taking a literary turn. The people on the street became: *The beautiful and the bizarre, teasers and pleasers, offering temptation at every turn. Dear oh dear,* he thought. *I need a drink.*

He was still dressed in his day clothes, a sure sign that he was feeling down, and couldn't be bothered to make an effort. He crossed the street into the 'lemon-light,' and stopped outside, The French House.

As usual, there was a diverse group of Friday evening revellers standing outside the pub, smoking, drinking, and putting the world to rights. John hesitated for a moment, and then squeezing past a man wearing, make-up, false eyelashes and a bowler hat, he entered the pub, and marched up to the bar like a man on a mission.

"A large gin and tonic, please?"

The young man, who took his order, had a curious looking wedge of hair sticking up from his head, and a carefully trimmed handlebar moustache. John thought he looked like a cartoon Frenchman. He had only been in this pub once before, and that was with Laura, who liked the atmosphere, and its bohemian history.

Sipping his drink, and taking in the surroundings, he started to feel a little better. *I hate feeling like this,* he thought. *It's so depressing, and must make you look very unattractive.* He had left work without saying goodbye to anyone, not even Laura; he couldn't, she would have immediately guessed he was in a mood. *It's strange,* he thought, *how sometimes, other people's happiness, highlights your own unhappiness. And even with people you adore, it sort of sucks away any joy you thought you had, and leaves you *feeling empty.* Thinking like this made him feel shallow and stupid, so he finished his drink, and ordered another, and tried to ease himself into some sort of good humour. His intention was to still go to the Jolly Gardener, but not yet.

* * *

Mary had gone out for the evening with some friends, and as Mickie was working, Billy was left to his own devices. He opened a can of lager, and then sat down at the kitchen table to consider his options.

As he didn't have many, this didn't take too long; in fact it took him less that a minute to decide on a quiet night in. He sighed, took another mouthful of beer, and then moving into the living room, picked up the phone and dialled the number of the local Indian Restaurant.

The waiter, who took his order, informed him that, as it was a Friday night, the restaurant was: "Very, very busy tonight, sir." And advised him to call by in about an hour. He sat in the silence of the living room mulling this over while finishing his beer, and then, brightening up a bit, he thought: *Och well, a wee bit of a stroll will be good for the appetite. And anyway, ah need more beer; no way can you have a curry without a lager.*

After leaving the flat, he wandered aimlessly through the local streets for a while, just taking in the evening atmosphere. But then, as he found himself nearby, he thought it might be a good idea to take a walk past Mrs McIntyre's house just to check if anything was amiss.

Acting on what Mickie had told him earlier in the week, he had made a few subtle enquiries about Sammie, but to no avail. Some people thought they knew him, but hadn't seen him recently; some of the younger black guys had blanked him with the usual, I know nothing, shrug.

As he got close to where Mrs McIntyre lived, he saw a young white guy sitting on the wall opposite her house. He kept on walking towards the youth, and when he got to within a few feet, he could smell the weed. On summer nights like this, it wasn't an unusual sight to see kids hanging out, especially in this neighbourhood. At first he didn't think too much about it, later, however, it struck him as curious that the youth was sitting alone outside Mrs McIntyre's house, as there was no attractions, it was a quiet street.

For an instant, he thought about crossing the street and checking on her, but then he decided it was probably better not to draw attention to the fact that he knew her, and so continued to walk casually towards the hooded figure. As he passed, the youth gave him the hard eye, and put a large spliff to his lips, so all that Billy could see on passing, was two defiant eyes staring up at him above the red glow.

Billy immediately felt pissed off; mainly he was annoyed at himself for letting the youth get to him. He didn't care what the guy thought of him personally, and he had nothing against kids, black or white, but why did they think they had to intimidate people to gain respect.

Billy knew all about the gang system; he had been through it growing up in Glasgow. He understood why some adolescent boys thought it was cool or even compulsory. But he had learned the hard way that it was stupid and dangerous. Billy was tough, and had a rapid rise up the ranks, and had no qualms about carrying weapons, or using them, if he thought it necessary. That's just the way it was.

It had been Mickie, who had eventually brought him to his senses. After one battle too many, Billy had been knifed in a revenge attack. Mickie, who had been coming to meet him, saw it happen, and his attackers run. Billy had been lucky, it hadn't been a serious wound, but Mickie had still insisted he take him to casualty, and wait while the overstretched, and not too happy medical staff, fixed him up.

"Ye've got to stop this. Ye've got to stop hangin about wi these fuckin arseholes!" Mickie had said, angrily. "Yer twenty years old, for fucks sake; catch a grip, ya tosser!"

Billy had never seen him so angry. Mickie was nobody's mug, but he was smart enough not to get involved with any gangs.; he was too self-contained, and into his own thing, even as a teenager, to get involved with anything so stupid and dangerous.

This time, Billy had listened, and deciding Mickie was right, had shortly after that, distanced himself from the gangs. He found he had an aptitude as a motor mechanic, and started working in a garage, getting properly trained, and even attending night classes.

After he had felt he had learned enough to be independent, he decided to leave Glasgow altogether, and six years ago, had headed for London. Mrs McIntyre's husband, Harry, had been a close friend of Billy's father, and so when Billy was thinking of leaving, his dad had arranged for him to stay with Harry and Lucy until he got settled. It didn't take him too long, however, to find a job and get his own place, and a few months after that, to his delight, he met Mary.

He was still deep in thought when he entered the off-licence.

"Hiya, Benno," he said to the big man behind the counter, and then walked over to the cooler, and took out four cans of Stella Lager.

"How ye Billy? My yer lookin very thoughtful dis evenin."

"Eh?" replied Billy, only half listening.

The big Irishman leaned forward, put both his large ham-like fists on the counter, and then sticking his chin out, said:

"I said, ye look like you've got somethin on yer mind."

"Oh, right. Aye, ye could say that," said Billy. "What is it with young guys these days? They all seemed to be pissed off, and have no respect for anythin, or anybody."

After voicing his frustration, Billy suddenly thought: *Fuckin hell, ah've just turned into my old man.*

"Oh yeah, dere's some nasty young pricks out dere, no doubt about it," agreed Benno. "A lot of young ones hang around outside here, because of the burger place next door. And I tink most of dem are good kids, but some are just vicious little bastards. Only a few days ago, somethin kicked off just outside."

"Oh aye?" said Billy, suddenly interested.

"Aye, Monday, it was. A black young one, a schoolboy, really, was bein laid into by dis bigger white one. I see dis youth around here a lot, I tink his names, Rob. I'm not certain,like, but I tink he might be sellin drugs to dese kids. His mother comes in here sometimes, and if she's not a Junkie, I'm fuckin Micheal Jackson. Annyway, he's an arrogant young fucker, and it could have ended badly, if the big fella hadn't stepped in."

"Big fella, what big fella?"

"Ah, an old black fella, but shockin big. He appeared from nowhere, and grabbed dis Rob by the arm, and pulled him off. It looked as if he was tryin to talk some sense into him. I couldn't hear what he said, but whatever it was, the young prick wasn't havin anny of it; he just stared the big fella down, and gave him some verbal. The cheeky young fucker was bein so arrogant, that for a minute, I thought de big fella was goin to lose it; his face just sort of froze. That's when Mrs McIntyre came over; she seemed to know the big fella, and took him by the arm and led him away."

"What?" Said Billy, wide-eyed.

"Mrs McIntyre; yer mate, Mickie's landlady; she came over and sort of calmed him down, and took him away."

* * *

As was customary for a Friday evening, The Jolly Gardener, was packed to overflowing; the music was loud, and the clientele colourful. John, having drunk four large gin and tonics in The French House, had managed to acquire a little more of that Friday feeling, although not enough to be in the mood for any jolly banter.

"Well, someone started early," said Paul the barman, who was tall, muscle-bound, and wearing an extremely tight, lemon yellow tee shirt.

John, having had trouble squeezing through to the bar, scowled at him, and said:

"Oh, shut up you big tart, and gimmie a gin'n'tonic."

"Oh, charming," replied Paul.

Paul, pretending to be offended, looked down his nose at John, and then, turning away, strutted off to fetch his drink.

I shall have to lighten up, here, thought John. *This won't do at all.* He then looked casually round the room, and, as he knew he would, saw the same old faces, and thought: *why the hell do I bother coming here?*

But then, to his astonishment, he caught sight of a face he certainly knew, but had never thought to see in here. Standing alone at the end of the bar, seemingly in a world of his own, was Tom Paine. John was instantly intrigued, and stared at the tall, slim figure, who stood out in his city suit, and freshly pressed white shirt.

Paul returned with his drink, and putting it in front of him, took the money. But John, without waiting for his change, lifted his glass, and walking up behind Tom Paine, said, somewhat mockingly:

"Well, well, well, what do we have here?"

Tom Paine turned slowly towards the voice, and seeing it was John, smiled sheepishly.

"Hello, I . . . I don't quite know what I'm doing here."

"Oh, I think you do," replied John, with a knowing look.

Paul put John's change on the bar, and gave him a smug look.

"Look, do you mind if we go outside?" said Tom. "I could do with a cigarette."

"Sure," replied John. "And maybe you could do with another drink."

"No, it's alright." replied Tom Paine. "And anyway, it's only water."

John's eyes widened for an instant, but he made no comment, he just turned and made for the door, with Tom Paine following him into the fading evening light.

* * *

It was a beautiful morning, and Laura was happy. She stepped out of the shower, dried herself off, and looked in the mirror. This morning she seemed to see herself with new eyes, lover's eyes, and thought, albeit with some modesty, that she liked what she saw. But then, feeling a little silly and self-conscious, she made a face in the mirror, slipped into her favourite dressing gown, and went to prepare her breakfast.

Opening the kitchen windows wide to let in the morning air, she made real coffee, warmed up the fresh croissants she had bought earlier, and then placed them, along with the coffee, hot milk, butter and blackberry preserve on a tray. While carrying her small feast through to the living room, she smiled to herself, and thought: *No counting calories today then.*

Mickie had phoned first thing, flirting with her, and making her laugh. He too had sounded happy, and his call had dispelled any doubts she'd had about seeing him again.

He had suggested they meet at one o'clock, have lunch at a pub on the river, and then walk along the embankment to Tate Modern. And then, he had said, teasingly:

"I'm sure we'll think of something else to do."

That was when she knew she was going to invite him back this evening, and the thought had made her feel excited, and nervous.

With Albinoni in Venice, her favourite Saturday morning music, flooding the room, she settled down on the couch with her coffee and croissants, and looked again at the photographs of Mickie's paintings. She knew the obvious person to ask, regarding what to do and who to approach on Mickie's behalf, would be Tim Farrell.

That, however, would have to wait until this latest job was over, as things were going to be hectic for the next few weeks. Before she realised it, she found herself thinking about what she still had to achieve at work next week, but happily, she came to her senses a few minutes later, and thought: *What am I doing? It's Saturday.*

After savouring the last morsel of buttery croissant, she poured some more coffee, and then, as she had been wondering why he had mysteriously slunk away from work yesterday evening, she decided to phone John.

She dialled his number, and after a few rings, a sleepy voice answered:

"Hello."

"Well, hello yourself. Where did you disappear to then?"

John answered through a yawn:

"Oh, hello Laura. What time is it?"

"Ten thirty. Where did you disappear to then?"

"Excuse me darling, but are you now working for the FBI?"

Laura suppressed a laugh.

"Well, pardon me for worrying about you."

"Were you? Aw, that's nice."

She couldn't quite work out if he was winding her up or not.

"Are you all right?" she asked.

"Hunky dory, darling."

"Oh, right," said Laura, a bit bemused.

"So what did you get up to last night?"

"If I told you, darling, you wouldn't believe me."

"Oh, really, why?"

"Oh, Laura, I'm sorry, I don't mean to be rude, but I really can't talk right now. I'll see you as usual on Monday, though. Okay, bye."

Laura sat for a moment with a puzzled look on her face, and then replaced the phone. *How very odd,* she thought.

* * *

Mickie was sitting in the shade, outside a café in Marylebone. He had been wandering around the area for most of the morning, and had come across the small café tucked away in this quiet back street. The old fashioned décor had caught his eye, that and the fact that it only had one other customer: a small elderly man, who sat gazing into the street, as if in a dream.

While waiting to be served, Mickie idly glanced at the play of sunlight moving across the facade of the red brick building opposite, and then, half-closing his eyes, tried to judge the colour of the shadows.

The young waitress, who a few minutes earlier had taken his order, now placed a foaming cappuccino on the table in front of him. Mickie smiled and thanked her. The coffee looked good, and as he had left the house too early to be bothered with breakfast, he was eager for a taste. He took a sip, and it was as good as it looked, but feeling he needed some sweetness this morning, he dropped two brown sugar lumps into the cup, and let them dissolve while he lit a cigarette.

He had been roused from sleep earlier than usual that morning by a police car speeding past the house with its siren wailing; the piercing sound coming so close, had awakened him in an instant. For a while after the wailing car had drifted into the distance, he had lain in the half-light of his bedroom, listening to the early song of the city birds, and staring at the ceiling.

Mona was never far from his thoughts, especially when he was alone, but it was always a bittersweet feeling, and he knew well enough the consequences of reflecting too long, on her being so far away; and he didn't want to be sad, not today. He had therefore decided, that rather than lying there brooding, it would be much better to get up and run a bath. An hour or so later, he was dressed and out of the house even before Mrs McIntyre was up.

On the journey into town on the Central Line, he had been wondering what he should do to pass the time until he had to meet Laura. But when the train had pulled into Marble Arch Station, he had taken the snap decision that this was as good a stop as any, and had got off to see where the mood would take him.

Since coming to live in London, he had spent many a solitary weekend exploring the different areas of the city. He soon found that it was more interesting to get away from the crowds, and blend into the quiet grandeur of the empty streets. The idea that you never knew what you would find, and could lose yourself for hours on end, appealed to him.

That he didn't know the exact location of the café he was now sitting in, didn't bother him, he really didn't care, that was the whole point of wandering. It suddenly struck him that his ex-wife would probably say that this was typical of his weak, aimless attitude to life.

Reluctant as he was to dwell on the past, particularly today, he found his thoughts drifting back to a conversation he'd had with Mrs McIntyre shortly after coming to London. He had been lodging with her only a few months, and was finding it hard to cope with the guilt of not seeing Mona.

The Falcon had been quiet, and as his shift had dragged, he'd had more time than usual to ponder on what he deemed to be his failures. Surprised to find Mrs McIntyre still up, and sitting at the kitchen table listening to the radio, he had popped his head round the door to say goodnight. What he didn't know then, was that she had this uncanny ability to sense when people were in need of someone to listen to their doubts and fears, and if she could help, she would.

She had somehow persuaded him to sit down for a while, and have a drink. At first, he had been shy and unsure of what to say, but she had gently eased him into talking about what was on his mind, and after a few rums, he had found all this despair and longing pouring out of him.

"Ah really did try to make it work, but it was a mistake from the beginning. If ah'm honest, ah only stayed as long as ah did, because of Mona."

Lucy nodded, but made no reply.

"When Mona was born ah couldn't believe the love ah felt for her, and then ah began to think that maybe things would be all right after all, but they weren't."

"How yuh come to meet your wife?" asked Lucy, although she already knew, Billy having told her the story before Mickie had come down.

"Aye, well, that was the whole root of the problem," said Mickie "We met at a party, got very drunk, and ended up going back to her flat, and two months later, she told me she was pregnant."

"Mi guessin it wasn't real love."

Mickie looked down into his glass, and shook his head.

"Ah feel like a bastard everyday for leavin but ah didnae know what else to do. She gives me dogs abuse about every simple wee thing, but ah canny really retaliate, because she knows ah never loved her, and ah know that hurts her more than anythin."

Lucy topped up his glass.

"We cain't choose who loves us, Mickie."

Mickie shrugged his shoulders.

"Och, ah don't know anymore. Ah just had to get away. Her anger was so cold and relentless, and ah hated Mona bein in the middle of something like that."

"Mickie, sometimes life is hard," said Lucy, a sad look coming into her brown eyes. "But darlin, the only way through it, is through it."

Mrs McIntyre was a wise woman, and talking to her had helped, but it was still sometimes hard to believe he had done the right thing. He crushed out his cigarette, took another sip of coffee, and thought of only a few weeks before, when after one of his daily calls to Mona, Sharon had come on the phone to tell him she had met someone else. He had said he was glad, and genuinely hoped she would be happy, but also voiced concern regarding his daughter:

"What about Mona?"

"What about Mona?" Sharon had said with the spiteful edge to her voice he had come to know so well. "At least Glen is up here, and not swannin about London, barely giving a second thought to his abandoned daughter."

A raw feeling went through him every time he thought of Sharon's bitter words. His only consolation was that he liked and trusted Sharon's mother, Peggy, and could rely on her to keep him informed about how Mona really was. He remembered how disappointed Peggy had been, when he told her he was moving to London, and how she had tried her best to convince him otherwise, even quoting him an old Glasgow saying:

"Ye've made yer bed, son, and should lie on it."

But Peggy, being an honest woman, had tempered her statement by reluctantly admitting that, unfortunately, her daughter could sometimes be spiteful and cruel. She was, however, also adamant that he should remember that Sharon truly loved Mona, and would never do anything to hurt her.

Coming out of his sad reverie, he lit another cigarette, and signalled to the waitress. When she came over, he paid for his coffee, and asked:

"What time is it, please?"

She looked at her watch.

"It's ten to twelve."

Oh right, thanks."

The girl then went over to attend to the elderly man. As Mickie watched, she gently helped the old man to his feet.

"Okay, Mr Mason," she said tenderly. "We'll see you tomorrow, same time. You take care, now."

The old man slowly nodded his head, and smiled, and then, to Mickie's surprise, he deftly unfolded a white cane. It was then that he realised the reason for the man's vacant stare. The girl watched him slowly make his way down the street, tapping his cane as he went, and then, smiling sadly at Mickie, she turned and went into the café.

Mickie finished his coffee, stubbed out his cigarette, and then placed a pound coin, and the rest of his change, under the lip of the saucer. He always tried to leave a tip, but didn't like handing it over personally; to him it felt too much of master and servant, as in: "There you go, my good woman." He was of course aware that people like the young waitress, actually depended on tips to boost their meagre wages, but he was just funny that way.

He left the café, and stepped into the sun, and then started walking in what he gauged to be a southerly direction, towards the river, and Laura.

Chapter 4

Lucy was sitting in her kitchen looking again at the old photographs. *Who were these young people,* she thought, *so full of hope and joy?* It was like looking at strangers. She held up one photograph that must have been taken at least thirty-five years ago, but she couldn't remember where. It was the young Lucy, sitting at a crowded table in a club somewhere, with Harry on one side, and Sammie on the other; and they were laughing, they seemed to laugh all the time back then.

She laid the photograph down, and began playing with her wedding band, as if she thought that perhaps caressing it so might cause some Genie to appear and grant her a wish. Seconds later, she was rudely stirred from her daydream by the sudden piercing ring of the doorbell, which made her jump in fright.

She went into the living room, and took a cautious peek through the curtains. It was Sammie; he was standing on the doorstep with his head down, and a forlorn look on his face. A light came into her eyes, and she smiled, but then she then quickly adjusted her face into a frown, thinking this an appropriate look for the occasion. She then opened the door, and pretended to be surprised.

"Oh, Sammie! Why yuh come here? We talk this over, so."

"Tch, Lucy, but mi cain't live like this. We have to find a way around this ting."

Lucy looked nervously up and down the street, and then at Sammie.

"Well, come man, come in if yuh comin."

Sammie stepped inside, closed the door, and followed her into the kitchen.

Lucy made coffee, and then they sat at the kitchen table, unsure how to begin. A jazz station played softly in the background. Sammie rolled a cigarette, lit it, and then looked at Lucy.

"Lucy girl, mi too old to change mi way a livin. Mi cain't let some nasty white rude-bwoy rule mi life."

Lucy looked down at her hands, and again played with her wedding ring.

"Mi know, Sammie, but that bwoy is bad; he been hangin around here most nights. Mi don't know if he just tryin to scare me, or if he gonna do someting. Mi don't know what to do. Yuh read about tings like this in the papers all the time."

Sammie was alarmed to hear this, but didn't show it.

"Yuh speak to the police about him hangin round?"

"Oh, they won't do anyting, and even if they did, it would only make tings worse. These youths don't respect nobody or anyting. Like a fool mi hopin him get bored, and leave we alone."

Sammie looked out the window and smoked in silence for a while. Lucy glanced at him, and then got up and went through to the living room, and came back moments later carrying a bottle of rum. Without comment, she poured a shot into each of their cups.

Sammie grinned, nodded his head, and took a long sip from his cup, and then, suddenly enthused, he said:

"Lets go out Luce. Lets show this blood-claat he cain't keep us out of the sun, cain't keep us away from the music. And you know what Harry would have said."

"Fuckum!"

Sammie said the expletive in a perfect Glasgow accent, and then adding, for emphasis: "And you know that's the truth, girl."

Lucy laughed out loud at the impersonation; she knew Sammie was right, that's exactly what Harry would have said, and it somehow gave her courage.

"Sammie, yuh right, why should we hide? Mi sorry mi made you stay away, but it vex mi to tink you gonna get hurt. Mi still scared, but mi cain't let that bwoy see that." She then rose from the table, and smiling at Sammie, said: "Help yuhself to rum, mi won't be long."

With that, she left the room, and Sammie poured another shot of rum into his cup, and smiled. A short time later, Lucy appeared back in the kitchen, only this time, she was dressed for town. Looking up this vision, a grin spread like the sun across Sammie's face.

* * *

"Hello! Is that you, Mary?"

Mary rolled her eyes, and shook her head in amused disbelief

"No, it's Nicole Kidman; I thought we could maybe watch the game, and crack a few cans."

Billy grinned.

"Oh, ah don't know about that, the wife gonnie be back soon, and she brings her own beer, you know."

Mary put her head round the living room door.

"Why do you always ask if it's me? Who the hell else would it be?"

"Oh, just to annoy you dear."

He was sitting on the couch with his feet up on the coffee table, watching the football. Mary crept up behind him and cuffed him on the back of the head.

"Ohya! Here there was no need for that," cried Billy, rubbing his head, while Mary made for the kitchen.

"Come on, get off yer arse, and give me a hand with the shoppin."

Billy leapt up and chased her into the kitchen, grabbing at her bottom, and making her shriek with laughter.

In the small kitchen, they worked together putting the groceries away in their proper place. They were good together, and it showed in the small details of their life.

While Mary finished putting the last of the shopping away, Billy filled the kettle, and flicked the switch. He then leaned against the sink and looked at his wife; he liked looking at her. He loved the way her full breasts swelled inside the black sweater she had nicked out of his drawer that morning, and the way that little flick of auburn hair curled at the back of her neck. She glanced round and caught him.

"Well! What are you lookin at?"

"What's up, can ah not look at my wife now?"

She smiled, and pinching his cheek, said mockingly:

"Of course ye can, wee chubby chops."

"What do you mean, chubby?" said Billy, sucking in his belly.

Mary laughed, and giving him a quick kiss, headed for the bathroom, and said over her shoulder:

"I'm goin to have a quick shower,"

Billy made coffee for Mary, and got a beer out of the fridge for himself.

After her shower, Mary came and joined him on the sofa, wearing a fluffy pink bathrobe, and looking glowing and fresh. She lit a cigarette, and took a sip of coffee.

"Ah found somethin out last night," said Billy, glancing at the silent TV screen.

"About what?"

"About Mrs McIntyre and Sammie."

Mary looked up from her magazine.

"Oh aye. What about them?"

"It seems there was a bit of trouble wi some kids outside that burger bar, ye know the one next to the off-licence. Well, it seems Sammie stepped in and broke it up, but the young guy he pulled off is a bit of a nutter, and ah think he's now got it in for Sammie; you know what they're like about this respect shite. Anyway, ah think this arsehole is hangin outside Mrs McIntyre's waitin for Sammie."

"How do you know that?"

"Because ah walked past there last night, and there was a hoodie sittin on the wall opposite her house, and there was just somethin about him that got to me."

Ye didn't say annythin?" said Mary, looking alarmed.

"No, mainly because ah didnae know anythin about this until later, but for some reason he really pissed me off. Anyway, ah then went to get some beer, and big Benno in the off-licence filled me in, as he saw it all kick off. He said Mrs McIntyre appeared while Sammie was confrontin the guy, and managed to coax him away, or it might have been worse."

"How do you mean?"

"Well, Sammie was tryin to reason with the guy, but apparently he was such a mouthy, arrogant fucker, that Sammie nearly lost it."

"Jesus! Do ye think Mickie knows annythin about this?"

"No, ah don't think so. If Mrs McItyre had wanted him to know, she would've mentioned it when Mickie found her all stressed out last week. I think she's hopin this prick will get bored, and doesn't want to worry anybody, and for the minute, ah agree with her, because Mickie probably would worry, what with Mona coming down. Ah also asked Benno not to mention anythin to Mickie if he sees him, but he rarely uses the off-licence, as he gets his beer at the pub."

Mary stubbed her cigarette out, and looked at Billy.

"Yer not goin to do annythin stupid are you, like confront this guy?"

Billy tilted his head, and shrugged his shoulders.

"Billy!"

"Okay, okay. Don't get excited. Ah just want to find out a bit more about this tosser, and keep an eye on things."

Mary looked sad all of a sudden, and started picking little bits of fluff from her dressing gown. Billy put his arm around her, and pulled her close.

"Honestly, darlin, don't worry. Ah'm not gonny do anything stupid.

* * *

He sat in the darkened room sucking on a can of lager, and staring at the TV screen. The room reeked of smoke and stale people.

Even though it was a summer evening, he was dressed as if he was cold, in a hooded jacket and a baseball cap. The windows were shut tight, and the curtains partially drawn. He was big for his age, almost a man, but his face had the cruel look of an indignant little boy.

In the ashtray on the littered coffee table, lay a large, newly rolled spliff. He reached for it, and firing it up, noisily took the acrid weed deep into his lungs, and then let go a thick column of smoke into the already airless room. A moment later, his mobile phone rang, but he let it go to voice-mail. He then clicked off the volume on the TV, and picked up the phone. As he listened to the message, his face gradually became a twisted mask of hate, and anger.

After the call, he replaced the phone back on the table, and for a moment sat motionless in the silence, but then, suddenly roaring like trapped animal, he stood up, and viciously threw his half-empty beer can hard against the wall.

* * *

To Laura and Mickie, the lights reflected in the river along the embankment looked dream-like. They had spent the evening talking endlessly in a bar, and now were tipsy and self-contained. As the Saturday night throng bustled all around them, they were content to stand in silence, and watch the river flow.

After a while, they continued to wander along Bankside, until they came across a busker filling the night with the Bach Cello Suite. He was playing so well, and with such passion, that Mickie was moved to throw what little change he had left into the young guy's instrument case; he guessed the boy was a music student, who was trying to supplement his meagre grant. The music enticed them to sit and listen for a while.

"What a magical night," Mickie said, almost to himself.

It was as if he had never really seen London before; it was so beautiful. He felt as though he had been walking around in some sad dream, but now his eyes took in everything with a new delight, the buildings, the people, but most of all Laura.

They had eased so naturally back into their love, that it thrilled, and scared him at the same time. They sat silent for a time, listening to the music, and then Laura, looking serious, turned to him and said:

"Mickie, would you like to come back and stay with me tonight?"

He looked into her eyes and saw that she was a little unsure as to what his answer might be, and that maybe she'd said the wrong thing. This just made him love her even more, but he couldn't resist teasing her a little; he scrunched up his face, as if pondering on the question, and then said:

"Well, ah don't know."

Laura looked downcast, and clasped her hands together, making Mickie immediately feel guilty.

"Oh Laura, ah'm kidding. Ah mean, look at you. Ah would have to be a blind fool not to want to spend the night with you. Ah'm sorry."

She looked up, and when she saw that he really did mean it, she gave a soft little smile, and then punched him surprisingly hard on the arm.

"Yeow!" he cried, clutching his arm.

Laura laughed, delighted at catching him off-guard, and getting her own back, while Mickie, still rubbing his arm, grinned at her sheepishly.

"Well, ah won't be doin that again," he said, giving her a wry look.

He'd had then just leaned in to kiss her, when suddenly, a fat man wearing a Tutu, sailed past them on a skateboard; they looked at one another, and burst out laughing.

Mickie was successful the second time, and kissed her sweetly on the mouth. Laura took him by the hand, and said:

"Let's go home."

As they made their way over the bridge towards Embankment Station, they couldn't help but stop and gaze at the moon. It looked huge, and was so low in the sky as to appear to have come to rest on the roof of the Savoy Hotel, as if taking time to survey the London night.

* * *

The boy heard them coming through the front door and immediately turned up the volume on the TV; it was a vain attempt to deflect the abuse he knew was coming.

The door to the living room was pushed open, and the clink of glass was accompanied by a hoarse laugh, which quickly turned into a hacking cough. He felt his whole body go tense; it was a sensation he knew well. He kept his eyes on the screen, and wished he were invisible.

Without acknowledging him, the man and woman went directly into the tiny kitchen, where he knew bottles would be opened and drinks poured. A few minutes later, the woman came into the living room. Her name was Patsy; she was thirty-nine years old, but with her unkempt dirty blonde hair, and sunken eyes, she looked much older. On the too rare occasions when she was straight and sober, you could still see in her face, traces of the very pretty girl she must once have been; unfortunately, alcohol and dope were now taking their steady toll.

She was obviously drunk, and sat unsteadily down on a chair at the bare table by the window, gulping greedily from a big tumbler of vodka. She then put the drink down, and proceeded to try and light a cigarette, only succeeding after a few attempts. The man then entered the room, and when passing behind the boy on the couch, smacked him hard on the back of the head.

"Watcha, wanker!" he said, as an added insult, before sitting down opposite the woman at the table. The woman gave a short gravelly laugh, and then started coughing. The boy remained impassive, afraid to react.

"Turn that fuckin volume down, willya," the man shouted above the noise of the TV. The boy turned it down, and stole a quick, furtive glance at the man.

"Don't you fuckin eyeball me, ya little prick!" the man snarled.

"Oh don't, Nazz," said Patsy, feebly interrupting. "He aint doin nothin. You two are always at it."

"Aw, fuck off! This wankers gotta learn respect."

Nazz took a slug of scotch, and then lit a cigarette, keeping his eye fixed on the boy the whole time. Nazz was black, and big, well over six feet; he had cold hard eyes and a misshapen, bulbous nose that was difficult not to notice.

"Just as well you took my advice not to fuck off until I got here," said Nazz, glaring at the boy. "And like I said on the phone, you're goin on a little oliday to the seaside."

"Whaddya mean oliday? I got somethin I gotta sort out," the boy replied feebly, still not daring to make eye contact.

"Ye'll do what I fuckin tell ya. I'm gonna be conductin a bit of business here, and I want you gone."

"Nazz took a drag of his cigarette, and then frowned at the woman.

"Oh, talk to him willya? He gets on my fuckin nerves. I'm goin for a piss."

He then stood up, and when passing behind the boy, he again delivered a cruel slap to the back of his head. The boy could only close his eyes in anger and shame.

The woman took another gulp of vodka, and glanced at the boy.

"I'm sure it'll only be for a couple of weeks, Rob, luv." Her voice was pathetic, pleading. "Yer Gran'll be pleased to see ya, and Kent's not that bad."

Rob turned on the woman, and hissed angrily, but not loud enough that Nazz would hear.

Kent? What the fuck am I gonna do in Kent? I hate the fuckin place. Why do you let him treat me like this, mum?"

For an instant, a shadow of genuine guilt crossed Patsy's face, but it was like a fleeting cloud passing in front of the sun, and was soon replaced by a phoney, yellow grin.

"Oh, come on, he aint that bad. He gives us money for this place."

"The council pays for this place, he's not even supposed to be livin here. I fuckin hate him, and I fuckin hate you. Yer supposed to be me mum, for fucks sake."

Nazz came back in the room.

"What you two whisperin about then?"

"Oh, I was just sayin his gran'll be pleased to see im," Patsy said quickly, flashing the yellow grin.

Nazz gave a low, humourless laugh, and sitting back down, knocked back his scotch in one swallow, and refilled the glass. He then reached for the half-smoked spliff in the ashtray, and lit it.

"Let's have some music," cried Patsy, in a feeble attempt to ease the tension. She then lurched over to a small CD-player, and fumbled with the discs; suddenly, the sound of raucous club music filled the room, and she made a pathetic attempt to dance, but vaguely resembled someone with an acute case of palsy, and soon gave up. Breathing heavily, she then sank awkwardly back into her chair with a sullen look on her face, and took a long swallow from her glass.

After a few minutes, she looked over at Nazz with raised eyebrows, while grinning stupidly, and nodding as if to intimate something. Nazz, still staring at the boy, took a small gelcap of white powder from his pocket, and threw it across the table. Patsy instantly grabbed it, and disappeared into the bedroom.

Rob sat for a long, excruciating few minutes with his arms tightly folded, staring at the floor. The dance music had become overpowering; it felt as if it was beating him down. Without warning, he leapt to his feet, and keeping his eyes fixed straight ahead, rushed from the room. Hearing the front door slam, Nazz sat motionless for a few minutes, and then grinning, relit the spliff.

* * *

Mickie opened his eyes, and was, for a few sleepy seconds, confused as to where he actually was, and then he became aware of Laura breathing softly by his side. He then lay very still in the half-light of the bedroom, staring at the ceiling.

He thought back to the previous evening, and remembered how at first they had both been a little shy, talking of nothing really. Laura had lit candles, and then put on some music; the mellow sound of the Miles Davis Quintet had somehow brought another element into play, and they had begun to feel a little more at ease.

Laura had told him to make himself at home, while she went into the kitchen to fetch a bottle of wine. He had wandered round the spacious room, intrigued by the odd collection of props Laura had acquired from the various projects she had worked on. He especially liked a large, beautifully shaped glass jar with a unique gold-plated lid; Laura told him later, that it was actually made from perspex and brass.

After he had opened the wine, they had sat together on the sofa, and Laura had shown him the photographs of his paintings. She had been delighted to see his surprise and joy at how professional they looked, and went on to tell him of her intention to show them to Tim Farrell, whom she thought would like them very much, and would be sure to help Mickie if he could. But she had also made clear that all that would have to wait until the commercial they were working on, had been filmed and edited.

Mickie couldn't believe she had done this for him, and had been so genuine and charming in his gratitude, that she had become a little embarrassed, and putting a finger to his lips, had whispered:

Shh, enough."

After a while, the wine and the music had made them feel languid, sexy, and suddenly they couldn't bear to be apart a moment longer. They simply stopped talking, and looked into each others eyes, and then Mickie, reaching over and tenderly caressing Laura's face with the back of his hand, had then pulled her to him.

They kissed, and passion had swept over them: hands, mouths, eyes closed to anything that wasn't part of this union. Mickie had then put his hand behind Laura's hips, and drew her to him, gently laying her down; Laura's dress riding up to expose her beautiful bare thighs. Lying on the sofa, now, he had felt Laura's hands pull free his shirt, and felt the touch of her hands on his skin. He was kissing her eyes, her neck, and the swell of her breasts above her dress. He had then reached down and gently stroked the silky, so soft skin on the inside of her thigh; and then slowly higher, feeling the moist heat of her sex through the thin cotton, making Laura moan softly, and hold him even tighter. He slipped his hand into the waistband of her pants, and the feel of her had made him gasp. He had then gently slid them down her slender legs, Laura arching her body to make it easier.

Laura had then loosened his belt, unzipped him, and guided his hardness into her. They had abandoned themselves to lovemaking heart and soul; the candlelight catching the rhythm of their bodies in its glow. Afterwards, their passion for the moment spent, they had lingered, joined in a loving embrace, not wanting to speak, not wanting to part.

After the last note of music had faded, Laura had kissed him, and whispered:

"Time for bed."

When Mickie had stood up from the sofa, his jeans had fallen to his ankles, making Laura giggle delightedly at the sight of him standing there trouser-less. She had then reached down, and plucking her knickers from the floor, gave him a sultry look, and sauntered sexily into the bedroom.

Grinning, Mickie had quickly pulled up his pants, and then followed her into the room. He had watched, entranced, as Laura had let her dress fall to the floor, and then lingering for a moment, had smiled shyly before disappearing into the bathroom.

Undressing himself, Mickie had then slipped under the covers, feeling strange and wonderful at the same time. When Laura had again appeared in the room, he had been delighted to see that she was still beautifully naked. He had then reached out to take her by the hand to kiss her, but had then suddenly realised he hadn't brushed his teeth, and Laura obviously had. Leaping from the bed, he had made an ungainly dash to the bathroom, leaving Laura looking somewhat puzzled at his rapid exit.

But finally, they were together in bed, locked in that beautiful sensation of skin to skin, and the delicious feeling of exploring each other's bodies. They had made love until sublime sleep had enveloped them, still wrapped in a warm embrace.

Mickie now turned to look at the sleeping Laura, her dark tousled hair, her long eyelashes, and her beautiful mouth. He put his hand gently on her belly, and felt the warmth of her skin. Still asleep, Laura had given a little moan, and then turning, had embraced him, and nuzzled into his neck. Mickie held her close and smiled, and then, closing his eyes, fell into a deep dreamless sleep.

*　*　*

Mary had left early to start her shift, and Billy had tried, without much success, to drift back to sleep. After restlessly tossing and turning for a while, he eventually gave up, and decided he might as well get up and make some tea. He was proud of the fact that Mary was a nurse, but when she had to work weekends, especially Sundays, he missed her, and got easily bored; and now, with Mickie otherwise engaged, it would be even more boring.

He put on his dressing gown, and went into the kitchen. After making his drink, he stood staring out of the window. As his and Mary's flat was on the third floor, he could look into various adjoining backyards. *It's weird,* he thought, *how one yard is so tidy and cared for, and then, the one right next door is a shit-heap, full of rubbish. It's funny how people can be so different.*

His thoughts turned to Mickie, and he wondered how his friend was getting on. He liked to think of him all loved up and happy; he certainly deserved some luck. He finished his tea and rinsed the cup, and then decided he might as well take a shower, get dressed, and go for a walk to pick up a newspaper.

The morning air made him feel better. He had over indulged a little too much the previous evening, but he was also feeling a little down for some reason. As Mary had an early start in the morning, they had both decided on a quiet night in, and Billy had offered to make dinner. He liked to cook, and as he was chef for the evening, he had decided to make his own favourite, steak and chips, while leaving Mary to relax with a drink, and sort out a movie for them to watch.

During the evening, Mary had only drunk one or two glasses of wine, while Billy had managed to consume more than his share of lager, and still managed to finish the wine; his excuse being, that Mary was working the next day, and he wasn't.

He pushed open the door of the little local shop, and then after nodding hello to the young Asian man behind the counter, he went and picked up a copy of the Scottish Sunday Mail. In the meantime, a big, stocky black guy had entered the shop, and now stood in front of him at the counter. Billy vaguely recalled seeing him around, remembering him mainly because of his nose; even now, it was hard not to stare. The big guy looked extremely disgruntled, and Billy couldn't help thinking: *Well, with a face like that, ah suppose he's entitled to feel pissed off.*

The guy gruffly asked for forty Camel cigarettes, and then, when handed the packs, tossed the money on the counter, even thought the Asian man had held his hand out to receive it. He then took his change without thanks, and just before he left, he swivelled his head round and gave Billy a cold look. Billy, however, just nodded, and said breezily:

"Mornin!"

The big man seemed unsure as to whether Billy was taking the piss or not, but he decided to ignore it, and turning away, left the shop. Billy smiled to himself, and thought: *You should be out haunting houses, pal.* And then, with the big man still in his thoughts, he put his paper on the counter, and suddenly deciding to buy Mary some cigarettes, he said:

"Twenty Malboro noses please?"

The young Asian man's eyebrows shot up, and Billy suddenly realised what he had just said.

"Tch, sorry. Lights, twenty Malboro Lights?"

The man turned and reached up to get the cigarettes, but then seemed to freeze, and remain motionless, except for a slight movement of his shoulders. Billy soon realised the man was actually silently laughing, and gave a wry smile. It took a good thirty-seconds or so for the young man to contain his amusement, but then he turned, and just managing to keep a straight face, handed Billy the cigarettes. Billy didn't dare look at him, but managed to keep his composure long enough to pay him, say thanks, and leave the shop.

Once outside the shop, Billy couldn't stop grinning. He peeked through the shop window, and could see that the young man was now leaning on the counter with his head in his arms, shaking with laughter. Billy grinned and shaking his head, continued up the street,

As he had no reason to rush home, he decided he would take a stroll past Mrs McIntyre's house, just to check, and then head back and make himself some breakfast.

As he approached the house, he saw, with some alarm, that something had been sprayed on the front door. He crossed the street to take a closer look, and was shocked to see, sprayed in big white aerosol letters, BLACK BASTARDS. For a long confusing few minutes, Billy stood stunned, unsure of how to handle the situation, but then thought: *How can ah ignore somethin like this?* He rang the doorbell. It took a quite a few minutes for Mrs McIntyre to answer, but eventually she opened the door, and looked surprised to see Billy standing there.

"Hello Billy. If yuh lookin for Mickie, mi don't think he's,"

"I'm sorry Mrs McIntyre," said Billy quickly cutting her off, and then pointing at the door, he added: "Ah was just passin, and ah saw this."

It took a few seconds for Lucy to register what she was actually looking at, but when it struck home, she covered her face with her hands. Billy suddenly felt his anger build, but pulled himself together enough to say:

"Why don't ye let me clean it off, Mrs McIntyre?"

Without saying a word, she let him into the house, and he followed her into the kitchen, where she sat down at the table.

"Do ye have anythin like paint thinners in the house?" Billy asked, as gently as he could.

Lucy seemed in a daze, but said in a thin voice:

"Maybe, in the cupboard under the stairs, mi not sure."

Billy looked, and found an old can of thinners, a scrubbing brush, and a couple of sheets of worn sandpaper.

"Why don't ye put the kettle on, and ah'll have this fixed in no time," he called through to the kitchen, trying his best to reassure her.

He set to work with the thinners and scrubbing brush, and thought how fortunate it was that the door was just plain wood, and with the paint still comparatively fresh, he managed to scrub off most of the paint without having to use the sandpaper. The scrubbed area, however, now looked lighter than the rest of the door, and so he mixed some dirt and water, and wiped it into the wood.

He stood back and examined his work, and thought: *Well, it's the best ah can do for now. Ah'll have another look when it's dried.* He replaced the items back in the cupboard, and then washed his hands at the kitchen sink. Lucy had made coffee, and the pot and two cups were now sitting on the table along with a bottle of rum. She poured them coffee, and then, without asking, put a couple of shots of rum in each cup. Billy sat down opposite her, and took a sip from his cup.

"Ah think we both know who did this, Mrs McIntyre."

She looked at him over the top of her glasses, and said, with a sudden hint of steely anger in her voice:

"Well, mi tink, mi know who did it. But how come you know?"

"Benno in the off licence told me he saw what happened when Sammie broke up the fight outside the burger bar. He said the guy Sammie pulled off was pissed off and mouthy. So it's not hard to make the connection."

Lucy took a sip of coffee, but made no comment.

"Did ye see or hear anythin last night?" Billy asked.

Lucy shook her head.

"No, mi was in bed asleep by ten-thirty. Sammie and miself had gone uptown in the afternoon to hear some music, and visit some friends' mi hadn't seen for a while. Mi left there about nine, as mi was a little tired, but Sammie stayed on to play for a while."

Lucy toyed with her wedding ring, while Billy tried to organise his thoughts.

"Look Mrs. McIntyre, ah happen know this guy has been hangin round yer house, and. . . "

He didn't get to finish, because all of a sudden, the anger and frustration Lucy had been holding back came pouring out in her native patios:

Yuh tink mi don't know dis, but if dis fool tink he can terrorise me, he got anudder tink comin. Mi bin through enough shit in mi life. Mi just don't want Sammie to be hurt; mi just don't want Samm..."

Her eyes gleamed with tears, but her mouth was set firm against crying.

Billy again felt his anger rise; he hated seeing her like this.

"Look Mrs McIntyre, excuse me, but ah'll take care of this arsehole; he disnae know me, but he will, because ah'll be keepin an eye on him. Ye know ah work at the garage, and ah hear things, and ah'm sure ah can find out where he lives and..."

Lucy cut in:

"Billy, mi don't want yuh getting into no trouble."

Billy looked at her tenderly.

"Oh, ah know. Ah won't dae anythin stupid; Mary's already marked my card on that score. But we've got to try and sort this out before it gets any worse. Yer gonny have tae trust me on this one."

Lucy sighed, and drank her coffee.

Ah think it's probably best if Sammie stays away from here for a wee while," added Billy. "And ah also think there's no point in worrying Mickie with this, if we can help it."

"Mi will explain to Sammie," replied Lucy. "He not gonna like it, but he'll understand. And mi agree, Mickie don't need to know anyting about this.

She then looked tenderly at Billy, and said:

"And Billy, thanks for today, mi really appreciate it."

Billy grinned, and then gave her a cheeky wink.

"Are ye kiddin, us Glesga folks have got to look out for each other."

Lucy gave him a crooked little smile.

Chapter 5 (2nd Monday)

As soon as the Monday morning meeting was over, Laura and Tim Farrell headed directly back to his office to discuss their next course of action regarding the new project.

"Okay, Laura," said Tim, sinking into his swivel chair. "As you know, the client gave us clearance on Friday; well, shall we say they have approved in principle, because as you also know, these people change their minds every five minutes. But we can't delay any longer, having only three weeks to get this into the studio. I've spoken to Mark at Magic Models, and set up a meeting for eleven-thirty. They've already made some small-scale mock-ups from your initial drawings, so we can assess how best to proceed with the full size models and rigs."

"Mark assures me they're ready to roll as soon as they get the go-ahead. And while they are normally very efficient, and hit the deadline, I just want to finalise a few things, and get some feedback."

"Of course," replied Laura. "I'll get all the relevant details together, and order a cab."

"Perfect," said Tim. "I have a few phone calls to make, so I'll be tied up for an hour or so, but if we leave around eleven, that should be fine."

Laura then made her way down to the kitchen; she was hoping to catch John, as she was dying to find out why he had been so mysterious on Saturday, but when she entered, he was nowhere to be seen. She made some coffee, and was about to go back to her desk when John came strolling in through the door.

"We-ll, if it's not Mr Ambiguous himself," she said, looking at him with a cheeky grin and raised eyebrows. "And how are you this morning?"

John wasn't taking the bait.

"Oh, I'm fine, thank you very much," he said in a breezy manner, and then proceeded to pour himself a coffee.

Laura smirked. "Nice weekend?"

"Oh, quiet, you know," he said, pretending to concentrate on stirring his coffee.

"Oh bullshit!" cried Laura, laughing out loud. "You've met someone, haven't you?"

John actually blushed, and she knew then that she had nailed him.

"I don't believe it, you're blushing."

"Okay! Okay! Bloody hell!" cried John, his face becoming even redder.

Laura bit her lip to stop from giggling; she was enjoying this.

"Well, don't you want to tell auntie Laura all about it?"

John grimaced.

"Oh, it's auntie Laura now, is it? It was Sherlock bloody Holmes a minute ago."

This made Laura giggle with delight, and John, eventually cracking, reluctantly joined in.

"Well?" said Laura, continuing the investigation.

"Well what?" answered John, continuing to be evasive.

Oh, come on!" said Laura in exasperation.

"Well, I don't have time to go into it all now, do I?"

Laura looked at him through half-closed eyes. "But you did meet someone?"

"Ye-es!"

Laura smiled in smug satisfaction.

"Tch!" said John, rolling his eyes.

Laura gave him a playful poke in the ribs, and then went off humming to herself. John sipped his coffee, and smiled.

On the taxi ride over to the Model-shop in Wandsworth, Laura, daydreaming of Mickie, and their weekend of love, was unaware that she had a broad smile on her face. Tim Farrell, glancing over at her, was instantly curious.

"Well, someone looks happy for a Monday morning."

"Sorry?'

Tim laughed out loud, and said in a pretty accurate impersonation of Barry White:

"Is someone on Planet Lu-rve?"

Starting to blush, Laura looked at him, and thought: *How did he know?* She now knew how John had felt, and made a face, as if to say: "What, me? Good grief, heaven forbid!" But then deciding it was futile she smiled sheepishly, and owned up:

"Yes, I am, actually."

Tim beamed a huge grin, and gave her a hug. He was very fond of Laura; he knew she was clever, and talented, but also knew she had a tender heart.

"Well, that's fantastic," he said, still grinning. "What happened to old tosser-bollocks, then?"

Tim had never liked Toby since first meeting him, and had there-after referred to him as, tosser-bollocks.

"How do you know it's not Toby?"

"Oh please."

Laura laughed, and looked at her boss with affection. He was a big balloon of a man, and that wasn't merely in reference to his shape, although he was fairly rotund. It was more that he had such a party zest for life, and his dress sense could only be said to be unique for a man of his age, not to mention size.

Tim didn't give a shit what people thought of him; he was an excellent Art Director, had a razor wit, and very few people got the better of him in an argument. Today he was wearing one of his large collection of Hawaiian shirts, faded pink calf-length shorts, and a red NY baseball cap. Laura didn't even question his style choices anymore, there was no point, it was just Tim.

"Well, come on, tell Timmy all about it."

He's an artist, a painter, and he's Scottish," said Laura

"What? Bloody Jocks, coming down here and stealing our woman," said Tim, pretending to be outraged.

Laura smiled, but then looked serious.

"Well, actually, I wanted to ask a favour. I've printed out some images of Mickie's paintings; three to be exact, there is a fourth, but he's still working in the bass player. It's a series of Blues Musicians waiting to play, and I know how much you love the music, so if you could cast your eye over them, and tell me what you think, and maybe suggest someone who might be interested."

Tim gave her a quizzical look.

"Well, it must be love."

Laura, who felt herself blushing again, pretended to look out the window, and then said in a rush:

"Oh, I don't mean now. I mean when this job is over."

Tim, who had only been teasing her, responded affectionally:

"Oh, Laura, I'm winding you up, of course I'll look at them, and if I can help I will. You know I respect your taste; well except for tosser-bollocks."

"Thank you, Tim," replied Laura, and smiling, she again looked out the window, and thought of Mickie.

* * *

Lucy was sitting in the kitchen, when she heard Mickie come in, and call out to her:

"Mrs McIntyre?"

It was somehow reassuring the way he called her name when he got home.

"In here, Mickie."

Mickie's happiness seemed to precede him into the room, and touch Lucy, who smiled knowingly on seeing him. There was a new light in his eyes, and he beamed the biggest smile.

"Hiya Mrs McIntyre, lovely morning, eh?"

Lucy just smiled and nodded. *Well, at least he hasn't noticed the door,* she thought.

"Would yuh like some coffee?"

"Oh, no thanks. Ah'm just gonny go up and change, and then ah'm off to the National Gallery, for my monthly fix of Rembrandt; and there's also an art store near there that does good quality oil paint at sale prices."

Lucy hadn't seen him so charged up before; he couldn't seem to stand still, and wandered round the kitchen, grinning. She shook her head, and smiled up at him.

"What?" he asked.

"Oh, nothin."

He gave her a shy smile, and then turned to leave the room, but just before he left, he heard Lucy say:

"Oh, Mickie? Mi glad to see yuh so happy."

He turned and said, softly.

"Ah know."

After Mickie had left to go uptown, Lucy sat for a while, lost in thought. She was thinking about love, and life, and how it seemed to fly by so fast. But mainly, she thought about Harry, who had died of cancer five years ago today, and remembered how he could always make her laugh. He had, of course, also been volatile and wild, with a temper that could flare like a match being lit; god knows how he would dealt with this mess. She still missed him everyday, but maybe it was time to move on.

Her thoughts then turned to Sammie, and she smiled, but then she quickly replaced the smile with a frown, as if she felt she had to admonish herself for being so silly. She had called him yesterday, after Billy had left, to explain the situation. He had initially been angry and concerned, but she had managed to calm him down, and convince him that it made sense for him not to come to the house until this thing was sorted out, one way or the other.

At least something had happened, and maybe the spraying of the door would be the end of it, but then again, maybe not. But even so, for some reason she now felt a little less anxious, maybe because they now had Billy as an ally.

She had also finally made up her mind about Sammie, and had decided to see more of him, and try to fill her life with some joy and meaning again. The phone rang, and she smiled, somehow she knew it would be Sammie, and this time, her smile was not followed by a frown.

* * *

Like a tiny ballet dancer, the little girl raised her arms in the air, and attempted a slow, jagged pirouette before the bedroom mirror. The morning sun, beaming through the window, fell on her like a spotlight. With every turn to the mirror, she checked her pose, and corrected what she considered wrong: her hands, her expression. She wanted everything to be just perfect.

"Mona! Come on. We have to go."

Mona made a face in the mirror; the voice had broken the spell. Hearing footsteps on the stairs, she turned towards the bedroom door, which then opened to reveal her mother framed in the doorway, looking flustered.

"Och, Mona! Yer still in your jim-jams, and ah'm already late."

The little girl struck her ballet pose again.

"But mammy, ah'm gonny be a dancer, and ah need to practice."

Sharon raised her eyes heavenward.

"Aye, but not right now, Mona. Come on, do ye want me to lose my job?"

Sharon hurriedly started undressing the little girl, and attempted to haul her pyjama top over her head. But then, muffled giggling, and strangled sounding words came from inside the top; it sounded to Sharon, something like: "head, and button."

She stopped tugging, and pulled the pyjama top down again to reveal the little girls wide-eyed expression.

"What?" asked Sharon, in exasperation.

"Yer pullin my head off. Ye need to loosen the top button."

"Oh, for God's sake, Mona

"Oh for God's sake," echoed Mona.

Sharon managed to get her daughter, sort of dressed, and then stuffed more of her clothes into a bag.

"Yer granny will have a fit when she sees the state of ye, but she'll have to sort you out when we get there."

She eventually got Mona strapped into the child-seat, and then drove the short distance to her mother's house; her mum looked after Mona on weekdays, and during school holidays.

"How long will it take to get to London when we go, mammy?"

Sharon looked at Mona in the rear-view, and thought: *Oh God, what is she like? Look at the state of her hair.*

"It takes about four hours from Glasgow by train, darlin."

"Will my daddy be there when we get there?"

"He bloody better be," replied Sharon, a little too sharply.

Mona frowned, and was silent for a few minutes, but then her curiosity again got the better of her.

"How long is an hour?"

"Eh? Well it's . . ." Sharon was stumped for an answer for a minute, but then she had a brainwave.

"It's . . . It's as long as four Tracy Beaker programs on the telly."

Mona considered this information, her little brow furrowed in concentration.

"Tch, does that mean London's nearly as far away as Edinburgh?"

Sharon smiled, and thought: *Oh, Mona, yer a funny wee thing, and definitely yer daddy's daughter, another dreamer.*

When Sharon's mother, Peggy, opened her front door, Sharon thrust Mona into her arms.

"Ah'm sorry, mammy, but ah'm really late, ah'll phone ye later on."

She turned to leave, and then immediately turned back.

"Oh Mona, darlin, ah'm sorry, give mammy a kiss." She kissed Mona, and was gone.

Peggy closed the door, and put her granddaughter down to have a look at her. The little girl's sweater was on back to front, and her hair was still sticking up after the tussle with the pyjama top. Peggy looked down at the little girl, who seemed totally unconcerned with her appearance, and stood beaming a big smile back up at her granny. Peggy stifled the urge to laugh.

"Well, just look at the state of ye. Do ye not have any mirrors in your house?"

Mona started giggling, and Peggy took her by the hand to lead her through to the living room.'

"C'mon, let's get you sorted out before the police see ye."

"I'm gonny be a dancer, granny," said Mona, nonchalantly arching her free arm above her head.

"Are ye, darlin?"

"Aye, in London, and that's nearly as far away as Edinburgh in Tracy Beaker time."

* * *

"Oh, Margaret, ah'm so sorry ah'm late, but this mornin's been a total nightmare," said Sharon, looking flushed, and anxious. She had just rushed through the door of, Cut'n'Dried, the local hairdressing salon, where she worked as a stylist.

"Oh, don't be daft," said Margaret. "Ye've only got wee Agnes, and she's not due in for another twenty minutes."

Sharon still looked around nervously.

"Oh, don't worry, baw-jaws hasn't made an appearance yet," said Margaret, grinning.

This cheeky Glasgow reference to her employer's chubby facial features, made Sharon smile, and feel a little more relaxed. She removed her jacket, and then walking towards the kitchen, she said over her shoulder.

"That'll be coffee for everybody, then."

The tiny, elderly woman, whose hair Margaret was attending to, whispered something to her, and then Margaret called through to Sharon.

"Oh, Sadie says can she have tea, she disnae like coffee." And then, as an afterthought, Margaret added: "Unless it's got a wee shot of rum in it."

Behind her thick glasses, Sadie's magnified eyes sparkled with delight, and she grinned broadly, revealing a gleaming wall of false teeth, that seemed too big for her face.

Sharon loved working with Margaret; she liked the fact that she didn't give a shit what people thought of her; though the fact was, almost everyone she knew thought the world of her. She was kind, and cared about people, and she could really make you laugh. She even had their boss, Boabie, or Bobby, as he insisted on being called in front of the customers, wrapped around her little finger.

She was a small, shapely woman of thirty-five, with beautiful big questioning eyes that could detect bullshit in seconds. And in contrast to a lot of hairdressers, her dark hair was short, and simply cut.

"Where is his nibs, anyway?" asked Sharon, coming through with the cups, a few minutes later.

"Oh, God knows. Ye'll not believe it, but he told me on Saturday that he was goin clubbin. Clubbin? Him? What's he like? The wee eejit."

"Och, maybe he's lookin for romance."

"Maybe he's lookin to get locked up. He's fifty-five, if he's a day."

They all started laughing, and Sharon suddenly had this vision of Boabie on a club dance floor, and then closed her eyes and shook her head, as if trying to rid herself of the image.

"Okay, Sadie, darlin, I'm gonny put ye under the dryer for a wee minute," said Margaret, gently guiding the little woman into the seat, and her roller covered head into the dryer.

With Sadie happily ensconced under the dryer, with her tea and a magazine, Margaret and Sharon had time to enjoy their coffee, and have a chat. They did this in the curious habit, seemingly common only to hairdressers, and addressed each other through the mirror.

"So, ye'll be lookin forward to goin to London, eh?" Margaret asked Sharon's mirror image. The image didn't respond immediately, but looked thoughtful for a minute.

"Aye . . . Ah suppose so."

Sharon was thirty-one, but sometimes looked older; her resentful nature was often mirrored in her face. She too frequently convinced herself that she hadn't many reasons to smile, but when she did, her whole face lit up, and she became the attractive young woman she really was.

"Ye don't sound very sure," said Margaret, giving her a questioning look.

"Oh, ah don't know . . . Ah'm really doin it for Mona, she's so lookin forward to it. Ah just hope it won't be too awkward . . . ye know, with Mickie. Ah haven't seen him for over a year." She hesitated for a second or two, and the said, with sudden venom:

"And ah don't bloody want to,"

Margaret knew this wasn't true.

"Oh, come on, Sharon, ye have to move on, darlin. That's all in the past. Ye've got Glen now."

"Oh, ah know. Glen's all right, but . . ." Sharon's voice trailed off.

"But ye don't love him," said Margaret, finishing Sharon's sentence.

Sharon frowned, and looked down into her coffee cup, and Margaret tried to think of something funny to say, but for once, she was unable to deliver. The awkward silence was thankfully broken a moment later, when the front door opened, and in floated Boabie on a cloud of aftershave. Margaret raised her eyebrows, and gave Sharon's mirror image a wry look.

Boabie stood posed in the middle of the salon. He was a small chubby man, not much over five feet tall. His face glowed from a recent session under a sun lamp. He had sharp blue eyes, and his dyed black hair was sculpted to perfection. He was dressed in a vivid pink shirt, and freshly pressed black trousers, which hugged his protruding little belly.

"Well, if it's not Boabie Travolta," said Margaret, grinning.

"Here, less of yer cheek," replied Boabie, in his whiney nasal voice. "And it's Bobby, as well you know.

"Tch, sorry Blobby," replied Margaret, pretending to be admonished.

"What?"

"Ah said sorry, Bobby," replied Margaret, giving him a cheeky grin.

"Aye, right," said Bobby, not fully convinced.

"Make me a cup of coffee." Although he didn't address her directly, the order was meant for Sharon, who looking as if she had just woken from a dream, stared blankly at him. Boabie turned and glared at her.

"Coffee, pour moi?" he said sarcastically. He knew he could never get the better of Margaret, and so tended to pick on Sharon, whom he knew would never dare to retaliate, being a single parent, and in fear of losing her job. He also resented the fact that she was an attractive young woman, who had spurned him when he had made an unsubtle pass at her shortly after she had started working there. Sharon gave him a brief forced smile, and then turned and went into the kitchen. Margaret looked him up and down, and then raised her eyes to the ceiling.

"What?" asked, Boabie.

"Aw, nothin," answered Margaret scornfully. Get outa my way, ah need to get Sadie from under the drier, while she's still got some hair left."

Margaret brushed past him, and rescued the old woman, and then led her back to her chair before the mirror. Sharon returned with Boabie's coffee, which he took from her sullenly, and without thanks, and then went and sat behind the reception desk.

The front door opened again, and in came wee Agnes, accompanied by her daughter, Moira. Agnes was another pensioner taking advantage of the cheap Monday deals. Margaret had suggested this scheme for senior citizens, as it was normally quiet on a Monday.

Having illusions of grandeur, Boabie hadn't been keen, but soon relented under a barrage of common sense from Margaret. She had quite rightly argued that it was better to have some money coming in at the beginning of the week, than none at all.

Boabie never even looked up from his paper when Agnes came into the salon, causing her daughter to stare at him for a minute, and then make a face, as if to say: "What's his problem?"

Sharon immediately went over and helped Agnes of with her coat, and got her settled in a seat. Margaret, who was removing the rollers from Sadie's hair, called over to Agnes's daughter:

"How ye doin, Moira?"

"Och not bad Margaret," replied Moira, and then pointing to her mother, she silently mouthed the words: "New medication."

Margaret mouthed back: "oh, right."

Moira then made to leave, and said to her mother:

"Okay, mammy, ah'll be back in an hour."

The old lady just smiled and nodded her head. Moira sighed, and gave a sad little smile. She made a final scornful face at Boabie, and then said her goodbyes.

"That's a lovely blouse ye've got on Agnes," said Margaret, trying to make the old woman feel at ease.

Agnes looked round, a little confused, as if Margaret's comment was taking it's time penerating the new medication, but then she smiled.

"Aye, it's all the colours of the railway," she answered dreamily.

Margaret raised one eyebrow; unsure she had heard properly, and Sharon bit her lip and looked away, trying not to laugh. Boabie looked over at Margaret, rolled his eyes, and shook his head. Margaret just laughed, and looking kindly at the old woman, replied:

"Aye, ah suppose it is."

They worked on quietly for a while, with radio two playing softly in the back ground, and then Margaret, helping Sadie from the chair and on with her coat, said:

"Well, Sadie darlin, that's you beautiful again for another week."

The old woman gave Margaret a soft little smile, and squeezed her arm affectionately. Margaret then saw her to the door, and watched her walk slowly up the street.

"Tch, God love her," she said to no one in particular. Sharon smiled at Margaret.

"She comes here for more than a perm, you know. She comes for the company, and because she knows you care about her, and of course for the patter; you can always manage to make her laugh."

Boabie gave a mirthless grunt of a laugh, and Margaret's head swivelled slowly, almost mechanically round to face him, her eyes burning into the top of his head. She felt herself losing patience with this ridiculous little man, and the icy tone in her voice more than conveyed that fact.

"What's the matter with you, torn face?"

"This is supposed to be a hair salon, not an old folks home," replied Boabie, loud enough for Agnes to hear.

Sharon instantly checked the old woman's image in the mirror, for any sign of hurt pride, but Agnes just kept her head down. Margaret continued to stare him down; she was angry now. She knew he couldn't run the salon without her; she was an excellent hairdresser, and in reality, managed the business, which allowed him to gad about like a half-pint playboy.

Boabie started to squirm under her gaze, having suddenly realised he had pushed his luck. Margaret decided to make him suffer a little more, and then maybe he would sidle off to one of his mysterious wee meetings, and leave them in peace. She smiled, wickedly.

Ah've just realised why ye're even more crabbit than usual this mornin. Ah'll bet it's because they wouldn't let a ridiculous wee chancer like you set foot in a club. Ye've got a cheek talkin about age, ye want to take a good look in the mirror, pal, yer way past eighteen. Or maybe ye didn't even try, eh? Ah think it was just another one of yer daft wee fantasies. And do ye know why? Because ah know for a fact ye were in the Quarter Gill on Saturday night, until way past closin time. Drownin yer sorrows were ye?"

Boabie squirmed even more, and tried to ignore her by hiding behind his newspaper, but Margaret wasn't finished.

"Well, Boogie Boabie, what have ye got to say to that, eh?"

Margaret knew she had him, when he abruptly stood up, lifted his car keys, and mumbled something under his breath.

"Sorry?" asked Margaret, trying not to smile.

"Ah have a meetin to go to," he said, a little louder, while edging towards the door without making eye contact. He then, without further comment, pulled open the door, slipped through, slamming it petulantly behind him.

"Bullseye!" said Margaret with a grin, and then turning to Sharon, she winked and started singing: "Night fever, night feveeer!" while boogieing into the kitchen to put the kettle on.

Chapter 6

The music, drifting through the open window was blue and bittersweet. The track opened with the piano and bass playing a simple two-note riff, and then the trumpet entered, soft, almost hesitating, and blew a languid phrase of soft breathy notes. Then came the alto saxophone, soaring like some beautiful bird, high in the air, sailing through a bright blue sky. The sound was pure and sweet, like honey and cream, but every note, while soothing Sammie's soul, carried with it some poignant memories.

It was mid-morning, and he was sitting at a table outside a Soho bar, reminiscing. The smoke from his cigarette seemed to curl and dance in time to the saxophonist's elegant, immaculate playing. He took a sip from his glass, looked up into the cloudless blue sky, and thought of his old friend. What times they had seen in this bohemian little corner of their adopted city.

He had first met Harry McIntyre in 1965, right here in this bar. You just couldn't fail to notice Harry, he was always right in the centre of the action. This tall skinny kid holding court, with his saxophone case propped up against the bar, and waving an ever-present cigarette, while relating some tall tale to an audience of fellow musicians, or anyone else within earshot. People just gravitated to him; he was wild and funny, and though he pretended not to give a shit, he had a heart.

From that first meeting, Harry and Sammie had an unbreakable bond, they never stopped to consider why; they were just united, in their playing, their humour, and their passion for Jazz.

There was, at first, the small problem of language, what with Sammie's thick Jamaican patios, and Harry, well Harry talked like he played; his Glasgow accent soaring over the noise of a crowded bar at speed, sounded to Sammie like something Charlie Parker could play. He just listened in wonder, not understanding a word, but loving the sound.

They soon became one of the killer duo's of swinging London's Jazz and Soul scene. They were part of a pool of talented professional musicians nicknamed, 'Soul-to-Soul' that was sought after for session work, and to play behind all the big names of that era. They could choose whom they wanted to play with, and while Soul Music was where the money was, at the end of the night, they always seemed to end up jamming someplace, playing their first love, Jazz.

Sammie relit his cigarette, took another sip of rum, and thought of Lucy. He had called her earlier, as he had taken to doing everyday now, just to check she was okay. They had talked briefly, and Sammie had been delighted when she had agreed to meet him here on Saturday. *Isn't it strange,* he thought*, how just a few words from the right person could brighten your day.*

His thoughts then drifted back to 1966, and the first time he ever saw her. In those days a lot of the musicians would drop into the late night bar at Ronnie Scott's Club. Sammie happened to be there one night, having a drink after a recording session, when in walked Derrol Brown, another Jamaican musician, with his sister, Lucy. They had eventually come over to where Sammie was standing at the bar, and Derrol, introducing his sister to Sammie, had asked if he would mind keeping her company for a while, as he had a bit of business with another musician.

Sammie, instantly smitten with this cool, sexy girl, and grinning like a fool, had readily agreed. They had talked for a while, and although he had turned on all his charm, he soon found out that she was no fool, she was smart and funny, and knew about music. After what seemed to Sammie, no time at all, Derrol had come back to tell Lucy that it was time to go. Sammie, his grin quickly fading as he watched them leave, couldn't believe that his plan to get closer to this woman had so soon been foiled.

A week or so later, he had again been having a late night drink, only this time with Harry, when to his delight, he saw Derrol and Lucy again enter the club. They had mingled in the crowd for a brief time, and then had come directly up to where he and Harry were standing at the bar.

Sammie had bought them a drink, and tried to take up where he had left off with the lovely Lucy. After a few minutes, however, he began to notice that Lucy's eyes seemed to keep drifting over his right shoulder to where Harry was standing.

Sammie had turned and gave Harry a quizzical look, which Harry didn't even seem notice, he was too busy gazing at Lucy. Sammie then felt obliged to introduce them, and that was it: he watched in stunned fascination, as Harry took her by the hand and totally, magically charmed her. They had instantly connected; it was like there was no one else in the room. From that minute on, they were like glue, and were married a month later. Sammie smiled and shook his head at the memory, and called through to Jack the barman, for another rum.

A young black guy, loping up the other side of Frith Street caught Sammie's attention. He was dressed up sharp in a dark suit and shades, and carrying a guitar case. He seemed oblivious to the world around him, and was grooving to some track on his headphones.

"Go to it, brother," said Sammie with a smile.

When Jack brought his drink, Sammie thanked him, and then waiting until he was again alone with his thoughts, he lifted his glass in a silent salute.

It was exactly five years ago today that he had lost his soul brother. He hadn't mentioned anything to Lucy when he called; he didn't have to, it was a precious, unspoken heart thing between them.

The last few months of Harry's life had been agony, and near the end, Sammie had organised a benefit gig at Ronnie's Club. All the old faces had turned out in force, and the place had been packed with musicians standing at the bar, drinking, laughing, and telling old Harry stories. It was like old times, and Sammie had wished Harry could have been there to see how much love and respect these people had for him.

When it came time to play, the stage was full of Harry and Sammie's long time friends, some of the best musicians in London. They had played a selection of Harry's favourites, with all their heart and soul, ending with Miles's So What, which both Harry and Sammie had loved, and had played so often in the past. After he had played his solo, and the saxophone had taken over, Sammie had stood rooted to the spot, tears streaming down his face.

After Harry's funeral, Sammie couldn't face talking to anyone, and had come here just to be alone with his thoughts and get slowly, sadly drunk. For a year or so after his friend had died, Sammie had drifted in and out of work, mostly as a sideman at recording sessions, and sometimes the odd club gig, but his heart wasn't in it, and he felt lost.

At one session, one of the other musicians, a younger guy who Sammie had often seen around, mentioned that he had landed a gig in a big band, playing on a luxury liner sailing to New York. He told Sammie they needed a trumpet player, and asked if he would be interested. Sammie had immediately said yes, as he knew he needed to get out of his funky rut, and find some new direction. He needed to head for some new horizon, and *New York, New York,* he had thought, *has always been a musician's town.*

* * *

Mickie stood in the silence of the National Gallery's Rembrandt room, studying one of the late self-portraits. He was looking so intently at the painting, that it was almost as if he thought by scouring the surface of the canvas, he would find the secret of this man's almost magical ability to conjure up with a few precisely placed strokes of paint, a scene of such tender realism, that you felt you could almost introduce yourself, and shake hands with the man.

He stood for a long time before the painting, his eyes taking in all the nuances of tone and colour; and then his mobile phone rang.

Shit, he thought, realising he had forgotten to switch it off.

He headed for the exit, smiling apologetically at one of the attendants, who frowned at him as he past. *Yeah, all right,* thought Mickie. *No need to get out yer pram.* When he got outside, he returned the missed call.

"Hiya, Billy. Sorry ah couldn't answer, ah was inside the National, when ye called. How ye doin? . . . Good, glad to hear it mate . . . Oh right . . . Well, that's fine, ah'll be workin in the Falcon from five o'clock onwards. Why, what's happening?"

Mickie laughed. "Oh, are ye? Well, ye don't have to bother checkin up on loverboy, loverboys doin just fine, thanks . . . Oh, aye, right," said Mickie, again laughing. "Okay, pal, ah'll . . ." Mickie didn't get a chance to finish, as Billy had hung up. *Why does he always do that? It's fuckin annoyin*, thought Mickie, looking accusingly at his phone.

Deciding he'd had enough culture for the present, he carried on down the steps of the Gallery onto Trafalgar Square, and then turning left into Charing Cross Road, walked towards one of his favourite art shops, just up from the Portrait Gallery. He bought a selection of cut-price tubes of oil paint, and then walking up past Leicester Square, turned left onto Lisle Street, and wandered through China Town, into Soho.

As he had a few hours to kill before his shift at The Falcon, he took his time and feasted his eyes on all the weird and wonderful sights the Soho streets had to offer. The City had somehow become more alive to him, and there was always something to see and remember. He turned into Frith Street, and took a few minutes to stop outside Ronnie Scott's Club to look at the posters advertising forthcoming attractions. He had just started to cross over to Bar Italia, when he caught sight of Sammie, sitting outside a pub further up the street.

As the man looked deep in thought, Mickie stood for a few minutes, uncertain whether to approach, and intrude into Sammie's reverie. But his curiosity was just too strong, and he found himself walking towards the pub.

One of the things that intrigued him about Sammie, was that even though his Bluesmen were totally a product of his imagination, Sammie looked so much like one of the men in his paintings, he could almost have posed for it. For this reason alone, he just had to talk to this man, he couldn't resist.

"Hiya Mr Turner," he said, approaching the table. "Do ye remember me? My name's Mickie, and ah live at Mrs McIntyre's."

Sammie looked up for a second or two, trying to register the face, and then he grinned and offered his hand.

"Sure, Mickie bwoy. How yuh doin?"

"Oh, ah'm fine. Do ye mind if ah join ye?"

"Sure, sure," replied Sammie, gesturing to a seat.

Mickie put his bag of paints on the table.

"Can ah buy ye another drink, Mr Turner?"

"Sure, if yuh stop callin mi Mr Turner."

Mickie smiled. "Okay, Sammie, what would ye like?"

"Thank yuh, Mickie. Mi would like a small rum."

Mickie went into the bar, and after ordering the drinks, stood taking in the interior of the pub. He then became aware of the music, and understood why Sammie would spend time here. When the drinks arrived, he paid the barman, and then eagerly went back to join Sammie.

"Cheers!" said Mickie, lifting his glass.

"Awrabest!" replied Sammie, in a perfect Glasgow accent, making Mickie laugh in surprise.

"Ah don't know if Mrs McIntyre has ever mentioned it, but ah'm a painter, and ah'm workin on a series of Bluesmen; and it's uncanny, but one of them looks just like you."

"Oh? He must be a handsome fella," said Sammie, looking up from rolling a cigarette, and smiling.

"Oh aye," replied Mickie, grinning and nodding his head. Sammie smiled, and lit his cigarette.

"Lucy did tell mi yuh were a talented bwoy. Maybe mi get to see your pictures some time."

"Are ye kiddin?" said Mickie, wide-eyed. "Anytime ye like. Ah would love ye to see them."

There was so much Mickie wanted to ask; it was like meeting someone who knew what it was like to spend your life trying to be the best.

"So, ye knew Mrs McIntyre's husband?"

Sammie closed his eyes and nodded, and then looked into Mickie's eyes, and said:

"Yeah man, mi knew Harry."

Mickie got the feeling that somehow, he had asked a stupid question.

"She doesn't talk about him much, and ah feel funny askin, as ah don't want to appear nosey, or rude. It's just ah love the music, and would love to learn more about that whole period, especially from somebody who actually was part of it."

The first few notes of Duke Ellington's 'In a Sentimental Mood', made Sammie smile, and then a sad look came over his face. He sighed a smoky sigh, and took a sip of his rum.

Mickie frowned. "Am ah intrudin on somethin here, Mr Turner?"

"Sammie."

"Sorry, am ah intrudin on somethin, here, Sammie?"

Sammie knew Lucy liked and trusted this boy, and now he knew why.

" Harry died five years ago today."

Mickie immediately felt stupid, and thoughtless.

"Och, fuck! Ah'm so sorry. Ah knew ah shouldn't have intruded. Ah'm a wank . . ."

"Hey! It's okay, it's okay," said Sammie, reaching out and grasping Mickie's arm.

"Mi done grievin for today; now mi want some company."

* * *

The bars of sunlight streaming through the half-closed curtains, made the squalid room seem even more depressing. Patsy lay on top of the bed, curled up in the foetal position, facing the wall. A syringe, a crumpled piece of burnt tin foil, and other junky paraphernalia, lay scattered on a small bedside table. The door, which had been slightly ajar, was suddenly kicked open, and banged against the wall with a crash, revealing the imposing figure of Nazz, who more than filled the doorframe. He looked down at the pathetic figure on the bed, and then frowning, as if at some bad smell, he walked over and opened the window. He then turned back, viciously booted the bed, and snarled at the still comatose figure:

"Get the fuck up. I got somebody comin that I need to talk business wiv, and I want you gone."

Patsy, now brutally jerked awake, started coughing, and slowly rolled over. It took a further couple of minutes of coughing before she spotted a crumpled, partially smoked cigarette in the ashtray. She immediately picked it up, and with shaking hands, lit it, sucking the second-hand smoke deep into her lungs. Nazz, shook his head, and then left her to it.

A little while later, still dressed from the previous day, and looking deathly pale, she appeared like a ghost in the living room. She stood, trembling, and looked over with pleading eyes, to where Nazz sat at the table by the window, smoking a cigarette, and drinking coffee.

"I need a little bit of somefing, Nazz; just to sort me out."

He didn't even acknowledge her presence until a hacking coughing-fit bent her double. He then turned, and looking at her with loathing, gave a mirthless laugh, and looked back out the window. With a final wheezing groan, she straightened up, wiped her mouth with her sleeve, and shuffled into the kitchen. He could hear the sound of glass on glass, and then she reappeared with a full tumbler of clear liquid, which he knew was vodka.

"Naaaazz!"

Aw, shut the fuck up ya dopey bitch. I aint got nothin for ya till later."

"Oh, please, Nazz."

"I told ya, no. Now fuck off out me face."

"She was sweating profusely now, and looked at him with pleading eyes.

"At least givvus a fag, Nazz."

He took a cigarette from his packet, and threw it across the room. It struck her in the face, and then fell to the floor. She reached down to retrieve it, spilling some of her drink in the process. She was shaking so badly, she had trouble lighting the cigarette, but eventually managed, and then sat unsteadily down on the couch.

"Where's Rob, then?" she asked, and then gulped down a couple of inches of vodka.

"Kent, if he's got any fuckin sense."

"Kent? What's he doin in Kent?" she asked, sounding pitiful.

Nazz shook his head in disbelief, and then dialled a number on his mobile phone.

"Hey, bro, change of plan . . . No, just listen willya? I'll be in touch with ya later, and we can meet up . . . Oh, yeah, yeah I know the place."

He stood up from the table, lit a cigarette, and then, without acknowledging the confused woman looking up at him from the couch, he took his jacket from the back of the chair, and walking from the room, he slammed the front door so hard, it drowned out Patsy's whining cry: "Naaazz?"

(2nd Tuesday)

Billy was sitting on a greasy old kitchen chair he had placed just outside the raised shutter door of the garage. It was lunchtime, but he hadn't felt like eating much, and now sat with his hands clasped around his nearly empty coffee cup, staring dreamily out into the street. The other two mechanics had gone to eat at the café, but sometimes Billy just liked to sit quietly on his own, and watch the world go by, especially when he had something on his mind.

A stout, elderly black lady, who passed by at this time almost everyday, caught his eye. It was her walk that always drew his attention: with every right step she took, the whole top half of her body swung to the left, and then, with the left step, it swung to the right; she was like a human metronome. He pondered on what could have caused her strange, almost mechanical gait. It looked as if it took tremendous effort on her part, just to lift her feet from the pavement.

He had recently been thinking a lot about the fragility of life, and how we have no idea what fate has in store for us. This thought made him shake his head, and smile a sad little smile. He threw the dregs of his cup into the yard, and got up to return to work, but then, for some bizarre reason, he decided to try and decipher the mechanics of the old lady's walk. He was attempting to imitate her waddling walk on his way back into the garage, when he heard a familiar voice behind him:

"Fuck me, Bill! You aint shit yerself, ave ya?"

Billy stopped suddenly, straightened up, and turned to see his two workmates standing in the yard, looking bemused. Billy gave them a sheepish grin.

"Naw naw. It's a long story, boys."

BeeJay grinned, and gave Billy a crafty wink.

"If you say so, Bill."

Billy laughed to cover his embarrassment.

"Okay, my secret's out. Ah was praticin my dancin."

BeeJay and Pete looked at each other and laughed; they were well used to Billy's somewhat eccentric behaviour.

Pete then went into the small office at the back of the garage to make a phone call, and BeeJay strolled over to his workbench. He switched on his radio, and then started pulling on his overalls. He was a tall, skinny, nineteen-year-old black kid, who Pete and Billy both agreed he had the makings of a good mechanic. He also loved to laugh, and that was always fine with Billy.

BeeJay took a few minutes to search for something in his toolbox, and then finding the appropriate tool, he turned and called over to Billy:

"Yo, Bill, you know you were askin about that bro wiv the nose?"

"Yeah."

"Well, I think I know who you mean, now. We just seen him come into the café. I fink he's a dealer, man."

"Oh aye?"

"Yeah man, but he aint from round here, that's why I couldn't suss him, innit? But as soon as I saw him walk in wiv his nose, I remembered."

"Remembered what?"

"Well, me uncle Darryl drinks in the Bulldog, and he said there's this junkie woman that sometimes drinks in there; well she drinks in there if somebody else is payin, innit. Anyway, I heard mi uncle Darryl tell me mum that he's seen her in there a lot recently, and that she comes in wiv this big ugly bro with a nose, that accordin to me uncle Darryl, looks like it's been badly chewed. A proper gangsta, man."

The words 'junkie woman' had made Billy stop what he was doing.

"What does she look like, this junkie woman?"

"Oh, man, she's hangin, innit; a real dog. She used to be lush, though, when we was kids at school."

"Ye went to school with her?" Billy asked, looking wide-eyed at BeeJay.

"No, man! I went to school wiv her son, Rob."
Billy raised an eyebrow.
"Rob?"
"Yeah."
"So he's a mate of yours, this Rob?"

"No, man! Never," replied BeeJay. "He's a fuck-up, and nasty with it. He's been pissed off since his old man left. I heard it was cause his mum would disappear for days with anybody who could get her smacked up. She always attracted a lot of bro's, and after her old man left, she would bring them back to the house."

"So, they live locally?"

"I think so, but I don't know where. I think they got moved a couple of times, but I never liked the geezer, so I never cared where he lived. Why you so interested, Bill?"

"Oh, no particular reason," replied Billy, not wanting to give too much away. "Its just yer man with the nose, he's hard not to notice."

"Well, I know one thing, Bill, if his mum is screwin around with another bro, old Rob's gotta be real pissed off. He's a real racist, man."

* * *

When Mickie saw Billy come through the front door of the Falcon, he picked up a fresh glass, and started to pour him a lager, and by the time his buddy got to the bar, a foaming pint was set up and waiting for him.

"How ye doin, pal?" said Mickie offering his hand.

"Och, not bad," replied Billy, briefly shaking Mickie's hand.

Mickie gave him a wry look; he couldn't help noticing his friend seemed somewhat distracted.

"Ye awright, mate?"

"Aye," said Billy, not too convincingly.

Mickie frowned, and looked at him through half-closed eyes.

"Tch, sorry, pal," said Billy, catching the look, "Ah was just thinkin about somethin at work. So anyway, how was your weekend?"

Mickie grinned.

"Oh, ah see," said Billy, with a knowing smile. "Done the deed, then?"

Mickie feigned innocence, and again beamed the grin.

"Ah canny lie to ye, pal; it's lo-ove."

"Oh right," said Billy, in a straight-faced, off-hand manner.

Mickie's grin sort of melted, and he suddenly felt something heartfelt and important, had been devalued. He glared at Billy, and with an edge to his voice, he said:

"Ah really mean it. This is new for me, Billy. Ah've never felt like this before."

Billy quickly realised his mistake, and tried to make amends:

"Oh, ah know. Ah'm sorry. Ah can be a insensitive prick, sometimes."

After a minute or so of embarrassed silence, Billy lifted his glass and took a long pull from his pint, and then putting it back on the bar gave Mickie a questioning look.

"Just one thing; if ye could possibly cut that fuckin grinnin down a bit, ah'd really appreciate it."

Mickie just smiled and shook his head, and then went to serve another customer.

Billy was genuinely pleased for Mickie, and decided he should forget the Rob issue for a while.

"Oh, by the way," said Mickie, while pouring a Guinness. "After ye called me, ah went for a stroll round Soho, and guess who ah met?"

Billy made a face, and shrugged his shoulders.

"The Pope?"

"The Pope? Naw, fuck off, he drinks up Mayfair. No, ah met Sammie, and we spent a couple of hours together, just talkin and havin a drink."

Oh, aye," said Billy, raising his eyebrows. "What was he sayin?" He hoped Mrs McIntyre had primed Sammie not to say anything to Mickie about the situation with Rob.

"Och, ah probably bored the arse off him, askin about Harry and the music, and . . . Oh, did ye know it's five years ago that Harry died? Anyway, ah told him that he looks the spitting image of one of the . . ."

The sight of Nazz suddenly appearing out of the gent's toilet, and then walking up to the bar, had instantly caught Billy's full attention. Mickie again glared at him.

"Ah'm obviously boring the arse off you as well, by the looks of it."

"No yer not. Ah'm interested, honestly," replied Billy, while cautiously watching Nazz in the gantry mirror.

Mickie wasn't convinced, and frowning, went off to serve Nazz. Billy heard the big man ask for two large scotches, no ice, and then continued to watch him in the mirror, as he paid for the drinks, and went to join another black guy at a table in the corner.

"What is wrong with you?" said Mickie, giving Billy a questioning look.

"What?"

"Don't give me that innocent look," replied Mickie "Yer startin tae piss me off. Ah know you, and there's somethin goin on, yer not tellin me about."

"Oh, awright, awright. Ah didn't sleep very well last night, and then ah had a big argument with Mary this mornin; and then to cap it all, Pete's been getting on my fuckin nerves all day. So, ah think to myself, ah'll go to the Falcon and have a quiet pint, and see my old mate, Mickie, and what do I find: you borin the fuckin arse off me. It's not fair. It's a cruel world right enough."

Mickie looked at him in dubious silence for a few seconds, and then a smile crept across his face, and he started laughing; Billy knew then he had got away with his fake excuse, but thought it best to keep up the pretence.

"Oh, that's right, just laugh at me."

"Och, stop moanin. Ah'll even buy ye another pint," said Mickie, grinning.

"Oh, awright, if ye insist," replied Billy, pretending to be consoled.

Mickie then went off to serve another customer, and Billy took this opportunity to check out what was happening at the corner table, and saw the two men were still deep in conversation. He sank about a third of his pint, and just as he put it back on the bar, he saw Nazz and the other man, drain there glasses, and stand up in readiness to leave. Billy immediately caught Mickie's attention.

"Forget that other pint, mate. Ah should really catch Mary before she starts her shift. Ah don't like leavin things bad between us."

With that, he quickly made for the main door, through which the two men had just left. Mickie stood gazing after him, with a look of total bewilderment on his face. It was only after a few minutes that he realised a customer was speaking to him:

"What?" said Mickie, in reply, but still looking towards the door.

"I said, a bottle of Budweiser."

Mickie reluctantly turned and nodded to the man.

"Sorry, mate, comin right up."

* * *

Billy caught sight of the two men as he left the pub, and keeping at a safe distance, tailed them up Ladbroke Grove Road, for a good twenty minutes. He stopped in a shop doorway when he saw them turn into the Treverton Housing Estate, and continued to watch as they walked towards a run-down block of flats. With Nazz leading the way, they went through the graffiti covered front door.

Billy now ran towards the entrance, as he wanted to see which flat they entered, but was also concerned he might be seen from the stairwell, or the communal walkway that leads to the flats. When he was safely inside, he could hear the footsteps of the two men ahead of him on the stairs, and silently started to follow in the hope they would lead him to where Rob lived.

He had only gone up a few steps, when he heard the front door opening behind him. He turned quickly, thinking he had been trapped, only to see a tragic looking figure at the foot of the stairs. He sighed with relief, while at the same time wondering how she could just appear from nowhere like that.

He took a guess, could this be Rob's mum, the 'junkie woman' that BeeJay had referred to. The woman certainly looked the part, and seemed to be out of it, on something. She was wearing a soiled blue shell suit, grubby trainers, and her matted blonde hair was scraped back from her face in a ponytail. As she started up the stairs, there was the clink of glass from the carrier bag she held in her arms. She didn't seem to be aware of Billy, until he spoke.

"Hello, love. Ye don't know if a Mrs MacGregor lives in this building? She's a friend of my mothers, and ah think ah've got the right place, but ah've forgotten the flat number."

She gazed up at him with glazed eyes, and then slowly shook her head.

"Oh, right," said Billy. "Thanks anyway."

"Givvus a fag, darlin," she said in a hoarse whisper, moving a step closer.

"Ah'm sorry love, ah don't smoke."

She received this news with no perceptible emotion, but Billy began to feel uneasy when she forced a crooked yellow smile, and moved another step closer.

"Couldn't lend us a fiver, could ya darlin? I'll make it worf yer while."

Billy recoiled slightly, but kept his composure.

"Ah'm sorry, love, but ah don't think so. You take it easy though, eh?"

He squeezed past her, retraced his steps down the stairs, and made for the door. He waited outside the entrance until he thought it safe, and then cautiously opening the door, went back inside. He got to the first floor walkway just in time to see her stop at a flat a few doors down, and fiddle with the key. After she was safely inside, and had closed the door, Billy walked quickly past, and noted the number: it was flat nineteen.

Chapter 7 (2nd Tuesday)

The light was fading as Rob crossed the street and sat down on one of the sea-front benches. He lit a cigarette and stared across the deserted beach at the distant, dancing lights on the pier. *Sand,* he was thinking. *I fuckin hate sand, and there's miles of it in this shithole.* He had only been here for three days, but already it felt like forever. His anger was a constant, and had been for years now: five to be exact, ever since his dad had walked out of his life.

He had threatened to leave so many times before that Rob began to believe it was just a ruse his dad used to get his mother to stop treating him like a fool. But it never worked. She would disappear for days, and then brazenly show up again, acting as if nothing was wrong, and she had just popped down to the corner shop. It drove his old man crazy.

They didn't exactly argue as such; his dad would shout and rave, while his mother would just sit there, smoking one cigarette after another. The fact that she didn't react one way or the other only made the poor man even more exasperated. He would once again threaten to leave, but somehow his mother always managed to charm him into staying, and then for a while things would return to some sort of normality.

One particular day, however, Rob came home from school to find his dad packing a suitcase, and with sudden, heart-stopping dread, he realised that this time it was serious. Once again, his mother had taken off without warning, and as usual his dad had been left seething with worry and frustration. But this time, she had finally tipped the balance of his endurance.

His dad couldn't even look him in the face, he was so angry. The sudden realisation that the man had finally had enough, and was really going to leave, struck Rob such an emotional blow that he broke down in tears. He begged, and pleaded with him not to go, but his tears were in vain. Confused and helpless, he watched as his dad walked out the door.

In his head, he replayed the last words his old man ever said to him:

"I'm so sorry, Rob, I just can't take it anymore. But I promise, I'll be in touch as soon as I get things together."

Rob was obviously aware that his mother's behaviour was erratic, and strange, but at this point, he was totally unaware that she was a heroin addict. His dad, it seemed, had long been shielding him from the truth, but it wasn't long before that changed. Within a week or so, Rob had to watch, as a string of surly, creepy men took advantage of his mother's growing drug habit, while he waited everyday for word from his dad.

After almost giving up hope, a letter addressed to him arrived from America. In this one and only correspondence, his dad had apologised for not getting in touch sooner, and went on to explain that he had been living in New York for over a year. He informed Rob that he had met a woman at the place where he worked, and that they were planning to settle in Ohio, where the woman had family. Although he finished the letter by saying he would be in touch very soon, Rob never saw or heard from him again, and from that day on, he never shed another tear.

He flicked his cigarette butt in a glowing arc onto the sand, pulled his hood over his head, and then got up and started walking towards his grandmother's house.

* * *

In just over a weeks time, Sally Toper would be sixty-eight; it didn't show on her. She was sitting in the quiet of her living room, reading, when she heard the back door being opened, and then noisily banged shut; she then heard the heavy clump of her grandson's feet on the stairs.

Sally closed her book, and sat motionless for several minutes, staring at nothing in particular, and then got up and went into the kitchen. She filled the kettle, flicked the switch, and then stood with her back against the wall. Her hands had turned into fists, and her face was now a mask of anger and frustration.

She was trying hard to understand, but in truth it was hard for her to comprehend just how much his mother's lifestyle had affected Rob's behaviour. She had somehow managed to block out her daughter's habits from her own day to day life, and convinced herself that it was just too hard to deal with at her age. But now, confronted with this bitter, angry boy, she realised that if she didn't attempt to heal the hurt and rage she saw in his face, he too would soon follow down that same path.

Rob was sitting on the bed rolling a spliff, when he heard his grandmother climb the stairs, and stop outside his room. She knocked on the door.

"Rob, open the door."

He raised his eyes to the ceiling.

"Whaaat?"

"Rob, open the door. I need to talk to you."

His face twisted in frustration, and he hid the makings of the spliff in the bedside cabinet drawer.

"Tch! Wha about? I'm busy."

"Rob, open the door." There was steel in her voice, now.

Angry, now, he got up, opened the door and glared at the elderly woman standing resolutely in the hall.

"Whaddyawant?"

"I've had enough of this. We need to talk."

"Tch! Aw, fuck off!"

The blow snapped his head back. He couldn't believe it; his granny had just slapped him, and hard. He was, stunned, rooted to the spot, but then his face crumpled, his head dropped forward onto his chest, and he started silently sobbing. He crossed his arms in a self-embrace, and his shoulders convulsed with every uncontrollable sob.

Sally Toper took a sharp intake of breath and immediately embraced her grandson. She then felt his arms enfold her, and hold on so tight that it felt it was like he was almost clinging to life itself.

(2nd Wednesday)

"Why are you being so secretive? You know I'll find out in the end."

"Oh for god's sake woman, will you give it a rest."

John and Laura were walking to the pub for lunch, and Laura was grilling John about his mysterious new man.

"Well, it's not fair. I tell you everything. Don't you trust me anymore, or what?" continued Laura, wickedly piling on the pressure.

John covered his face with his hands in a theatrical gesture of frustration, and then gave a loud groan. Laura bit her lip to stop from laughing.

She knew of course, that John had been lonely and unhappy for quite some time, and she was delighted that he had apparently found someone. And while she could certainly relate to his present loved up state, the secrecy of the whole thing was just too intriguing, she couldn't resist winding him up.

They entered the pub, ordered their lunch, and then taking their drinks, went out into the garden and found a table in the shade.

"All right," said Laura. "I'll leave it for now, but I'm not giving up."

"Bitch."

Laura smiled, and changed the subject.

"So, are you coming on this shoot?"

"Oh God, I hope not. I hate shoots, they're so boring."

"Oh, I don't know about that," replied Laura. "I think this one's going to be pretty intense, it being the first project for a new client."

"Oh God, that's even worse."

They sat in silence for a while, sipping their drinks, and then John, without really thinking, asked:

"Do you ever hear from Toby?"

Laura gave him an enquiring look.

"No, why?"

John suddenly realised he had made a mistake, and thought: *What am I doing?* He then tried to make light of it, and answered, casually:

"Oh, no reason in particular, just making conversation, dear."

Laura continued to look at him suspiciously, and he started to feel a little hot.

"Why would you ask me that?"

"Tch, I don't know. Just being nosy I suppose. Anyway, what have you got planned for the weekend?" he asked, in the hope of getting her off the Toby trail.

"I don't know yet. What about you?"

"Oh, probably go for a drink somewhere I suppose, and . . ."

"Oh, where?" said Laura, cutting in. "Maybe Mickie and I could meet you and . . . What's his name again?"

"Tch! You know very well I haven't told you his name. You're so sneaky, honestly."

Laura fluttered her eyelashes, and smirked.

* * *

Out of the corner of his eye, Tom Paine spotted Toby Sutton making his way across the office towards him. He pretended to be engrossed in his work.

"Well, hello there old chap, and where have you been hiding for the last couple of days?" asked Toby, in his usual breezy manner.

Tom looked up at the tall figure standing before him, and forced a smile.

"Oh, nowhere, really, I just fancied a bit of a long weekend, what with my sister being down. We went to Brighton for the day on Sunday, and then stopped with an aunt who lives on the coast."

As all this was coming out of his mouth, Tom suddenly thought: *This is madness. Why am I telling lies to this ridiculous man? I don't actually care what he thinks.*

The truth was, he'd had such an unexpectedly enjoyable weekend with John, that he couldn't bear the thought of coming into work. He simply wanted time on his own to get his head round this significant event in his life.

"Oh, right," said Toby, looking somewhat bemused.

As the man was obviously in no hurry to leave, Tom felt obliged to respond in some way.

"What about you? How was your weekend?"

Toby's face clouded over, and he seemed unsure of how to answer.

"Oh, it was all right, quiet, you know. What with Laura . . . " He looked away, and never finished the sentence.

Tom suddenly realised, that for all his silliness, and boorish behaviour when drunk, Toby had been hurt and embarrassed by Laura ending their relationship. The fact that this had never occurred to Tom, made him feel vaguely guilty about lying. And then out of the blue, he heard himself say:

"Well, that seems to be lunchtime. Fancy a pint?"

Toby's face lit up with an almost cartoon grin.

"Bloody right, old chum. I've got a thirst you could photograph."

Tom made an effort to smile.

They walked to the local pub near the office, and managed to get a table outside. During lunch, Tom had let Toby do most of the talking, and then after they had eaten, and while Toby continued to prattle on about some other bore's silly antics, he lit a cigarette and drifted into a dream.

He thought about John, and how easy he had felt in his company; he had been thoughtful, funny and smart, and had really made him laugh. There had of course been a little initial awkwardness, and as yet no real physical contact, apart from when they had crashed out fully clothed on top of John's bed, after drinking, laughing, and talking until dawn. But he didn't feel scared about that anymore; in-truth he felt somehow, free.

"Hello?"

Tom heard Toby's voice as if from a distance.

"What?"

"I was asking, what are we going to do on Friday? Are you all right? You seem a little preoccupied."

"Oh, sorry, what about Friday?"

"Oh, you can't have forgotten. It's my birthday of course."

"Is it?" asked Tom, looking at the grinning figure opposite.

"Yee-es! So what I thought we'd do is . . . "

Tom listened while Toby listed the coming highlights of his birthday bash, but then he drifted off again, and found himself thinking: *I can't do this anymore. I've got to tell him.*

"I'm gay!"

Toby's mouth continued to move up and down, but there was no sound. To Tom, he vaguely resembled a fish staring at him from within a glass bowl, and somewhat captivated by this spectacle Tom continued to stare until, after what seemed like ages, Toby cleared his throat and said:

"I'm sorry?"

"I'm gay," repeated Tom. "And I've met someone."

(2nd Thursday)

The only sound in the room came from the brush scumbling oil paint onto the canvas. The morning sun had for the moment disappeared behind a cloud and dimmed the light coming in through the open window. But Mickie, who was in effect, creating his own light, continued undisturbed.

He continued to work on for a while, and then taking a step back, scrunched up his eyes, and scrutinised his work. He had picked up this habit after reading a book of Van Gogh's letters: Vincent had apparently used this odd technique to examine his own paintings, and for some reason, it seemed to work. He studied the bass Player in this fashion for a few minutes, and then laid down his brushes.

While still studying the painting, he drew up a chair, and then plucking a Malboro Light from the pack on the table, put it between his lips. He then picked up his lighter, and with a smooth one-handed action, flicked it open, fired the flame, and lit the cigarette. He was just about to replace the lighter on top of the pack, when something made him hesitate, and he found himself gazing down at the silver object in the palm of his hand. He had suddenly become aware that although he had been using this familiar object for many years, he had never really taken the time to look at it properly.

The Zippo had belonged to his dad, and after he passed away, it had come down to Mickie. The lighter was one of the few things belonging to his dad that he had taken; this, and a couple of old photographs. *Not much to show for a life,* he thought.

The name, 'Johnny' had been inscribed diagonally across the steel face of the lighter. The 'Y' was slightly distorted because of a dent on the bottom right hand corner.

"Johnny," he said, softly, and rubbed the engraved name with his thumb. It then struck him that he hadn't thought of his dad in a long time.

He obviously had memories of his father, but he somehow found it difficult to recall the man clearly in his mind; it seemed, looking back, that he hardly knew the man at all. Or had he just forgotten? How could that be? It was only eight years ago that he died.

He mostly remembered him as a homebody, a quiet man. That of course was until he got drunk, which regrettably happened every weekend without fail. This alarming ritual always began on Friday, payday. After work, instead of going home, he would take his wages and make his way directly to one of the local pubs. He would remain there until they closed, by which time the beer and whiskey would have spawned a Mr Hyde type character, who bore no resemblance to the man he knew as his dad.

This man was often cruel and frightening, and Mickie had memories of hiding under the bedcovers and listening to his mother trying her best to placate the strange being that had returned home. Mickie remembered blows being struck, and dinner plates being swept off the table on to the floor. Saturday would be a repeat of the night before, and sometimes worse, as his dad would go into town in the morning, and spend the whole day drinking.

And then came Sunday; Sundays were just very odd for Mickie, as the house would be so quiet. His mother, who was always an early riser, would wake him, and get him ready and dressed for church, and then after church, she would drop him off at Sunday School.

He dreaded this, and found it deadly boring, mainly because after the teacher was told by his mum that he was very: good with his hands, he seemed to be continually modelling Jesus and his disciples out of plasticine. The funny thing was, when he returned the next Sunday, they were nowhere to be seen. *What were they doing with them?* He remembered thinking.

After a while, he began to rebel in his own small way, and started modelling Jesus with lurid tattoos. And even his disciples became decidedly odd looking, with helmets, goggles and capes, but no one seemed to notice.

As for Mr Hyde, he would spend most of the day in the bedroom, only appearing at dinner, looking beaten and ashamed. After this silent meal, which to Mickie seemed to last forever, his dad would then skulk back to his hiding place.

It wasn't until early evening, when a saviour, in the form of the ice cream man, would arrive, and things would start to ease back into some sort of normality. As soon as he heard the van's chimes, Mickie would stand outside the bedroom door, knowing his dad would open it, and slip him money to go down and get them all treats, especially a double nougat wafer for his mum. His mother's mood seemed to melt with the ice cream, and they would all end up watching the Sunday night movie.

His dad loved him, he was sure of that, and when he was a little boy, despite everything, they had spent some good times together. It was when Mickie had gotten older that things became somehow different. His father seemed to disappear into himself, and Mickie knew he was partly to blame for this, but being a young man on fire, he didn't think to spend time trying to understand his dad. They soon became virtual strangers, so much so, that some of Mickie's teenage friends had later said they couldn't remember if they had actually ever met his dad.

Mickie thought another factor in the distance between them could have been age: his father had been a bachelor well into his forties before finally getting married. His mother had been married before, but her first husband had tragically died eighteen months after the wedding, leaving her to cope with bringing up Mickie's half-sister, Ellen, on her own. His parents had met when they had both worked in the same engineering factory, his dad on the shop floor, and his mum in the canteen. Mickie now believed it hadn't been a love match, but more a marriage of convenience, although his mother would never have said so.

The sun again shone through the window. Mickie laid the lighter down and looked out the window, and made a mental note to phone his mother and sister. He then thought of Mona: *How would she remember me in years to come?* The thought began to make him feel sad, and he quickly dismissed it from his mind. He crushed his cigarette out in the ashtray, and then slipping a John Lee Hooker disc into the machine, turned up the volume.

"YA GOT DIMPLES IN YER JAW," John Lee's blue, guttural voice wailed over the raw guitar riff.

Mickie scrunched up his eyes, and picked up his brush.

(2nd Friday)

It was almost five o'clock as Mickie approached the Falcon to begin his Friday night shift. He was only a few yards from the main door, when all of a sudden, it was pushed open, and two men came striding out on to the street, and started walking towards him.

When they got close, the big man in front, who Mickie vaguely recognised, seemed intent in making Mickie move out of his way, and almost shouldered him aside. The other one, *a flash little fucker,* Mickie later remembered thinking, came strutting up behind, and stared hard at Mickie, as if challenging him to react in some way. When Mickie didn't respond, flash boy grinned, and then followed the big man to a parked car. Mickie took a deep breath to suppress his anger, and then continued towards the door and entered the pub.

Flash boy, whose name was Toto, used the fob on his key ring to unlock the doors of the BMW, while strutting towards it. The big man settled himself in the passenger seat, and then helped himself to a cigarette from a pack of Malboro Reds that Toto had left on top of the dashboard. He then lit it with a Dunhill lighter, that Toto had also left, and then slipped it into his pocket. Toto saw this, and sucked his lips in indignation, but made no comment; he just slid under the steering wheel, turned on the ignition, and drove off.

He drove aimlessly for a few minutes, waiting for the big man to give him a clue as to where they were supposed to be going, but Nazz didn't seem to be in any hurry to do this. Toto stole a quick glance at his passenger, and decided he should probably wait a few more minutes. But when the information was still being withheld, Toto cleared his throat, and asked as casually as he could:

"Nazz my man, wha happenin?"

Nazz inhaled deeply through his nose, making sure the two lines of coke he had just snorted in the pub toilet, were getting home. He then made a low growling sound in the back of his throat, and then opening the window, spat into the air.

"I've got a meet in Brixton at six, and then we pick up the new batch. After that, your gonna drop me off someplace, and then your gonna head back to the flat, and get your boys to cut and bag the white stuff."

Toto's face creased in a scowl, and he whined:

"Aw, man! Is that scuzzy bitch gonna be there? She's hard to take, bro."

Nazz took one long final pull on his cigarette, and then flicked the butt out the window.

"You mind your business, and leave her to me. Just do what your told. I need this bitches flat as a base."

Out the corner of his eye, Toto gave the big man a quick, cautious glance. He hadn't known him very long, and now wasn't sure he wanted to. They had met at a poker game in Clapham, and near the end of the night when everybody was getting a little too wired, something had kicked off. One of the brothers had accused Toto of cheating, and it was just about to get ugly, when Nazz had cooly placed his cards on the table, and then slowly tilting his head, had stared hard at the accuser.

"Chill, bro. I'll stand for the man."

There was a stand off for a few minutes, but then the accuser grinned.

"Aw. Man. Mi was just foolin wit de bwoy."

Nazz had reacted with a slight lift of his chin, and the game had continued. Toto was relieved, but also surprised; he had never met the big man before, and had thought: *Why is he doin this?* It didn't take too long before he found out.

The game had ended shortly after that, and it was then that Nazz had bluntly told Toto he needed a ride, and as his accuser had continued to give him the hard eye, Toto, was more than happy to oblige. As soon as they had got into Toto's car however, Nazz had turned and stared steadily at Toto, until the little man had begun to feel the sweat cling to his back. He tried to keep cool, and avoid eye contact, but his nerve soon gave out, and swallowing hard, he gave a nervous little laugh, and said:

"Wha appenin, man?"

Nazz had almost smiled, but then said, almost matter of factly:

"You can cheat all ya like, bwoy, but ya aint cheatin me."

He had then extended his right hand, snapped his fingers twice, and then held it there, palm up.

Toto had been too stunned to resist. He just looked at that big scary face, and handed over his winnings. Nazz gave short rolling laugh, and Toto could tell that somehow people didn't hear that sound very often.

"Relax," Nazz had then said, handing Toto back a few bills. "I got a business proposition for ya."

That was three weeks ago, and Toto was yet to be convinced he wasn't being played for a fool. But he couldn't for the moment figure out how, and he certainly didn't want to make waves until he was sure he could get out of the deal intact. Of course, the over-riding factor in his compliance was that he was a very greedy man, and could never resist the chance of so-called easy money.

The deal, according to Nazz, who seemed to be a man in the know, was that he had access to serious amounts of heroin, but he needed a partner with enough money to put towards buying a sufficient supply to get started, and then they could start making a real profit, and Toto, despite all his flash, fitted the bill. It was also Toto's job to get together a crew of youths to deal it on the street. Nazz never saw or had dealings with these kids, except one, who helped them count the cash. He also made it more than clear that if the kid, or Toto, ever tried to scam him, it would get nasty, very nasty.

After a silent journey; it hadn't taken Toto long to find out Nazz wasn't a great conversationalist, they pulled up outside a terraced house, in a sunlit square in Brixton. Nazz started to get out of the car, but then turned and lifted the almost full pack of Malboro's from the dashboard. Toto scowled at the big man's back, and thought: *Oh right, just steal my fuckin smokes as well, man.* He had the urge to say it out loud, but didn't.

Nazz told him to stay in the car, and then walked up to the front door and rang the bell. The door was eventually opened by a tall, attractive, brown skinned woman, who was dressed simply in jeans and a white t-shirt. If she recognised Nazz she didn't acknowledge it, she just cooly stood aside to let him enter, and then closed the door behind him.

Around forty minutes later, the door again opened, and Toto saw Nazz and the woman make their way to the car. Toto immediately brightened up at the sight of this pretty woman, and as soon as she was seated in the back, he turned and beamed her a ridiculous grin.

"Well, hello there. You lookin goood, girl."

The woman said nothing in reply, but slowly slid her dark glasses down ever so slightly on her nose, and looked over them at Toto. His grin began to melt when he saw that she was gazing at him like he was something the dog had brought up on the carpet. Nazz's big head then swivelled round, and he too stared at Toto, and then made a slight movement with his chin, as if to indicate that Toto should: *Just drive the fuckin car.*

Toto scowled, but instantly got the message, and started the engine.

Chapter 8 (2nd Friday)

"BABY- PLEASE- DON'T-GO,
BABY-PLEASE-DON'T-GO,
BABY-PLEASE-DON'T-GO-DOWN-TO-NEW-OR-LEANS,
YOU KNOW I LOVE YOU SO,
BABY-PLEASE-DON'T-GO."

It was Friday night, and The Scotia Bar was crammed with happy, noisy, liquid refreshed clientele. It was reputed to be one of Glasgow's oldest pubs, and live music had been a feature of the bar for a long time. Glaswegians love music, especially music with soul; it can be happy or sad, but it has to have one vital ingredient: heart. The Frank O'Hagan band played music with heart and soul every Friday night, and by ten-o'clock, the place was jumping.

Sharon had to keep standing up in an effort to catch a glimpse of the band through the crowd. She would much rather have been sitting at a table closer to the music, but Glen, in one of his awkward moods, had perversely wanted to sit as far away from the band as possible, and as a result, they were seated right at the back of the pub. Sharon, however, couldn't be bothered making a fuss, she was just happy to be here.

She had made a special effort in the way she looked, and was smiling, and rocking back and forth in time to the music. It had been a long time since she had visited The Scotia, and it brought back good memories; Mickie had brought her here when they had first started going out together. He liked the diverse crowd of local people, artists, writers, and of course, he loved the music; Glen, on the other hand, didn't.

When Sharon turned to pick up her drink, she could see he was still sulking. He was sitting, hunched over the table, his back to the band, and his face all sort of scrunched up, sipping moodily at his orange juice.

She had been more than aware that all he had wanted to do was go somewhere quiet, and local, so they could just sit and talk, or to be more accurate, so he could talk. He had suggested as much when he had phoned her earlier that day, but as that was all he ever seemed to want to do, she was getting pretty bored with it; she was also, as she now realised looking at his pained face, getting more than a little bored with Glen.

At this point they had been seeing each other on and off for just over three months. In the beginning, Sharon had been content enough to be the focus of Glen's attention, as it had seemed like a release from the monotonous, lonely routine that she considered her life had become. She loved her daughter dearly, but the long months of having to deal with the circumstances of being the sole parent had begun to weigh heavy on her; she felt weary and alone, and couldn't help thinking: *Is this it? Is this my life, now?*

She had first met Glen through his mother, who came to the Salon every Friday afternoon to get her hair done for the weekend. On this one particular Friday, Sharon had been perched on a stool polishing one of the large mirrors, when the sound of the front door opening, had made her turn in time to see this smartly dressed man breeze into the Salon.

He was wearing a dark grey suit, a bright red tie, and was carrying a blue plastic folder; she remembered thinking at the time how fastidiously clean and shiny he looked. He was under medium height, with an amiable, if somewhat flushed face, and short sandy hair.

As soon as he caught sight of Sharon, still attractively poised on her plinth, he had beamed, what she later learned was a well-rehearsed grin, and wasted no time in introducing himself in his faux, refined accent:

"Oh, hello there, I'm Glen Baxter. I've just popped in to pick up my mum."

Sharon gave him a brief, quizzical look, and then stepped down from the stool.

"Oh, right," she replied, sounding decidedly unimpressed.

"Well, in that case, why don't ye take a seat? She shouldn't be too long now."

Glen looked around the Salon, and appeared a little confused. His grin began to fade slightly, but then, spotting his mum under a drier reading a magazine, he had inadvertently cried out:

"Oh, there she is."

Whether through nervousness, or surprise, this statement came out of Glen's mouth in a rather higher register than he had obviously intended, causing Sharon's eyebrows to shoot up in surprise. He'd given an embarrassed little laugh, and then, in a much lower voice, said:

"Oh, I didn't see her there."

Sharon had bit her lip to stop from laughing, but then quickly composed herself enough to say:

"Oh, right, aye well, we always try and hide our clients from their relatives, they insist on it."

Sharon had obviously been joking, but it had come out sounding a little too sarcastic, and Glen's face had taken on a peeved look. Catching the look, and remembering that his mother was a good customer, she thought she had better make an effort to placate him, and flashed a smile.

"Oh, ah'm sorry. Ah'm only kiddin. Ah'm actually just about to rescue yer mum from under the drier. Oh, and ah'm Sharon, by the way."

"Very nice to meet you, Sharon," replied Glen, in his new low voice.

With his grin back on full, Glen had then sat down, still clutching his blue folder, and watched as Sharon retrieved his mother from under the drier. Mrs. Baxter had emerged looking a little flushed, but then, catching sight of Glen, she had smiled.

"Oh, hello son," she said, and then turning to Sharon, she added: "Oh Sharon, this is my boy, Glen. He's an estate agent you know."

"Oh, mum, I wish you would stop telling everybody that. It's only a job," said Glen, looking embarrassed.

Sharon had then got Mrs. Baxter settled in the chair before the mirror she had been polishing, and started to remove the rollers from her hair. She was beginning to feel slightly irritated by Glen's constant gaze, and felt the need to break the silence.

"We shouldn't be too much longer now, another twenty minutes at the most."

"Oh, you take your time, I'm in no hurry," said Glen, and then proceeded to chat away like he had known her for years. She hadn't thought too much about this at the time, and had merely assumed that a big part of his job was to have, as they say: the gift of the gab, and anyway, she wasn't really listening.

Margaret, who having no client at present, had been tidying up the kitchen, but on hearing a man's voice, couldn't resist coming out to have a bit of a nosy. She had stood silent for a few minutes, bemused by Glen's relentless stream of chatter, and waited for him to take a breath. But it didn't take her long to realise that this man was not going to stop talking anytime soon, and so, after waiting another minute, she realised that her only option was to butt in:

"Would you like a tea or coffee?" she asked the back of his head.

"Is it instant?" replied Glen, without even turning round.

"Well, it'll not be that instant, ah need to wait for the kettle to boil," dead-panned Margaret.

"Eh, no thanks," replied Glen, and then without missing a beat, carried on giving Sharon his full attention. Sharon tried not to laugh, when she caught Margaret making faces at her in the mirror, as if to say: "Who's a popular wee hairdresser, then?"

The following Friday, Glen had again popped in, even earlier this time, and again Sharon was the sole focus of his attention.

The first time she had witnessed it, Margaret, surprisingly enough, hadn't made any comment on Glen's obvious attraction to Sharon. But following the second visit, she hadn't been able to resist teasing Sharon, and as soon as the obviously besotted Glen had escorted his mum from the Salon, she had given Sharon a wry look.

"Well, somebody's keen, eh? Ah'll bet ye anything ye like, wee Glenny boy is getting up the courage to ask ye out. And what's yer answer gonny be, ah wonder? That is, if he ever stops yakkin long enough to let ye answer."

Sharon had frowned, but made no reply.

Margaret, however, was proved right, for on the following Wednesday afternoon, Glen had called the Salon, and asked to speak to Sharon. Margaret, having answered the call, had passed the phone to Sharon, and then, with raised eyebrows and an exaggerated smile, she had silently mouthed the word, G-l-e-n.

"YOU-KNOW-I-LOVE-YOU-SO,
BABY-PLEASE-DON'T-GO."

As the band finished the song, Sharon turned and gave Glen a brief, tight-lipped smile, and then slipped a cigarette from her pack on the table.

"Ah'm just gonny nip out for a cigarette, ah won't be long."

Before he had a chance to reply, she picked up her lighter, and disappeared through the crowd.

Once outside, she leaned against the wall, lit her cigarette, and blew a smoke-filled sigh up into the cool night air. There was a full moon, which at first appeared to be moving swiftly across the starless sky, but she soon realised it was actually the ever-drifting clouds that were creating this illusion. Standing there gazing up at the vast dark sky, she found herself thinking: *How many other people in the world, are at this minute looking up at the same moon with the same sense of wonder and longing?* But then, almost immediately, she gave an embarrassed little smile, and thought: *Catch yourself on, Sharon.*

During the past week or so, she had been experiencing mixed emotions: anxious one minute, and elated the next. She couldn't help wondering what fate had in store for her. In a week's time, she and Mona would be in London. In a week's time, she would see Mickie again.

Sharon had only relayed this information to Glen earlier in the evening, as he was driving them across town. It was shortly after being told of the London trip that he had gone into a mood, and become, which was certainly unusual for him, silent. At first, Sharon had felt a little guilty for not telling him about the trip before now, but then she began to feel irritated, and thought: *Why am I feeling guilty? It's none of his business;* and during the latter part of the journey, she actually began to consider Glen's childish behaviour a bonus, and made the most of the silence.

She was still weighing up love and life, when her thoughts were interrupted by the laughter of two young men who came bustling out through the door of the pub, and then strolled over to lean against the wall on the opposite side of the door to her. Sharon glanced over, and recognised them as members of the band. The one with the pork-pie hat began to relate some musical anecdote, while the taller of the two, took a pack of Malboro reds from his shirt pocket, and then pulling out two cigarettes, offered one to the storyteller.

It suddenly struck Sharon that the band were obviously having a break, and for an instant, she thought she should perhaps go back in and sit with Glen, but then decided she was entitled to linger over her cigarette. Moments later, she stubbed it out the on the metal box attached to the wall, and reluctantly turned towards the door, but then something made her stop. She didn't really know why, maybe she just didn't feel like sitting opposite a grumpy little boy. *It's a beautiful night,* she thought. *Why shouldn't I enjoy it a wee bit longer?* The decision seemed like a release, and she returned to her place against the wall, and again gazed up at the moon.

She was just beginning to wish she had brought the rest of her cigarettes with her, when the pub door was again pushed open. Through it came a tall, lean young man with longish dark hair, who casually ambled over, and stood next to her. Sharon glanced out the corner of her eye, and saw him purse his lips, as if to whistle, but no sound came.

He reached into the pocket of his leather jacket and pulled out a pack of Camel cigarettes, and then turning towards her, gave a hesitant little smile and held out the pack. At first, she was unsure of what to do; she looked down at the cigarettes, and then up into the man's face. She saw something in his eyes that made her decide to trust in fate, and she withdrew one of the offered cigarettes.

"Thanks," she said, and put it between her lips.

The guy flicked his lighter, and Sharon held a stray lock of blonde hair back from her face, and allowed him to light her cigarette. She looked up as he was doing this, and saw that he was gazing right into her eyes. She then turned away, and they smoked in silence for a long minute, and then the man spoke:

"Nights are fair drawin in, eh?"

It was such a hammy line that Sharon couldn't help but laugh.

"Aye, ah suppose they are," she replied, glancing round to see his reaction.

He was raising his eyes heaven wards, and shaking his head.

"Ah've always had rotten patter." He seemed to be talking to himself, but then he turned to Sharon with a mischievous glint in his dark eyes.

"Just as well ah'm good lookin, eh?"

Sharon shot him a quizzical look that made him laugh out loud.

"Ah know, ah know. Ah can tell what yer thinkin," he said, closing his eyes, and again shaking his head. "Has that boy not got a mirror?"

Sharon grinned, and then bit her lip and looked up at him. She guessed he was in his late twenties, maybe a little older. There was definitely something about him: he seemed perfectly at ease in himself, but at the same time, he had this humility, and obviously had a sense of humour. She gently let go a stream of smoke, and said:

"Are ye one of the musicians?"

"Aye, the drummer," he replied, quietly, nodding his head.

"Oh, right," said Sharon. "Ah'm afraid I can't see very well from where ah'm sittin."

"Oh, why don't ye come and sit up the front?" he said, not looking at her.

"Well, ah'm with somebody," she replied, trying to not sound too disappointed.

"Oh right. And yer da disnae like the music?"

"My da?" Sharon cried out, in wide-eyed disbelief.

This again caused the man to laugh out loud, while Sharon could only look on bemused. But then she relented, and her face broke into a wide grin, and she too had to laugh. They again stood in silence for a minute, smiling, and smoking their cigarettes.

"Ah'm sorry," he said, again without looking round. "It's just ah noticed ye as soon as ye walked in through the door. Ah was setting up my kit, and ah couldn't help thinkin: what's a lovely girl like that doin with Mr Cardigan? He disnae exactly look like he's a laugh a minute."

Sharon gave him a wry look. Although he had sounded sincere, and she did feel flattered, she was unsure and didn't want to appear foolish; he was, after all, a musician. And how long had she known him, all of five minutes? She gave a short mirthless laugh, and said in a flat cynical voice:

"Oh, really?"

His face instantly changed, and he looked uncertain, as if he had made a mistake. Sharon too, instantly regretted her brusque manner, and felt a sudden empathy with him.

"Ah'm sorry. It's not workin out," she said, softly.

The young musician released a stream of smoke, and nodded, as if in resignation.

"With Mr Cardigan, ah mean," added Sharon.

"Oh, ah'm sorry," he said, but his face had noticeably brightened.

Sharon thought for a moment, and then said:

"Oh, don't be. Ah'm not. It's time ah started livin again, and ah've only just realised that tonight."

He looked somewhat taken aback by this remark.

"Oh aye? Ye've obviously come to some sort of decision."

"Yeah, ah have." Sharon smiled, and felt like a weight had been lifted.

The two other musicians were making ready to go back inside, and the drummer looked over and acknowledged this with a slight lift of his chin.

"Well, back down the mines," he said, smiling tenderly at Sharon. A cloud of regret passed over her face, but then she looked up at him and returned his smile.

He dropped his cigarette on the ground, and extinguished it under the heel of his boot, and then holding out his hand, he gave her a shy smile, and said:

"Well, it's been good talkin to ye, eh . . . "

She looked up at him in anticipation, and then realised he was waiting for her to finish his sentence.

"Sharon," she said, taking hold of his hand, which felt smooth and strong.

"Well, it's been great talkin to ye, Sharon."

"Oh, and you, eh. . ."

He made a face, and wrinkled up his nose.

"Bamma."

"Sorry?"

"BAMMA!" he repeated a little louder.

Sharon's eyes inadvertently shot up, and she had to bite her lip.

"Bamma?" she said, giving him a teasing look.

"Yep!" he replied, nodding, and then gave an embarrassed little snort of a laugh.

They then both seemed surprised to suddenly realise that they were still holding hands. Bamma reluctantly released hers, and then turned to make his way back into the pub, but when he was just about to go through the door, he stopped and looked back.

"Oh, Sharon?" she liked the way he said her name.

"Yeah?"

"Ah'll keep a seat up the front for ye."

Sharon smiled, and gave a slight nod of her head, and then saw broad grin spread over his face as he entered through the door. She rolled her eyes, and then took a minute to finish her cigarette. She again glanced up at the moon, but this time, she would have sworn it looked bigger and brighter than before.

Chapter 9 (2nd Saturday)

Laura and Mickie were sitting at a table on the terrace of the Town House Hotel in Dean Street. Mickie, after eventually catching the eye of a waiter, had ordered a beer for himself, and a gin and tonic for Laura.

They had earlier left a late afternoon showing at a cinema in Leicester Square, and decided, as it was still early, to take a leisurely stroll through Soho. While walking down Dean Street, soaking up the Saturday evening atmosphere, they had come upon the Town House.

"Oh, Mickie, let's go in here," Laura had said. "They have a lovely bar, which has a great collection of contemporary art." Laura had once attended a production lunch there, and knew the bar to be a very select place.

On entering, Mickie had looked around somewhat nervously; it was indeed classy. The clientele, the art on the walls, the whole ambience of the room had instantly made hime feel, socially, and financially out of his depth.

The room was packed with people talking, laughing, eating and drinking. The collective sound of their voices almost drowned out the music coming from the expensive speakers on the walls. After standing marooned in the middle of the busy room, while waiters in striped waistcoats slid past them carrying trays loaded down with food and drink, it quickly became obvious that there was virtually no chance of getting seated anytime soon.

Much to Mickie's relief, they had just stepped back onto the terrace with the intention of leaving to find another bar, when Laura spotted a couple getting ready to vacate their table. She had then convinced Mickie, that as it was a beautiful evening, a table on the terrace would be ideal.

When the waiter brought their drinks, Mickie paid the tab, and tried not to look too shocked at the prices. He poured some beer into his glass, lit a cigarette, and then leaning an elbow on the table, cupped his head in his hand, and slowly released a long smoke-filled sigh. In contrast, Laura, sitting comfortably back in her chair, looked perfectly at ease in her surroundings, casually sipping her gin and tonic, while cooly surveying the comings and goings of Soho street-life. She certainly looked the part, dressed as she was in a midnight blue silk blouse, and perfectly tailored black trousers.

After a few minutes of people watching, Laura put down her glass, and then reaching over, cheekily plucked the cigarette from between Mickie's lips. She took a puff, and then smiling coyly, handed it back to him. Mickie, trying hard to conceal his irritation, and his unease with the surroundings, kept looking straight ahead.

"Ah'm getting to be a bad influence on you," he said.

"Phooey," replied Laura.

"Phooey?" echoed Mickie, glancing round, bemused.

Laura giggled, but Mickie on the other hand, frowned, shook his head, and returned to his thoughts. Although he would have openly admitted that the interior of the bar was beautiful, he would never have thought of drinking in a place like this; it just wasn't him. It struck him as ironic, that just as he was thinking this, a shabbily dressed man came shuffling onto the terrace, and shoved a stained, crumpled copy of the Big Issue in front of his face.

Mickie looked up at the man's forlorn, gaunt features, and for some reason he found himself trying to guess the man's age. The beggar wore a full scraggy beard, and as he had his mouth tightly clamped shut, this obscured most of his face. But something in the beggars glassy blue eyes, made Mickie think that he couldn't be much older than himself. It was so obvious, just by looking at him, that the man slept rough, and so Mickie didn't stop to consider why he was begging for money, he just placed a pound coin in the man's grubby hand, and waved away the offered Big Issue.

At this very moment, one of the waiters, the big Italian guy, who had just served Laura and Mickie, came out on to the terrace. On seeing the beggar, he immediately came strutting over, and brusquely told the man to move away from the table and stop annoying the customers. When the man ignored him, the waiter then gripped the beggar by the arm in order to escort him off the terrace. This immediately incensed the man, who spun round, and snarled:

"Don't put yer ands on me man, don't put yer ands on me man, don't put yer ands on me man."

It became a mantra, and the big waiter, releasing his grip on the man's arm, raised his hands in a pacifying gesture, and said, firmly.

"Well, just leave."

The beggar stared wildly at the waiter, for what seemed to Mickie, a uncomfortably long time, and then, giving the big Italian a final, scathing, dismissive look, he turned and walked in a jerky, erratic manner into the middle of the street.

Laura couldn't help but notice the look on Mickie's face as he watched the homeless man disappear into the crowd.

"I'm afraid it happens a lot around here," she said, in explanation, "especially in the evenings."

Mickie muttered something under his breath that Laura didn't quite catch.

"Sorry?" she asked.

"Ah feel like a fake sittin here," he repeated, louder than he meant to.

Laura looked a little taken aback, but then asked:

"Why? You have as much right to be here as anyone else."

"He disnae seem to have many rights," answered Mickie, a little petulantly.

"Look at me, Mickie."

He gave her a sideways glance, causing Laura to raise her eyes heavenward.

"He's a junkie, Mickie. He pesters people for money to buy drugs. He'll be back again in half and hour, pestering someone else. What do you expect the management to do? I'm not condemning the poor man, he's sick and desperate, but that's not our fault."

She took a large swallow of her gin, and then turned and looked away, as if interested in something at the other end of the street. Mickie knew she was right, but he couldn't help the way he felt; he did feel like a phoney, sitting somewhere like this with just a few pounds in his pocket.

They sat in silence for a time, while Mickie, who was well aware it was down to him to break the tension, tried hard to find the right words. He nervously flicked the lid of his Zippo back and forth a few times, and then, staring straight ahead, took a deep breath, and said:

"Ah'm sorry, Laura. You're probably right, and ah honestly don't want to spoil the rest of the evening, but ah just feel awkward."

He felt the warm touch of her hand on the back of his neck, and when he turned to face her, she smiled teasingly at him.

"Phooey," she said, with a certain amount of comic glee.

She then closed her eyes, tilted her head back, and feigning a haughty expression, majestically turned her head away. This made him laugh. He didn't want to argue, and he was relieved that Laura was charming and clever enough to cajole him out of his Celtic gloom; although there was still one question he had to ask:

"Okay, ah give in. What is it with this phooey stuff, then?"

Laura giggled.

"Oh, that, it's just something John said, and it sort of stuck in my mind."

She took a sip of her drink, and seemed lost in thought for a minute.

"Look, Mickie, we don't have to stay here if you feel uncomfortable, we can find somewhere else, I really don't mi . . . "

Her voice suddenly trailed off, and when Mickie turned to see why, he found her staring open-mouthed at something on the other side of the street.

"I don't believe it," she said, still looking intently at the object of her disbelief. But then, a grin began to light up her face and to Mickie's total amazement, she suddenly leapt out of her chair, and cried:

"Quickly! Drink up."

Mickie, confused to say the least, just sat in stunned silence gazing up at her.

"Oh please Mickie, we can't afford to lose him," she pleaded, while looking earnestly down the street.

Mickie was still bewildered, but he stubbed his cigarette out in the ashtray, and then leaving his beer unfinished, joined her on the pavement. Laura immediately grabbed his hand and pulled him across the street in pursuit of whom or what, he had no idea.

"Laura! What the hell is going on?"

Keeping her eyes focused straight ahead, she replied:

"Oh Mickie! I know you'll probably think I'm a silly cow, but I've just seen John walking past, and as he's been so infuriatingly secretive about his new man, I've just got to find out why, and perhaps this is a chance."

"Oh, right," said Mickie, with a hint of sarcasm. "Ye had me worried there for a minute, ah thought it might be something trivial."

Laura ignored the jibe, and held fast to his hand while negotiating them through the crowd. Mickie, who was in fact more than happy to be led away, was thinking: *maybe now we'll find something resembling a proper pub.*

Keeping at a safe distance, they followed their prey as he continued down Dean Street, and then saw him take a left onto Old Compton Street. He walked halfway down, and then crossed the street and entered a pub named Molly Mogs. As they approached the front door of the pub, Laura said in a whisper:

"We'll give him a few minutes to get settled, and . . . Oh, Mickie, don't look at me like that, I know I must seem like a madwoman."

She turned and caught Mickie grinning at her.

"Well, not mad exactly," he replied, pretending to be alarmed. "By the way, why are ye whisperin?"

She punched him lightly on the arm, and then said in a droll Scottish accent:

"Humour me, Jock."

This amused him no end, he loved that she could make him laugh. He smiled at her, and then put on a mock serious face.

"Okay Clouseau, what next?"

She looked thoughtful for a few seconds, then sat down at a table and started poking around in her handbag. Mickie pulled out his cigarettes, lit one, and then sitting down beside her, watched, captivated, as she then pulled out her purse, plucked a ten-pound note from it, and said:

"Right, okay. Here's what we should do. He doesn't know you, right? So, I think you should go in and have a quick shufti."

She handed him the money, and saw he was trying not to laugh.

"Shufti?" he said, grinning. "What are ye like?"

"Oh, shut up," she replied, but couldn't help smiling.

Mickie placed his cigarette in the ashtray, and then walked towards the door and entered the pub. Laura sat in contemplation for a time, and then picked up the still smouldering cigarette, and took a puff.

As Mickie squeezed through the mainly male punters to reach the bar, he began to feel a little self-conscience; he had the distinct feeling he was being watched. The pub walls were filled with posters advertising drag nights and other gay events. *But at least it was a real pub,* he thought.

He ordered a pint of Guinness and a gin and tonic from the blonde tattooed barman, and as the drinks were being prepared, he casually looked around the room in search of John. He caught sight of him standing at the other end of the bar, in the company of another man, and thought: *could this be the mysterious new man?* They were engrossed in conversation, which gave Mickie the chance to slyly observe them, and, as it were, report his findings back to Laura at HQ. He smiled at the thought.

John, slightly built, with thinning blonde hair, was dressed in a crisp white shirt and tan chinos, and seemed to be describing something to the other man in an animated manner. The other man could hardly be said to be responding in kind, however. He was just standing there, impassive, with his hands in his pockets, wearing a thin smile, and giving barely perceptible nod of his head at appropriate intervals. He was tall and skinny, and was wearing an open-necked shirt under a dark suit. He struck Mickie as having the look of the city-boy about him.

When the barman came back with his order, Mickie paid him, and then with a final quick glance at the two men, he made his way back outside. He found Laura smoking his cigarette, and staring dreamily into space, but as soon as he sat down, she extinguished the cigarette.

"Well?" she asked.

"Well, what?" replied Mickie, dumbly, winding her up.

She glared at him, and Mickie quickly held his hands up and cried:

"Ah'm kiddin, ah'm kiddin."

"Well?"

"Well, he's just standing at the bar, talking to some tall, skinny, city-lookin type."

Laura looked unconvinced by this information.

"City-looking type, surely that can't be his new man?"

Mickie made a face, and shrugged his shoulders.

"How would ah know?" he replied, and lit another cigarette. Laura sipped her gin and looked thoughtful.

"Are ye gonny go in and surprise him?" asked Mickie.

Laura made a face, and let out a little groan of doubt.

"I don't know. This needs a bit of thinking about. Why would we, out of the blue, go into a gay pub that John had just entered? It would just look suspicious, and he might guess we had been following him."

Mickie smiled at her; he still couldn't get his head round the fact that fifteen minutes ago, they were on the brink of an argument. And now, here they were, sitting outside a gay bar, playing detective. *Life certainly wasn't dull with Laura,* he thought.

He slowly released a stream of smoke, and then after taking a long pull of his pint, continued to watch Laura for signs of an emerging plan. She pondered on the problem for a few minutes more, and then appeared to have come to some decision. She seemed just about to speak, when suddenly, Mickie heard the pub door open behind him, and saw Laura stare open-mouthed at whoever had just appeared.

Mickie turned in the direction of her stare, only to find John and the city-boy wearing equally stunned expressions. An awkward silence ensued, until the new man, who Laura was now looking at with evident distaste, spoke up:

"Why, Laura, what a pleasant surprise," he said, in what Mickie thought was a somewhat smarmy voice.

Laura responded to this with a sibilant, dismissive hiss, and turned her head away, while Mickie, once again totally confused, sat looking back and forth, tennis-fashion, from one to the other, trying to figure out what was going on. John, now sporting an embarrassed grin, suddenly stuck his hand out.

"You must be Mickie," he said, in a flustered voice. "I'm so pleased to meet you. I've heard so much about you, I'm John."

Mickie dumbly took the offered hand, and cleared his throat.

"Oh, right. Well . . . Eh . . . Nice to meet you, too."

Laura had now transferred her look of distaste onto John, and sat scowling up at him, which had the effect of making his grin sort of crumple.

City-boy piped up again, in his too smooth voice, and casually offered Mickie his hand.

Hello there, I'm Tom. It's so nice to meet you at last."

This was too much for Laura, she rolled her eyes, and then abruptly standing up, barged past Tom Paine and disappeared into the pub. Mickie, now more than ever, was at a loss to know what was going on, he stared at the pub door for a few seconds, and then up at the two men.

"It's been a funny sort of day," he said, almost to himself.

John wrinkled his nose, and then looked down at Mickie, as if to say: "Awww, bless." But when he spoke, he sounded sincere.

"I'm so sorry, Mickie, I'm afraid this is a bit of a long story, although I have no doubt Laura will tell you all about after we've gone. It really was nice to meet you, though, and please tell Laura I'll explain everything on Monday. I can only hope she will have calmed down by then. I'm sorry again if we've spoiled your day."

He then turned to Tom Paine, and said:

"Okay trouble, I suppose we better be going."

Tom Paine returned this comment with a brief, tight-lipped smile, after which, they said their goodbyes, and leaving Mickie to his confusion, strolled off down the street. He was still gazing after them, when all of a sudden he became aware of a burning sensation between his fingers.

"Yeow! Fuck!"

He had forgotten all about his still smouldering cigarette, and now flicked it into the ashtray, and started flapping his hand in front of his face, while blowing cold air onto his scorched fingers. However, finding this did practically nothing to soothe the pain, he took the reckless, and comical step of plunging his hand into his Guinness, which caused him to groan audibly with relief. He began to think: *Have I somehow become the innocent party in some sort of secret farce?* He became even more convinced of this, when he looked round and saw the startled look on the faces of the two older gay men, sitting at the next table.

Chapter 10 (2nd Sunday)

"Happy birthday, gran!"

Sally Toper looked up into her grandson's face, and then down at the badly wrapped little package he had just placed in her hand. She found it hard to believe that this was the same bitter, angry boy, who only a week ago, had broken down and sobbed uncontrollably in her arms.

The ever-present scowl had, for the time being, been replaced by a fleeting, sad little smile. And although she was delighted to see any glimmer of hope, however brief, light up his face, it also more than ever convinced her that her grandson hadn't had much reason to smile for quite some time. It almost looked as if he was trying to remember the fundamental mechanics of how to actually do it. If it weren't so sad, she would have found it comical.

On that night of tears, after she had managed to somehow console him enough to lead him downstairs, she had sat him down at the kitchen table, and poured him a small brandy. While he had sat looking mournfully down into the glass, she had silently busied herself making them both some tea. This was a delaying tactic, she was playing for time, trying to find out the best way to proceed in such a delicate situation. When she had felt ready, she had placed the tray on the table, and then sitting down opposite him, had gently encouraged him to talk.

Although she had perhaps been afraid to confront it before now, she knew in her heart, even before he opened his mouth, what was causing him all this anguish. But she also instinctively knew that he, now more than ever, needed to open up and talk about it. And of course, she was right, for when he started talking, he couldn't stop. It was almost as if he hadn't really spoken to anyone for years; all the pent-up rage and fear simply flooded out of him.

She was, of course, more than painfully aware that her daughter was a serious drug addict, and had been for many years. And although she had more or less given up any hope of that ever changing, it was only now, listening to her grandson, that she became fully aware to what an appalling degree Rob had been suffering as a result.

She had listened, with mounting horror and shame, to the unfolding story of how he had been forced to leave his mother to the mercy of some low-life named, Nazz. She'd had to bite her lip and endure the tears of rage that fell from his eyes, because he blamed himself for being too weak and scared to prevent any of this from happening.

So wretched and helpless had he looked, that Sally had immediately felt guilty for her past, what on earth am I supposed to do about it, attitude. Her guilt was especially acute, when he had told her, somewhat bitterly, that the only reason he came to her door, was because he had nowhere else to go.

Dismissing these thoughts for now, she opened the gift; she had guessed it was a paperback book by the feel of it, but was genuinely surprised to see it was by one of her favourite authors.

"For some reason I remembered you liked her. Ye've probably read it, so I could always change it if . . . "

She held up a hand, and smiled.

Oh Rob, I'm so touched you even remembered; and you've somehow managed to pick the only one I haven't read."

This happened to be a lie, but under the circumstances, she felt it was justified. While she was pretending to read the synopsis on the back cover, the doorbell rang. At the sudden, shrill sound,

Rob's face took on a suspicious, alarmed look, but Sally gave him a reassuring smile, and then placing the book on the table, got up to see who was calling.

Hearing the voices coming from the hall wishing Sally happy birthday, Rob had a sudden urge to flee. To say his environment had done nothing to hone his social skills, was an understatement. Whenever he felt awkward and out of place, he would become suspicious and sullen, or, as with kids his own age, would take some innocent remark as a slight, and react, sometimes violently. But now, for the sake of his gran, he felt he should, make an effort.

Sally entered the living room accompanied by a teenage girl, and a tall, stern looking woman. Sally smiled, made a small self-conscience hand gesture of presentation, and then introduced them to Rob.

"Rob, this is my good friend, Jenna Brown, and her daughter, Louise."

Rob shuffled his feet, and looked across at the two strangers, his blank expression giving nothing away. Jenna, who appeared to Rob quite a few years younger than his gran strode across the room towards him. And in the few seconds it took her to cover the short distance between them, this tall, stern looking woman's face, broke into a smile of such warmth and beauty, that Rob could hardly believe the transformation; he stood momentarily mesmerised by her charm.

"Hello, Rob, it's so nice to see you again. You probably don't remember me, you were only a little boy the last time I saw you."

Rob clasped her hand briefly, and then looked at the floor. The young girl didn't move, but smiled at him with the same dazzling effect as her mother.

"Hi Rob, nice to meet you."

Rob flicked a look at her, and practiced another one of his fleeting smiles. Like her mother, Louise was tall and slim. She was wearing a pink top and faded jeans, and with her short blonde hair and healthy tan, she looked every inch the outdoor girl.

"Can I offer you a sherry, Jenna?" said Sally. "It's a little early I know, but it is my birthday after all."

"Oh, go on then, just a small one," replied Jenna.

Sally went to a glass fronted cabinet and took out two small schooner glasses, and a bottle of sherry.

"I don't suppose you'll want sherry, Louise. I know Rob wont, but unfortunately I seem to have run out of anything you would like. Rob seems to go through gallons of the stuff."

Rob looked slightly embarrassed, and then gave a nervous little cough.

"I could easily nip down the shop and get somefing, gran."

"Oh would you, darling? That would be good." Then while pouring the sherry, she added:

"Maybe Louise could walk down with you, and help you choose something you both like."

Rob's eyes widened for a second, and then again looking down at the floor, he swallowed audibly, but said nothing.

"I don't mind," said Louise, brightly.

Sally went into her bag, and taking a five-pound note from her purse, handed it to Rob. He quietly thanked her, looked briefly at Louise, and then made for the door. Louise raised her eyebrows, and gave Sally and her mum a wry little smile.

"Okay, won't be too long. Don't drink too much," she said, and then followed Rob out the door. Jenna gave Sally a look, but then smiled, and shook her head.

"She's getting so grown up. I can't believe where the time has gone."

Sally nodded, and handed Jenna her sherry.

"Oh, she's a lovely girl, and she's got spirit."

"Oh, she's got plenty of that," said Jenna, laughing.

The midday sun was high and hot as Rob and Louise walked down to the little parade of shops opposite the beach. Rob, still feeling nervous, looked straight ahead; he had no idea what to say. He was dressed in his usual urban uniform of hooded tracksuit, and trainers. Louise gave him a sideways glance.

"Aren't you hot dressed like that?"

Rob's head instantly snapped round, and with his scowl back in place, he glared at her, as if ready for some sort of confrontation. In his world a comment like that could only mean one thing, someone was trying to diss you. But when he saw that she continued to smile back at him without any trace of malice in her calm blue eyes, his expression softened, and he felt his anger recede.

"I aint got nuffing else to wear," he said.

"Oh, I'm so sorry. I didn't mean to be rude."

"Ah, don't worry about it," he said, shaking his head.

Someone being sincere, and apologising to him was certainly a novel experience.

Meanwhile, back at the house, Sally and Jenna were sitting at the kitchen table sipping their sherry. Having got their small town talk out of the way, Jenna got down to a more serious subject.

"So what are you planning to do now, Sally?"

Sally sighed, and looked out the window, as if searching for an answer.

"Well, I know one thing," she said with conviction. "I'm going to do my level best to try and get Rob to stay down here for as long as I can. It just breaks my heart every time I think of what he's been going through up there. He's just so full of anger. I'm afraid for him."

"Well, that's hardly surprising, considering what you've told me," replied Jenna. "When did you last actually speak to Patsy?"

Sally blew air through her mouth, and rolled her eyes.

"Oh, quite a while now, I'm ashamed to say. Up until about six months ago I used to try and call her at least once a week, and then one day the phone was dead. I assume they must have cut her off, and as she never ever called me back, and I'm afraid I just sort of gave up. But most of the time, even when she did answer the

the Gambling Commission. The principal office of Camelot is Tolpits Lane, Watford WD18 9RN.

GAMES RULES AND PROCEDURES

National Lottery games are subject to the relevant Rules and Procedures which set out the contractual rights and obligations of the player and Camelot. Games Rules and Procedures are available to view at retailers or on the website, and copies can be obtained from the National Lottery Line. Camelot is entitled to treat a ticket as invalid if the data on it does not correspond with the entries on Camelot's central computer. Players must be 16 or over. Play responsibly.

If you are concerned about playing too much, call GamCare on 0808 8020 133 (freephone).
www.gamcare.org.uk

TR12

THE NATIONAL LOTTERY®

For information visit the website at www.national-lottery.co.uk or call the National Lottery Line on **0333 234 50 50**. Calls cost no more than calls to 01 or 02 numbers. If your phone tariff offers inclusive calls to landlines, calls to 03 numbers will be included on the same basis. A separate MINICOM line for the hard of hearing is also available. A proportion of National Lottery sales goes to the Good Causes. For further information please refer to the Players' Guide.

GUIDANCE ON HOW TO PLAY

For how to play and prize structures see the Players' Guide (available from retailers), see the website, or call the National Lottery Line. Results can be found through recognised media channels, retailers, the National Lottery Line or the website. Tickets issued in error, illegible or incomplete can be cancelled if returned to the issuing terminal within 120 minutes of purchase and before close of ticket sales through that terminal on that day.

GUIDANCE ON HOW TO CLAIM A PRIZE

For details about how and where to claim prizes see the Players' Guide. If you hold a winning ticket you must claim your prize by post, or in person at a retailer, or Regional Centre as appropriate, within 180 days of the applicable draw date, or within this period notify the National Lottery Line of your intention to claim, and then claim within 187 days of that draw date. Claims over £50,000 must be made in person. **If you believe you have won over £50,000 telephone the National Lottery Line.** For all claims over £500 (over £5,000 if claiming by post) you will be required to complete a claim form and show proof of identity. For a claim form telephone the National Lottery Line.

To claim by post, please send your ticket (and completed claim form for prizes over £5,000), at your own risk to The National Lottery, PO Box 287, Watford WD18 9TT.

SIGN YOUR TICKET. MAKE IT YOURS.

Name

Address

Post Code

Signature

Safe custody of your ticket is your responsibility. If your ticket is lost, stolen, damaged or destroyed, you can make a written claim to Camelot no later than 30 days after the winning draw date, but it will be at Camelot's discretion whether or not to investigate and to pay the claim.

THE OPERATOR OF THE NATIONAL LOTTERY

The National Lottery is operated by Camelot UK Lotteries Limited under licence granted by the Gambling Commission. The principal office of Camelot is Tolpits Lane, Watford WD18 9RN.

GAMES RULES AND PROCEDURES

National Lottery games are subject to the relevant Rules and Procedures which set out the contractual rights and obligations of the player and Camelot. Games Rules and Procedures are available to view at retailers or on the website, and copies can be obtained from the National Lottery Line. Camelot is entitled to treat a ticket as invalid if the data on it does not correspond with the entries on Camelot's central computer. Players must be 16 or over. Play responsibly.

If you are concerned about playing too much, call GamCare on 0808 8020 133 (freephone).
www.gamcare.org.uk

TR12

LOTTO

Good luck for your
1 x Sat draw
on Sat 29 Feb 20
1 play x £2.00 for 1 draw
£2.00

0287-030179685-089679 010092

YOUR NUMBERS

A 13 20 21 31 37 44

THANKS TO NATIONAL LOTTERY PLAYERS
AROUND £30 MILLION IS RAISED EVERY
WEEK FOR GOOD CAUSES ACROSS THE UK

CHECK YOUR TICKET THE EASY WAY
SCAN WITH THE NATIONAL LOTTERY APP

0287-030179685-089679 010092 Term. 47021601
[. . . .] Fill the box to void the ticket

phone, I couldn't get any sense out of her. Rob has given me her mobile number, which I tried to call yesterday, but that too was dead; Rob says she often forgets to top it up, and so I dread to think what state she's in."

Jenna could see Sally's eyes glisten, and thought she may be about to cry, but she managed to steel herself, and took another sip of sherry.

"Well, I wonder how the kids are getting on," she said, brightly, changing the subject.

Jenna looked over and smiled at her friend; she did feel great sympathy for the predicament in which Sally now found herself, but she also couldn't help thinking: *Thank God it's not me, and thank god it's not my daughter.*

On a sea-front bench, looking out over the water, Louise and Rob sat in quiet contemplation. A large open packet of crisps lay on the seat between them, and they both held their own individual bottle, Coke for Rob, mineral water for Louise. Rob had even removed his hooded top, and although he was squinting against the sunlight, he appeared, at last, to have mastered his fleeting little smile.

* * *

Piles of used banknotes lay on the grubby surface of the coffee table. A solidly built black youth, known on the street as Shank, was pulling handfuls of the bills from a satchel, and then conscientiously sorting, £5, £10, and £20 notes into £100 stacks. Toto, who was sitting next to the youth on the couch, then transferred these stacks, ten at a time, into another bag, and then noted the amount in a notebook.

Nazz, who was presiding, ominous and silent, over this procedure, sat opposite the two men, smoking a cigarette. His gaze was fixed, and never for an instant, did he take his eyes off the money.

Toto, as usual, was feeling the tension; he didn't like the way the big man always seem to treat him with no respect whatsoever. *It's me that's doing all the fucking work,* he was thinking. *It's me that's bringing in the fucking money.*

It was uncanny, but right at that precise moment, Nazz snapped the fingers of his right hand, twice, and then holding it out palm up, glared at the little man. It was almost as if he knew what was going through Toto's mind, and wanted to remind him who was boss by checking the figures in the book. Toto, trying hard not to let Nazz see he was almost shaking with rage, instantly produced a not too convincing grin, and reached over the table to pass the book to the big man,

"Lookin good, boss," he said, hanging on to his grin.

Nazz made no comment, but took a few minutes to study the figures, before throwing the book back across the table. Shank could feel the bad feeling in the room, but was smart enough to keep his head down, and carry on with his work.

"Naaaz!" The sound of the woman's voice through the closed door, was grating, especially to Toto.

"Aw man! What does that scuzzy bitch want now?"

Shank looked up, and Nazz made a slight movement of his chin towards the door. The youth rose, and went out into the hall to deal with Patsy; Nazz had earlier ordered her to stay in the bedroom, as he wanted her out of the way while they counted the money.

A brief mumbled conversation took place behind the closed door, during which, mainly Patsy's pitiful, whining voice could be heard, pleading. The boy then re-entered the living room and closing the door behind him, remained standing.

"She says she's run out of cigarettes, and feels bad," he said. "Says she needs a little bit of somefing."

Toto scowled at this.

"Fuck off! Somefing," he said, sarcastically. "That fuckin bitch is jackin up all the profits."

Nazz ignored Toto's comment. He took air in through his nose, held it for a couple of seconds, and then let it go with a groan.

"Tell her to stop whinin, or she'll get fuck all," he said, loud enough for Patsy to hear. "She'll get a taste when I'm ready." He then withdrew a few cigarettes from his pack and handed them to Shank. The boy took the smokes, and went back through the door, closing it behind him.

Chapter 11 (3rd Monday)

"Och, ah know, darlin . . . Are ye kiddin? Ye've no idea how happy ah am that yer comin down . . . Oh really? Well ye know yer uncle Billy canny wait to see you again, either . . . Och, ah know . . . Well, it won't be long now, eh?"

Mickie was cradling the phone between his chin and shoulder, while struggling to lace up his boots.

"Ah know, ah know." He was grinning; the sound of his daughter's voice always had that effect on him.

"Of course ah'll be there to meet ye . . . Does it? What in Tracy Beaker time? Wow! Really? Ah didnae know that . . . Yeah, you bet were gonny have a fantastic time . . . Yeah, yeah."

He laughed out loud and nearly dropped the phone.

"Yer a mad woman!" He heard delighted laughter coming from the other end of the line; he loved to hear her laugh.

"Listen, darlin, ah've got to go now, but thank yer mum for lettin ye phone. Ah'll call ye back in a couple of days, okay. And then, on Friday ye'll be here . . . Ah love ye too, darlin, bye, bye."

He replaced the receiver, but lingered in the silence of the hall, staring at the floor.

"Hey, daddy, yuh got time for cup of coffee?"

Lucy had become curious at the silence, and when she had looked round the kitchen door and saw Mickie still sitting on the steps, lost in thought, she knew exactly what he was feeling.

He looked round and smiled.

"Yeah, thanks. That would be good."

He got up and walked into the kitchen, and then stood by the open door, looking out into the yard.

"Everything okay, Mickie?"

"Yeah," he said replied, a little hesitantly. "She's just so excited, and ah'm just a wee bit nervous. Ah really want everything to go all right."

Lucy put his coffee on the table.

"As soon as yuh have her in your arms again, everything will be all right. Yuh love her, and she loves you, that's all that matters."

He turned from the door and sat down at the table, and looked up into Lucy's dark brown eyes.

"Thanks, Mrs McIntyre. Ah'm sure yer right."

She sat down opposite him, and noticed he was looking at her as if he wanted to ask her something. She peered over her glasses at him.

"What is it, bwoy?"

He seemed embarrassed.

"Oh, ah was just wonderin if you and Harry had any kids. Ah never hear ye mention anybody."

At first, Lucy didn't reply; she looked down, and blinked nervously. She made a futile little gesture with her hand, and then let it fall onto her lap. Mickie immediately sensed that he had overstepped some mark. He was beginning to regret having asked the question, when Lucy lifted her head, and looked him straight in the eye.

"Mi couldn't have babies."

She said it like it was a phrase she'd had to utter too many times for too many people. She again lowered her eyes.

"Mi didn't know at first, but it didn't matter too much then anyway, because there was so much goin on: the music the gigs, the parties; we was young and rippin it up, and havin a time. It was later, when Harry and Sammie started to get a lot of work on big name tours. It became too much for me, and mi started to get weary of the road. And by that time, we had moved into this house, and mi felt the need to make a home. Yuh know, a solid base where we could live a normal life away from the road. That's when we found out mi couldn't have babies."

She swallowed hard, like her mouth was dry, and then took a sip of coffee. Mickie sat motionless, trying desperately to find the right words to convey how sad he felt for her. He had instantly realised he had opened an emotional wound, and now felt guilty for being so thoughtless.

"Oh, Mrs McIntyre, ah don't know what to say, sorry doesn't seem to be enough."

"Oh, Mickie, darlin, mi know yuh have a tender heart, and that's enough." She attempted a brief, sad smile, but then lifted the coffee cup to her lips to conceal her failure.

***

Unusual though it was for a Monday lunchtime, Billy was sitting hunched over the bar of the Falcon. That he had something on his mind would have been obvious to anyone taking the time to notice, simply by the fact that an untouched pint of lager had been sitting on the bar in front of him for more than ten minutes.

Since he had given his word to Lucy that he would take steps to find out about Rob, and somehow sort things out, he had taken to walking past her house at different times every evening. He had hoped to catch the youth in the act of intimidation, as it were, but even after more than a week, Lucy and Sammie's stalker was still nowhere to be seen.

He had wasted most of yesterday afternoon sitting at the window of a large, rowdy pub named The Bulldog. It was directly opposite the block of flats where the woman he assumed to be

Rob's mother had confronted him, but the only people he had seen, immediately recognising the big guy with the nose, were the two men he had initially followed from the Falcon. They had got out of a car and entered the building accompanied by a younger man. It seemed that all his detective work had come to nothing; the boy had mysteriously disappeared from the streets.

"Well, hello mister Dunn."

The greeting broke into Billy's thoughts, and he looked up in surprise. Mickie had suddenly appeared from nowhere.

"What the hell are you doin here? Ye don't usually start work until five on a Monday."

"Ah'm workin all the shifts ah can get this week, so ah can have more time with Mona. Ah was just grabbin a wee bit of lunch in the back."

"Oh, right," replied Billy, brightening up. "Ah completely forgot that she's comin down on Friday,

"Aye. Ah spoke to her this mornin. She's so excited, and she said she canny wait to see ye."

"Och, the wee darlin," said, Billy, delighted.

"She was really makin me laugh. She's apparently got a hamster called William."

"Och, ah always wanted a hamster," said Billy, with a benign smile.

Mickie gave him a look.

"Ah did!"

"If you say so," said Mickie, not entirely convinced, and then added:

"Anyway, what are you doin in the pub at this time of the day? Are ye a wee secret drinker, now?"

Billy pulled a face, and then remembering his pint, lifted it to his lips, and took a long pull, and then, putting the half-empty glass back on the bar, wiped his mouth with the back of his hand, and then asked:

"Never mind that, how was yer weekend, then?"

"Oh, interestin."

"Lucky you."

"Oh, why?"

"Ach Ah was just bored shitless. Ah hate it when Mary has to work the weekend."

"Is that why yer drownin yer sorrows? Ye looked really pissed off when ah came in."

Billy obviously didn't want to disclose what he had actually been thinking.

"Did ah? Ach no, it's just that Monday feelin, innit? And sometimes Pete gets on my nerves, so ah thought ah'd grab a quiet pint."

Mickie looked at him curiously, and then slowly bobbed his head up and down.

"Oh, by the way," he said, changing the subject. "Did you know Mrs McIntyre couldn't have kids?"

"Ah did actually. Why?"

"Because ah opened my big mouth, and asked her if she and Harry had any kids. The thing was, ah had just been talkin to Mona, and it was then it struck me that I had never heard Mrs McIntyre mention anything about children. The question was out of my mouth before ah really thought about it, but then, when I saw her face, ah instantly felt like a thoughtless prick. It was almost like ah'd punched her."

Billy took a sip of beer, and sighed.

"Well, ah can imagine, It's got to be a very painful subject for her, especially as Harry fathered a son with a younger woman."

Mickie's face crumpled with remorse.

"What? Aw yer kiddin?"

Billy shook his head.

"Well, as ye know, Harry and my old man were close mates, even after he moved to London. When ah left to come down here to stay with them, he told me all about Harry and the other woman. Ah think the only reason he spilled the beans, was in case ah asked the same question as you."

"Oh cheers, pal. Now ah feel even fuckin worse," Mickie said, squirming with guilt.

"Ah'm sorry mate, ah suppose ah should have mentioned it, but it just never occurred to me. It was so long ago, a good eighteen years at least. Ah don't really know how, but one way or another, the situation was resolved. Although ah don't think either of them ever got over it; my old man reckoned it killed Harry in the end. Mrs McIntyre and him were such a love-match, that he felt the guilt for the rest of his life. As ye can imagine, it was never mentioned when ah was stayin there, and ah obviously never let on ah knew anythin about it. It was none of my business."

"So what happened to the woman and her kid?"

Billy shrugged his shoulders.

"My da thinks Harry made some sort of money deal with her, and then she apparently moved away. Ah don't think Harry ever saw her or the baby again."

Mickie was silent for a moment, shaking his head in disbelief, and then looking a Billy, he asked:

"Do ye think Sammie knows?"

Again, Billy shrugged his shoulders.

"Ah don't know, Mickie, but ah would have thought so. Accordin to my da, they were like brothers."

Mickie gave his friend a sad helpless look, and then said, mournfully: "Life is just shite sometimes, innit?"

* * *

The morning had come and gone, but Lucy was still sitting at the kitchen table, lost in thought. It was unusually quiet; there was no jazz drifting softly from the radio, no favourite songs to help her sing and sway her way through her daily chores. By now, she would normally have washed up after lunch, and be busy checking what groceries she needed at the market. But in the hours since Mickie had left to go to work, she had sat here motionless, unable to generate any enthusiasm for the simplest task.

She had always tried not to dwell on bad memories. What was the point? It only made you blue. But, unfortunately Mickie had asked that question; an innocent enquiry of course, but nevertheless, it had been a long time since anyone had brought up the subject of why she had no children. Perhaps it was thinking recently of Harry's death that had made the memory of it more than tender, more than a little hard to bear.

Anyone who had ever thought the whole affair hadn't torn her heart was a fool; she thought she would die of the pain. On the day Harry had told her, she watched dumbly as tears of remorse had flowed from his eyes. She was so shocked and hurt, that she didn't know how to feel. Her first furious instinct was to drive her fists into that stupid sorrowful face; but she couldn't, all she could do was sit there in stunned silence, until Harry had told her everything.

"Oh, darlin," he had pleaded. "What have ah done? Ah'm so sorry. Ah don't know what to do. Ah don't want to lose ye."

These clichéd words were more than she could bear; she put her hands over her ears, and lowering her head to her chest, had wept uncontrollably. How could he let this happen? How could he let this happen to her? She wasn't stupid, she had been around musicians long enough to know the score. She knew Harry liked to flirt, but that's all it had ever been, until now.

It was a tough year for both of them. There were times when Lucy thought she wouldn't make it. But she knew in her heart that Harry loved her, and that it was tearing him up dealing with the whole sorry mess. But deal with it he did, and it cost him more than money.

Lucy hadn't wanted to know anything about the aftermath of the affair, it hurt too much. Harry had respected her wishes, and had taken care of the situation. The woman had wanted to keep the baby, and so he had worked out a financial settlement with her, after which, as far as Lucy knew, he didn't see her, or the baby again.

Something changed in Harry after that, it was as if he couldn't bear to live with himself. He smoked and drank much more than he had ever done before. Unusual as it was for a musician, he had never been a big drinker; he just seem to have this sort of built in natural-high, it was one of the things that made him such an attractive man.

Lucy had never doubted that Sammie had been aware of the affair, and would have been privy to the details of the settlement. But he never uttered a word to her, and Lucy would never have pressed him for information. She could, however, tell by his face that he felt for her, but what could he do, he was caught between two people he loved.

All the time she had been thinking these sorrowful thoughts, her little cat had been stretched out on her lap, as if sensing her need for some silent company. Lucy had been distractedly stroking him under the chin, which had eventually caused such a soporific effect on the animal, that now, so deep asleep was the little cat that he was in imminent danger of sliding head first off her lap. But Dizzy, instinctively becoming aware of the danger, jerked awake, and jumped to the floor. This in turn, brought Lucy out of her sad contemplation. She shook her head, and looked down at the little face that was now yawning, and gazing up at her, in the hope of being fed.

"This won't do, darlin. Mi cain't sit here all day."

She got up, switched on the radio, and started to prepare Dizzy's food.

* * *

John returned to the office after a solitary lunch, and again, just as he had done before lunch, searched everywhere for Laura. When she was still nowhere to be seen, it was obvious that she was avoiding him. She had positively blanked him during the Monday morning meeting, and then afterwards, had made a point of marching off, with a confused looking Tim Farrell trailing behind her.

By this point, John's frustration was such that he even took the reckless step of trying to enlist the help of the biggest, nosiest creep in the company. As he approached Lewis's desk, he just knew he was going to regret it.

"I don't suppose you have any idea where Laura might be?" said John, forcing a smile.

Dick Lewis smirked, and John, who was in no way physically aggressive, immediately felt like poking him in the eye with one of the perfectly sharpened pencils, that for some reason, Lewis kept in an open-mouthed, bright pink plastic hippo on his desk.

"Oh, had a little tiff, have we?" said Lewis, in his irritating whine. 'I wondered why you were wandering around like little boy lost."

"Oh just answer the question, will you?" replied John, in exasperation.

"All right!" snapped Lewis, and then added in an irritatingly clipped voice:

"No, I don't know where she is."

He then closed his eyes, and turned his head away, as if to say: "Our business here is concluded, please leave."

John gritted his teeth, and let air out through his nose. He was seriously considering using the whole contents of the hippo on Lewis, but instead he strode off towards the kitchen to calm down.

He had just turned to go through the open door, when Laura virtually bumped into him coming out.

"Aha!" said John, with a tad too much drama.

Laura rolled her eyes, and tutted.

"Excuse me please," she said, coldly. "I'm in rather a hurry."

"Oh Laura! You can at least let me explain."

She gave a deep, exaggerated sigh.

"How could you keep something like that from me? You know how much I detest that creep."

"Well, there you go. That's the very reason. I didn't know what to do for the best."

Laura hissed through her teeth.

"It's true," continued John. "How on earth could I start explaining something like that? Especially knowing how you felt. It just happened, and I was trying to get my head round it myself."

She scrunched up her face, but made no effort to leave.

"Oh please, Laura," John said, with a sigh. "I'd hate it if we fell out over this."

Laura fluttered her eyelids, looked away, and took a deep breath.

"But Tom Paine?" she said, with a puzzled look on her face. "I mean . . . " She was lost for words for a moment. "Tom Paine?" He's not even gay."

"Oh, yes he is," replied John, raising his eyebrows for emphasis.

"I knew it the first time I met him, that evening you broke up with Toby. I had decided to confront him about it only because he was being such a pain. But when he came back to the table, and found that you two had gone, he became a very different person. He was, however still pissed, and I couldn't resist getting my own back on him, and winding him up. In the end he became so flustered and embarrassed, that he too, stormed off; it certainly seemed the thing to do that evening. The funny thing was, after he'd gone, I found myself actually feeling sorry for him."

Laura hissed again.

"He's still a creep."

"Actually, he's not. Although I will admit, he has what you might call, an unfortunate manner if you don't know him very well. But he's really very nice; he doesn't even really drink anymore."

Laura hissed yet again, and John rolled his eyes.

"Will you please stop doing that? You sound like a leak."

Laura frowned. "Tch, well honestly, what do you expect?"

John smiled at her.

"Look, just say you'll let me take you for a drink after work, so we can talk properly."

Laura sighed.

"Well, okay, but I'm not promising anything."

"Of course, of course," John said, eager to placate her. But he couldn't help grinning, nonetheless.

* * *

The phone call had been strangely unsettling for Sammie. Although Lucy had tried her best to disguise it, there had been a certain blue quality to her voice. Sammie remembered hearing the same tone in his late mothers voice, in times of sorrow.

She had kept it brief, simply saying that she would like to see him, and would he mind coming over to the house. A request like this would normally have made his day, but for some reason he felt uneasy at the prospect.

That he had received the call just as he had been packing away his horn, after a particularly soul destroying muzak session, only added to his general mood of despair. He hated these gigs, but for a musician his age, quality work was becoming harder to find, and he needed the money.

As he approached Lucy's front door, he was still pondering on the reason behind her phone call. It was then a chilling thought entered his head: *That bloodclaat of a bwoy has come back.* Sammie felt his anger rise, and he stood looking up and down the street before walking up to the door and ringing the bell.

Lucy answered his ring almost immediately, as if she had been watching out for him, which of course she had. She smiled at him tenderly, and gave a slight lift of her chin in greeting.

"Hey, Sammie, it's good of yuh to come. Come in, man, come in. Mi got the coffee on."

Sammie laid his trumpet case down in the hall, and followed Lucy into the kitchen.

"Is everyting okay, Luce?" he said, trying not to sound anxious.

"Everyting is fine, man. Sit down while mi fix tings."

Sammie took out his tobacco and papers, and proceeded to roll a cigarette. While he did this, he stole furtive glances at Lucy;

he was still trying to gauge from her mood the reason for his visit. But after completing his task, he decided to let fate take its course, and sat back in his chair, lit his smoke, and slowly nodded his head to the sounds coming from the radio.

Lucy brought over a tray containing the coffee pot, two cups, and an unopened bottle of Jamaica rum, and placed it on the table. After she had poured the coffee and added a shot of rum to each cup, she sat down opposite Sammie at the table.

Mi been doin some tinkin, Sammie. In fact, mi been doin a whole lotta tinkin."

Sammie looked uneasy, and took a pull of his cigarette.

"Yuh sounded different when yuh called mi Luce, like yuh were scared or someting. Wha appenin?"

"Oh, mi sorry, Sammie, mi mood take over mi voice, but yuh have nothin to feel bad about. Mi just come to some big decisions."

Sammie sipped his coffee, but didn't look any less anxious.

Lucy looked him straight in the eye

"Mi want us to be together, man; mi mean, really together. Mi want yuh to move in here with me, what yuh tink?"

Sammie appeared momentarily stunned; his mouth was moving, but there was no sound. Lucy gazed at him over her glasses, and then said, a little impatiently:

"Well, man! What yuh tink?"

It started as a low rhythmic rumble, deep in his throat. But then the sound began to build until Sammie was laughing out loud with uncontrollable delight, and slapping his thigh, as though to further emphasise his joy.

At first, Lucy could only stare at him in wonder; she was not sure what to make of his reaction, but then a smile spread across her face, and she too began to laugh.

Sammie eventually managed to refrain from laughing long enough to wipe the tears from his eyes.

"Oh, Lucy, darlin, yuh sure had this old man fooled; mi was tinkin something bad had happened."

Lucy poured some more rum in their cups, and then looked tenderly at Sammie.

"Yuh home now, Sammie. Yuh home now."

Chapter 12 (3rd Wednesday)

Sally and Jenna, were for the moment, comfortable in their silence. For the last hour or so they had been sitting in the quiet of Sally's living room, where their conversation had flowed easily from one note-worthy topic of local gossip to another. But now they had re-convened to the kitchen, in order to make yet another pot of tea. They were sitting in the sunlit room, nursing their teacups, and looking out at Rob and Louise larking about in the garden.

The change in her grandson's whole demeanour continued to strengthen Sally's resolve to try and keep the boy here with her for as long as possible. He had now begun to trust her enough to open up and tell her more about his life, which in turn, made it a whole lot easier to understand his previous behaviour. She soon came to realise it was a small miracle that he had actually managed to survive at all, without succumbing to hard drugs, or ending up in prison.

They continued to watch as Rob attempted to mend the dilapidated framework of the clothes carousel, situated at the end of the garden. Sally, until recently, had used it to hang her washing out on warm days. But the wire in the mechanism had snapped, and it now stood useless, with its tubular arms hanging down pathetically from the main pole; it vaguely resembled a sad, skinny man.

Rob was trying his best, but Louise, who was reclining in a deck chair, kept making him laugh, and he would then lose concentration, and drop the pliers.

"You don't know how happy it makes me to see him laugh," said Sally, gazing at the young couple through the open door. She then turned to Jenna.

"I can't believe the change in him since he met Louise on Sunday. In four days she has somehow transformed him; he even looks different."

Jenna looked down into her teacup.

"This is going to sound hypocritical, but I have to be honest with you Sally, when I first saw Rob, I was more than a little concerned. I thought: *Oh dear, I don't want my daughter to get involved with this scowling, London hoodie.* I felt guilty making assumptions, and thinking like that, but I couldn't help it. I was instinctively afraid for her, but somehow, she was able to see something more in him than just this sullen boy, hiding behind this hoodie façade. And perhaps she's right, for I have to admit I find I'm actually coming round to him myself."

Sally's eyes flashed for a second.

"Listen, Jenna," she said, looking intently into her friend's eyes. "I totally understand why you felt like that. When Rob first arrived unannounced at my door, I'm ashamed to say I didn't want anything to do with him either. And I certainly didn't want him near anyone I cared about. I just couldn't seem to get through that veneer of anger and hate, and to be honest I began not to care. But oh God, when he broke down in tears, I knew in a heartbeat how blind I had been. And when I look at him now, my only fear is what will happen if he goes back to that horrible environment."

They then sat in silence for a time, each alone with their thoughts, until the sound of laughter made them once more turn their attention to the teenagers in the garden.

Having somehow managed to get the carousels arms to stay upright, Rob had then stood back to admire his handiwork and await his due praise. But then, something had snapped, and the metal arms had collapsed and again hung useless from the main pole. Louise instantly became helpless with laughter, while Rob could only stand looking at the device in disbelief, while muttering under his breath: "Poxy fing." But then he couldn't help but see the funny side, and he too started to laugh.

Sally came to the kitchen door.

"Oh, Rob, don't worry about it, love, the stupid thing is just too old to be mended. I really need to get one of the new plastic ones. You just relax for a bit, I'm going to start making us some lunch now."

Rob sat down on the deck chair next to Louise, lit a cigarette, and then lying back, closed his eyes against the bright sunlight. Louise took this chance to glance over at this London boy, and she could see a change in him. He was dressed in jeans, and one of the plain white t-shirts she had encouraged him to buy, instead of the garish printed ones, he had seemed to favour. The sun had begun to colour his pale city face, and even the ever-present scowl had mostly disappeared.

Considering the short time she had known him, she was surprised to find how much she cared about him. She hadn't quite figured out why yet; perhaps it was because there was such sadness in his eyes when he thought no one was looking. She would normally have stayed well clear of a boy like Rob, but somehow she sensed that underneath all that street bravado, he was vulnerable and scared, and after the initial awkwardness, she felt he found her easy to talk to. There was one subject however, about which he remained reticent: his mother. She decided to take a chance, and broach that tender issue.

"So, have you managed to get hold of your mother yet?" she asked, feigning a matter-of-fact manner.

Rob was silent for a long minute.

"I ave, as it appens, yesterday," he replied, keeping his eyes closed.

"Is she okay?" Laura asked, tenderly.

"Well, she was out of it, but then she always is, when she can get hold of it. And wiv that black bastard usin the place for bizness, there'll be stuff there most of the time."

Louise furrowed her brow, and tried desperately to think of something positive to say. But she had no experience of his world, and didn't want to say something stupid or flippant. She felt she should, however, say something, even if it was stating the obvious.

"Couldn't you tell the police what this guy is getting up to in your house?"

Rob shook his head and hissed with sudden angry vehemence.

"He would know it was me what did it. You don't know im, he's a fuckin animal. He would fink nuffin of hurtin me mum, just to get back at me."

They sat in silence for a few awkward minutes, and then, to Louise's relief, Sally appeared at the kitchen door and announced lunch was ready. Rob flicked his cigarette butt away in a defiant gesture, and then jumping up, strutted towards the house. His sudden emotional outburst had left Louise in no doubt that there was still serious hurt and anger lodged deep inside this London boy.

(3rd Friday)

Mona gazed out the window of the 10.25 London bound train as it slowly pulled out of Glasgow's Central Station. Due to her insistence that they be at the station well ahead of time, she and her mum had been first to board the train. As a result, they were now settled comfortably into their window seats.

Sharon glanced across the table at her daughter, and smiled. The little girl was wide-eyed with excitement, and attempting to take everything in at once: the passengers struggling with their luggage, and searching for their seats, the unique view of the city from the train. She didn't seem to have enough eyes, and her head was turning this way and that. She caught her mother looking over at her, and flashed her a huge happy grin. Sharon rolled her eyes, and thought back to the previous evening.

As was usual after work on a weekday, she had arrived to pick Mona up from her mum's house. She had rung the bell, but had been to busy looking for something in one of her shopping bags, to notice anything amiss when Peggy had opened the door. But when she had looked up into her mum's face, she knew at a glance, that something had happened.

Filled with a sudden panic, she had rushed past her mother, and dropping her bags in the hall, went straight into the living room. What she had expected to find, she hadn't dared to guess, but what she had actually found was Mona sitting on the floor, happily drawing a picture. That she had happened to be wearing one of her granny's berets was also nothing out of the ordinary: Mona loved hats.

Sharon's confusion had been obvious by the puzzled way she had looked over at her mother, who for some reason was looking decidedly guilty. Seconds later, however, when Mona had turned to greet her, and Peggy had reached down and plucked the beret from the little girl's head, it all became clear, someone had cut Mona's hair.

To say it had been cut was something of an understatement. Mona's hair had been chopped different lengths, and was sticking up scarily in all directions; she looked remarkably like a little punk rocker.

Sharon smiled at the memory of her mother trying to explain what had happened; she had apparently drifted off to sleep in her chair, and when she had woken up and saw what Mona had done, she had almost passed out again.

"Ah didn't know what to do," Peggy had said. "Ah just kept lookin at her, and thinkin, oh, God, what is Sharon goin to say?"

As Peggy had continued to look at her granddaughter in silent confusion, Mona had calmly related how her wild new style had been achieved. On noticing that her granny had fallen asleep, she'd had a sudden, wonderful idea: she would, as a big surprise, give herself a new hairstyle for the holidays. She had then gone to the full-length mirror in the hall, and set about re-styling her shoulder length hair with a pair of small, not too sharp, safety scissors, which she had earlier been using to cut patterns out of sticky coloured paper.

The state of her daughter's hair had momentarily struck Sharon speechless, and she had stared, open-mouthed at her mum, who had gazed sheepishly back at her, while wringing her hands in a gesture of helplessness.

"Oh Mona! Look at ye. Yer a menace," Sharon had at last cried in frustration.

Mona's reaction was to look up, bewildered, wondering what all the fuss was about. Sharon, however, had quickly regained her composure, and realised the only thing she could do, was to take her daughter home and try to repair the damage.

Sharon smiled again at the memory of securing Mona into the car, and asking her, more in frustration than anger:

"Did ye really want to look like Johnny Rotten?"

"Who's Bonnie Rotten?" Mona had asked, wrinkling up her nose, causing Sharon to bite her lip to stop from laughing.

"Oh, forget it, darlin, mammy's only trying to be funny. Let's go home and try and get ye sorted out."

Although she looked cute, the result of this misadventure was that Mona's hair was now cropped as short as a little boys, it was really all Sharon could do to make her look presentable.

"Okay, baldy, do ye want yer crisps and fizzy drink, yet?" asked Sharon, making her eyes go squint. This made Mona giggle, and she tried to copy her mum's funny look.

Sharon rummaged in the plastic bag containing the snacks she had bought for the journey, and passed a packet of cheese and onion crisps over to Mona. She then opened a can of Irn-Bru, plopped a gaily-coloured straw in the hole, and placed that on the table in front of Mona.

It was then that she noticed the struggle going on between Mona and the crisp packet, and quickly plucked it back to open it, fearing that any minute now, there was going to be an explosion of crisps and Irn-Bru. Mona then decided to concentrate on making a show of drinking her Irn-Bru, by popping her eyes, and sucking in her cheeks. Sharon rolled her eyes, and shook her head.

"Yer a wee weirdo."

Mona responded to this remark by putting on a pretend haughty expression, she closed her eyes, tilted her nose in the air, and turned her head away. And then, as if to dismiss her mother still further, she made a noisy slurping sound with her straw. Sharon laughed out loud at this little pantomime – Mona could always manage to make her laugh. But then, her mood changed, and she found herself thinking of Mickie, and all that he was missing, and would miss, as his daughter grew up.

This thought, and the realisation that they would very soon all be together again after such a time apart, somehow tangled her emotions. She gave Mona a reassuring little smile, and then gazed pensively out the window at the passing landscape.

The rest of the journey was uneventful, and they were fortunate in that the seats next to them remained vacant all the way to London. Sharon looked at her watch and was surprised at just how quickly the journey, for her at least, had passed. Mona, of course, after the initial excitement had worn off, had become restless, and eager to arrive and see her daddy, and Sharon had been relieved when she had finally dropped of the sleep.

Sharon closed her magazine and looked out at the London suburbs, and then across at Mona, who was still sleeping, all the anticipation having finally got the better of her. She looked so helpless and small, and seeing her like this, always made Sharon feel torn between love and fear: love for her daughter, and fear for the future. As if she sensed her mum was looking at her, Mona's eyes fluttered open, and she yawned widely. Within seconds however, she was fully alert, and ready with the questions:

"Are we nearly there yet? Is this London?"

* * *

All last night, Mickie's mind had been buzzing so much with thoughts of seeing his daughter again for the first time in over a year, that he had hardly slept at all. Now here he was, outside the main door of Euston Station, nervously smoking a cigarette and pacing up and down like an expectant father, which in an odd way he was.

The train was due in at approximately 2.30, and he had another long ten minutes to wait. He was clutching a small fluffy rabbit he had bought on impulse yesterday, but was now unsure; maybe Mona had outgrown fluffy bunnies.

He continued to pace up and down for what seemed like ages, and then squinted through the glass at the digital clock, completely forgetting he could just as easily look at his mobile phone. *Seven minutes to go. How can time go so slowly?* He thought.

He knew he couldn't stay out here forever, and feeling he should be there when the train came in, he extinguished his cigarette, and entered the main hall. He had nearly got as far as the entrance to platform 12, when he saw them coming through the crowd towards him. For a few seconds it felt as if his heart had stopped.

Mona was the first to see him, she squealed with delight, and running towards him, flew into his arms. He hugged her tight and swung her round and round until they were both dizzy. Sharon, coming up behind with the luggage, stopped, and stood looking at the father and daughter reunion, without comment. As usual, Mickie couldn't gauge from her expression, what was going through her mind.

He managed to peel Mona off him long enough to give her the rabbit, with which, to his relief, she immediately bonded. He then greeted Sharon with a nod, and thought how different she looked. Something about her had changed; she looked good, slimmer, maybe, or perhaps her hair was different. She gave him a curious look, and he suddenly realised he had been staring. He shook his head, as if clearing it of recent thoughts.

"Okay ladies," he said, with a beaming smile. "Lets dump yer luggage, and hit the town, eh?"

He took one of the wheelie-bags from Sharon, and then taking Mona by the hand guided them towards left luggage. On the way, he informed them that he was taking them out to lunch, to which of course, Mona had to state her preference right away.

"Can we have pizza, daddy? Ah luuuve pizza," she said, closing her eyes, and making a comical face for emphasis.

Mickie's heart thumped in his chest, and it suddenly struck him just how much he had missed his little girl.

"You can have whatever you want, darlin," he said, smiling down at her. It was only then that he noticed her new hairstyle.

"Well, hello shorty. What happened to yer hair?"

Mona giggled

"Oh, it's a long story," said Sharon, rolling her eyes. "She'll no doubt tell you all about it when we get to the restaurant."

"Well, anyway, ah think ye look fantastic," said Mickie, grinning down at his daughter.

Mona beamed him back a big smile, and he felt her hand squeeze his a little tighter.

Mickie had worried that the reunion, especially with Sharon, would turn out to be awkward. But to his joy, Mona had been so funny and enthusiastic about everything that he'd soon managed to forget his concerns and relax.

Although he couldn't help but notice that Sharon hadn't said much, he was at least thankful that she hadn't spoiled things by making any of her usual sarcastic remarks. Mona however, had made the whole occasion so spontaneously enjoyable, that he hadn't wanted it to end. He had even insisted on escorting them to Sharon's aunts house in Ealing, to prolong their time together.

It was afterwards, when returning home alone, that he began to feel troubled. He found himself evaluating his life in London, and comparing it with the few happy hours, he had just spent in his daughter's company. And the unfortunate result was, he started to feel melancholy, and lonely.

He came out of Notting Hill Station, and then stood in the middle of the busy thoroughfare, pondering on his situation. He remained there, unsure of what to do, but then the solution became obvious; what he really needed right now was to see a friendly face. Spurred into action by this decision, he made his way towards Ladbroke Grove.

A short time later, he was sitting in Billy and Mary's living room, smoking a cigarette and gazing dreamily out at some cloud formations floating above the roofs of the building opposite.

"So, how was my wee pal? Was she askin after me?" said Billy, coming in from the kitchen, and putting a can of beer and a glass in front of Mickie on the coffee table.

"Oh aye," said Mickie smiling. "She certainly asked after her uncle Billy."

Billy wiggled his head from side to side, and smirked comically.

"Aw, man, it was just so great to see her," continued Mickie. "Ah mean, she's just so funny; she had me in stitches impersonatin her teacher and her school mates. Ah canny believe how quickly she's growin up."

After uttering that last statement, Mickie's expression changed. He had suddenly realised that he had put into words the regret that he had been feeling for quite some time: the fact that he was missing important stages in Mona's life. He stubbed out his cigarette, and then, with more than necessary vehemence, cracked open his can of beer.

"What's up, mate?" asked Billy, noticing the sudden change.

"Oh ah don't know," said Mickie, with a sigh. "Ah sometimes wonder what ah'm doin down here. Am ah just wastin my time or what? When ah saw Mona walkin towards me today, it just struck me how much a miss seeing her everyday. My wee girl looked so beautiful."

Billy took a minute to open his can and fill his glass. He was aware that Mickie needed to open up and talk, but he also knew that he was finding it difficult. And so, when Mickie remained silent, Billy decided to broach a tender subject.

"And what about Sharon, how was she?"

Mickie shrugged and made a face.

"Well, Sharon was Sharon. But to be fair, she didnae say anythin to piss me off, which was unusual. She seemed different, somehow, but that could just be a ploy. And ye know as well as ah do, that her track record disnae inspire trust."

Billy looked at his friend, and was about to comment further, when he heard the front door open. A moment later Mary sauntered into the living room.

"Hiya boy's, startin without me, eh?" she said, with a grin.

"Hello darlin," replied Billy.

Mickie didn't say anything, but got up to greet Mary with a hug, and then settled himself back on the couch.

"So, howye, Mickie? Did Sharon and Mona get in on time?"

"Yeah, they did," he replied, a little impassively it seemed to Mary. When he appeared reluctant to say anything else, she flashed a glance at Billy, who then rose from his seat.

"Sit down, darlin, and let me get ye a drink."

"Oh that would be great," replied Mary, tossing her jacket on a chair. "It'll have to be a quick one, though, I'm meetin Caitlin and the girls at seven."

She searched in her bag to find her cigarettes, and then sat down next to Mickie and offered him one. Mickie lit both their cigarettes, and then sat back in his seat.

"So, yer wee lassie, eh? I'll bet she was happy to see ye"

"Oh aye," said Mickie, but then he seemed to pause, and Mary sensed he was still somehow unwilling to expand on the subject. She was relieved when Billy came back into the room and placed her vodka and tonic on the table; however, she decided to persevere, and tried another topic.

"How's Laura? We'll need to get to meet her sometime."

Mickie seemed a little more at ease with this subject.

"Oh, she alright. Ah'm seein her tomorrow. The thing is, she's got this big job on at the minute, and as it's for a new client, she's under a bit of pressure. It's hard to say, but maybe when that's over we could get together."

"Oh, that would be good," said Mary, nodding and smiling. "She sounds like an interestin girl."

"Oh yeah, she's a talented girl, and nice with it. She's even taken the time to show the photographs she printed of my paintings to her art director friend, who she reckons has contacts, and maybe could help me in some way."

"Well, that's good," said Mary, and then, couldn't think of anything else to say, which was rare for her. There was an awkward silence, for a minute or so, and then Mickie, putting his cigarette in the ashtray, cleared his throat, and rose from the couch.

"Excuse me a minute," he said, not looking at anyone. "Ah need to use yer toilet. That beer's goin right through me."

When he was safely out of hearing, Mary looked at Billy, and frowned.

"Jesus," she said, in a hushed tone. "It's like pullin teeth, askin him about Mona. What's the matter with him?"

Billy made a face.

"Well, ah think he's been building this up in his mind for a while now, ye know, about how great it was gonny be when Mona came down. And of course it is, but at the same time, seein her and Sharon today, has knocked him a bit, his emotions are all over the place. He's upset that he's missin her growin up. I was actually tryin to get him to open up about it, when you came in."

Mary looked hurt.

"Oh, look," Billy, said quickly. "Ah don't mean he disnae want to talk to you, but ye know what he's like. He's not bein awkward. Ah just think he's feelin guilty, and tryin to get his head round them bein here, but at the same time, not make a big thing about it. Don't take it personally."

Mary sighed, and rolled her eyes.

"Jesus. Now ah really don't know what to say to him."

They heard the toilet being flushed, and Mary stubbed her cigarette out, and then finished her drink in one gulp. She looked over at Billy, and gave him a tender little smile, and then got up from the couch just as Mickie was coming back into the room.

"Well, ah've got to go and get changed, and get the auld lippy on," she said to no one in particular. And then, to Mickie's surprise, she hugged him, and then left the room. Mickie glanced over at Billy.

"Tch, woman, eh?" said Billy, beaming a silly grin.

Mickie gave him a wry look and sat down. And then, noticing his cigarette had burned down, he lit another one.

"So, do ye fancy goin out for a pint, or what?" aked Billy, more to have something to say, than anything else. Mickie seemed to brighten at this suggestion.

"Oh aye, and it won't just be the one, either."

Billy shot him a glance, but decided not to comment on the implication. *At least,* he thought, *it might help him to open up and talk.*

"Right, you finish yer beer," said Billy, draining his glass. And ah'll nip to the bog, and then we can go. He took a final quick glance at Mickie, and left the room.

Mickie took a pull on his cigarette, and then when he looked down to lift his glass, something caught his eye on the shelf under the coffee table. It was a book, half hidden by a magazine, but he recognised the familiar black and yellow cover of the 'Book for Dummies' series. Curious, he pulled the big paperback from its hiding place, and when he read the title, he nearly laughed out loud. At first, he was a little confused as to why Billy, or Mary, for that matter, would have a book with that particular title. But then he remembered that he had recently told Billy about Mona's pet: William.

At that moment, Billy came back in the room, and Mickie couldn't resist giving him a mischievous look.

"Ah worry about you, sometimes," he said, holding up the book. "Hamsters for Dummies?"

Billy looked momentarily embarrassed, but then he poked his nose in the air, and declared in a mock, posh voice:

"It's educational. I didn't want my wee pal thinkin I'm ignorant."

Mickie laughed out loud, he was glad he had Billy as a friend.

Chapter 13

John was midway through what he thought was a very funny anecdote, but when he became aware that Laura was staring into space and not really listening, he tutted in frustration and stopped talking.

They were having a Friday evening drink in a wine bar in Holland Park. As a rule, they frequented another bar not far from the Martin & McLean Agency, but Laura, having had more than enough of the advertising industry for one week, and knowing the local bar would be full of colleagues and clients, had suggested they go somewhere else; though in truth, she would much rather have gone straight home.

She had certainly felt that way when they had first entered the bar. It had seemed to her far too noisy and crowded. She obviously knew this typical end of the week ritual very well, and normally loved it. The Friday night after work buzz, the fun of trading banter with John, but not tonight, tonight she had other things on her mind. John, however, had managed to talk her round.

"Oh, come on, it's Friday night," he'd said beaming with enthusiasm. "You'll feel better once we've had a drink."

They had actually been lucky enough to get seated and served almost immediately, and were now perched on stools at the bar, working their way through a bottle of Petit Chablis. Laura, though, as John couldn't help but notice, was not her usual self. He had been trying for at least the last half an hour to tease her out of her sullen mood and make her laugh, but Laura was having none of it. This lack of success in the funny story department was beginning to irritate John, so he decided to try another tack.

"So the other woman, eh?" he said, raising his eyebrows.

Laura flashed him a look, but didn't take the bait, and silently refilled her glass. She was beginning to regret mentioning to John that Mickie's daughter and ex-wife were travelling down from Glasgow today. And she wasn't entirely sure she had forgiven him for not telling her about Tom Paine.

"Well, this is jolly," said John, sarcastically.

"What?" snapped Laura. "Your like a dog with a bone."

"Oh, that's nice, that's very nice. I'm a dog, now."

Laura suddenly looked tired.

"Oh, I'm sorry," she sighed. "It's just that this week, everything seems to be coming at me all at once."

John felt a sudden empathy, he knew it had been a stressful week for her: the new client was being particularly difficult.

"No, Laura, I'm sorry. I should know better by now. I was trying in my usual tactless way to cheer you up."

"Oh, I know," Laura, answered wearily. "It's just I'm not up to the game this evening."

At that very moment, a big, butch looking girl chose to approach the bar, and, so it seemed to John, stand rudely between them and wave a twenty-pound note around, while shouting out her order in an effort to attract one of the bar staff.

"Excuse me!" said John. "Were trying to have a conversation, here."

The woman swivelled her head round, and gave John a look such as you might give someone trying to peddle a selection of nasty smells. And then, without even bothering to comment, she rolled her eyes and turned her attention back to shouting out her order.

John gritted his teeth, and was about to get even angrier, when Laura suddenly plucked their bottle from the bar, and made for a pavement table she saw a couple just vacating. When he joined her a moment later, John was still seething.

"Did you see the biceps on her? She looks like Arnold fucking Schwarzenegger. If she's a woman, I'm Mike fucking Tyson."

That did it; Laura laughed until the tears fell from her eyes. She was still dabbing them with a tissue, when the big girl walked past with her drinks, and gave them a filthy look. That of course, just set her off again, and it took a few minutes before she managed to control herself.

"Oh, John," she said, sniffing and dabbing her eyes. "Thanks for that, I needed that."

"All part of the service," said John, grinning with delight. "Shall we have another bottle?"

* * *

"Why doesn't somebody write a book for tossers, and call it, Love for Dummies? Eh? Tell me that," asked Mickie, gazing up at the sky as if expecting an answer.

Billy, who was guiding him home from the pub, said nothing in reply, but just shook his head, and continued to propel his unsteady friend gently along the street.

Mickie had certainly achieved his earlier aim of having more than one drink; he was in fact ,as Billy had put it when later relating the tale to Mary, pissed as a puddin.

"Ah mean, come on, Surely that's got to be a big seller, eh?" continued Mickie, twisting his head round, and squinting in an effort to bring into focus, the two Billys by his side.

"Cause ah'll tell ye somethin, ah don't know what it's all about . . . Alfie. And ah'm sure ah'm not the only wanker in the world.

Alfie? Who the fuck's Alfie? Thought Billy, but then made an effort to reassure his babbling friend:

"Yer not a wanker."

"Oh, listen, ah think ye'll find ah'm a total wan . . . Hold on," said Mickie, suddenly realising they were passing a brightly lit pub. "Where are we goin? The pubs are still open."

Billy steered him a little more forcibly along the street.

"Love for Tossers, now that would be a much more accurate title," said Mickie, somehow remembering his train of thought.

A few hours earlier, when they had first got to the pub, Mickie had started in earnest, and immediately ordered a Guinness for himself, a lager for Billy, and two large Jameson's whiskies. After the first Jameson, Billy refused to have any more, rightly anticipating that it would be advisable for one of them to remain reasonably sober.

As the evening progressed, Billy had looked on as Mickie became increasingly drunk. At first, it was fine; the initial couple of drinks had actually helped loosen him up, and he spoke with true tenderness of his concerns regarding his daughter. He had also been very funny, and had Billy really laughing at his spiky humour, which he aimed mostly at himself. But after a while, the whiskey began to have an adverse effect, and when he started getting a little too loud, and wasn't being particularly funny anymore, Billy knew it was time to go.

Arriving at Mrs McIntyre's front door, Billy held the swaying Mickie with one hand, while searching for his key with the other. He had foolishly hoped to use Mickie's key to get him in and up to bed without disturbing Lucy and Sammie. Mickie, however, had other plans, and decided this would be a good time to compose a blues to fit his mood. To Billy's horror, Mickie's voice suddenly boomed out into the night.

"AH'M A TOSSER FOR YE BABEE. AH'M A WANKER FOR YER LUUUVE."

Billy immediately attempted to shush him up, but too late, the front door suddenly swung open, and the imposing figure of Sammie stood glaring down at them. But he quickly realised the situation, and with a grin spreading across his face, he helped Billy get the now rapidly melting Mickie through the door, and up to bed. They pulled back the covers, and gently laid him down, and within seconds, he was gone. He mumbled something unintelligible, sighed deeply, and then fell fast asleep.

When they came back down, Lucy was waiting for them in the hall.

"Hello Billy," she said, looking at him over her glasses. "Is the Bluesman okay?"

"Oh aye, he's sound asleep. Sorry about that, but it was a big day for him, and his emotions sort of got the better of him. Ah don't think he's gonny be too clever tomorrow, though."

Lucy smiled briefly, and nodded her head. It was an old story, and Lucy knew it well.

"Well, mi just made some coffee. Why don't yuh come in and sit for a while?"

Billy followed Lucy and Sammie into the kitchen, and took a seat at the table. It felt good to be in the warm homely room, after the noisy environment of the pub. The radio played softly in the background, and Billy felt himself relax, as he watched Sammie roll a cigarette, and Lucy prepare his coffee.

Lucy placed the already sugared coffee on the table in front of Billy; she seemed to have this ability to remember people's individual tastes. And then, without asking, Sammie poured a shot of rum into his cup, from the bottle on the table. Billy smiled, and lifted his cup in silent salute. The hot sweet liquid tasted good.

"So, how have things been?" he asked, and then, suddenly remembering what Mickie had told him earlier, he grinned.

"Aw, congratulations, by the way," he said, with genuine affection, and again lifted his cup in salutation.

Sammie grinned at Lucy, who briefly smiled back. Billy was amused to see that they looked almost coy.

"Mickie only told me about it tonight, and we both thought it was great news. Ah'm well chuffed for ye both, and Mary will be too."

They were quiet for a minute or so, and then, after lighting his cigarette, Sammie looked at Billy, and said:

"Mi don't want to spoil tings, but Luce and me were wonderin if yuh had lately caught sight of the youth that been harrasin her? Lucy aint seen him round here for a while, now."

Billy looked solemn, and slowly shook his head.

"No, ah haven't. He seems to have totally disappeared. Ah don't really know why. Maybe he got nicked. But ah've been lookin, ah can tell ye that."

"Well, we appreciate yuh takin the time to look out for us, Billy," said Lucy

"Aw, listen," answered Billy. "Ah just wish ah had caught up with the fucker." And then realising emotion had got the better of him, he added quickly: "Oh, ah'm sorry Mrs McIntyre, that was the auld drink talkin there."

Lucy shook her head, and raised her hand. She had been around musicians long enough not to be bothered by the odd emotional expletive.

"Ah've even kept an eye on the flat where ah think he lives with his junkie mother, but he was nowhere to be seen," continued Billy. "Ah don't know if him not showin his face, is a good thing, or not."

Lucy had noticed a certain look flash into Sammie's eyes when Billy had mentioned the flat, and she somehow knew what he was thinking. Sammie took a cool minute to relight his cigarette.

"Well, mi just content enough right now to know that he's not out there every night, scarin Luce." And then almost like an afterthought, he asked:

"So, the fool must live round here, huh?"

"Well, not too far away," replied Billy, and then turning his attention to Lucy, he said: "Ye know that estate on Weir Road, opposite the Bulldog pub?"

Lucy only nodded in reply. But Billy noticed that she glanced briefly at Sammie, who taking in smoke from his cigarette, looked up, and blew it slowly towards the ceiling. Her eyes then flicked back to Billy.

"Mi just hope he got bored or someting, especially as Sammie here now. Mi don't understand why these kids got to take tings so far. Sammie was only tryin to stop somebody bein hurt."

Billy took a sip of coffee.

"Well, BeeJay, the young guy ah work with, knew this Rob at school, and he reckons yer boy is pretty screwed up, and a real racist. He's apparently been pissed off ever since his old man walked out on him and his mum, ah few years back. It seems the man couldn't take livin with a junkie anymore. Since then, again according to BeeJay, the mothers had a string of iffy boyfriends, and most of then, ah'm sorry to say, have been black. Right now in fact, she seems to be involved with a dealer, who BeeJay described as, 'a particularly nasty lookin bro'. And he is, ah've seen him. So, all in all, this isn't doin a whole lot for this tossers disposition."

Sammie poured another shot of rum into his cup, and then offered the bottle to Billy, who held up his hand.

"No thanks, Sammie. Ah should really be goin."

He drank the last of his coffee, and then rising from the table, shook hands with Sammie, and then turned to Lucy.

"Try not to worry, Mrs McIntyre. If this guy turns up again, ah'll know about it, believe me."

Before he turned to leave, he smiled at Lucy.

"Thanks for the wee heart-starter, ah always loved yer coffee. Now don't get up, ah'll see myself out."

When she heard the front door close, Lucy looked sternly over her glasses at Sammie.

"Mi know what yuh tinkin, Sammie Turner," she said, with steel in her voice. "And mi don't like it. Yuh hear me?"

Sammie looked back at her, and then lowering his gaze, said nothing in reply. Lucy gave him a final questioning glance, and then started to clear the table.

(3rd Saturday)

Mickie woke up drenched in sweat, and made the mistake of trying to open his eyes, but it felt as if they had somehow been glued shut. He managed it a moment later, but on viewing the dizzying display of sunlit patterns on the ceiling, he quickly closed them again. To accompany a rising nausea, vague feelings of paranoia and guilt began to seep into his brain. But worse still, was the worrying sensation that he had been beaten up. He buried his head back under the duvet, and thought: *Oh God, what the hell have I been doing?* It didn't take long, however, for him to realise that this pathetic ruse wasn't going to work, and these feelings weren't going to go away.

He heard Mrs McIntyre calling for, Dizzy, and his face scrunched into a frown. He knew the first thing he had to do was to apologise to her and Sammie. The problem was, apart from the obvious fact that he must have been extremely drunk, he wasn't at all sure what he was supposed to be apologising for. No matter how hard he tried, the latter part of the evening remained a total blank.

These worrying thoughts continued to buzz round and round in his head until he had no choice but to try and get himself together enough to go downstairs. He slid one tentative leg out from beneath the cover, followed by the other, and then sat up.

"Aw, man," he groaned, on discovering he was still fully clothed.

He flopped back down on the bed, and realising he was still fully clothed, struggled to take of his jeans. *This is not looking good,* he thought. With effort, he managed to stand, and then wobbled about on one leg, pulling on a pair of tracksuit bottoms. The buttons on his shirt were another challenge. He ended up pulling it off over his head in frustration, but then had to wait until the room stopped spinning. Surprised to find a clean t-shirt, he slipped it on, and then stood blowing air through his mouth until he felt able enough to make an unsteady exit from the bedroom.

His whole body ached, and he felt like an old man as he hobbled down the stairs one timid step at a time. As he took the final step into the hall, he saw that the kitchen door, which was always open, was closed. This immediately struck him as strange, but what he thought was stranger still, was that there was no sound coming from inside, no music, no voices, nothing. *They have to be in there,* he thought. *I just heard Mrs McIntyre.* He took a final deep breath, and pushed open the door.

The sight that greeted him, made him stop dead, as if nailed to the floor.

Lucy and sammie were sitting side by side at the kitchen table, wearing the same look of stern disdain. He was so startled by this, that for a few seconds he was unable to say anything, but then attempted to blurt out a pitiful apology:

"Eh . . . Ah just . . . Oh."

He was already feeling guilty, but having to stand there in their solemn, judge-like presence, made him feel even more like a criminal; he couldn't help feeling that any minute now, he was going to be sent down for a long stretch.

But as he continued to stand there with his mouth slowly flapping up and down, he became aware that Lucy and Sammie seemed to be experiencing some sort of inner turmoil. The effort to keep this under control was beginning to be mirrored on their faces. Mickie was to say the least, confused. While he remained rooted to the spot, trying to think of something to say to relieve the tension. Lucy all of a sudden, cried out:

"Oh, Mickie!"

This cry, apart from causing Mickie to recoil in fright, was all Lucy had time to utter, before she and Sammie became helpless with laughter. It took a few minutes, and much puffing and wiping away of tears, before they managed to control themselves long enough for Lucy to explain:

"Oh Mickie, darlin. Mi sorry mi couldn't resist teasin yuh, but seein yuh standin there like a condemned man was too much. Mi hadn't the heart to keep it up any longer."

Mickie tried to respond, but felt sick, and again began to sweat. Lucy seeing this, and feeling a little guilty, got up and started fussing over him. She sat him down at the table, and prepared him a coffee, complete with her obligatory shot of rum. This made Mickie shudder, and scrunch up his face, but it seemed to help.

Lucy opened the fridge, and then turning, looked over at Sammie, who now sat lost in thought, rolling a cigarette. For a second she wondered what was going through his mind, but all she said was:

"Sammie, go get some more milk. Mi need to get some food into this bwoy."

Sammie looked up, lit his cigarette, and before rising from the table, he put his big hand gently on Mickie's shoulder.

"Oh Mickie bwoy. Yuh gonna be fine. Lucy'll look after yuh. The woman had a lot of practice." He then gave Lucy a tender look.

By the time Sammie got back from the corner shop, Lucy had cooked up a big batch of bacon, scrambled eggs, and hot buttered toast, which Mickie ate in slow grateful silence.

After he had eaten, bathed and changed, Mickie felt a little better, but not that much, he was still suffering from sudden waves of nausea. He had hoped that getting out in the fresh air would make him feel better, but he soon found out as he made his way to the station, that the muggy, overcast weather didn't help his delicate condition one bit.

He had arranged to meet Laura in town, but now he was beginning to wish he had suggested somewhere local. He just knew that travelling in a crowded weekend tube train with a hangover was going to be awful. However, he hadn't the heart to call her and explain.

His prediction regarding how bad his journey would be, was evident when he emerged from Oxford Circus tube station with his sweat sodden shirt sticking to his back. It had been uncomfortably hot and crowded on the train, and now, to add to his woes, the sun had come out and seemed to be focusing its stinging heat directly on him alone.

The one good thing in his favour was that he was early. He didn't have to meet Laura until two o'clock, and so, having nearly an hour to kill, he turned off the hectic bustle of Oxford Street, and headed for the nearest pub. With a sigh of relief, he entered the cool shade of the big room and walked up to the bar, but then had to lean on the counter for a minute until his head stopped spinning.

He was fortunate in one respect, in that for a Saturday afternoon the bar wasn't too busy, and he soon managed to get the attention of one of the bar staff. He had noticed previously, when on the rare occasions he'd been stupid enough to wake up with a particularly bad hangover, that there was this odd sensation of things appearing strange; it was as if some higher power was toying with you, and playing mind games. One look at the barman convinced Mickie that here was an individual who could easily be a prop for some God's celestial trickery.

The man had shoulder length wispy hair, which clung to his neck as if it didn't have the strength to hang free, while the top of his head was completely bald. He was tall and skinny, with a pale face and sad eyes. Apart from the fact that he was wearing a black t-shirt with 'God's Bollocks' printed on the front, he looked almost Dickensian.

Mickie took note of this without much interest. Had he felt better, he might have enquired if this was a rude criticism of the almighty, or was the guy perhaps a fan of some obscure Christian Heavy Metal Band, but he hadn't the will, or the energy.

From behind the bar, the man gazed at him, sullen and silent. Mickie, who couldn't help but notice, that apart from his slack-jawed expression, the guy also had extremely bad dandruff. This was surprising, considering how little hair he had. And then, without a muscle moving on his face, the man uttered the word:

"Yeah?"

Mickie slightly taken aback by this sound suddenly emanating from that face, coughed, and said:

"Eh, a pint of Guinness, please?"

The barman's expression never changed, he just turned and wandered off to fetch the order. That was when Mickie saw, printed on the back of his t-shirt, the words, Nuff Said, and assumed this to be some sort of conclusion to the legend on the front. He considered this for a moment, but, as before, he just couldn't be bothered to try and figure it out.

After being served, he took his pint, and trying in vain not to spill any, navigated his way to an empty corner table, well away from the window. He had just sat down, when his phone rang: it was Billy.

"Oh, hiya, mate," Mickie said, mournfully.

"Oh, don't even ask . . . Oh, ah know, ah know . . . Gonny not cackle, Billy. Ah'm not a well man, ye know . . . Oh, that's right, state the fuckin obvious, why don't ye."

While Mickie was listening to Billy admonish him over the phone, he watched the barman that had just served him, go over to a nearby table to retrieve some empty glasses. As the man bent down to pick them up, Mickie noticed a little cloud of dandruff drift off his head and dance through a beam of sunlight.

"Ah know yer only winding me up, but ah'm really sufferin here, man. Ye know that weird anxiety thing ye sometimes get when yer really hung-over, and everythin seems to out to mess with ye? Well, that's what's happenin. When ah was walking to the station, today, ah nearly stepped into the biggest dog shite ah've ever seen in my life. Ah mean, ye wouldn't want to make this animal angry. Know what ah mean?"

Mickie had to wait for Billy to stop laughing, before he could continue.

"Ah'm serious. Anyway mate, thanks for last night, ah really appreciate it . . . No, ah mean it. Oh, and tell Mary ah'm sorry for actin like a weirdo . . . Oh aye, very funny . . . Ah know, ah know. Anyway, ah've got some medicine goin flat here . . . Yeah, ah'll talk to ye tomorrow."

Mickie replaced the phone in his pocket, and then, picking up his pint, he drank almost half of it, quietly burped, and then gave a deep sigh.

* * *

Laura had slept late, and on rising, had felt thickheaded and listless. She had a long hot shower, which did little to revive her. She then brewed a pot of coffee, and warmed up some croissants, but after loading the tray, and getting settled on the sofa, she'd found that she wasn't all that hungry.

An hour or so later, she was still sitting in her dressing gown, sipping lukewarm coffee, picking distractedly at one of the pastries, while staring out of her living room window.

She was trying not to think of work, but the anxiety she had been experiencing for most of the week, kept returning, and she was finding it difficult not to let her mind wander in that direction.

She was feeling so drained, and hung-over, that she could easily have gone back to bed and curled up under the covers. But deciding she should make an effort to get things together, she dragged herself off the couch, and went to the computer to check her e-mails.

Finding nothing there that couldn't be dealt with later, she was just about to close down when a loud ringing tone almost made her jump: someone was trying to contact her on FacetTme. After connecting, she was surprised to see John's grinning face come up on the screen.

"Hello, what an earth are you doing," she asked.

"Oh, I just wanted to see your cheeky little face, darling."

He seemed a little too cheerful, but Laura decided that was probably just her mood.

"Oh John, I'm sorry. I'm afraid I'm not at my best today."

John tilted his head, and put on his, 'aw, bless' face.

"Oh your not still worrying about whether Mona will like you, are you? I told you I was only teasing when I made that other woman remark. You know what I'm like. I mean look at you. Mickie's got to be absolutely mad for you. And Mona will be too."

"Aw, thanks for being so sweet," Laura said. "And thanks again for last night. At least I managed to forget about things for a while, thanks to you."

"Oh, sweetie, I do wish you would cheer up," said John. "I hate to see that lovely little face all scrunched up in misery."

Laura tried to smile, but looked almost close to tears.

"Oh, I don't know what wrong with me. I just have this awful feeling of foreboding, and it's affecting my judgment about everything, even Mona's visit. I think it has a lot to do with this commercial for Morgan's. I've been desperately trying not to think about it, but you know how difficult and picky they've been all week. I keep having this urge to call the model-shop to check that everything is okay. And I know it's silly, because I only spoke to them yesterday."

She suddenly bit her lip, and put a hand up to cover her eyes. It took her a minute or so, before she managed to compose herself enough to look back at the screen. But when she did, she couldn't quite believe her eyes: there was a giant rabbit looking back at her, while drinking what appeared to be red wine from a large glass, with the aid of a straw. For a few seconds, Laura was speechless, and then she felt her anger rise.

"What are you doing? Are you drunk?"

The rabbit said something she couldn't quite catch, mainly because it still had the straw in its mouth. Laura could no longer control her temper, and yelled at the screen:

"Oh, I'm not in the mood for this. Here I am, worried sick and trying to deal with issues I feel are beyond my fucking control. And now, now I've got Bugs Bunny calling me up pissed. What is the matter with you?"

John instantly put down his glass, tore off the rabbit mask, and said, all in a rush:

"I'm sorry, I'm sorry. I got it for a fancy dress party. I was only trying to make you laugh."

"Oh, really?" said Laura, "well it didn't work, did it? And anyway, what are you doing drinking so early?"

John looked confused, and wrinkling up his nose, replied:

"It's gone half-past one in the afternoon."

"What? Oh shit!" cried Laura, staring at him wide-eyed, and open-mouthed. "Why didn't you say so before? I'm supposed to be meeting Mickie in town, at two o-clock. I'm sorry, but I've got to go."

With that, she pressed a button, and John's bemused face disappeared from the screen. She spent a frantic few minutes running around searching for her bag, which she finally spotted under a chair. She made a grab for it, pulled out her phone, and sent a hurried text message to Mickie, apologising, and saying she was going to be a little late.

* * *

An hour or so later, Mickie having informed her where she would find him, Laura pushed open the door of the pub. She scanned the room for a moment and then caught sight of him, sitting hunched over a table in the corner. He appeared to be frowning at his mobile phone, as if something on the screen was troubling him. She brushed a lock of sweat-dampened hair from her forehead, and walked over to the table.

"Hello Mickie. I'm so sorry I'm late. I don't know where the time went. I . . . " She had said this all in a rush, but now stopped, as he appeared not to be listening.

"Mickie!" she said, a little irritated.

He seemed reluctant to drag his attention away from the phone. But as she stood there, trying to figure out what was going on, he slowly raised his head and peered up at her. Laura stared back at him in confusion, until, after a few puzzled seconds, his eyes widened in recognition.

"Oh, hiya, Laura."

At first, she was unsure why he was acting like this, but when he rose unsteadily to his feet, and grabbed hold of her shoulders, to plant a feeble kiss on her cheek, she smelt the whiskey on his breath.

Mickie feeling the tension in her body, drew back.

"Are you okay?" he said, a little slurred.

Laura sighed, and looked as if she may be about to cry. Mickie gave her a curious look.

"What?"

"Oh, nothing, I'm just being silly."

Laura thought he accepted this a little too readily, for he instantly flashed her a silly grin.

"Sit down," he said. "Ah'll get ye a drink. What would ye like?"

Laura took a deep breath, made a face, and sighed. She felt anxious, and on edge. Mickie, however, completely misreading the signs, decided to make an ill-timed attempt to get her to smile. He tilted his head to one side, arched his eyebrows, and again displaying the silly grin, asked in a very bad cockney accent:

"Large navy rum, luv or perhaps a little drop o gin?"

This ridiculous attempt at humour only made her more aware of how drunk he really was. She looked down at the floor, feeling awkward and embarrassed.

"I'll have a spritzer, please," she said softly.

Mickie rolled his eyes, and then turned and went to the bar. Laura sat down, all of a sudden she felt exhausted. She searched in her bag for a small mirror, withdrew it and scrutinised her face.

My God, she thought. *What a fright.* She never over-used make-up, but in her haste to meet Mickie, she had forgotten to use any at all, and so now, applied a little lipstick. She replaced the mirror, and then glanced over to where Mickie was standing at the bar; she couldn't help noticing that he was looking more than a little dishevelled.

After being served, he tottered back and placed Laura's drink safely on the table in front of her. But in attempting to sit down, he managed to spill a good amount of his pint over his hand,

and the table. Laura glanced down at the Guinness, and then raising her eyebrows, gave him a wry look.

"I have the distinct impression you may be feeling a little delicate."

He rolled his eyes, and blew air though his mouth to indicate that she was spot on. Laura flashed a brief, brittle smile, and took a sip of her drink.

"So, why is that?" she said, looking straight at him. "I thought you would be all bright and happy today, after seeing Mona."

Oh yeah? Well so did ah," he said in an abrupt, bitter tone; and then looking away, continued in the same resentful manner:

"But seein my daughter for the first time in a year, only made me feel like a wanker. A wanker that was too stupid to realise how much he was missin."

Laura didn't quite know how to take this. She looked down into her drink, and said, almost in a whisper:

"Oh."

Mickie appeared not to notice her reaction.

"Ah mean don't get me wrong, seein Mona was fantastic; she was so beautiful and funny. But after bein with her for only a few hours, ah had to watch her leave again. It nearly broke my heart. Ah felt so guilty and pissed off that all ah wanted to do was get drunk. And now that bitch won't even let me talk to my own daughter on the phone. She said ah sounded drunk; of course ah'm fuckin drunk."

Laura listened to this rant, but could find nothing to say in reply. She felt confused and angry. Mickie took a big gulp of his Guinness, and then after an awkward few minutes' silence, he finally seemed to notice the look on Laura's face.

"How about you, then? You seem unusually quiet," he asked, without much real interest.

Laura didn't look up, but shook her head impatiently. She could tell he wasn't in the mood to listen, and under the present circumstances she certainly didn't feel like discussing things with him, however, she gave a resigned sigh, and said, with some effort:

"The new client is being extremely difficult, and so, to say the least, it's been a trying week."

Mickie nodded, dumbly, and it was another uncomfortable minute before he muttered:

"Oh aye, why is that?"

Laura frowned at him, then looked away and began speaking in a clipped professional tone, as if explaining to a not too bright stranger.

"It's a rig, and model heavy commercial; which is basically down to me, as I came up with the original concept. The client, however, is now picking fault with this concept, and with only a week before we go into the studio, this is causing serious problems."

Mickie gave her a blank look; he was experiencing another wave of nausea. Laura drew in breath, and when she released it, it carried these words:

"Look, Mickie, I'm not feeling too good right now. I'm very concerned about quite a few issues, but I really don't see any point in discussing anything with you at this time. Your priorities are clear, and I sympathise with your problems, I really do, but I too, need comfort and sympathy. Your relationship with your daughter is, quite rightly, your main concern, and I can't compete with that, nor do I wish to try."

Mickie sat silent and expressionless, and so Laura continued:

"I've decided to go to my parents for the weekend. I need time to think. I thought about calling you this morning to tell you this, but then kept changing my mind. I hoped that seeing you would help, but this is not helping either of us. And so, assuming that you too, could do with some space, I think it's probably best, for now, for us to be apart."

Laura, looking again as if she maybe about to cry, quickly stood up, and reaching across the table, kissed Mickie tenderly on the mouth. She then turned and walked away, leaving him looking sick, and stunned.

(3rd Sunday)

"Mi getting worried about that bwoy," Lucy had said to Sammie earlier that morning. "When he come down, mi need some time alone with him. Mi need to find out what vexin him. He cain't go on like this."

She understood that Mickie had gotten drunk on Friday because he was torn up about Mona, but last night was worse. They had heard him struggling to get his key in the lock, and when they opened the door, he almost collapsed into the hallway. Neither Sammie nor herself could then get any sense out of him; he wouldn't be comforted, and kept crying and mumbling something about Laura.

Mickie at last appeared in the kitchen, looking sick, and miserable. Sammie took this as his cue to make a discreet exit, and rose from the table, saying he had to fetch something from the bedroom. He then left, closing the door behind him, and waited in the hall until he heard Lucy start to console the boy.

"Sit down, bwoy, yuh look like death sittin on your shoulder. Yuh need to eat someting."

In the hall, Sammie took his jacket and hat from the hook, and careful to make as little sound as possible, seized this chance to make his escape. The air had cleared overnight, and there was now a fresh breeze blowing as he left the house, and walked down the street like a man on a mission.

Since the other night, when Billy had revealed that he knew where Rob's mother, and possibly Rob himself lived, Sammie hadn't been able to get it out of his mind. Lucy's warning, however, still sounded in his head as he walked along. And although he was well aware of the consequences if she ever found out that he was going against her wishes, he somehow couldn't rest until he had checked things out for himself.

He stopped outside the local corner shop and checked to see if he had remembered to bring money before entering. He fumbled in one of his trouser pockets, and pulled out his sole capital, three ten pound notes, and change.

Once inside the shop, he had to wait while the young Asian man behind the counter, nodded in silent response to the constant chatter of the only other customer, a tiny, elderly Irish woman.

If she had heard Sammie enter the shop, she didn't acknowledge it. She ignored his presence, and continued with her unbroken narration, rattling on and on in her sing-song voice. She seemed to be in the middle of relating intimate details of her life to the young shopkeeper, as if convinced that this was important stuff, and he needed to be told all about it:

"Take me late husband, you wouldn't believe the lies dat man could tell, devious he was, devious. And dat big tart at number twenty-three was no better, she encouraged him."

As the old woman prattled on regardless, the young Asian man kept glancing at Sammie, obviously hoping the old woman would notice, and stop talking long enough for him to carry on with his business. After a while, however, Sammie got fed up waiting.

"Mi sorry, darlin," he said, firmly, but politely. "But mi in a bit of a rush, ya know."

He then pointed to the tobacco shelf.

"A half ounce of Old Holborn, please my friend?"

The old woman's face scrunched up like fist, and she turned and stared up at Sammie with her hard little eyes.

"Thank you my man," said Sammie, after receiving his tobacco and change. He left the shop without saying anymore to the old woman, he didn't see the point. Although he had been in the shop quite a few times, he only now realised that he had never heard the man speak, and thought: *maybe this was the reason.* He smiled at the thought.

Sammie had never been in the Bulldog. In the sixties, there were pubs a black man just didn't frequent, and this was one of them. But when he entered and walked up to the bar, he saw there were quite a few black faces, mostly older men, sitting playing dominoes at a table near the window.

"A large rum, please darlin?" he said, giving the fat, tattooed, and unsmiling barmaid, a friendly grin.

Sammie guessed she was in her thirties, but her, dour, pasty-faced attitude, gave her the appearance of someone older. After fetching his drink, she banged it down on the bar, and then without a glimmer of acknowledgment, gave him his change. *Maybe things haven't changed that much,* thought Sammie. He took his rum, and then went and sat at a window seat were he could see the coming and goings of the flats opposite.

For the next half an hour, nothing much caught his attention; he ordered another rum, and then, having rolled a cigarette, took his drink and sat at a table outside. He lit his smoke, and then, glancing over in the direction of the flats, he saw a man and a woman come out of the main door of one of the blocks. They came walking towards the pub, the man keeping a few steps in front of the woman.

As they crossed the road and came closer, Sammie kept his head down, but still managed to catch a look at them. The man was black, and big, as big as Sammie, but younger. The woman was white, with dirty blonde hair, and looked worn down by life. As they passed Sammie's table, she was taken by a sudden coughing fit, which shook her whole body, and caused her to stop until it had passed, after which, she continued to suck on her cigarette. The man, however, hadn't even looked back, but had carried on into the pub. For some reason, Sammie found himself trying to determine the woman's age, there was something about her.

When he had finished his smoke, he went back into the pub and ordered yet another rum. He then sat in a corner seat at the back of the room, where he could observe what was going on without being too obvious.

The man was sitting at a table on his own, looking sullen, and talking to no one. The woman, however, was flitting about from table to table, talking rapidly to anyone who would listen. It seemed to Sammie that most people were humouring her, and looked relieved when she moved on. It also struck him that she was high, speeding on something.

She began talking to an elderly couple at a table near him, and Sammie noticed they were at least taking the time to listen, and looked as if they actually knew her well. She stayed with them longer than anyone else, giving Sammie the chance to try and figure out what it was about her that intrigued him. He decided she was definitely high; she couldn't stay still, and when she suddenly threw her head back, laughing at something the old man had said, Sammie's jaw dropped in shocked recognition. He knew this woman, it had been seventeen, eighteen years or more, but he knew this woman.

Chapter 14 (4th Monday)

"But it will be all right, won't it? It will be ready to go into the studio?"

Laura was speaking on the phone to Mark Shaw, one of the managers at Magic Models & Effects. She was frowning, and had her hand up covering her eyes. The conversation was starting to make her feel anxious.

"I can't believe this is happening. When we were there on Friday everything was on course, but now from what you're telling me, there's a good chance we're not going to make the deadline . . . Yes, Mark, I do realise it was an accident, but this is Monday, and the rigs are supposed to be ready to be taken into the studio after the meeting on Friday morning."

Under the desk, Laura's right foot was keeping up a constant tap on the floor.

"Yes, I know you're doing your best," Laura continued, trying not to sound desperate. "But as you well know, when we come down again on Friday it will be with the Director, and it's going to be embarrassing, not to say expensive, for both of us I may add, if he's not completely satisfied with the work. And I don't even want to think about what will happen if the client finds out."

Laura looked over, and could see Dick Lewis smirking and enjoying every minute of her discomfort. She gave a mirthless laugh into the phone.

"Is that supposed to make me feel better? Well, Mark, I'm afraid it doesn't . . . No, no I don't . . . Oh, look, just keep me posted, all right?"

She banged the phone down, and apart from the tapping of her foot, sat in stunned silence, letting the bad news sink in. She knew the problem wasn't going to go away, and so, after a few minutes, she gathered up some relevant documents and went to find Tim Farrell.

On entering his office, she found him gazing at his computer screen, while listening to someone on the phone. She waited just inside the door, and after a few seconds, he noticed her out the corner of his eye, and then turning, made a face to mime that he wouldn't be long.

"Okay dokay, Nigel. I'll email that over to you straight away . . . Okay, Bye" He replaced the phone.

"Fuck! That man can talk," he said to no one in particular, and then turned his attention to Laura.

"Hello darling," he said in a comic posh voice. "How long have you been standing there?"

He instantly knew by her face that something was troubling her.

"What's wrong?"

"Mark Shaw has just called, and by the way he tried to call you first, but you were engaged for ages. Anyway, there's been an accident, our main rigged model has come cropper, and will need extensive repairs, if not remade entirely."

"What?"

Tim got up and closed his office door, and guided Laura to a seat.

"How the fuck did this happen?"

Laura took a deep breath, as if it was a struggle to get air. And then said, all in a rush:

"As you saw on Friday, the rig had just been sprayed, and looked beautiful. Well, it appears they were moving it from the spray booth to another part of the workshop yesterday evening. The thing is, it couldn't have been secured properly on the forklift, because it somehow slipped off and fell onto the concrete floor. The mechanism is only slightly damaged, but the outer part, the casing, is badly crushed, and they don't know if it will be possible to repair it. I'm almost sure it will have to be remade, which is not a quick job, and the whole commercial hinges on the look of that rig."

They sat in silence, for what seemed to Laura, an age, and then she saw Tim pick up the phone and dial a number.

"Hello Mark, it's Tim . . . Yeah yeah, never mind all that old bollocks. I'm just phoning to say were coming down . . . Yeah, yeah, we'll see you in an hour."

* * *

Mickie threw down his brush, and reached for another cigarette. He lit it with a flick of his Zippo, and then glanced at his painting. *What is the point?* He thought. *What is the fuckin point?* He rose from his chair, and taking the pack with him, sat by the window and gazed out at the familiar setting.

Two days, he thought, *two days, that's all it's taken for me to fuck everything up.* Although he'd been drunk, he remembered the look on Laura's face before she turned and left the pub, and the thought still made him squirm with shame. *What a wanker.*

He looked down at his paint stained hand holding the cigarette, and watched it burn down to the filter, he then stubbed it out, and lit another. He blew a column of smoke towards the ceiling, and the air from the open window made it curl and drift across the room towards his painting.

He gazed over at the canvas he was working on, and saw that even after a whole morning's work, the face still looked lifeless. He had repeatedly applied the paint, only to decide when he stood back to study his work, that it was awful, and then had to scrape it away and start again. It was obvious to him now, that there was no point in continuing to work under this cloud of guilt. He was getting nowhere.

While sitting in this black mood, he became aware of Mrs McIntyre and Sammie talking in the hall. After a minute or so of muffled conversation, he heard the front door open, and Sammie's resonant voice rise in frustration:

"Oh, darlin, mi just goin to check someting, mi won't be long, y'know."

Hearing the door close, Mickie sat for a minute, mulling things over. The previous day, after he had managed to drag himself down to the kitchen, Mrs McIntyre had tried her best to get him to open up and talk to her. But being yet again, hung-over and depressed, he hadn't wanted to discuss anything with anybody, and had behaved like a sulky fool.

With Sammie gone, he decided now would be as good a time as any to go down and face her. At least if he attempted to smooth things over with Mrs McIntyre, he might find a solution to his major source of guilt and heartache, Laura.

"Hello, Mrs McIntyre."

He remained on the threshold of the kitchen, uncertain of his status in the McIntyre household.

"Ah'm so sorry," his voice broke a little, as he said the words.

Lucy, who was at the sink washing dishes, let a minute pass before acknowledging him, and then turned and looked at him over her glasses. He knew this look, he had seen her use it on fools before.

"What yuh playin at bwoy?"

Mickie didn't know what to say. He stared at the floor.

"Sit down," Lucy said. "We need to sort a few tings out, y'know."

He took a seat at the table, while Lucy started to prepare coffee.

"Yuh want someting to eat?" she said, her voice softening a little.

Mickie shook his head, and lit a cigarette.

"Well, mi makin it anyway; eat it, don't eat it," Lucy said with a shrug. She then fell silent, and concentrated on cutting up bread for toast.

Dizzy came slinking in from the backyard, and after rubbing up against Mickie's chair, sat down and gazed up at him. Mickie couldn't help noticing the animal's relentless stare; it was hard not to see it as a look of severe distain.

Oh, not you as well, he thought.

When she was ready, Lucy placed the tray on the table, and sat opposite Mickie. She filled two cups with coffee, but there was no rum, not today. Dizzy turned his attention to his mistress, and jumped up on her lap. Mickie took a sip of coffee, and then let out a sigh.

"Look, Mrs McIntyre, about the last few days . . . Ah don't really know what to say. Ah canny blame ye for bein angry. Ah know ah . . . "

"Mi not angry," cut in Mrs McIntyre. "Mi disappointed. Mi disappointed to see yuh become such a fool, y'know. Mi don't poke mi nose in your bizness, but mi got to say someting, yuh actin like a baby drunk."

Micke squirmed, but took it on the chin.

"Ah know. Ah'm sorry."

Lucy made a dismissive kissing sound.

"What's the matter with yuh bwoy? Grow up and deal with what vexin yuh."

Mickie looked down and stubbed out his cigarette.

"Ah think ah might have messed things up with Laura."

Lucy peered at him over her glasses.

"Ah've tried phonin her mobile all mornin, and left umpteen messages, but she hasn't got back to me."

Lucy sipped her coffee, but made no comment.

"When ah saw her on Saturday, ah was really drunk, and behaved like an arsehole." He made a face. "Sorry."

Lucy shrugged.

"It was seein Mona again. Spendin that short time with her made me feel so good, but then, afterwards, I . . . "

He shook his head and sighed.

"Afterwards ah began to feel guilty about bein absent from her life, and not seein her for so long. Ah got myself so worked up, that the only solution ah could think of, as you well know, was to get drunk."

Ah still had a hangover when ah went to meet Laura, but as ah was an hour or so early, ah thought if ah went to a pub and had a hair of the dog, it might help. But then, after ah had been sitting there drinkin for a while, ah started thinkin again about Mona, and the old guilty feelings came back. And then, to make things even worse, Laura sent me a text to say that she was going to be late. By the time she did arrive, ah was a drunk, maudlin, pathetic mess, and poor Laura had to sit there and suffer me babblin on and on, while ah took my drunken frustration out on her. Ah mean her of all people.

Ah love Mona Mrs McIntyre, but Laura has made me happier than I have felt for a long time. And ah know we haven't been together that long, but it just feels so right. Ah love her, and the stupid thing is, ah only realised it when ah saw her walkin away. Ah hurt her, and it makes me feel like a real arsehole . . . Sorry"

Lucy rolled her eyes.

"Mi a sixty-five year old black woman. Yuh tink mi gonna cry cause yuh swearin. Mi been called tings yuh wouldn't believe."

"Sorry," said Mickie.

Lucy's eyes widened, and she started to laugh. Her whole body shook so much with the rhythm of it, that Dizzy looked up like he feared he might be in danger of being shaken off her lap. Mickie was puzzled for a minute, but then smiled like an embarrassed little boy.

"Oh Mickie, bwoy, what we gonna do with yuh?" Lucy said, shaking her head. Mickie flashed a brief smile, and then sighed.

"When yuh gonna see Mona again?" asked Lucy.

"Ah'm pickin her up from Sharon at Lancaster Gate Station at one o'clock. Ah thought ah'd take her to the park, and then for somethin to eat. It's just gonny be the two of us, which will be nice, as my ex-wife doesn't go out of her way to ease the situation."

Lucy looked down, silent for a heartbeat, and then lifted her head, and looked him straight in the eye.

"Mickie we only get one chance at this life, so yuh got to grab happiness anywhere yuh find it. Mi got no doubt your baby girl loves yuh, and from what yuh've told me, she's got spirit. Tell her about Laura, and how important she is in your life. Yuh got to be honest with these two people, or yuh gonna lose them."

Mickie turned and looked out the window for a long silent minute, and the turning back, he smiled a soft, sad smile, and said:

"How did you get to be so wise?"

"By bein a fool," replied Lucy.

* * *

"Hey man, can we talk?"

Billy recognised the voice, and ducked from under the hood of the car he was working on, to find Sammie peering at him from beneath the rim of his hat.

"Hiya Sammie. What's up?" said Billy, wiping his hands on a rag.

"Mi need to ask yuh someting."

Billy shrugged.

"Ask away."

"Not here. Mi thought maybe the Falcon."

Billy was intrigued, but his face gave nothing away. He turned to look at the clock on the office wall.

"Sure," he said. "But ah need to get cleaned up first. You go ahead, ah'll catch ye in there."

Fifteen minutes later, Billy entered the Falcon. Among the usual scattering of local punters, he saw Sammie sitting alone at a table in the corner, nursing a glass of rum. Billy walked up to the bar, and ordered a pint of lager, and another rum for Sammie. Paddy the landlord was on his own behind the bar.

"Howye Billy?" said the big Irishman.

"Aye, not bad Paddy. Yerself?"

"Oh, don't fuckin start me off," said Paddy, grinning to show he had a few dental issues.

"How was yer man, Mickie, after Friday? Sure I've never seen him neckin the auld drink like that before."

"Aw, he's awright," replied Billy, not wanting to give too much away. "He was celebratin seein his daughter again, and got a wee bit carried away."

"Carried away is fuckin right, and you were the one doin the fuckin carrying."

Billy acknowledged the remark with a brief smile. He liked Paddy well enough, but he knew the man was nosy, and wanted to know all your business. Without another word, Billy pocketed his change, and then lifting the drinks from the bar, walked over and sat down opposite Sammie.

He guessed by the look of him, that the big man had something serious on his mind, but he took a long pull of his pint, and waited for Sammie to get to the point. Sammie topped up the rum he already had, with the one Billy had just brought over, and then swirled the dark liquid round inside the glass.

"This junkie woman's man," he said without looking up. "What does he look like?"

Billy refrained from asking why.

"He's big, about forty, and has a nose that looks like somebody's worked on it, if ye know what ah mean."

Sammie drank most of the rum, and looked Billy directly in the eye.

"Mi saw them. Mi went to that pub, yknow, The Bulldog."

"Oh aye," said Billy, not too surprised. He knew Sammie had clocked the name of the pub, and he remembered Lucy had clocked Sammie. He stayed silent, and let Sammie continue.

"Mi grateful yuh helpin us, man, but mi had to see for myself, y'know. Tings is good for me right now, better than for a long time, and mi don't want no young blood-claat messin it up."

Billy nodded, and then raised his eyebrows.

"What, ye mean ye saw the boy?"

Sammie shook his head, and finished his rum. And then, as if just realising something, he looked at Billy.

"Mi don't want Lucy knowin anyting about this, y'know. Mi love the woman, and don't want her to get hurt."

Billy nodded.

"Mi appreciate what yuh doin, Billy. Mi just got crazy not doin anyting, but mi realise now, it's best to leave it to you. Lucy would be mad, tinkin mi getting involved."

Billy tilted his head, and shrugged.

"Another rum?"

"No man, mi got to get back," said Sammie, and then held out his hand.

"Thanks man. Mi really do appreciate it."

Billy grasped the big man's hand, and then watched him rise from the table, and leave the pub.

* * *

Mickie leaned back and felt the tension of the last few days ease away. The sun was hot, and he and Mona had taken refuge from the heat on a bench under the shade a big oak tree. For the moment, they were happy to be silent, concentrate on their ice creams, and watch the world go by.

Mona was fascinated by the diverse array of colourful characters that had been lured into the park by the warmth of the sun. She grinned up at Mickie when a group of black girls, who were sitting only a few feet away, got up and started singing and dancing to the music coming from a player they had placed on the grass. The girls looked good and sounded good, and didn't care if people stared; they were young and having a time in the sunshine. And Mona couldn't take her eyes off them.

On catching Mona's gaze, one of the girls, dressed in tight zebra-print pants and a oversized black t-shirt, smiled and called over:

"C'mon, girl, show us your moves."

Mona looked up at Mickie, her eyes wide with wonder.

"Go on," Mickie said, "Ye know ye like to dance."

The girl came over.

"Hi, I'm Rita, wanna dance?"

Mona smiled, shy for a second, but then handed Mickie her ice cream, got off the bench, and took the girl's hand.

"Just a minute," Mickie said, taking a tissue from his pocket, and gently wiping ice cream from Mona's mouth. "Let's make ye a wee bit more presentable."

Mickie watched in delight as Mona and the girls danced and laughed in the sun. She would look over and grin at him, and again, her joy filled him with bittersweet feelings.

An hour or so later, they were facing each other over a table in a Pizza Express: Mona's favourite. Mickie looked over at her and shook his head; she had somehow managed to smear the tomato sauce from her pizza onto her nose.

"Can ye not get anythin in yer mouth without spreadin it all over yer face, first?" he said wiping the stain away with a napkin.

Mona just giggled. She's had a fabulous (her word) time in the company of the dancing girls. They had fussed over her, let her try on their cool hats, and complimented her on her hairstyle. She even forgot about her ice cream, which Mickie had gladly eaten.

When it had been time to go, Mickie had thanked the girls for their kindness. They in turn had flirted with him, and called him a cool dad, which had made Mona laugh. She had then called him cool-dad, all the way to the restaurant.

He poured some more Peroni beer into his glass, and watched Mona finish the last slice of pizza.

"That was great, daddy," she said sitting back in her chair.

"Ye'll not be wantin any puddin after all that, eh?" Mickie said, teasing her. Mona put on her mock disappointed face, which made Mickie laugh out loud.

"Awright, awright. Whaddya want?"

"Chocolate cake and ice cream," she cried. And then giving him wry look, she added: "cause somebody ate my last ice cream."

Mickie made a face.

"Okay, but ah'll just get the waitress to spread it all over yer face, and save you the bother."

Mona made her eyes go funny. Mickie smiled, and then called the waitress over and ordered the sweet for Mona, and a coffee for himself.

"So, are ye lookin forward to comin to stay at Mrs McIntyre's? She canny wait to meet ye."

"Oh aye," replied Mona, grinning, and holding her spoon upright in her little fist, in readiness for her chocolate cake.

"And yer uncle Billy canny wait to see ye again, either."

Mickie waited until Mona was tucking into her cake and ice cream, before bringing up the topic of Laura.

"There's somebody else ah'd like ye to meet," he said, and then thought: *if she ever lets me see her again, that is.*

Mona's looked up at him, her eyes wide for a moment.

"Ah've met this girl. She's really nice. Ah'm sure ye'll like her. Ah know she's dyin to meet you."

Looking at Mona's expression, Mickie realised that this information had come out all in a rush, however, as she didn't say anything in reply, he felt the need to keep talking.

"Listen, darlin, ah'm so sorry we haven't seen each other for a while, and ah'm really gonny make sure it won't be as long again."

He looked at his silent little girl, who had now managed to get chocolate on her forehead. He loved her so much it hurt.

"What's her name?"

"What?" After the silence, the question had surprised him.

"What's her name?" repeated Mona, and then shoved another spoonful of cake into her mouth.

"Laura," Mickie said. "Her name's Laura."

"Is she yer girlfriend?" Mona asked, round the chocolate cake.

"Well, aye."

Mona giggled.

"Oh, ye think that's funny do ye?" said Mickie, smiling, relieved.

Mona grinned to reveal chocolate covered teeth.

"Look at the state of ye. Yer a chocolate monster."

Mona savoured another spoonful.

"So, if she comes over to Mrs McIntyre's to meet ye, ye won't mind?"

Mona thought for a few seconds, and then shook her head.

"Thank you darlin. Ah love you."

They were silent for a while, and then when Mona had finished her pudding, Mickie gently cleaned her up with some wet-wipes that Sharon had put in Mona's little satchel; he now knew why.

"So how do ye get on with Glen?" Mickie asked, "Does he talk to ye much?"

Mona reacted to the question by comically raising her eyebrows, and making a face.

"He never shuts up. He yaks non-stop, but only to my mum. Ah think it was getting on her nerves, because she's chucked him."

"Oh aye," replied Mickie. "When did this happen?"

"Ah don't really know," said Mona, shrugging her shoulders. Ah heard her tellin my granny that he was too borin to live, and that she had met somebody else."

Mickie stifled a laugh.

"And who's the somebody else?"

"Ah don't know, she disnae tell me things like that, but they didnae know ah was in the kitchen getting a drink of juice. Ah think she said he was drummer in a pub called the 'Squashier'."

Mickie was quiet for a minute; he wasn't quite sure how he felt about this new development. He then drained his beer, and called for the bill.

"Okay darlin," he said looking fondly at his daughter. "Ah suppose ah better get ye back to Ealing."

* * *

"The thing is, ah canny quite figure out why he came to see me," said Billy, opening the fridge. He took out a can of lager, and stood in the middle of the kitchen pouring it into a glass.

Mary, who was preparing dinner, was standing with her back to him, chopping vegetables. She turned to fetch a pot from the cupboard, and knocked Billy's arm, spilling some of his beer.

"Tch, yer in my way, go and sit down."

Billy sidestepped her.

"Yes dear," he said, making a face, and then sat down at the kitchen table, and took a sip of beer.

"Why would Sammie want to know what this guy looked like?" he said, to the back of Mary's head. She shrugged her shoulders.

"Ah just know he's worried about somethin; ah mean apart from yer man Rob comin back on the scene. But he never got to the point of sayin what it was."

"Why didn't ye ask him?" Mary said, still concentrating on her task.

Billy thought for a moment.

"Ah don't know," he said, looking out at the evening sky. "Ah think it was the look on his face; he looked more sad than worried, thinkin back on it."

Mary turned to look at him.

"Billy, I hope yer not thinkin of getting involved with anythin to do with drug dealers. Everyday at the hospital, I see first hand what happens when ye cross these bastards."

"Tch, naw!" replied Billy, a little too readily. He was wishing now that he hadn't mentioned anything to Mary about Nazz.

Mary shook her head, and turned back to her chores.

"Och Mary, ah'm just lookin after Mrs McIntyre, and keepin an eye out for this Rob. His mother's boyfriend disnae come into the picture, as far as ah'm concerned. Ah'm just curious why Sammie was askin about him, that's all."

Mary made no reply, and Billy thought he should perhaps change the subject.

"It'll be great seein wee Mona again, eh?"

He watched, as Mary slowly turned and gazed at him, and then tilting her head and raising her eyebrows, she said:

"You must think I'm stupid."

Billy made no reply, he couldn't think of anything to say. Mary turned away, and they fell silent, the only sound was the laughter of kids playing in the backyard opposite.

"I just worry. I can't help it." Mary said, without turning round. Billy looked up from his beer, and saw she had stopped what she was doing and was staring at the wall. In a second, he was on his feet, and had her in his arms.

"Och, Mary darlin. Ah'm sorry. Ah didnae mean to upset ye. Ah'm just talkin."

They stayed like that for a few minutes, until Billy broke the silence with a pretend nervous request:

"Eh, any chance of ye puttin that knife down?"

Mary pulled back and tried to hold on to her concerned expression, but couldn't.

"Tch, look at that big daft face, " she said, smiling.

Billy kissed her, and then said:

"Don't worry Mary, ye know ah'm no a mug, and ah'm only lookin."

Chapter 15 (4th Wednesday)

Mickie stood on the pavement gazing up at the impressive facade of the Martin & McLean building. It was taking him some time to get straight in his head what it was he wanted to say. He let a few more minutes drift by while he lit another cigarette, and then blew a long slow draught of smoke into the air. The decision, when it came, was like a reprimand to someone else.

Fuck it, he thought. *Yer here now, so ye might as well get on with it.*

He dropped the unfinished butt into the gutter, and then, as if to prevent any further indecision, mounted the steps up to the entrance two at a time. A motorcycle courier, who was just leaving, held open the heavy glass door, and with a nod of his crash helmet, allowed Mickie to step into the smart, minimalist interior. Mickie took a few seconds to survey the steel and glass splendour of the foyer, and then walked over to reception.

The stylishly dressed black girl behind the desk looked up as he approached and beamed him a well-practiced smile.

"Good afternoon," she said.

"Hiya," Mickie replied, a little nervously. "Ah wonder if ah could speak to Laura Taylor?"

"Do you have an appointment?"

"Eh, no, ah'm afraid ah don't. But as ah happen to be a friend, and was just passing, ah thought it would be nice to pop in and surprise her, maybe take her to lunch."

The girl's eyes widened for a second, and Mickie began to feel he had made a mistake blurting out too much information.

"Actually, I think she may be out," said the girl, looking down at a large diary on the desk. "I'll just double-check."

She picked up the phone and pushed a couple of buttons.

"Hi, John. I have a gentleman here asking for Laura. A mister, I'm sorry what's your name?"

"Mickie, Mickie Lee."

"A mister Mickie Lee . . . Okay, I'll tell him. Thank you John."

"Yes, I'm afraid she's had to go to a meeting at the model-shop, but if you would like to take a seat, John Light will be down in a minute to explain."

"Oh, ah know John," Mickie said, somehow feeling he had to up his image.

I could really do with a fag, he thought, as he sat down on a bright yellow designer chair. But then had to shake his head at his choice of phrase when he saw John come tripping down the stairs.

"Well, this is a pleasant surprise, I must say," said John, almost dancing across the polished floor.

This exuberant greeting caused Mickie to be at a loss for words for a few seconds, but he rose to shake John's offered hand, and then said, again all in a rush:

"Thanks for takin the time to see me, John. Ah hope ah'm not keepin ye from yer work. The thing is, ah just canny seem to get a hold of Laura. Ah've tried her mobile umpteen times now, but she disnae answer. Ah just hope she's all right."

John tilted his head, and smiled at Mickie, but before he had time to say another word, Mickie's paranoia kicked in. His first thought on seeing the look on John's face, was: *don't even think of patronising me, ah'm not in the fuckin mood.* Whether John sensed this or not, his manner changed.

"I'm sorry Mickie, but all I know is, she's having a difficult time right now."

Mickie looked at the floor, and nodded, but made no comment. On seeing this, John's natural kindness came into play, and he said:

"Listen Mickie, I haven't had lunch yet, and we can't talk properly here. Why don't we go to the pub, and I tell you what little I know."

"Oh, that would be great," said Mickie, looking up. "Ah'd really appreciate that."

John then turned and called over to the receptionist:

"Susie, darling, if anybody's looking for me, I'll be in the pub."

Susie grinned,

"Of course you will, darling," she replied, imitating John's fruity tone, which made him laugh.

"Bye, bitch," he called over, beaming her a big false grin.

Twenty minutes later Mickie was sitting at a table just outside the main entrance to the Castle Pub.

One Guinness," said John, coming through the door and placing the pint glass in front of Mickie. He was about to sit down when he noticed, that having just lit his cigarette, Mickie was now repeatedly flicking the lid of his Zippo lighter, up and down. John was trying not to say something bitchy, but he couldn't stop himself from frowning down at the irritating clicking lighter. Mickie looked up, wondering why John was still standing over him, but on seeing the look on his face, he placed the lighter on the table.

"Tch, sorry, nervous habit."

"Oh Mickie, don't worry. I'm sure everything will be all right," said John, settling himself down on the bench. He sucked up a mouthful of spritzer through a multi-coloured straw, and then bit into his cheese and tomato baguette.

"So, have ye had a chance to talk to Laura?" asked Mickie.

"Well, sort of," replied John, trying to talk round the food in his mouth.

He concentrated on chewing for a few seconds, and then, with an effort that made his eyes bulge he swallowed.

"We had a brief chat after the meeting first thing on Monday morning," he said, and then coughed to dislodge a blockage.

"But she didn't seem very happy, and wasn't too forthcoming as to why; but then again, I'm not her favourite person at the moment."

"Tell me about it," said Mickie, rolling his eyes.

"And then later," continued John. "To add to her woes, she got a call from Model-shop to inform her that the main rig for the commercial she's working on, had somehow got badly damaged over the weekend."

"So, she didn't say anything about me?"

"Well, no," said John, shaking his head, and looking at Mickie as if to say: "Aren't you listening?"

"Ever since the accident she's been flying in and out of the office, trying to make sure the rig will be repaired in time for the shoot. And so, she really hasn't had time for a heart to heart, as it were."

Ah just wondered why she's not returning my calls," said Mickie, labouring the point.

"For the self same reason, I would imagine," replied John, becoming a little impatient.

"Look Mickie, as it's a new client, this job is very important to the company, and the aforementioned new client, who is of course a bit of a pain, was being very picky even before this happened. And as it was Laura who placed the job with this particular model-shop, she feels responsible, and is therefore taking the brunt of the pressure."

Mickie squirmed with regret, and thought of the last time he had seen Laura.

"Ah'm afraid ah behaved like a drunken prick the last time ah saw her."

"Oh dear," said John. "No wonder she wasn't looking very happy. Déjà vu, or what?"

"Oh, ah know," Mickie, groaned. "My timing's good, eh? Just what she needs right now, another wanker for a boyfriend."

John couldn't help smiling.

"Oh, don't beat yourself up, I'm sure Laura doesn't think that."

Mickie rolled his eyes, and blew air through his mouth, as if to say: "Oh, ah'm not so sure about that."

They were silent for a time; John finished off his lunch, and Mickie, left alone with his thoughts, stared off into the distance. After swallowing the last of his sandwich, John dabbed his mouth with a napkin, took a sip of spritzer, and then looked over at Mickie, sitting there lost in thought.

"Look, Mickie, I don't know what happened between you two, but I know Laura, and I know by the way she talks about you, that she's crazy about you. If she's not answering your calls, there's got to be a good reason. And as I've just said, that's probably because she's at her wits end trying to do her job, and can't deal with emotional stuff on top of that."

Mickie looked at John, and could tell he was being sincere, and trying to help.

"Oh, ah know, John, ah do realise that now. Ah just feel so bad, and want to tell her how sorry ah am. My emotions got all twisted up when ah saw my daughter again. And it appears that fate has decided to be a bastard by also makin Laura's life a misery at the same time."

I can't stand it, he looks so bloody miserable, thought John, and decided he should at least try to give Mickie a flicker of hope.

"Listen Mickie, I'm not entirely sure how accurate this information is, but shortly before you came, I heard a rumour that there is a more than good chance the model and rig will be completely repaired for the director's meeting on Friday morning. If you leave off phoning Laura until after then, I'm sure I will have a chance to speak to her before you do, and I will make sure she knows how you feel."

Mickie thought about this for a moment, and then gave John a tender look.

"Thanks, John. Ah would appreciate that very much."

John smiled back, and then noisily sucked up the last of his spritzer.

"Another?" said Mickie, pointing to John's empty glass.

"Oh go on then, you big temptress," replied John, fluttering his eyelashes. Mickie, smiling for the first time that day, went to fetch the drinks.

* * *

On her way back from the model-shop, Laura stopped off to pick up some lunch from the local deli. In the two days since the accident with the rig, she had hardly eaten a thing. She would buy a sandwich, take a bite, and then put it aside while she worked, only to find it curling up on her desk at the end of the day. But now, she was ravenous; the relief she felt after learning the damaged rig would be completely repaired for the meeting on Friday, had given her an appetite. She ordered a big helping of four-cheese pasta, green salad, a ciabatta roll, and a slice of apple tart.

When she entered the main office and walked past Dick Lewis's desk, she was glad his smug little face was nowhere to be seen. Since eavesdropping on the bad news from the model-shop on Monday morning, he had been a real pain, and had relished every minute of her misery.

She had just checked her emails, and was settling down to enjoy her lunch, when she caught sight of John going past her door. A couple of minutes later he again appeared at the door, sipping from what she assumed to be a cup of coffee. He then sauntered over to her desk, and stood looking down at her with a silly grin on his face.

"What?" she said, looking up at him, while holding a forkful of pasta midway between the plate and her mouth.

"Peace be with you," he said, his grin melting a little.

Laura frowned, and dropped the pasta back on the plate.

"What on earth are you on about?"

"I'm just checking what sort of mood you're in," said John. "And if I'm still in your bad books."

"I'm fine," replied Laura. "The rig is going to be fixed in time; of course we still have the client to contend with, but I'll have to deal with that when it happens. And anyway, you're not in my bad books."

"Well, in that case, after you've had your lunch, I've got something to tell you," he said, reconstructing his grin, and raising his eyebrows. "You know where to find me, tatty bye for now."

Laura watched him saunter away again, and, although intrigued, she couldn't help thinking: *tatty bye for now? He's definitely getting worse.*

After savouring the last mouthful of apple pie, she leaned back in her chair and let out a deep sigh. *I could easily go to sleep now,* she thought. But that of course, was out of the question, so she took her plates and cutlery to the kitchen, and put them in the dishwasher. She then poured herself a cup of black coffee, and taking it with her, walked towards John's office.

"Okay, John-boy, what's the big secret?" she said, popping her head round the door.

"You had a visitor," he said, looking coy.

"Oh?" replied Laura entering the room, and giving him a questioning stare. "And are you ever going to tell me who it was?"

"Are you sure I'm not in your bad books?"

"JOHN!"

"Oh all right, all right. It was Mickie," he said, trying not to look too smug.

"Mickie?" said Laura, in genuine surprise. "What, he came here?"

"Yep." replied John, grinning.

"I don't quite know what to say," said Laura.

"Well, he certainly did, and all of it about you."

Laura sat down, and placed her untouched coffee on the desk. She was silent, and looked pensively at the floor.

"So, you spoke to him?" she said looking up at John.

"Well, more listened, really. He obviously needed to talk, so I took him to the pub."

"He's been calling, and leaving messages on my mobile," said Laura. "But I just couldn't deal with it, not on top of everything else."

"That's more or less what I told him," said John. But when Laura looked as if she may cry, John began to feel guilty for initially being flippant about an obviously tender subject.

"How did he seem? Was he all right?" she asked.

"Well, no not really. He feels terrible about everything that happened the last time you met, and knows he behaved like a shit. He said he really needed to talk to you, and wants desperately to make amends. He really loves you Laura."

Laura gazed at John, as if gauging his sincerity. He in turn looked tenderly back at her, and giving her a brief smile, prepared to dunk a biscuit in his coffee.

"Look, Laura, it's your decision, but I think I know you well enough to see that you feel the same about him. I told him that all I could do was talk to you, and tell you how he felt. I also said he should refrain from calling you until after the meeting on Friday. I think he now understands the pressure you've been under, and knows he's behaved like a fool."

Laura looked at John, and smiled.

"You're a darling, really, aren't you? You pretend to be this cynical joker, but it's just a front, because you have a wise head, and a tender heart."

"Oh look!" John cried, suddenly. "Now look what you've made me do, I dunked my biscuit too long, and now it's sunk to the bottom of my cup."

Laura rolled her eyes, and grinning, got up and left him fishing in his cup for his sodden digestive.

* * *

Sharon was sitting in her aunts garden, sipping a coffee, and watching the smoke from her cigarette drift lazily up into the sky. She was distracted, and was thinking of recent events, and of one person in particular. *That bastard still manages to get under my skin,* she thought. She took a final petulant puff of her cigarette, and then crushed it out in the ashtray. *Margaret,* she thought. *I need to talk to Margaret.* She then fumbled in her handbag, pulled out her phone, and dialled a number.

"Hiya Margaret. How ye doin? . . Well, it's the first chance ah've had to phone ye . . . Och, not too bad . . . Oh she's fine. Sadie's taken her for a walk round the shoppin center . . . Och, ah just fancied a wee chat about you know who . . . Oh aye, ah saw him on Friday, he came to meet us at Euston . . . No, ah haven't had a chance to talk to him properly about anythin yet . . . Well funny you should mention that, because Mona told me he's met a new woman, and ah get the feelin things are not goin too good . . . What do you mean, wishful thinkin? Cheeky bitch."

Sharon pretended to be annoyed, but then laughed.

"Well, okay, maybe it is, a wee bit. All ah know is he phoned on Saturday afternoon to speak to Mona, and sounded so drunk that ah wouldn't let Mona anywhere near the phone . . . Ah know, normally

he doesn't, but he must have been really pissed off about something, but ah couldn't get any sense out of him."

She lit another cigarette.

" . . . Oh, ah don't know, Margaret. All ah know is when ah saw him again, all the old feelins came floodin back. He looks great, and he was so funny; Mona and him were crackin each other up . . . Oh, it does, does it? Well, ah don't know about that, love's a big word . . . Okay, but the only chance ah'll get is when he brings Mona back on Monday, which of course is her birthday . . . Well, it's easy for you to say. You're so bloody smart, you."

She could hear Margaret laughing on the other end of the phone, and was about to say something in reply, when she heard the front door open, and voices in the hall.

"Listen, Margaret, that's them back, so ah better go," she said stubbing out her half-finished cigarette. " . . . Oh aye, of course ah'll keep ye posted . . . You too, and thanks for listenin, pal . . . Yeah, okay, bye."

Mona came running into the garden.

"Mammy, mammy, look what auntie Sadie bought me."

She held up a new top, in a pretty shade of blue.

"Oh that's fantastic, darlin," said Sharon, embracing Mona. "Lucky you to have such a great auntie, eh?"

Mona nodded enthusiastically.

"That was really nice of ye, Sadie," Sharon called through the kitchen window.

Sadie made a face, and a dismissive gesture with her hand.

"Don't be daft, it's lovely to see ye both. By the way, ah've got us some nice lamb cutlets for our dinner. Ah'm gonny grill them to have with new potatoes, and green beens. And what do we have for puddin, Mona?"

"Chocolate ice cream," cried Mona.

"Oh, wow! Yer favourite," said Sharon, making an excited face.

Ah'm goin up for a bath, Sharon," said Sadie, from the kitchen door. "And then ah'll get the dinner on."

"Okay, Sadie. Do ye want me to do anythin?"

"No, just relax for a wee while, and then when ah come down you and Mona can set the table. Oh and ye can fix me a gin and tonic in about fifteen minutes."

Sharon watched as Mona held her new top against herself, and pretended to be a model.

"Ye can wear yer new top when yer daddy comes to pick ye up on Friday."

"Oh, that'll be great. Ah canny wait."

Sharon lit another cigarette, blew a stream of smoke into the air, and then smiling at Mona, casually asked:

"What did you and yer daddy talk about, when you saw him the other day?"

Mona looked thoughtful for a minute.

"Eh, ah don't really remember, just things."

"Did he talk much about his new girlfriend," asked Sharon, again as casually as she could.

Mona frowned and looked away, as if the topic embarrassed her.

"What's the matter, darlin?"

"Does my daddy not love ye anymore?"

The question caught Sharon unawares, and her heart skipped a beat, as she frantically searched for something approaching an answer.

"Aw, Mona, ah'm sorry. Ah didnae mean to make ye feel sad. Ah'm sure yer daddy loves me, but in a different way now. Sometimes things just happen to mummies and daddies, and they find it difficult to live together, and have to go their own way."

Mona remained silent, and looked at the ground. Sharon felt useless and guilty, and had to fight back the tears. She dropped her cigarette in the ashtray, and looked in misery at her little girl.

"Come here darlin," she said, holding out her arms. "Ah think we both need a cuddle."

Mona turned, and Sharon could see she was on the verge of tears. Sharon pulled her close, and held her tight in her arms.

Mona's emotions gave way.

"Ah miss my daddy," she said, as the tears filled her eyes.

Chapter 16 (4th Friday)

Mona narrowed her eyes from the glare of the morning sun, and looked out from the bedroom window onto the quiet suburban street; she was waiting impatiently for her daddy to arrive. Mickie had arranged to pick her up at ten-thirty, Mona, however, had been dressed and ready, and at her place at the window, since well before ten o'clock. When she at last caught sight of Mickie walking up the street, she started waving, and bouncing up and down on the bed. Mickie saw her the minute he turned into the path leading to the house, and grinned.

"Mammy, mammy, daddy's here," cried Mona, as she leapt off the bed and dashed down the stairs to open the front door

"Hello darlin," said Mickie, scooping her up in his arms.

"Ah thought ye were never comin daddy," said Mona, pinching his cheek.

Oh, ah'm sorry darlin, but ah'm only a few minutes late."

Sharon's aunt Sadie stepped into the hall.

"Hello Mickie," she said, smiling a brief, tight-lipped smile. "Have ye eaten? Would ye like a cup of tea, or anything?"

No thanks, Sadie, ah'm fine. Ah'd like to get Mona settled at Mrs McIntyre's. And then," he added, looking wide-eyed at

Mona, "ah'm gonny take her for lunch, but ah'm not sure if she likes pizza, or not."

Mona gave him a exaggerated grin, and he laughed and set her down.

"Right, let's get ye sorted. Where's yer stuff?"

"It's here," said Sharon, from the kitchen.

Mickie led Mona by the hand into the kitchen. Sharon was standing at the kitchen door, smoking a cigarette. She was still wearing her dressing gown, and Mickie thought she looked tired.

"Hello Sharon. How ye doin?"

'Ah'm all right," she replied, without turning round to acknowledge him.

Mickie nodded, unsure of what else to say.

"Right," he said, turning his attention back to Mona. "Have ye got a jacket?'

"It's in my bag, daddy. It's too sunny for a jacket."

"Aye, right, fair enough," Mickie said, picking up Mona's bag. "Right, ah'll bring trouble here, back first thing Monday mornin."

Mona looked up at Mickie and playfully punched his leg, and then looked over at her mum. Sharon stubbed out her cigarette, and turned towards Mona.

"Come and give mammy a kiss, darlin."

Mona ran over to embrace and kiss Sharon.

"You be a good girl for yer daddy, okay?"

Mona nodded, and Mickie thought she looked a little sad, but then she looked over and grinned at him, and raising her eyebrows, said:

"Okay, trouble, let's go."

* * *

Mickie watched as Billy lifted Mona into his arms, and whirled the laughing little girl above his head.

"Hello my wee darlin. How ye doin?" he asked, carrying her into the living room.

"Ah'll bet ye've missed yer uncle Billy, eh?"

"Yeah!" cried Mona, wrapping her arms round his neck.

Mickie stood silently watching this affectionate reunion. He loved to hear Mona laugh, and had forgotten how infectious her laughter was. Now that she was going to be staying with him for the weekend, made everything he had gone through in the last few days, seem almost worthwhile. Earlier this morning, when he and Mona were leaving, he had half expected Sharon to make some sarcastic remark, and the simple fact that she hadn't, only added to his delight at having this quality time with his daughter.

"My, yer getting awful heavy," said Billy, sitting down with Mona on his knee. "What's yer auntie been feedin ye?"

"My daddy took me for a pizza," said Mona, and then balloned her cheeks out and made her eyes go funny, which cracked Billy up.

Mickie rolled his eyes, but was delighted to see his daughter and best friend together again.

"Mary'll be back from work in a minute," said Billy. "And then ah'll take ye down the shops, so we can get yer daddy some beer."

"Okay uncle Billy, but ah need to go to the toilet."

Billy let her slip to the floor.

Okay, darlin. The bathroom is the one with the blue door. Ye'll find it no bother, eh?"

"Aye," answered Mona, nodding her head.

When she had left the room, Billy grinned, and shook his head.

"Oh, man, what is she like? She's a riot. And ah canny believe how big she's getting."

"Ah know, it's a wee bit scary," said Mickie, flopping onto the couch, and looking wide-eyed at Billy.

Billy looked down, and was silent for a few seconds.

"Ah'm sorry ah don't have a beer for ye, pal," he said, still looking down. "Ye've sort of caught me between cans."

"Och, no worries," said Mickie.

Billy again seemed to hesitate.

"Have ye heard anythin from Laura," he asked, tentatively, and picking up a magazine, pretended to be interested in flicking through it.

"Aye, she phoned me this afternoon. She still sounded a wee bit stressed, but she's comin over tomorrow."

Billy looked up, and frowned.

"Tch! Well ah wish ye'd told me. Here ah am worried about whether ah should mention anythin."

Well ah'm sorry," replied Mickie. "But ah've not exactly had a chance, have ah? Ah've only been here five minutes."

Aye, ah suppose so," said Billy, reluctantly, but then a grin spread across his face.

"Och well, that's great, innit?" he said, and then hearing the front door opening, he added in a whisper: "Try not to fuck it up this time, eh?"

"Hello, it's only me," cried Mary from the hall, before going into the kitchen. A moment later, she appeared in the living room.

"Ah! Howye Mickie?"

Oh, ah'm fine, Mary. How'a yerself?"

Oh, don't ask. But I know one thing, I could do with a large . . ."

"Auntie Mary!"

Mona calling her name from the hall cut Mary of mid-sentence.

"Oh, my god, Mona. I forgot yer daddy was bringing ye over from Ealing today."

Mona ran into the living room, and into a big welcoming hug from Mary; she had loved Mary, right from their first meeting.

"Listen, my wee nursin suger-plum," said Billy, addressing Mary with a comical adoring look on his face.

Mary looked down a Mona, and rolled her eyes.

"Ah'm gonny take Mona for a wee walk down the shops, because she wants to get her daddy some beer."

Mona looked up at Mary, and rolled her eyes.

Mickie loved this (the craic) but what he loved even more, was that his daughter was part of it.

"Okay dokay," said Mary, but us girls want chocolate, and plenty of it."

"Nae bother," said Billy standing up and winking at Mona. He then took her by the hand and led her into the hall, where there was a minute of whispered conversation.

"Okay, we'll be right back with the goodies," they both cried in unison, before laughing, and closing the front door.

Mary smiled at Mickie, and shook her head.

"Right, first things first," said Mary, taking off her jacket. "I need a large vodka and tonic. How about you, Mickie?"

"Aye, go on then, that would be good," said Mickie, lighting a cigarette.

A few moments later, Mary came back in the room carrying two large vodka and tonics, with ice and lemon.

She handed one to Mickie, and then sank into the armchair, and took a long slow drink.

"Oh my, that's good," she said with a sigh. "I've been thinkin about this all the way home."

"Hard day?" asked Mickie, offering Mary a cigarette.

"Och, not really," she replied, accepting a light. I just get fed up with the bullshite, sometimes. Annyway, let's not talk about that, ye must be happy to have yer wee girl to yerself for a while?"

"Oh yeah, it's great." Said Mickie, grinning. "But the icing on the cake is Laura's gonny come over tomorrow and meet her."

Oh, that's fantastic, Mickie," said Mary, genuinely pleased, but then she added: "Try not to mess it . . . "

"Ah know, ah know," Mickie cut in. "Billy's more or less just said the same thing."

Mary laughed and took another sip of her drink.

"Oh, god, I nearly forgot," she said, putting her drink down and rising from the chair. She went into the bedroom, and a moment later returned and handed Mickie a wrapped gift, and a card.

"Mona's present. I hope she likes it."

" Aw, thanks Mary, ah'm sure she'll love it," Mickie said, and tucked it away in his bag.

Mary settled herself back in the armchair, and picked up her drink.

"So, ye obviously got Mona settled in Mrs McIntyre's?"

"Oh aye, first thing. Her and Sammie were great. Mona was a wee bit shy at first, but after a while, she had them in stitches."

"Well, she is a funny wee thing," replied Mary. "And I love her hair, it really suits her."

"Aye, well, that's another story," said Mickie, smiling, and rolling his eyes. He then reached over to flick ash into the ashtray.

"Listen, Mary," he said, looking earnestly at her. "Ah'm really sorry ah was a bit weird the last time ah was here. That was just rude."

"Och, away ye go. Don't be daft," said Mary, making a face.

"No, ah mean it. It was seein Mona again, and realisin how much ah'd been missin; it just hit me funny."

"It's okay, Mickie, honestly. I understand."

Mickie smiled a brief little smile, and nodded his head. He was having trouble thinking of something else to say, but was saved by the sound of the front opening. Seconds later, Mona came running into the room and jumped onto Mickie's lap.

"Uncle Billy's really daft, isn't he?" she said, grinning at her dad, and Mary.

Both Mary and Mickie nodded their heads enthusiastically.

"Hey, ah heard that," said Billy, from the kitchen.

Mona giggled, and snuggled into her daddy's shoulder.

* * *

Sally turned down the radio when she heard the doorbell ring, and then wiping her hands on her apron, went to see who was calling.

"Oh, hello Louise," said Sally, surprised to find Jenna's daughter on her doorstep. "I'm afraid Rob's just gone up for a shower."

She hesitated for a few seconds, and then realised she was staring.

Oh, I'm sorry, Louise. What am I like? Please do come in. I'm just a bit confused, I was under the impression that Rob was supposed to be calling for you."

"Well, yes he was, but somehow I was ready early for a change, and I got a bit bored waiting." And then she added with a self-conscience smile:

"To be honest, my mum was getting on my nerves."

"Oh dear," said Sally, giving the girl a knowing smile.

"Well, it's always lovely to see you, come into the kitchen and I'll make us some tea. I've just finished baking some scones, and I'm sure I could tempt you to one with some of my homemade strawberry jam."

"Oh, I should think so," said Louise, following Sally into the kitchen. "I wish I could bake."

"Oh it's not so hard, especially something like scones. You could do it easily. You just have to know a few little tricks. I could teach you sometime, if you like."

"I would like that, even if it's just to get this fantastic aroma filling the house."

Louise sat down at the kitchen table, and watched Sally prepare the tea. Sally was dying to ask what Louise's mother had said to get on her nerves, but decided she shouldn't be nosy.

"So, how do you find Rob these days? To me, he's almost like a different person to the scowling boy who arrived at my door only a few weeks ago. But then, maybe that's just wishful thinking on my part; you probably have a better understanding of how he really feels."

"No, I think you're right," said Louise. "I think he's more settled, you know, relaxed. And he's certainly more open with me now, than when we first met."

"Oh, I'm so happy to hear you say that," said Sally, placing a plate of scones on the table. "I worry about him all the time; guilty conscience, I suppose."

"Oh, you shouldn't feel like that; he talks about you with real affection. I've never heard him criticise you."

Sally brought a tray containing the teapot, milk, two cups, butter, and strawberry jam to the table.

"Well, that's nice to know, but I still feel guilty. My only consolation is that I've managed to give him some respite from his dreadful existence in London. And, I may add, his present disposition is in no small way down to you."

Louise gave a shy smile, and looked down at her hands.

"Oh, I'm sorry darling," said Sally, realising she may have embarrassed the girl.

"Oh, no, that's okay," Louise, said, looking up. "I'm happy to help. He's really very sweet underneath all that bravado. But as you must know, he still worries about his mum all the time, and it clearly makes him angry that he's so helpless to do anything about her situation. After the few occasions when he has managed to contact her, he just goes quiet and tries to hide it, and unfortunately, when that happens, I don't really know what to say to make it better."

Sally looked at the girl, and smiled fondly.

"I know darling, me neither. But at least he has contact with her, she won't even answer my calls."

They were quiet for a minute or so, while Sally poured the tea.

"Please help yourself."

Louise concentrated on buttering a scone, and then after adding the homemade jam, took a bite.

"Mmmm, oh these are delicious."

Sally smiled, and was about to comment further on her concerns for Rob, but stopped short when she heard the heavy clump of his feet on the stairs.

Chapter 17 (4th Saturday)

Mona and Sammie were sitting at the kitchen table. Mona was gently caressing the loudly purring Dizzy, who had jumped up on her lap, and made himself comfortable. Sammie, still wearing his hat after coming back from the corner shop, looked on, while contentedly smoking a cigarette, and sipping his coffee.

"Well, Dizzy sure fell for yuh, girl," he said, smiling down at Mona. "He don't usually do that with nobody but Lucy."

Mona smiled back at him, delighted.

Lucy came in from the garden with a basket of washing, and glanced at Dizzy stretched out on Mona's lap.

"Typical tomcat, cain't resist a pretty girl, " she said, grinning at Mona, and then placing the basket on the draining board.

Mona smiled back; she felt at ease in the warm cosy atmosphere of Lucy's kitchen.

"Have yuh had enough to eat, darlin?" said Lucy, clearing away some of the breakfast things.

"Oh aye, thanks very much, Mrs McIntyre," said Mona, nodding her head. "Ah really loved that eggy toastie thing ye made, it was absolutely fabulous."

Lucy smiled, more at Mona's expression than at the actual compliment.

"Oh, yuh welcome, darlin," said Lucy. "And yuh can call me Lucy, us girls got to stick together."

She then gave Sammie a knowing look, and following Lucy's gaze, Mona looked up at Sammie, who winked at her, and removed his hat.

The sound of footsteps clumping noisily down the stairs caused everyone to look towards the door, where, seconds later, Mickie, still glowing from his bath, stood posing comically in the doorframe.

"Hello everybody," he said, grinning. "Did ye all miss me?"

Lucy gave him a wry look, and then turned to Mona, who tutted, and rolled her eyes.

Mickie laughed and then went over and planted a noisy kiss on the top of Mona's head.

"Ah'll just have another quick cup of coffee, darlin," he said sitting down at the table. "And then we'll get ye ready for a wee bit of uptown top rankin, eh? What do ye think?"

"Yeah!" cried Mona, catching Mickie's infectious happy mood. "Ah'd like to wear my new blue top, and my black trousers."

"Ye can wear whatever ye like darlin," replied Mickie. "Ye would even look fabulous wearin a bin-bag."

"Ah'm not wearing a bin-bag," said Mona pulling a face. "Why would ah want to wear a bin-bag? Do people in London really wear bin-bags?"

Sammie looked over and grinned at Mickie, as if to say: "Get out of this one, sonny."

"Eh, no, not really," answered Mickie, somewhat flustered. "Ah just meant . . . Oh, never mind. Ye'll look fabulous in anythin ye want to wear."

Mona then looked down and stroked Dizzy, and asked softly:

"Is yer girfriend still comin round, daddy?"

"Aye, she'll be here in an hour, so we better get ye ready. And ye can call her Laura, ah'm sure she'd like that."

Mona looked thoughtful for a moment.

"Does Laura ever wear a bin-bag, daddy?"

Mickie raised his eyes to the ceiling, and then lifted his hands palms up, as if seeking assistance from above.

"What have ah done?" he said to the ceiling.

Sammie's big deep laugh rumbled through the kitchen, and even Lucy couldn't stop herself from joining in. Mona looked up at them, puzzled, but then she too started to laugh. Mickie rolled his eyes, and shook his head, and then, grinning, leaned over and gave his daughter a big soppy kiss.

"Okay, trouble," Mickie, said, trying to keep a straight face. "Let's go up and get ye into yer bin-ba . . . ah mean clothes."

Mona grinned up at him, and he couldn't remember the last time he felt this happy.

* * *

"I love your hair, Mona," said Laura. "Did your mum cut it for you?"

Mona glanced up at Laura, and nodded; her silent response conveying that she was taking her time opening up to her daddy's new girlfriend.

"Yer bein very quiet, darlin. Are ye okay?" asked Mickie, ruffling Mona's hair.

"Ye normally can't shut her up," he said, giving Laura a sad, apologetic smile.

They were sitting in the dappled shade of a café terrace at the edge of the Serpentine. Mickie, nervous of how quiet Mona had become since meeting Laura, found he was talking more than he normally liked to, trying to fill Mona's silence. He could tell, however, that Laura was aware of his predicament, and was grateful for her patience, and understanding.

When Laura had first arrived at Mrs McIntyre's, looking beautiful in a simply cut, pale yellow dress, there had been the usual few awkward minutes of introductions, and a lot of smiling and nodding. But as soon as she was settled at the table with a coffee, she was her usual charming self, chatting away to Lucy and Sammie, and of course making an extra effort to get to know Mona.

Mona, however, had seemed to become inhibited, as if finally meeting the new woman in her daddy's life had made her unsure of how to feel, or act. This of course, hadn't helped Mickie's nerves, and Laura could tell that he was anxious for things to be just right, especially after their last encounter.

Earlier, when they were walking through the park, Laura kept catching the little girl giving her quick furtive glances, when she thought Laura wasn't looking. In an attempt to get the little girl to respond, Laura had tried smiling back, but so far she had remained guarded.

"Ah need to find the gents toilet in this place," said Mickie. "Will you two girls be all right for a minute?"

Mona appeared to be momentarily alarmed by this statement, and flashed a glance up at her dad, but then, just as quickly looked down again at the table.

"We'll be fine," said Laura, giving him a reassuring smile.

When Mickie had gone, Laura thought that now was as good a time as any to try and put Mona at her ease.

"Mona," she said softly. "I really do want us to be friends. I understand how difficult it must be for you to see your dad with someone else, but I'm not trying to steal him away from you. He loves you very much, and you will always be his number one girl; he talks about you all the time. I do wish you would tell me about yourself. It would make your daddy so happy if we were friends."

Mona remained silent, staring down at the table for a minute or so, but then, just as Laura was finally about to admit defeat, Mona looked up, and flashed the briefest of smiles.

"Ah love yer dress," she said, and then looking down again, sucked some chocolate milkshake through a fluorescent green straw.

"Oh, thank you," said a relieved Laura. "It's one of my favourites, too."

Mona took another suck, and then appeared to ponder on something for another minute. She then raised her head, and gave Laura a wry look.

"Ah'm just glad yer not wearin a bin-bag," she said, shaking her head, and rolling her eyes, as if still puzzled by this bin-bag phenomenon.

Laura was at first a little surprised by this comment, but soon she was biting her lip in an effort not to laugh out loud. It was useless however, for soon she was shaking with laughter, and it took a couple of minutes before she could dip into her bag and search for a tissue to mop up the tears streaming down her face.

Mona looked round at the other tables to see if she could spot what was so funny, but when she turned back and realised she had been the cause of Laura's hilarity, she grinned, and soon she too began giggling.

When Mickie chose this precise moment to come walking back to the table, he was, to say the least, surprised.

"We'll, what's happenin here then? What have ah missed?" he asked, obviously bemused, but also more than happy to see Mona laughing again.

It took Laura a few minutes to contain herself; she kept thinking of what Mona had said, and that set her off again. And of course, Mona couldn't help but join in.

"What have ye done to poor Laura?" said Mickie, grinning at his daughter.

"Oh, that was so funny," said Laura. "I needed that."

"So, what was so funny?" asked Mickie.

"Well, I'm afraid that's just between us girls," said Laura, winking at Mona.

Mickie gave them both a quizzical look, but he was as relieved as Laura that Mona had finally relented.

"Okay, girls," he said. "If yer both finished laughin at yer secret joke, ah think we should make a move; Mrs McIntyre is cookin us a special dinner."

He stroked his chin, and pretended to look thoughtful.

"She said somethin about somebody's birthday comin up soon. Ah wonder who that could be?"

Mona pretended to scowl up at him, and Mickie grinned, and then leaned over and gave her a big kiss.

"Yuk!" said Mona, and squished up her face. Mickie reached over and tickled her, and she squealed with delight. She then finished her milkshake in one noisy slurp, and looked up at Mickie.

"Ah need to go to the toilet, daddy."

"Okay, darlin, it's just through that door there. Come on, ah'll take y . . . "

Mickie didn't get to finish.

"Would you like me to take you?" asked Laura, smiling at Mona, and mopping up the last of her tears. Mona glanced briefly up at her dad, who mimed that it was okay with him. Mona then looked at Laura, and nodded.

"Oh, thank you," said Laura. "You can help me repair the damage. Goodness knows what I must look like."

Mickie lit a cigarette, sat back in his chair, and watched them walk away hand in hand. Could he dare feel that things were finally going his way for a change?

* * *

"Mrs McIntyre that was fantastic," said Mickie leaning back in his chair.

Lucy beamed him a big smile.

"Mi like to see a man enjoy his food, yknow."

Mona ballooned her cheeks out and made her eyes go funny, and then let out a noisy stream of air.

"Ah think ah'm gonny burst, daddy," she said, making everybody laugh.

Lucy had prepared a wonderful dinner of traditional Jamaican dishes: jerk chicken, peas and rice, broad beans, and dumplings. Mickie was initially worried That Mona wouldn't like any of the food, or might find it too spicy, but his daughter surprised him and tried everything with relish.

Rising from the table, Lucy went to the oven and took out Mona's special birthday treat: an upside down pineapple cake. She brought it hot from the oven to the table, while everybody sang happy birthday. Mona beamed with delight, when Lucy asked her if she would like to try it with some homemade mango ice cream.

"Oh, yeah, please, ah want to try everythin. Yer much better than Jamie Oliver, Mrs McIntytre."

Lucy couldn't help grinning as she went to fetch the ice cream from the fridge. After she prepared a dish for Mona, all eyes were on the little girl as she sampled the first spoonful.

"Hmmm," she hummed with delight, seemingly forgetting that only a few minutes before, she was about to burst.

For a while, all that was heard was the click of spoons hitting plates as everyone concentrated on scooping up every morsel of the delicious dessert.

"That's it, definitely," said Mickie, again leaning back in his chair. "Ye've definitely done it now, Mrs McIntyre. I couldn't eat another thing."

"Me too," said Laura. "That food was delicious. Thank you so much, Mrs McIntyre."

"Oh, yuh more than welcome, darlin. Mi so happy to meet yuh at last."

Laura smiled, and looked over at Mona and Mickie, who were looking at each other, and again pretending they were going to burst; she felt happy for him. Mickie refilled his glass from one of the bottles of Guinness, he had bought for himself, Lucy and Sammie. Laura and Mona had favoured Lucy's homemade lemonade.

"if you don't mind, ah'm gonny sit on the step for a minute, and have a smoke," he said, looking over at Laura. "And then, we'll do the dishes."

"Oh, no," replied Lucy, waving her hand. "Mi will do the washin, and Sammie will do the dryin."

Sammie feigned shock and horror at this suggestion, and clasped his hand to his chest, which made Mona giggle.

While Mickie sat surveying the evening sky, Lucy switched on the jazz station, and started preparing the coffee. Sammie rolled a cigarette, and gently nodded his head to the music.

"The sixties must have been an exciting time to be a musician, Mr Turner," said Laura.

"Sammie," said Sammie, turning to Laura. "Yuh makin me feel old, darlin."

Lucy looked round and made a face.

"Yuh is old," she said, and Mona giggled again; she was enjoying the banter.

Sammie smiled to himself, and lit his cigarette.

"Okay, Sammie, it must have been an exciting time," repeated Laura, smiling.

"Oh, yes indeed, darlin; we sure had some high old times back then. Maybe Lucy will get the old photos out to show yuh later. Mi sure they will make yuh laugh."

"Speaking of photographs," said Laura. "I have yet to see a certain person's paintings for real, having only seen the photographs."

Mickie looked round and grinned at her.

"Tch, of course," he said. "It just went out of my head, what with everything else goin on."

He stubbed his cigarette out in the ashtray at his side, and got up from the step

"Okay," he said, smiling and taking Laura hand. "Treat me gently now."

"We won't be long, Mrs McIntyre, be back in time for coffee."

Lucy smiled to herself as they went out the door, and Mona made a face and rolled her eyes at Sammie.

When they were alone in the bedroom, Mickie arranged the four now finished paintings around the small room.

Oh, Mickie, they really are wonderful," said Laura, studying the Bluesmen. "The colours are beautiful, so subtly done."

She reached out to gently touch the surface of the guitar player, and then, when she turned to comment further, she saw that Mickie was gazing at her.

"What?" she said, half smiling.

"Ah didn't think ah would ever see ye again. Ah'm so sorry for the way ah behaved. Ye must have thought ah was some sort of drunken caveman."

"How do you know I don't like cavemen?" She replied, teasing him.

He looked so sheepish that she went over and took him by the hand. Her touch must have awoken that inner caveman, for he grabbed her in his arms, and kissed her long and hard.

"Ah've certainly missed doin that," he said, with a sigh, and holding her at arms length. "Ah canny believe yer really here. Ye look so beautiful in that dress."

Laura smiled up at him.

"Thank you. I've really missed you too. Oh and before I forget," she said, reaching into her bag. "I got a little something for Mona, but I didn't want her to think it was a bribe, so could you give it to her when I've gone."

Mickie smiled, and again took her in his arms, and kissed her.

"Ah suppose we better go back down, or we'll be getting a bad name," he said, grinning, and then added:

"Oh, and thanks for today; ah know how hard ye tried with Mona,"

Laura shook her head.

"It was a pleasure; she's great. I can see why you miss her so much."

Mickie touched her cheek, and then again kissed her tenderly on the mouth.

They entered the kitchen, just as Lucy was pouring the coffee. She had also laid out a dish of homemade gizzada coconut tarts, which Mona was already sampling.

"Ye've got to try these, daddy," she said, wide-eyed.

"And ah better be quick by the looks of it," he said, grinning at his daughter's munching face.

Sammie was sorting through a pile of old photographs that he had picked from the shoebox that Lucy had brought from the cupboard under the stairs.

"Oh, great," said Mickie. "Wait till ye see some of these, Laura. Do ye mind if ah look through them, Mrs McIntyre?"

"Sure, help yuhself," said Lucy, pouring a shot of rum in her coffee.

Mickie looked through a handful of the old images, and then smiling, handed one to Laura, and pointed to the two grinning men in it.

"Ah remember this one from the last time, that's Harry and Sammie."

Laura studied the photo, and a smile spread across her face.

"Oh, wow, I can't believe how cool you all look, Mr Turner, sorry, I mean, Sammie."

Sammie closed his eyes, and nodding, smiled at the memory.

"Oh, we certainly thought so, darlin. And we sure had a time, huh, Luce?" he said, looking fondly at Lucy, who just smiled, and nodded her head in time to the soft jazz coming from the radio.

"Who is this sharp looking man in the picture with you and Harry?" said Laura, holding up the black and white image.

Oh, that's Wilson, Wison Pickett. Lord, that man is one funky cat," said Sammie.

"Mmm hmm," echoed Lucy, "And a real charmer."

Laura looked at Mickie.

"Wilson Pickett? I don't think I know him."

"What?" said, Mickie. " Ye must have heard Midnight Hour, surely?"

"Midnight Hou . . . Oh, I love that song. Oh, wow," said Laura.

Sammie grinned at her response, and he too poured a shot of rum into his cup.

Sammie and Harry played with all the great American soul stars when they came over to the UK," said Mickie. "Otis, Soloman Burke, the Isley brothers, all of them."

"Well, if they could, they would try and bring their own rhythm section with them," explained Sammie. "But that was fine with Harry and me, because we got to play with some great musicians."

"Mrs McIntyre, Ah think yer tryin to kill us with food," said Mickie, through a mouthful of gizzada tart. "These are fantastic."

He noticed Mona's eyes were blinking, and then she yawned, but still munched away at her tart.

"Ah think we have to get this wee lassie ready for bed," said Mickie, smiling down at Mona. "Ah reckon it's the only thing that will stop her eating."

"Aw, daddy, it's still only early," replied Mona, putting on her pitiful face.

"Och, darlin, it's nearly nine o'clock, and ye've had a big day. Look, why don't we get ye into yer jammies, and then we'll see."

"I'm afraid I have to make a move quite soon, too," said Laura, giving Mickie a tender look. "I have a big day at the studio on Monday, and I still have a few things to sort out before then."

Disappointment showed on Mickie's face for a second, but then he gave her a brief smile.

"Give me half an hour, and ah'll walk ye home," he said, and then, pretending to frown at Mona, he added: "Okay, trouble, let's get ye sorted."

Chapter 18 (4th Sunday)

Billy watched as the Bulldog gradually filled up with Sunday lunchtime regulars. He was sitting at a window seat nursing a pint of Stella, and pretending to read his newspaper. Since arriving at the pub not long after it had opened, he had been keeping an eye on the estate opposite, hoping for a sight of anything that might lead him to Rob. Boredom however, was beginning to get the better of him, and he yawned, blew air through his mouth, and then tossed his paper on the table.

Mary had a Sunday shift, and so, yet again, he had been left to his own devices. Earlier that morning, long after she had gone to work, he had remained at the breakfast table, mulling things over. Foremost in his mind had been the recent promise to his wife that he would be careful not to get too close to any gangsters. His dilemma of course, was that he had also made a promise to Lucy and Sammie. He had chewed over this problem for quite some time, but in the end had convinced himself that the latter promise was still paramount, and justification enough to put his Sunday boredom to good use.

He reached for his lager, and had just lifted the glass to his lips, when his attention was drawn to a car, which was pulling to a stop on the street outside. Three men got out, and Billy's eyes widened when he realised they were the same guys he had observed on his previous watch.

This time, however, instead of heading for the estate, they started walking towards the pub. The big guy with the nose led the way, followed by the small, flashier dressed man, who was strutting as if he considered himself someone to be reckoned with. There was something about him that irritated Billy. He instinctively knew that here was a type that he had been well acquainted with in the past: stupid, sneaky, and vicious.

The youngest of the three, the last out of the car, strode along a few yards behind the strutting figure. Billy thought he saw the youth shake his head, and smile to himself.

Billy picked up his paper again, as he didn't want to appear too obvious when surveying the trio entering the pub. He saw the big guy and Mr Flash, go and sit at a table at the other side of the room, while the younger man walked straight up to the bar and stood a few feet from Billy.

From behind his newspaper, Billy managed to catch a good look at the youth, and couldn't help thinking he had seen his face somewhere before. He had just started wracking his brain trying to remember exactly where, when to his surprise, the boy looked over and nodded a greeting. Billy was puzzled for a few seconds, but then it came back to him: BeeJay, of course, the boy had come into the garage one lunchtime a few weeks ago to see BeeJay. Billy acknowledged the greeting with a slight lift of his chin, and then went back to pretending to read his paper.

He recalled how BeeJay had greeted the boy warmly, and then introduced him to Billy, saying he was an old buddy from school. The youth, who BeeJay had referred to as Shank, had been respectful and friendly but hadn't said too much with the exception of the admiration he had shown for a shining, big BMW Billy was working on. Billy had been amused at the teenage way he had freely displayed his high regard for the car. There had been a lot of cool gestures, finger snapping, and cries of:

"Aw, man, lush!"

Billy remembered something else that might have some relevance to the company the boy was keeping today. BeeJay had just gone to change out of his overalls, when Shanks mobile phone rang. The youth had immediately turned his back on Billy, and talking in hushed tones, had walked to another part of the yard. Billy hadn't thought too much about it at the time, but he now wondered whether BeeJay was aware that his old school pal was hanging out with drug dealers.

As Billy continued to watch, he saw Shank take the drinks over to the other two men at the table, and then, taking his own drink, he walked over to one of the fruit machines near the door. Billy considered now was as good a time as any to try his luck, and tried not to think of Mary. He finished his pint, and then went to the bar to order another.

He gulped down an inch from his new pint, and then walked over and stood in front of the machine next to Shank's. Without looking at the boy, Billy placed his glass on the window ledge, and dropping a few coins into the machine, set it in motion. He was hoping the boy would speak first, but Shank kept his eyes on the revolving barrels of printed fruit.

"Is this yer local, then?" Billy asked. He knew it was a lame question, but for the moment, it was all he could think of.

Shank didn't reply immediately, but just kept whacking the buttons on the machine, trying to nudge the fruit round to a win.

"Naw, man, just visitin," he said, after putting more coins into the machine.

"Oh, right," said Billy, again trying to think of something to further the conversation, and then, surprising himself, he said:

"Ah only use it when ah'm visitin my auntie."

The boy turned his head for an instant, and gave him a look. Billy immediately thought: *vistin my auntie? What the fuck am ah on about?* But then felt he had no option but to continue with the scenario.

"She lives in the block across the road, but ah always need a couple of pints first, as it get's a wee bit borin."

Shank only nodded his head and gave a brief smile. Billy almost smiled himself, because he could tell what the boy was thinking: *and he thinks his auntie's borin?* But then it occurred to Billy, that maybe it wasn't such a bad thing if the boy initially thought his conversation innocuous. He could then perhaps feed in a pertinent question.

"Ah mean, don't get me wrong, she's a nice old soul, and the wife likes me to keep an eye on her, especially as there's some nasty young arseholes on that estate."

Shank remained silent, but Billy thought: *fuck it. It's too late to stop now.* "Talkin about young arseholes, BeeJay was tellin me about some fucked up kid you and him went to school with. He reckoned he lives round here somewhere. Ah think he said his name was Rob."

Again, there was no reaction from Shank, who just kept banging buttons.

"Do ye ever see him these days?" Billy asked, as casually as he could; he knew he was pushing it.

At that very moment, Shank punched a winning line, and a clatter of coins came down into the machine's metal cup. Billy couldn't tell if the boy had been about to answer his question, or if his sudden windfall had made him feel generous, but Shank turned and grinning at him, said:

"No, man, I aint seen him. I eard e's livin down the coast somewhere, innit."

Billy was about to respond to this information, but then became aware of someone standing close behind him. He turned his head and saw Mr Flash giving him the hard stare. Billy, having kept his attention focused on the machine and the conversation, hadn't noticed him come silently up behind him, and didn't know how long he had been standing there, or what he had heard. He decided to play dumb and flashed a grin at the little man.

"It's awright for some, eh?" he said, nodding towards Shank.

The little man's expression never changed, and Billy was really trying not to say something that would inflame the situation, but he could feel his anger rise. And then, out of the corner of his eye, Billy saw the big man stand up, and for a few tense seconds, he thought he was in trouble. But the big man completely ignored what was going on, and casually left the pub.

"Okay, bwoy, time to go," said Mr Flash, without taking his eyes off Billy.

Billy first thought was: *cheeky little fucker,* and he was on the verge of telling him where he could stick his orders, but then, without taking his eyes off the machine, Shank spoke up:

"You go ahead, bwoy, I'll be along."

It was then that Billy realised that the little man had been talking to Shank. He could see that the youth's retort had got to him, for Flash turned his attention away from Billy, and scowled at the back of Shank's head. The boy continued to ignore him, and play the machine. Billy couldn't resist flashing a grin at the deflated little man, who then attempted to give him a pathetic, final hard stare, but then made a brief hissing sound, and strutted away.

"Friendly little fucker, eh?" Billy said, watching Mr Flash follow the big man out the door.

Shank made a dismissive kissing sound.

"The man a blood-claat," he said, retrieving his winnings from the cup. He finished his drink, and then turning to Billy, held out some pound coins.

"Here, get some juice for your boredom," he said with a wry look.

"Oh, cheers mate," said Billy, smiling briefly at the boy's teasing cynicism, but then his expression changed, and he looked earnestly into the boy's eyes.

"And you take it easy, eh?"

Shank gave a slight lift of his chin, and then walked towards the door.

(5th Monday)

Sharon stood at the open kitchen door smoking a cigarette, and looking on as Mickie and her daughter sat happily side by side at the kitchen table. As arranged, Mickie had brought Mona back to Ealing earlier that morning. All the way back Mona had been so excited, and couldn't stop chattering on about how she had never had two birthdays before, referring of course to Lucy's treats.

On arriving, they saw that Sharon had laid out Mona's presents on the dining room table, to which Mickie had added his. To everyone's surprise, Mona had taken her time, and opened every gift carefully, and then smiling, had shyly thanked each person in turn. Mickie's emotions nearly overwhelmed him, as he watched his little girl being so humble, and grateful for people showing how much they cared for her.

Sadie had then told Mona to close her eyes, and then taking her by the hand, had led her through to the kitchen. When Mona was asked to open her eyes, there, sitting resplendent on the kitchen table, was a beautiful pink cake with Happy Birthday Mona written in white icing, and topped with seven candles.

"Auntie Sadie baked it especially for ye," said Sharon.

Mona looked up at Sadie

"Thanks auntie Sadie," said Mona, again with a shy little smile.

"Och, darlin, it was my pleasure," said Sadie, scooping the little girl up in her arms.

"Now we have to light the candles, so ye can blow them out, and make a wish."

Mickie went over, and using his Zippo to light a taper, set the candles alight. Sadie then stood Mona on a chair, where she again closed her eyes, and blowing as hard as she could, managed to extinguish all the candles in one go. The three adults then cheered, and sang happy birthday.

Sadie had prepared them all a special birthday treat of homemade pancakes, maple syrup, and ice cream. Mickie had been relieved to see that Mona had relished this treat with a return to her usual joyful self, laughing, and managing to get more cream on her face than in her mouth.

For her birthday, he had bought her a big, good quality watercolour pad, brushes, and a palette of large discs of watercolour paints. It was obvious, even to Sharon that he wanted to encourage his daughter's creativity. He had taken the time to gently show Mona the best way to use the materials, and now she was totally concentrated on what she was doing. He was delighted to see that she was mixing the different pigments on a plate, just as he had shown her, and not going for the easy option of using a primary colour.

"That's really good, darlin," he said

"It's gonny be a pink dancer, daddy,"

"Oh, wow! Ah canny wait to see that."

He looked over at Sharon, who gave him a brief tight-lipped smile, and then went into the garden.

"Ah'm just gonny nip out for a quick smoke, darlin. Will ye be all right?" he said, ruffling the little girl's hair. Without turning her concentration away from her painting, Mona nodded her consent, and Mickie went into the garden to join Sharon.

"Yer doin a fantastic job with Mona, Sharon," he said, sitting down, and lighting a cigarette. "No matter what's gone on between us in the past, ah've got to be honest, and admit to that."

"It's not a job, ah'm her mother," Sharon said sharply.

Mickie shook his head, and smiled a bitter smile.

"Ah know yer her mother. It was meant as a compliment. Fuck, ah'm trying to build some bridges here, but if ye keep trying to twist everythin ah say, it's not gonny help anythin."

He looked round to see if Mona had caught him swearing, but she was still bent over her work. He took a deep pull of his cigarette.

"Look Sharon, ah just want to do what's best for Mona."

Sharon gave him a sideways glance.

"Oh, and how can ye do that when ye never see her?"

She pulled a cigarette from her pack on the table, lit it, and then blew a stream of smoke into the air. Mickie was at a loss as to what to say; he looked down at his hands, and sighed. Sharon glanced over at him, and her expression softened.

"Ah'm sorry, Mickie, but it's awful hard for me not to feel hurt and abandoned, but ah'll really try and make an effort not stick it to ye, all the time."

"Ah'd appreciate that," he said frowning.

Sharon gave a fleeting smile.

"So, is it love?"

Mickie looked at her with suspicion.

"Is what love?"

"The lovely Laura."

Mickie looked away, and took a pull of his cigarette.

"Ah don't think ah want to get into that with you. As usual, ye'll only make me feel bad about myself."

"Oh, thanks. Ah was only askin."

"Aye right," Mickie said, not convinced.

"And anyway, what about you and the drummer boy?"

Sharon looked surprised

"Oh, come on. Did ye think Mona's wasn't gonny tell me about something like that."

Sharon shrugged her shoulders, but made no reply.

"So, what's his name?"

Sharon gave a dry laugh.

"Oh, so you can question me, but ah canny ask you anythin. Typical Mickie, one rule for him, and one rule for everybody else."

Mickie couldn't help smiling.

"Ah was only askin."

They smoked in silence for a minute or so,

"His name's Bamma," said Sharon, suddenly, stubbing out her cigarette.

Mickie slowly swivelled his head round to face her.

"Bamma?" he said, trying not to laugh. He could see that Sharon was also trying to keep a straight face.

"His name is actually David, Bamma's just a nickname."

"Getaway," said Mickie, grinning.

They were again silent for a few heartbeats.

"Is it love?" Mickie asked, grinning.

Sharon gave him a wry look.

"He makes me laugh."

"Well, he'd have to be funny with a name like Bamma," replied Mickie, crushing out his cigarette in the ashtray.

"Och, don't be an arsehole all yer life, Mickie. Have a day off."

Mickie frowned, but took the reprimand on the chin.

"Ah'm sorry," he said. Ah really ah'm glad ye've found somebody."

Sharon glanced at him, and sensed he was being genuine.

"He's actually a nice guy, but it's not a big thing, or anythin, well, not yet. Ah'm just glad he's not Glen," she said, rolling her eyes.

"Oh aye, and what happened to him?"

"Aw, Jesus," replied Sharon, shaking her head. "That man is just too borin to live."

This remark made Mickie laugh out loud, which then started Sharon off.

"So," said Mickie, when they had settled down again. "Is Bamma a good drummer, and would ah know the band?"

Sharon made a face, as if to say, "how would ah know?"

"He's playin with the Frank O'Hagan's band at the minute, but he says he wants to get a band together with his brothers."

"Oh right," said Mickie, and then they were both lost in thought for a few minutes.

"So, is it love?" Sharon asked again.

Mickie lit another cigarette.

"You smoke too much," said Sharon, frowning at him.

Mickie nodded, and blew smoke into the air.

"Well?" said Sharon.

"Well what?"

"Oh come on. Why are ye bein so evasive?"

"Ah just don't feel comfortable talkin to you about this."

"Oh, well, that means it is, then," said Sharon, looking away.

Mickie again looked down at his hands.

"It's early days," he said

"What the hell does that mean?"

Mickie continued smoking, and looking at the sky, playing for time. He hated being questioned like this. Why should he have to disclose how he really feels? Sharon continued to stare at him.

"It means she has a stressful job that takes up most of her time, and ah don't know if ah'm as important to her as her career."

He knew the latter part of this statement was a lie, but he hoped it would be enough to satisfy Sharon's curiosity. The ruse seemed to work, for Sharon's expression brightened.

"Oh, right. So when will ye see her again?"

Mickie blew air through his mouth, and shook his head.

"To be honest, ah don't actually know. Ah have to wait until she calls me. They're apparently gonny start shootin the commercial today, ah think." Mickie said, pretending to be unsure.

Sharon rolled her eyes, and grinned.

"Well, it disnae sound as if she's that enamoured with the famous Mickie Lee charm after all, eh?"

Mickie shrugged and extinguished his cigarette. He was torn, in one respect, he was glad Sharon seemed to accept that his affair wasn't going anywhere, but he also had a great urge to tell her what he really felt for Laura, and that he had never felt this way before, about anyone.. He glanced over at Sharon, who was looking at him with a self-satisfied smile on her face.

"Poor Mickie," she said, and made a mock sad face.

Mickie's anger almost came to the surface, and he was on the verge of retaliating, when Sadie, fresh from the shower, called from the kitchen:

"Okay, kids, time for lunch, and then we can cut the cake."

With a final smug look, Sharon rose, and went to help Sadie set the table.

* * *

At the very moment Mickie was trying to control his irritation in Ealing, Billy was sitting on his greasy old chair just outside the garage workshop, staring pensively out into the street.

"Hey Bill, wanna a coffee, bruv?" asked BeeJay, popping his head round the open shutter door. When he received no answer, he guessed Billy's mind must be elsewhere, and repeated the question:

Billy man, do ya wanna coffee?"

"Eh?" said Billy, jolted out of his daydream. "Oh aye, thanks, Bee."

BeeJay gave him an indulgent smile, and then strode off towards the kitchen. One of the issues Billy had been considering, when BeeJay interrupted his thoughts, was whether he should mention to the boy that he had met his buddy, Shank, yesterday, and that he was in decidedly dubious company.

After yesterday's encounter in the Bulldog, Billy had decided to forgo Shank's advice about having another pint, and had gone directly round to Mrs McIntyre's. He felt he should immediately deliver the good news that Rob had apparently moved down the coast somewhere, and with any luck, would stay there. When he had repeated what Shank had told him, Lucy and Sammie were of course relieved, and Lucy had immediately got out the rum, and insisted that Billy stay for dinner. She said it would be like a little celebration, as Mickie and Mona, who had gone out to get some beer, would be back soon; but all three of them still thought the subject of Rob should remain strictly between them.

It had been nice for Billy to be included in a family get-together, especially on a weekend when Mary was working; for now that his best buddy was now otherwise engaged, he sometimes found these weekends long and dull.

Although Mickie had been initially surprised to see Billy sitting at the table, he had been easily convinced that he had just dropped round on the off chance because Mary was working, and he had been bored.

Mona had been delighted to see him, and straight away came and sat on his lap and told him all about the Jamaican feast Lucy had cooked for her birthday. After a few beers, Mickie had also been in good form, and had kept everybody amused with stories of some of the more eccentric punters in the pub. But most of all, the thing that gave Billy real pleasure, was that Lucy and Sammie had kept beaming contended looks at each other all through lunch.

BeeJay arrived back with Billy's drink, and again caught Billy lost in thought.

"You all right, bruv?" he said, handing Billy the cup.

"Yeah, yeah. Just got a few things on my mind."

Billy took a sip of coffee, and then looked up at BeeJay.

"Oh, ah bumped into yer mate, Shank, yesterday."

"Oh yeah?" said BeeJay, grinning and bobbing about in front of Billy, as if to some dance beat only he could hear.

"Yeah, as ah was at a bit of a loose end, ah decided to go for a walk, and somehow ended up in the Bulldog." Billy watched to see if this statement got any reaction from BeeJay, but the boy just kept grinning and swaying. Billy found it hard to judge whether the youth already knew, and was playing dumb, or that he genuinely didn't have a clue. Billy found the latter, hard to believe, especially as BeeJay had said the Bulldog was his uncle's local. He decided to get right to the point.

"Did ye know yer mate was hangin out with gangsters?"

Billy let the question hang in the air for a few seconds, and BeeJay's grin began to lose its glow.

"In fact, he seems to be well acquainted with the big guy with the badly chewed nose; remember, the one yer uncle Darryl told ye about."

BeeJay stopped moving, and looked away. Billy remained silent for a moment longer, but then felt he had to get things out into the open.

"Look, Bee, ah normally don't give a fuck what other people do, that's their business, but when vulnerable people ah care about are bein threatened by some arsehole, then ye can bet yer life ah give a fuck big time."

BeeJay looked confused.

"Billy man, I don't know what yer talkin about; I don't hang with Shank. We was close at school, but he goes is own way, innit?"

"So, ye knew he was hangin out with these guys?"

"Well, yeah, me uncle told me he'd seen Shank hangin with the big bro with the mash-up nose, but I didn't see no reason to mention it. I figured that was his business, and I didn't want to get involved."

"Well, ah'm glad to hear it, because ah know all about gang life, and ye really don't want to get involved in that shite."

BeeJay looked lost, he had never had this type of conversation with Billy before.

"Billy man, I'm sorry. If Shank been hasslin somebody you know, I'll have a word, but it aint like him. Sure he's a tough bro, but he aint a bully, he looked out for me at school, man."

"Ah'm not talkin about Shank, ah'm talkin about Rob."

"Rob? Rob's been freatnin somebody you know?"

"Look, it's a long story, but yeah; that arsehole has been stalkin Mrs McIntyre's house, and intimidatin her and Sammie. That's the real reason ah was in the Bulldog, ah've been lookin for him, to mark his card. Ah was keepin a watch on the estate, when Shank and the big guy came walkin into the pub with this other little fuckin weasel."

BeeJay still had a puzzled expression on his face.

Aw for fuck's sake, Bee," said Billy, in exasperation. "Ye told me yerself that Rob's junkie mother was involved with the big guy. And it wasn't long after ye told me, that ah got a chance to follow him and the weasel from the Falcon, and they led me straight to Rob's mothers flat on that estate. Ah canny be bothered goin into details of how ah found out it was her flat. But the bottom line is, Shank told me he thought Rob was now livin down the coast somewhere, which would explain why ah haven't come across him, but before ah could get him to elaborate, the weasel came up and told him they were leavin."

BeeJay slowly nodded his head, but said nothing. Billy rolled his eyes.

"What ah'm tryin to say, is, after they left the pub, ah watched the three of them walk over the road, and into the buildin where Rob's old lady lives. And so, as Shank's obviously had contact with her, did he ever mention anythin to you about seein Rob, or about him movin away?"

BeeJay looked at Billy, and shook his head.

"The last I heard anyfing about Rob was over six months ago. I heard he had started doin a bit of dealin, but only blow. This other bro I knew from school told me he saw Rob hasslin this couple in the street; he said they looked like students, but with money. Anyway, this bro said that Rob started slappin the youth about, until the girl started cryin and handed over money. But Shank never said anyfing about him or is mum to me, innit."

Billy looked steadily at BeeJay, until the boy's nerves got the better of him, and he again started moving to his silent beat. But Billy could tell he was telling the truth.

"Look, Bee, ah don't mean to hassle ye, it's just ah'd feel a lot better if ah knew where that fucker Rob was hangin out, and if he's gonny stay there. If ye hear anythin, will ye let me know?"

"I'll try, Bill," BeeJay sighed. "Me uncle Darryl is good at findin fings out."

Billy looked at the boy's forlorn features, and smiled.

"Don't look so worried, Bee, ah know yer bein straight. Come on, it's my turn to make you a coffee."

BeeJay looked relieved, and managing to retrieve his grin, followed Billy into the garage.

Chapter 19 (5th Wednesday)

Toto counted the money, folded it, and then slid it down the side of his right Timberland boot. Shank, who was helping Toto cut and package the dope, couldn't help noticing this, but he made no comment.

"Whatchoo lookin at?" Toto said, peering at the boy through half-closed eyes.

Shank knew Toto liked to sample the merchandise, but stealing from Nazz, that was different; he wondered how long it had been goin on.

"I'm the one doin all the fuckin work around here," Toto whined. "I deserve a little bonus from time to time."

The boy shrugged his shoulders, and carried on with his work. *The asshole sounds as if he's tryin to convince himself, more than me,* he thought.

Although he didn't know too much about Nazz, Shank was smart enough to know he was a man you didn't cross, not unless you were a fool. As for Toto, Shank and the rest of the youth crew had sussed, and it didn't take long, that here was a man so weak and stupid, he didn't even know he was a fool.

The mobile phone on the table rang, and Toto looked down to see who was calling. He hesitated for a moment, but then picked it up and pressed the call button.

"Hey, boss, wha appenin?"

As he listened, his face twisted with irritation, and he silently mouthed the word: "motherfucker."

"Yeah, man, yeah. It's a done deal, innit?" he said, trying to sound in control, but the whine in his voice gave away his emotions.

"Aw, man, I don't know. The bitch left about an hour ago . . . Well I know, bro, but I can't be baby-sittin that slag all the time . . . Okay, okay, I'm doin it."

Toto held the phone to his ear for a few more seconds, but then realising Nazz was gone, he scowled, and threw it down with a clatter on the table.

"Motherfucker!" he said in a rage. "That motherfucker treats me like a fool, innit. Well, he's gonna be sorry before too long, man."

Guessing this was just more of Toto's bullshit, Shank didn't really give this threat much credence,

A few ready rolled spliffs were lined up on the table; Toto snatched one up and lit it, sucking the weed down in noisy tokes, while his right leg twitched with nervous rage.

At the sound of the front door opening, Shank looked over his shoulder, and noticed Toto's twitchy leg gain speed. As soon as they heard the hesitant footsteps in the hall, they knew it wasn't Nazz.

Rob's mother, Patsy, came hobbling into the living room hugging a plastic carrier bag. She ignored the two men and went straight into the kitchen.

With shaking hands, she removed a bottle of cheap vodka from the bag, lifted a mug from the odd assortment in the sink, and giving it a token wipe, then filled it from the bottle. She put the mug to her mouth with both hands to minimise the shaking, and then greedily drank half the contents. A shudder ran through her, and she had to stand clinging to the counter for a time, before she managed to refill the cup.

When he heard her shuffling steps coming in from the kitchen, Toto started shaking his head, and blowing air. She stopped behind his chair, but it was Shank, to whom she spoke:

"Got a little somefink for me, darlin?" she asked in her hoarse, cigarette blasted voice.

But before the boy could answer, Toto was up, and in her face.

"Listen, bitch. I'm getting so sick of seein your fuckin junkie face always meddlin in my bizness."

Patsy staggered back, spilling vodka down the front of her already soiled top. But Toto clung to his anger, and moving with her, kept his face inches from hers.

"I don't give shit if ya jack-up and die, ya scuzzy bitch. But when I'm here, keep the fuck outtta my face, ya . . . "

"Here, Patsy, we got some spare, innit."

Shank had risen from his seat, and cut in on Toto.

The small man swivelled his head slowly from Patsy to the youth.

"What the fuck is this shit?"

Ignoring him, Shank handed the shaking woman a little gelcap. Toto looked from one to the other, as if he couldn't believe what was happening, but Shank turned away, and said over his shoulder:

"I'm just doin what I'm told. You know what Nazz's orders are."

"Orders? Orders?" raged Toto, moving towards the boy.

But he stopped dead, when he saw Shank spin round in a heartbeat, and look hard into his eyes. Shank was young, tough, and powerfully built, and Toto knew he had gained the respect of the rest of the crew for not taking any shit.

Toto tried to hold the boys gaze, but couldn't, and after a few seconds he looked away and with a dismissive hiss, and picked his phone up from the table. Shank's eyes never left Toto; he could see the little man was shaking with anger, and he was waiting to see if the fool was stupid enough to pull the blade he knew he carried. But then, without warning, Toto spun round and slapped Patsy with such force, that she crumpled to the floor like a broken doll, and before Shank realised what was happening, Toto was gone, slamming the front door behind him.

The boy helped Patsy to her feet; he could feel her shaking, and saw that she had a painful looking welt below her right eye, which had obviously been caused by one of Toto's flash rings.

"Are ya okay?" he asked.

Patsy didn't answer, she kept her head down, and looked as if she may be about to cry. She then turned away from the boy, and took slow shaking steps towards the bedroom.

(5th Thursday)

Mickie sat motionless, staring vacantly out of his bedroom window. The house seemed awfully quiet without Mona. Behind him, propped up on his easel, was a streaked washed off canvas, and on the coffee table lay his discarded paint-clogged brushes and palette. His attempt to start a new painting had come to nothing. He pulled a cigarette from his pack, lit it, and thought back to Mona's birthday on Monday.

For him, the latter part of the celebration had been marred by Sharon's behaviour towards him. But what really got to him was the realisation that he was still pathetically vulnerable to her wiles; even now she knew which buttons to press to make him feel bad about himself.

The trouble was, she had unknowingly struck a nerve. Although he had purposely made Sharon think his new affair was somehow doomed to fail, he was, in reality, somewhat uneasy about Laura's commitment to the relationship. In his heart, he knew he was being stupid, for in the short time they had known each other, she had shown him with every word and gesture that she loved him. But his confidence had always been easily shaken, it was one of the things he hated about himself. He couldn't help thinking: *why can't I just man up and make a stand for what I truly want?*

There was of course Mona to consider in all this. He was always going to be emotionally tied to Sharon through his daughter, and he had to find a way to live with this. He also knew he had to rise above his ex-wife's mind games, and make a new life for himself. That, however, was the hard part, as it really tore him up to watch Mona's face cloud over every time they parted. He sighed, and exhaled a plume of smoke, which curled and billowed, and then sailed out the window on the breeze.

Laura again filled his thoughts, and he picked up his phone to check if there were any messages. A few hours earlier, he had sent a text enquiring how her shoot was going, but so far, there had been no reply. He hadn't heard from her since Saturday evening, but she had made a point, when speaking to him then, of saying that things would be full on until the shoot was over, and not to feel she was neglecting him.

As he was pondering on this, his phone rang, making him jump. He dropped his cigarette in the ashtray and answered:

"Hello . . . Oh, hello," he said, without much enthusiasm, recognising Sharon's voice.

"Oh, ah'm all right," he said, again without enthusiasm.

"What's up? . . . Oh, right, ah see. So, out of the blue, it's now all right for me to see my daughter today. Why the sudden change of plan, did ye get a better offer? . . Well, ah'm not surprised she's upset, ah promised to take her to the National Gallery today."

As Sharon continued to rant, his eyes inadvertently went to Mona's painting of the Pink Dancer, which he had pinned to the wall.

"Why the fuck shouldn't ah make promises? She's my daughter too . . . Look, ah don't actually care why you've changed yer mind, ah'm just happy that ah'm gonny see my daughter. But what really pisses me off, is that you use that wee girl like a weapon, and in doin that ye hurt her as well as me . . . No, ah'm not bein paranoid, Yer a manipulating bitch, and ye know exactly what yer doin . . . "

Mickie pulled another cigarette from the pack, and lit it his hands shaking with emotion.

"Okay, okay, whatever. We'll just have to agree to disagree. Ah'll meet Sadie and Mona outside Queensway Station at four, but ah'll tell ye somethin, ye better pack her jim-jams, and a change of clothes, because she's stayin the night . . . Ah don't care, ye canny phone up at three o'clock in the afternoon and expect me to jump just because ye've decided to make other plans. Mona is staying the night, and ah'm takin her to the National tomorrow . . . Oh, really, well, okay, I'll bring her back tomorrow evening, but on the condition that ah also spend Saturday with her . . . Listen, you get to see her all the time, so it's only fair for me to spend as much time with her as possible while she's here; yer goin back on Monday, for fuck's sake . . . Oh don't start with the emotional blackmail, ah'm well aware it was me that moved to London. Don't ye think it hurts me everyday to be away from her? . . Aw, cheap shot, Sharon. Look us chewin each other up like this isn't helpin anybody, least of all, Mona. Ah just want to spend sometime with my daughter . . . Okay, so long as were clear on that. Ah'll be there at four."

He tossed his phone down, and taking a final drag of smoke, stubbed out his cigarette. He was shaking with emotion, but somehow felt better. At least this time she hadn't managed to manipulate him into feeling bad. He had made a stand for his rights as a father, and surprisingly, Sharon gave way.

A faint smile creased his lips as he picked up his dirty brushes, and started to clean them. He just had time to get the place looking half decent, before he went to pick up Mona. His smile widened at the thought.

(5th Friday)

For Laura, it felt like the day had already been way too long, and it seemed there was to be no respite from the disagreeable comments coming from the clients, especially the youngest, and most vocal of the group.

David Osbourne was a tall, imperious looking individual, with slicked back hair, and a superior attitude. He was always dressed, even in the studio, in an expensively cut suit, the jacket of which he would hang on a hanger suspended from a light stand, much to the annoyance of the lighting guys.

He would alternate between posing irritatingly close to the to the set, with his hands behind his back, showing off his bright yellow suspenders; or else sit with his legs crossed, hands forming a steeple, on which he rested his chin, all the while wearing an expression of haughty, scowling, superiority.

Laura had retreated for a few moments relief into the darkness at the back of the studio. She actually felt like running away, but the best she could do was to pace nervously up and down. She was also, not too realistically, hoping that if she kept out of sight, perhaps they would stop blaming her.

Why are they being such shits? She thought. *We've done everything they asked. The model-makers especially are doing everything humanly possible to make their product look good.*

With some trepidation, she glanced at the text messages on her phone. Since yesterday, Mickie had now left four messages, the last one asking him to call him about Saturday. She felt guilty for not calling him, but under the circumstances, she had been, and still was, in no mood to talk to him. She had texted him a brief message first thing this morning, saying she would try and call, but as things were pretty tense, and she was constantly being confronted by the clients, it was difficult.

Her only crumb of comfort was that Tim Farrell had called over an hour ago to say he was held in a meeting, but would be there as soon as he could. She was hopeful that he would be able to bring some sort of logic to the proceedings, as she obviously held no sway with these people. But it was already five o'clock, and the way things were going, she was starting to think that they would be here all night.

She saw the silhouetted figure of a man coming towards her from the brightness of the set: it was Mark Shaw. She assumed by his agitated stride that he was searching her out because they had found something else to complain about. *Oh, what now?* She thought.

"Laura?" he called out, adjusting his eyes to the gloom.

"Yes, Mark. What is it now?"

"Oh, it's okay. That last shot was great. I just had to get away for a minute, or I'm gonna deck that arrogant bastard."

Laura had to stifle the urge to laugh out loud.

"Join the club," she replied.

"I hate bastards like that," Mark continued, with some venom. "They have no respect for anyone; even the director is beginning to grit his teeth."

"I know. He's making things difficult for all of us. It seems to be the one thing he's not being picky about."

Mark uttered a dry scoffing laugh.

"Listen, Mark," said Laura, attempting to lighten the mood. "Thanks again for all the work you and your guys have done. The models look great; I'm grateful, even of that officious wanker isn't."

"Oh, no worries, Laura, were used to it. But on this occasion, we seem to be well behind you in the queue when it comes to shiny boy's disrespect. Although it seems almost perverse, because I think he fancies you."

"Oh, God!" Laura shuddered at the thought. "He's the last per . . . " her comment was cut short by the sound of the studio door opening.

Through it came the unmistakable figure of Tim Farrell. As usual, he was dressed in the eccentric choice of clothing styles that always made him a unique sight. Today, he sported a red baseball cap, a loose fitting shirt, adorned with bright red tropical flowers, faded pink calf length shorts, and Timberland boots. He strode over to where Laura and Mark stood, and immediately gave Laura a supportive hug, and then shook Mark's hand.

"So, what's the story so far?" he said, glancing at the technicians setting up the next shot.

"Well, we'd get on a lot faster if shiny boy kept out of the fuckin way," said Mark. "I've worked with some pains in the arse, but he's something else."

Tim nodded his head.

"I know; he's been on the phone to Andrew, who fortunately, is well aware that the man is a jumped up prick. But unfortunately, he also seems to be the golden boy of the moment. Andrew has therefore asked us to be patient, and try and humour him, which I do realise is easier said than done."

"I'd like to humour him with a fuckin length of scaffold pole," said Mark.

Tim Farrell's big face broke into a grin, and his body shook with silent amusement.

"Stay cool, chaps," said Tim. "I'll go and have a word with golden bollocks."

With that, he then strode across to where the clients were seated in a semi-circle in front of the set.

As they looked on, Laura and Mark observed Tim taking David Osbourne aside for a chat. It was always fascinating for Laura to watch the way Tim could work these people. For a minute or so, the client stood posing with his hands behind his back, looking down his long nose, at what he obviously considered a ridiculous looking underling. But before long, he seemed to be captivated by whatever spiel Tim was feeding him. He began nodding his head in serious agreement, and even, to Laura and Mark's astonishment, broke into laughter on more than one occasion.

When Tim had finished with shiny boy, he spent time talking and joking with the crew, shaking hands, and slapping backs.

The crew knew it wasn't bullshit; they respected his wit and experience.

Laura then saw him come strolling back to where she stood with Mark, and wondered what he had managed to achieve.

"Well, there's good news, and bad news," he said, matter of factly. "The bad news is he wants to shoot at the weekend, as he thinks things need to be speeded up."

"He's the sole, fuckin reason were behind," said Mark, with some passion. "If he had kept . . . "

"I know, I know. I'm well aware of that, but the quicker we get this done, the quicker I can take you all down the pub for a skin-full. And of course, I've told him he will have to pay overtime."

"What's the good news?" asked Laura somewhat dolefully.

"The good news is, Mr Slick is not going to be here at the weekend, or on Monday, and I doubt whether the other's will be willing to give up their weekend, either. So, hopefully, you can crack the guts out of this thing in the next three days, and have a reasonably easy few days next week. And also, as from Monday, I'm going to be here for the rest of the shoot, as Andrew thinks there is a chance to wangle another job from this mob, and he wants me to butter them up a bit."

Laura and Mark looked at each other, and rolled their eyes. Laura looked especially glum.

"What's the matter, lovely?" said Tim. "I'll make sure golden bollocks and crew keep out of your way for the rest of the shoot."

"Oh, it's not that, apart from being a bit frazzled, I really don't mind working the weekend. It's just I think Mickie was hoping that I could spend Saturday with him and his daughter, as she goes back home on Monday."

"Well, I'm sorry, Laura, but its little Polly's birthday party on Saturday, and my mum and dad are coming over for the weekend. And so, I'm sort of locked into being there, being her dad and all."

"Oh, of course you must, Tim," said Laura, feeling suddenly pathetic. "I'm sorry, I didn't mean to imply anything. It's par for the course of this job, I know that. I'm sure Mickie will understand if . . . "

Their conversation was cut short when one of the other model-makers approached and said they were about to shoot the next set-up. Mark and his colleague went onto the set, and took up their positions. Tim was about to follow to observe the action, when Laura touched his arm.

"Tim could you cover for me for a minute, while I call Mickie?"

She looked so sad, that Tim gave her another reassuring cuddle.

"Course I will, lovely. You take your time."

Laura then turned, walked into a corner of the studio, and dialled Mickie's number.

* * *

Mickie tossed his phone down on the coffee table, hung his head, and releasing a deep sigh, gazed into his beer. He was confused, and angry, but he also felt guilty for feeling that way. He knew that only a moment ago, he had behaved like a petulant little boy. He also knew that was the last thing Laura needed right now; as was evident in the manner she ended the call, by cutting him off mid rant.

The sound of the front door opening made him look up, and a moment later Billy ambled into the room.

"Hiya mate," said Billy, eyes widening in mock surprise. "What are you doin here?"

"Hiya Billy. Ah just popped round with Mona in the off chance Mary would be in."

Billy sensed a certain flat tone in Mickie's voice, but let it go for the moment.

"Oh, right, and where are my two favourite girls?"

"Mary's taken Mona down to the shop for chocolate and beer."

"Ooh, my favourite combination," said Billy, throwing his jacket onto the seat. He then went into the kitchen, and Mickie heard the fridge being opened.

"Another beer?"

"Aye, that would be good," Mickie called back.

A moment later Billy came back into the room carrying two cans, which he set on the table, and then with a sigh, sank into his favourite armchair. He removed his work-boots, and then wriggling his toes, he uttered ooh and aah noises of obvious relief. Mickie lit a cigarette, opened his new can, and refreshed his glass, but remained quiet. While reaching for his beer, Billy gave him a sly glance.

"Ye all right, mate? What did you and Mona get up to today?"

"Eh, we went to the National Gallery," said Mickie, without much enthusiasm.

"Oh, right," said Billy, and then took a long swig from his can.

He looked at Mickie, who was staring sullenly into his beer. Billy felt vaguely irritated by his friend's reluctance to talk. He could always tell when Mickie was fretting about something, but he sometimes got a bit tired of trying to drag it out of him.

"What the fuck is wrong with ye now?"

Mickie looked up with a frown, and blew out a column of smoke.

"Ah've upset Laura."

Billy shook his head.

"When are ye gonny fuckin catch yerself on?" said Billy, his patience for once slipping. "How do ye manage to fuck it up all the time?"

Mickie looked annoyed, but made no reply.

"What have ye done, anyway?"

Mickie took a deep drag of his cigarette, and then crushed it out in the ashtray.

"She called me just before ye came in, to tell me she apparently has to work over the weekend, and ah sort of over-reacted a bit." His face creased in a grimace. "It was obvious she was upset, as she cut me off mid sentence."

"Well, ah'm not fuckin surprised. What is she supposed to do, walk out of her job?"

"Ah know, ah know. Ah'm a wanker, what can ah tell ye," said Mickie, turning away, and looking out the window.

Billy sighed, and took another long slug of beer.

"Why don't ye phone her back, and apologise for bein a tosser?"

Mickie's eyes flashed with anger.

"Yer not bein a lot of help, Billy."

"Hey, listen, ah don't know what ye expect me to say," replied Billy, looking directly at Mickie. "Ah'm well aware yer in the middle of a fuckin horrible dilemma, but that's just the way it is, and ye have no choice but to deal with it. And maybe ah don't have any answers, but ah'll tell ye something, if ye don't start cuttin Laura some slack, yer gonny lose her."

Mickie held Billy's gaze for a few seconds, and then slowly lowered his head. A minute later, the silence was broken by the sound of the door opening, and Mona racing into the room, holding a bar of chocolate in each hand, and wearing a broad grin.

"Aw, ye've bought me chocolate. Och, ye shouldn't have bothered," said Billy stretching out his hand.

"It's not for you, uncle Billy; it's for meee," cried Mona, comically clutching the sweets to her breast.

"Oh, right, fair enough," said Billy, pretending to be sad. "Ah suppose ah'll just have to have beer, then."

He rose from his seat just as Mary came in through the door.

"Well, hello, petal," he said, giving her a peck on the cheek. "Can ah get ye a wee voddy?"

"No, ye can get me a large voddy," said Mary, giving him a comical smile.

"Well, Mickie, ah've heard all about your cultural afternoon," said Mary, throwing her bag onto the chair.

"Aye, it was aw right," said Mickie, and then drained his glass

Billy came back in the room, and handing Mary her vodka and tonic, then turned to Mickie.

"Another beer, mate?"

"Naw thanks," Mickie replied, not looking up. "Ah think it's time we were goin. It's been a long day."

Mary looked at Billy, who rolled his eyes, and shook his head. Mona, sensing something was going on in the adult world she didn't understand, looked confused, and anxious.

"Ach surely ye can stay for a wee while longer?" said Mary, smiling at Mona.

"Naw, honestly," Mickie said. "Ah just want to pick up Mona's stuff from Mrs McIntyre's, and then get her back to Ealing. Like I said, it's been a long day."

With that, he stood up, and lifted Mona up into his arms.

"Okay, darlin, say goodbye to Mary and Billy."

Mona looked close to tears, as she reached out, and in turn, warmly hugged and kissed the embarrassed couple. Mickie gave Mary a quick peck on the cheek, and then turning away, made for the door.

"Ah'll see ye later," he said.

When they heard the door close, Mary turned to Billy, her face a mask of confusion.

"What the hell was all that about?" she asked.

"Oh, don't even ask," replied Billy.

Chapter 20 (5th Friday)

Rob and his grandmother were sitting in the quiet of the living room. They had finished lunch a short time before, and Sally was now settled comfortably in her favourite armchair, reading her book. Rob, who was never still for long, was on the couch, fidgeting with something caught in the tread of one of his trainers.

"Oh, Rob," said Sally, looking up from her book. " You do remember that I will be staying with old Sylvia tonight, as she goes into hospital tomorrow for a hip replacement, and I said I would stay over and keep her company, and then help her get ready in the morning. I'm going to pop over after you've gone, and tomorrow I should be back before lunch."

There was no answer. Sally rolled her eyes.

"Rob?"

"Yeah, yeah, no worries, gran," replied Rob, still concentrating on his task. "Sorry, this bleedin fing's been annoyin me for ages."

He had been about to go up and get changed, having earlier arranged to call for Louise around three o'clock, but then decided to investigate what was causing this annoying, clicking sound, whenever he walked. He had just managed to remove a small stone, with the help of Sally's crossword pen, when the sound of his mobile phone's ring-tone cut through the silence of the room.

Sally looked over and frowned. *Why do we have to endure such a horrible racket every time his phone goes off?* She thought. *Rap music indeed.*

Rob immediately pulled the phone from his pocket, and looked down at the screen. The identity of the caller, whoever it was, caused him to leap up from the couch, and rush out into the garden before answering the call.

Sally, catching sight of him through the French windows, guessed by the agitated way he was striding up and down the garden, that he was talking to his mother. He had been trying to get hold of her for over a week, but either she couldn't be bothered answering, or hadn't topped up her phone. Sally always felt helpless on these occasions, for it was difficult to know what to say to calm him, as he always imagined the worst.

After a short while, Sally heard the back door fly open, and Rob come storming back into the kitchen. It was quiet for a minute, and then she heard the fridge being opened, and knew by the hiss of the can, that Rob was drinking beer. She thought it best to leave him alone until he was ready to talk.

* * *

Louise sensed there was something amiss when she answered her front door and found Rob on the doorstep; he was standing with his back to her, and bouncing from one foot to the other in an agitated manner.

"Oh, hello," she said. "You're early."

Rob spun round.

"So what? That's all right, innit?"

Louise was a further taken aback by his brusque manner, but gave a brief, hesitant smile.

"Sure, of course," she said. "But you'll have to give me time to change."

"Yeah, yeah, no worries," he replied, repeatedly nodding his head.

"Are you okay?" asked Louise.

"Yeah, yeah, no worries."

He was beginning to make her nervous, but she let him in and showed him into the lounge.

When Laura left to get ready, Rob couldn't stand still, and kept bobbing around the room, looking at nothing in particular. Laura's mother, Jenna, having heard Louise answer the door, popped her head round the kitchen door, and was somewhat bemused to see Rob aimlessly wandering around.

"Oh, hi, Rob. I thought I heard the door. Everything okay?"

"Yeah, yeah, no worries," he said, pretending to look out the window.

Jenna gave him a wry look.

"Can I get you a drink of something, tea or coffee?"

"No fanks," he replied, keeping his back to her.

Jenna frowned, she felt anxious all of a sudden, but for the moment went back into the kitchen. A short time later, Louise came back into the lounge wearing loose fitting blue shorts, and a white t-shirt. She glanced at Rob, still bouncing by the window, and then called through to her mother.

"I'm off now, mum. See you later."

Jenna came in from the kitchen, and walked over to Louise.

"Oh, you look lovely, darling," she said, lightly touching her daughter's face. "Have a nice time, but don't be too late."

She then looked over at Rob, who seemed oblivious to what was happening, and was still standing gazing out the window. Jenna gave her daughter a concerned look, but Louise only made a face and shrugged her shoulders.

"Okay, Rob. Shall we go?" she asked.

"Yeah, yeah, whatever," he replied, and then, without acknowledging Jenna, he strode out of the room and made for the front door. Louise gave her mother an embarrassed little smile.

"Don't worry, I won't be late."

Jenna nodded, and then, as an afterthought, she asked:

"Oh, you do have your phone with you?"

Louise silently mouthed the word, yes, and then followed Rob out the door.

Jenna frowned as she watched them walk down the street, and then, as soon as they were out of sight, she walked over to the phone and dialled a number.

"Oh, hello Sally, it's Jenna."

* * *

Closing the door behind her, Lucy put her bags of shopping down on the hall floor, and removed her damp raincoat. But before she even had time to hang up it up on the coat-rack, Dizzy appeared, as if from nowhere, and greeted her with a hungry meow, as if to say: "where have you been, don't you know I'm starving?" She grinned and shook the coat, sending droplets of water into the air, and onto Dizzy, who then beat a swift retreat into the sitting room.

On entering the kitchen, she found Sammie sitting at the table, gazing out through the open back door at the summer rain. The room was silent, but even so, he seemed not to have heard her enter the room, and flinched at the touch of her hand on his shoulder.

"Oh, mi sorry, darlin, mi thought yuh heard me come in," she said, and then started to unpack the grocery bags.

"Oh, hey, Lucy girl. Mi just tinkin, and enjoyin the rhythm of the rain."

"Uh huh," replied Lucy, giving him a wry smile. "What yuh tinkin about?"

"Oh, nothin much."

Lucy gave him another quick glance. He had been unusually quiet the last couple of days, not sullen, or blue, just quiet.

"Yuh wanna go hear Bobbie play tonight?" she asked over her shoulder.

He didn't answer right off, but started to roll a cigarette.

"Huh?" she said, turning to look at him when he didn't answer.

Mi don't tink so, darlin," he said, and then lit his cigarette.

"Well, now. Sammie 'Toots' Turner don't want to hit the town on a Friday night, huh?" she said, teasing him.

He gave her a soft smile.

"Oh, mi content to stay here with you, darlin," he said, looking up into her eyes. "Mi never felt so happy in a long time."

Lucy made a dismissive kissing sound, but when she turned away, she smiled.

"Well me suppose mi better get busy cookin yuh favourite dinner then, huh?"

Sammie gave a rumbling laugh, and rising from the table, put his big arms around her, and kissed her bare shoulder.

"Well, mi suppose mi better get us some more Guinness."

With that he went into the hall to fetch his hat and jacket., and then came back to pick up his lighter and cigarette.

"Oh Mickie say he'll bring Mona back to say goodbye."

"They gone already?" said Lucy in surprise. "What vexin that bwoy, now? He up one minute, and down the next. Mi could tell someting was wrong when I pass him earlier on the street. He hardly said a word, and the child look like she been cryin."

"Well," said Sammie. "I only seen them for a few minutes, but he didn't seem to want to talk too much about anyting, and Mona was way too quiet."

Lucy made the kissing sound again, this time in real irritation.

"Okay darlin, mi won't be long," said Sammie heading for the front door.

Lucy put Mickie and Mona out of her mind for the present, as she didn't want to spoil her mood. She switched on the radio, and when she heard Billy Eckstine singing 'Prisoner of Love' she turned up the volume, and began swaying gently to the music. In a singsong voice, she then called for Dizzy, and at the sound of her spooning food into his yellow bowl, he came scurrying into the kitchen, and meowed his appreciation.

As he tucked greedily into his food, Lucy gently scratched his neck, which he totally ignored, and then she went to the back door to check on the weather. The rain was easing off, and the sight of the sun creeping over the rooftops made her smile. She felt life was good; it felt like a new beginning, and she was grateful to whatever fates had brought Sammie back into her life. Feeling like little treat, she opened a bottle of Guinness, and then turned her attention to preparing her man's favourite meal.

* * *

Louise stole a furtive glance at Rob, and tried to think of something to say that would break the silence. He had been in a strange mood all evening, and she was at a loss to know quite what to do about it. Earlier when he had called at her house, she could tell he had been drinking, but there was something else, he had been edgy and offhand, and she suspected he had taken something else. What was worse, was that she knew her mother had also been aware that something wasn't right.

He had insisted they go directly to a pub, and when she refused to drink anything alcoholic, it had seemed to irritate him further. Her refusal was not because she didn't drink, but she just had a feeling that tonight, it would be a bad idea.

They were sitting on a seafront bench opposite a McDonald's, which was a regular haunt for local teenagers, especially at this time on a Friday night.

"Would you like something to eat, Rob?" asked Louise. "I'm starting to feel a little hungry."

He lit a cigarette, and shook his head. She noticed he kept tapping his feet, in a constant nervous way.

"I'm just going to pop across and get something, okay?"

Rob shrugged his shoulders and took a long pull on his cigarette. Louise crossed the road, and was just about to enter the burger bar, when one of the boys standing around outside, called out to her:

"Hey, Louise, not speaking tonight?"

She looked round, and saw it was a boy named Gary; he had gone to the same school as Louise, but had left the year before.

"Oh, hi Gary, I was in a bit of a dream, there."

Gary was stocky, of medium height; he had gelled, spiky hair, and was wearing low-slung, baggy jeans, and an oversized black t-shirt. Louise didn't actually know him that well, as he was that bit older than her, but she could instantly tell he had been drinking by the stupid way he was grinning at her.

"Lookin lush, Louise," he said, leering at her. "Lookin lush."

Oh, god! Thought Louise. *That's all I need.*

She knew he had been a bit of a prat at school, and he obviously hadn't changed. She felt embarrassed, and at a loss to know quite what to say, or do. She looked at the ground, and gave a brief smile.

"Thanks," she managed to say, and then quickly turned to go into the bar.

"You were always a stuck up cow, though," said Gary, with some vehemence, causing a few of the by-standers to laugh. Louise froze, she didn't know what to do, and was close to tears; it was turning out to be a very strange evening.

It went quiet all of a sudden, and then she heard Rob's voice, only it sounded strangely strangled by emotion:

"Hey, dickhead!"

Louise spun round in time to see Rob flick his cigarette butt into Gary's startled face, and then pounce on him like an animal. He head-butted Gary hard in the face, and then sweeping his legs away, got him down on the ground, and started kicking him repeatedly in a frenzy of vicious blows. Gary, obviously in shock at the ferocity of the attack, could only lie helpless in a foetal position, and pray his grunting assailant would soon tire of hurting him. Unfortunately for him, however, all the frustration that had been building up inside Rob for most of the day, was now being released in this enraged assault.

Louise stood open-mouthed, numbed by the spectacle, as did most of the people standing by. A few had walked quickly away, not wanting to be involved.

"Rob, stop! Please Rob, stop!" Louise screamed, suddenly terrified.

Rob ignored her frantic cries, until the oncoming sound of a Police siren seemed to bring him to his senses. His breath coming in short audible gasps, he stood hunched over, looking down at the stricken figure at his feet. It was then, as if waking up from some bad dream, he looked at Louise, and for an instant she saw the confused, pitiful mask his face had become before he turned and ran into the night.

Chapter 21 (5th Saturday)

"Hey Mickie, give me a call back. Ah know yer pissed off, and probably don't want to talk, but ah hate leavin things like this, we need to sort it out. Awright, mate, hopefully speak to ye soon."

Mary, still in her dressing gown, came into the living room carrying a tray containing two cups of coffee, and a plate of toast.

"No answer, then?" she said, placing the tray on the coffee table.

"Naw, ye know what he's like," said Billy, chucking the phone down beside him on the couch. "He can be a really obstinate fucker, when he wants to be."

Mary lit a cigarette, and then took a sip of coffee.

"What are ye goin to do?"

Och, ah don't know; maybe ah should go round to Mrs McIntyre's this afternoon and see if he's there."

Billy took a bite of toast, and munched it moodily. Mary felt she should say something.

"I don't know why you're feelin so bad, from what ye told me, he was behavin like petulant wee boy, and you just pointed that out."

Och, ah know, he irritates the hell out of me sometimes, but even so, he got a lot to deal with right now."

Mary cupped her chin in her hands, and looked at him.

"Well, he's in a quandary that's for sure. There's no way he can deal with a situation like this without somebody bein hurt, especially him."

Billy threw down his crust, and sat back in his chair. Mary couldn't for the moment think of anything else to say, so she smoked her cigarette, sipped her coffee, and gazed out at the sky above the rooftops opposite. After a few minutes silence, she decided to try a change of subject.

"Well, at least Lucy and Sammie are happy," she said, smiling at Billy. "I met Lucy in the market on the way home yesterday, and she was like a young thing, all smiles, and chattin away about her and Sammie. It made me feel good to see the change in her. And it was you that helped make that happen, Billy."

Billy shrugged. "Aye, but for how long?"

"Why, what do ye mean?"

"Aw, nothin, ignore me, ah'm just pissed off. Ah didn't sleep very well last night."

Mary gave him a stern look.

"Is there something your not tellin me, Billy," she said, stubbing out her cigarette.

"Naw, everythin's fine," replied Billy, while thinking: *me and my big mouth.*

"Look, Mary, honestly, ah don't want ye worryin, because everythin's fine, well, apart from the Mickie thing, that is."

Mary looked unconvinced, so Billy made a funny face, as if to say: "now, would I lie to you." Mary still looked unconvinced.

"Okay, well ah'm gonny jump in the shower," Billy said, rising from his seat, but he still felt vaguely guilty, and stopped at the door.

"Are ye all right?"

Mary didn't feel all right, but she nodded anyway. After Billy left the room, she lit another cigarette, and again gazed out the window at the clouds moving across the rooftops.

* * *

Sally dialled the number, and then held the phone to her ear. The sun had thrown a beam of light across the floor of the lounge, and she gazed, as if in a trance, at the rich colours highlighted in the rug at her feet.

"Hello Jenna, it's Sally again," she said, trying not to sound irritated. "I've been trying to catch you since I came back from Sylvia's about an hour ago, and listened to your voicemail message. As you're normally there when I phone at this time on a Saturday morning, I don't know what to think. But anyway, could you please call me back, as I don't know where Rob is, and I'm extremely worried. His bed hasn't been slept in, and his clothes are gone."

When I heard your message from yesterday, I could tell immediately by your enquiry that you were concerned that something was troubling Rob. Has something happened I should know about? I do know that before he left to go round to your house, yesterday, he got a call from his mum, and whatever she told him, really upset him. But as usual, I couldn't get any sense out of him, and what little he did say, was about going back to London, which of course worries me. If you can shed any light on any of this, I would be grateful. Please do call me back."

She replaced the phone, and was trying to make sense of the situation, when the doorbell abruptly roused her from her thoughts. She felt a sudden sense of doom as she rose to answer the door. The sight that greeted her more than convinced her that her instincts were somehow horribly accurate: a policeman and policewoman stood on the doorstep.

"Sally Toper?" asked the policewoman.

"Yes," answered Sally, feeling the panic rise in her chest. "Wha... What's happened?"

"Do you mind if we come in?" said the policewoman. "We don't want to discuss things on the doorstep."

"Of course, of course," said Sally trying to remain calm.

When they were seated in the living room, the policewoman again spoke:

"Mrs Toper, I'm constable Wendy Cole, and this is constable Paul Drummond." The big policeman nodded, but said nothing.

"We called round last night to make some enquiries, but there was apparently nobody home."

"Could you please get to the point," said Sally, her voice taking on an edge. "Something has obviously happened."

"Mrs Toper, we believe your grandson has been staying with you?"

"Yes," answered Sally, a little tartly, and then a sudden panic overcame her. "Oh, my God! What's happened? Is he all right?"

"Mrs Toper," continued constable Cole, in a business-like tone. "We believe your grandson, Rob, was involved in an incident last night outside the McDonald's restaurant on the seafront We would like to ask him a few questions regarding the incident, as another boy was badly beaten up."

Sally suddenly looked as if she had been slapped; she bowed her head, and started to wring her hands.

"Are you all right, Mrs Toper, can we get you anything?"

Sally closed her eyes, shook her head, and sighed.

"No, I'll be all right. Just tell me, how do you know it was Rob?"

"We got a good description of him from witnesses to the assault, and of course we've spoken to miss Brown."

"Louise?" said Sally in surprise. "I've been trying to call her mother for the last hour, but didn't get an answer."

"We advised Mrs Brown not to speak to you until we got a chance to interview you and your grandson."

"Oh, I see," said Sally, looking down at her clasped hands.

She was quiet for a few seconds, and then looked up and said, with renewed concern:

"Oh God, is Louise all right? She's such a nice girl. She shouldn't have to experience something like this. What am I going to say to her mother?"

"Well, she was still there when we arrived at the scene, and although she was in some distress, she managed to give us the relevant information, but even so, she is pretty shaken up. It was a particularly vicious attack, Mrs Toper."

Sally let go an uncontrollable sob, and put her face in her hands. Constable Cole looked at her colleague, and nodded to the selection of alcohol and glasses in the cabinet. The policeman rose, poured a brandy, and brought it back for Sally.

Constable Cole placed the glass gently into Sally hands, and let her take a few sips, before continuing.

"Do you have any idea where your grandson might be, Mrs Toper?"

"No," answered Sally, without looking up. "After he went out yesterday afternoon, I went to stay the night with an old friend who was going into hospital today. I said I would keep her company, and then help her get ready this morning, before the ambulance came. I only came back home a short while ago."

"Is there any sign that your grandson returned here last night, for instance is there anything missing?"

Sally wasn't sure what the policewoman was trying to imply, and again became a little irritated.

"No, nothing's missing," she snapped, and then realising she was being paranoid, continued in a quieter tone: "Well, apart from whatever little clothes he had, and also, his bed hasn't been slept in. I can only guess he has gone back to London. He was concerned about his mother."

Constable Cole jotted down a few details down in her notebook, and then glanced briefly at her colleague.

"I'm afraid there was another incident, and of course we don't know for sure it's related, but one of your neighbours, a Mr Grant, was assaulted, and had his car stolen."

Sally started to shake her head, as if trying to wake up from a bad dream.

"Mr Grant was assaulted approximately two hours after the incident on the seafront, around 11.30. He didn't get a good look at the assailant, as he was temporarily bewildered when he was knocked to the ground, and his head came in contact with the road."

At this, sally gave another sob, and put her hand over her eyes. The policewoman again glanced at her colleague, and then with a sigh, continued:

"Mr Grant managed to give us a vague description of his attacker, and although he didn't see his face, we have reason to believe, from the way he was dressed, it may have been your grandson."

Sally remained silent, and hidden behind her hands until the policewoman felt the need to proceed with her enquiry:

Mrs Toper, we need an address in London where we could possibly locate your grandson. And if you could also supply us with his mobile number, assuming he has a mobile, that would be very helpful. The sooner we get this cleared up the better."

Sally nodded dumbly, and looked at the floor.

"Have you spoken to your daughter lately, Mrs Toper?"

The question made Sally look up.

"No," she said in a sudden, clipped way. "You may as well know, as you'll probably find out anyway, my daughter is a heroin addict, and isn't easily contacted."

Constable Cole didn't comment, but wrote in her notebook.

Sally laid down the unfinished brandy, and lifting a pen and a small yellow pad from the table, wrote down the requested information, and handed it to the policewoman.

"Thank you for you help, Mrs Toper," she said, placing the yellow page carefully in her notebook. I think we have enough to be going on with, but one last thing, I wonder if we could have a look in your grandson's bedroom?"

Sally looked away, her face set in a mask of anger and shame. She was silent for moment, and then took a deep breath, and let it go.

"First right at the top of the stairs," she said, without turning to face the police officers.

***

Nazz finished his whisky, and then walked up to the bar for a refill. The fat tattooed bar-maid saw him out the corner of her eye, but continued talking to another customer further along the bar. When Nazz rattled his glass noisily on the bar-top, she gave him a sharp look, and then waddled over to serve him. He didn't speak, but stared right into her eyes and pointed to his empty glass. He could see she was on the verge of making some sarcastic comment, but his silent, unblinking stare made her think better of it.

Being Saturday lunchtime, the Bulldog was busy, but Nazz took his drink back to an empty table. He had earlier come back from dealing with some business in Brixton for a few days, and had initially gone to the flat to check things out. Finding nobody there, he had called Shank and arranged to meet him in the Bulldog; his instincts told him something had gone down while he was away. Nazz hadn't spoken to Toto since Wednesday, and now he wasn't answering his phone. Nazz had a feeling Shank knew why.

He was considering this when he saw Shank come in through the main door of the pub and look around the room. The boy caught sight of Nazz, and strode over to the table. The big man eyed the youth for a few seconds, and then dipped into his pocket and tossed a five-pound note on the table. Without a word, Shank lifted the money and went to the bar. He came back with a beer for himself, and another whisky. Nazz poured the new spirit into his glass.

"What appenin?" he said staring at the boy. "Why aint that sneaky little fucker answerin his phone?"

Shank took a sip of beer.

"Have ya seen Patsy?"

Nazz gave him a questioning look, and slowly shook his head.

"No, she weren't there when I looked in earlier. Why?"

"She aint good, bro. I been worried since Tot . . . " he didn't finish, but looked down, and took another sip of beer.

Nazz stared hard at the boy, but remained silent.

"Toto banged her bad, bro," said Shank, with sudden venom. "I gave her a taste, to keep her sweet like you told me, but then flash boy started mouthin off, tryin to play tough. But when he suss I was real sweet for rippin him up, he turned and slapped Patsy real hard, and then was gone before I knew what was appenin. I aint never seen her like that before, man, her face just sort of crumpled like she was gonna weep, but she didn't. I tried to help her, but she pushed me away, and then slunk off to the bedroom. I carried on doin the job, and when I was leavin, I knocked on the door, but she never answered. When I came back the next day to check on her, she weren't there. I aint seen either of them since."

Nazz said nothing in reply, but stared at Shank until the youth looked down into his beer, but after a moment, he looked up, and said, again with anger:

"I hate workin with that fucker, blud," and then, as if to add weight to his story, he added: "And e's been dippin money, innit. I seen him do it, bro."

Nazz downed his whisky and then slammed the glass on the table, causing a few heads to turn, and then just as quickly, turn away.

"Greasy fuck," said Nazz, in an edgy controlled voice. "Ya need to find that blood-claat, bwoy."

Shank didn't show any reaction to the referred slight in the use of the term, bwoy, but looked Nazz straight in the eye, and asked:

"What about Patsy?"

"If the bitch hangin, who knows what she'll do. I aint finished my business yet, and I need that flat to be safe. I don't want her bein bait for the Feds. Once they start pokin around, it's over. I'll find her, you worry about the weasel."

With that, Nazz slid his glass across the table towards Shank, who lifted it, and without further comment, went to the bar.

* * *

For a long time after the police had left, Sally sat in a daze. She couldn't even talk things over with her best friend; she wasn't even sure she had a best friend anymore. Her head was spinning, and she felt sick with worry at the thought of what was going to happen to both Rob, and her daughter; but she also couldn't help thinking that it was now too little too late.

Remorse was weighing heavy on her, and she began to question her lack of empathy in the past: *Why hadn't she taken responsibility for Patsy, and tried to help her more? What was the point of being a mother, if you ignored your own child's plight because you didn't want to deal with issues you thought were beyond your control?*

Since the police left, she had made at least four calls to Patsy, but as usual, there was no reply. And of course, there was no way Rob would be answering his phone. She had called anyway, and left a message, hoping upon hope that he would get back to her.

On top of everything else, there was poor Duncan Grant. What on earth was she going to say to him; she felt so ashamed. She had known him and his wife for years; the three of them belonged to the same bowling club. And in all that time, she had found him to be the most kind and considerate of men, a perfect gentleman in fact.

As if things weren't bad enough, a worrying additional factor of the awful attack on Duncan was that he had only recently started to adjust to life again after the death of his wife. Diane had passed away just over a year ago, and something like this could send him back into the deep depression from which he had only just emerged.

Sally had thought long and hard about phoning him, but had then decided against it. What could she possibly say? She longed for the police to call and say it had been a terrible mistake, and the attacker had been identified as another boy; but in her heart, she knew it had to be Rob.

She was so lost in contemplation of her failures that the sudden shrill ring of the doorbell made her jump.

"Oh God, what now?" she muttered, as she rose from the sofa to answer the door. When she opened the door and found Louise standing there, looking confused and forlorn, she was so surprised that for a few seconds she was unable to speak; but then, an overwhelming feeling of such protective tenderness overcame her, that she instinctively took the girl in her arms.

"Oh, Louise, I'm so sorry, what a thing to happen."

In the act of comforting Louise, Sally in turn, found the she too had been in need of a hug.

"I just had to come and see you," said Louise. "Do you mind if I come in?"

"Oh, of course," said Sally, realising they were still on the doorstep. "What am I thinking?"

She stepped aside, and allowed Louise to enter.

"Lets sit in the kitchen and I'll make us some tea," said Sally, ushering the girl into the bright sunlit room.

Louise sat down at the kitchen table while Sally prepared the tea. She glanced at the girl, and could sense she was struggling with her thoughts.

"My mum doesn't know I'm here," said Louise, after a few minutes silence. "She's very upset and angry, and I thought it best not to tell her."

Sally turned to face her.

"Look Louise, I completely understand why your mum feels that way. You should never have had to witness something like that. I really don't know what to say, apart from I blame myself for a lot of thi . . . "

"He was protecting me," said Louise, suddenly cutting Sally off.

"What?" said Sally, gazing at the girl in surprise.

"Rob was helping me. That boy was being horrible. I think he had been drinking, and he just started picking on me."

"Did you tell the police this?" asked Sally, sitting down at the table.

"Yes, but they still said it was a serious assault, and that was no excuse."

"Yeah, I suppose they would," Sally replied, with a hint of scorn.

"I didn't know what to do. I had never seen anyone act like that before; I had never seen anyone that angry before. It was like animal instinct, he just exploded into violence."

Sally remained silent; she felt the girl had a need to talk. She rose and went to fetch the tea things, and brought the tray back to the table.

Louise was fidgeting with a gold band on her wrist. Sally poured the tea and added milk to both cups.

"Sugar?"

"Sorry," replied Louise.

"I'm sorry, love, I can't remember if you take sugar," said Sally, looking tenderly at the girl.

"Oh, no thank you," replied Louise, and continued to tinker with her bracelet.

Sally sipped her tea, and watched Louise across the table.

"Why is he so angry?" Louise asked, suddenly looking up at Sally.

"Oh, God," said Sally, with a deep sigh. "Where do I start?"

She stared out the window as if searching for answers, but sadly, she was more than aware why her grandson was such a broken boy. Louise felt the need to break the silence:

"I got the feeling, from what little he said about it, that things really started to fall apart for him after his father left."

"Rob never knew his father," Sally said, abruptly, while continuing to stare out the window.

Louise looked confused, as if she had misheard what had just been said. Sally turned and looked at her.

"The man that left wasn't his father. He tried to be, for a long time, but my daughter eventually drove him away. In the end, he could no longer take the frustrating arguments, or the disappearing for days at a time with any man that provided her with drugs. I'm actually surprised he lasted so long."

"Are you serious?" cried Louise in astonishment. "Why didn't anybody tell Rob this? He surely has the right to be informed that the man he believed to be his father, wasn't, especially as it caused him, and is still causing him so much heartache."

Sally looked down in shame; she knew Louise was right, but she had no plausible answers to her questions, but felt she should at least try to explain:

"Everything you say is true. I could make the same excuses as I did then: that I wasn't even aware that Patsy was pregnant until after the baby was born, and that she refused to discuss who the father was. She came here shortly after the birth, and I cared for her and the baby. That was, of course until she got bored, and we started arguing. It was after one particularly horrible argument that she took the baby and went back to London. I heard nothing from her, and she wouldn't answer my calls. In the end, I'm ashamed to say, I just gave up. If her dad had still been alive, maybe it would have been different; she loved her dad."

As these words were coming out of her mouth, Sally felt bitter tears of shame fill her eyes, and she hung her head. Louise looked tenderly at the old woman, and felt her pain, but was unsure of what to say.

"I'm sorry, Louise, I just feel so sad that I didn't do more to prevent all this. Patsy was fifteen when her dad died. She couldn't believe that someone she loved so much was suddenly gone. She always favoured Micheal, I was the disciplinarian, and he was the one she went to for comfort and love. It wasn't long after he died that she began to change. It was then that I became the enemy. Nothing I did was right. She didn't once consider that I too might be heartbroken. I came home from work one day, it was almost a year after Micheal had died, and there was a note on the kitchen table, saying she had gone to stay with a friend in London."

Sally was silent for a moment, and then with a sigh, she looked up into Louise's worried face, and forcing a brief sad smile, she said:

"I never did find out who the real father was, and I really don't know if it would have made any difference telling Rob the truth. Unfortunately, darling, it's too late, the damage has been done, and God only knows what's going to happen now."

* * *

The light was fading, but it was still warm and muggy as Shank entered the estate and made his way to the main door of Patsy's block. Since leaving Nazz in the Bulldog earlier, he had, as instructed, been busy trying to locate Toto. After checking various likely places and people, he had still come up with nothing; Toto had simply disappeared. Shank, however, wasn't in the least surprised by this, Toto was a fool, but not that much of a fool.

He had often boasted of frequenting a particular West-End cocktail bar, where he was apparently treated with respect, and the woman couldn't get enough of him. Shank sensed this was just more bullshit, and he was probably only tolerated because he had money, and coke; Shank had gone there in the vain hope that Mr lover-man would show.

After a couple of hours, however, Shank had felt bored and out of place, but before he left, he thought it worthwhile to make enquiries of the bar staff. He wasn't too surprised when his questions were met with total apathy. Toto, it seems, wasn't the well-respected stud he had claimed to be, and if he was remembered at all, it certainly wasn't with fondness. When Shank had described who he was looking for to one of shapely young blonde girls behind the bar, she had been especially scathing:

"Oh, that creepy little pimp looking guy? No, he hasn't been in, and he won't be missed if he never comes back."

Shank couldn't help smiling. It was unanimous, old Toto was like poison all over town.

Before finally giving up for the day, and reporting back to Nazz, Shank had decided he might as well go and check out the flat, having not been there since his brief visit on Thursday. He approached the front door, and was about to put the key in the lock, when he saw that the door was slightly ajar.

He slowly pushed the door open and stepped inside. As soon as he entered the hallway, he sensed someone was in the flat. There was the sickly smell of freshly cooked dope, which could only mean Patsy had returned; but because the door had been open, Shank wasn't taking any chances.

He stood motionless for a minute or so, gauging his next move, and then, tensing his body against any sudden attack, he slowly and silently moved along the hall. When he looked in the living room, it was empty, and looked much the same as when he had left on Thursday. He let out a controlled sigh, and again moved silently along the hallway. The first bedroom door was wide open, and he checked the room was empty, before making his way towards Patsy's room. Her door was partly open, and the acrid smell of vomit filled his nostrils as soon as he got to the doorway. From where he stood, he could only see a pair of filthy trainers lying on the floor; he recognised them as Patsy's.

He had an instant feeling of foreboding, and when he entered the room, he could see his instincts were right on the money. Patsy was on the bed, lying on her back; her face had a bluish pallor, and her eyes were open, staring at the ceiling. A syringe was hanging from her left arm, and a stream of vomit ran from her mouth onto the pillow.

Shank was stunned; he had seen some bad things in his young life, but this was different. He remembered Patsy as a young mother, and how all the boys had lusted after her whenever she had to come to the school sort something out for Rob; and now, here she was, dead.

He felt as if he was going to throw up, and rushed into the kitchen. There was an unopened bottle of vodka on the worktop; he opened it and drank down a good inch and a half of the spirit. He shuddered, took another mouthful, and thought: *What the fuck. This is bad.*

His first instinct was to get out of there, fast, but he soon realised that there had to be evidence of some description over most of the flat, that he, Nazz and Toto, had been using the place to cut and package drugs. He took another slug from the bottle, and then, taking his phone from his jacket, dialled Nazz's number.

"Hey, boss, we got a big problem," he said, his own voice sounding strange to him. "I just come to the flat, and I . . . " he hesitated, hardly knowing what to say. "Patsy's OD'd, bro . . . I don't know, man. I just got here . . . Well, I spent most of the day tryin to find Toto, like ya told me . . . Well, yeah, I know that."

He was trying not to sound angry.

"No, man, no way; I aint doin it on my own, ya gotta come over here . . . What, not before then? . . Okay, okay, I'll start, but . . ."

Before Shank had finished speaking, his phone went dead, causing him to smack his lips in irritation, and then cry aloud:

"Fucker aint got no soul."

He put his phone back in his pocket, took another hit of the vodka, and then went into the living room. He sat down at the table by the window and stared out at the darkening sky.

* * *

An hour or so later, the big man stepped out of a cab, and walked casually towards the door of Patsy's block. His every step, however, was being watched by a hooded figure slumped down in the front seat of a blue Vauxhall. The car had been parked in a part of the street where the overhead lighting had failed, and far enough away not to be conspicuous.

When he saw Nazz enter the building, Rob lit a spliff and blew the smoke out the partly open car window. His right foot was keeping up a constant drumming beat on the floor; a sign that his customary edginess had been topped up by a lack of sleep, alcohol, and the mishmash of pills he had been popping. This combination was going a long way to exacerbate the anger that had been building up ever since he had received the call from his mother on Friday.

Such was the surge of rage that had rose up in him when she had told him what had happened with Toto, that in the end he had been unable to control it. All that pent-up fury had finally erupted, and had been violently directed at the youth who had been unfortunate, and stupid enough to say the wrong thing to Louise at the wrong time.

Panicked by the realisation of what he had done, Rob had run from the scene, and didn't stop until he reached his grandmother's house. His goal had been to get there before the police, and hide out while trying to figure out what to do next.

After making it safely to the front door and catching his breath, he had glanced round the other houses on the street to check that he wasn't being watched, and then had quietly let himself in. Careful not to switch on any lights, he had then closed the living room curtains, and waited by the window. He didn't have to wait long.

At the sound of a car stopping outside, he had peered through a crack in the curtains, and saw two police officers, one of which was a woman, get out of a squad car. They took a few minutes to look around the street, and then walked up the path to the front door. The sudden shrill ring of the doorbell had made him jump, and he drew back from the window and held his breath. The bell was pushed longer the second time.

He could hear the officers talking, but couldn't make out what was being said. And then, seconds later, a sudden beam of torchlight had shone through the crack in the curtain. He had stood rigid with fear, but after a few seconds, it was switched off again, and then he heard them walk round the side of the house. The handle of the back door was rattled, as one of them checked to see if it was open, and then the beam from the torch shone through the kitchen window.

The beam scanned the interior of the kitchen for what seemed to Rob, a long time, but was then again switched off. Rob had stood motionless in the living room, with his back against the wall, until he heard the officers walk back to the front of the house.

He had then chanced another cautious look through the curtains, and saw the policeman sitting in the squad car, and guessed he was reporting back to the station. After a final look back at the house, the policewoman had joined her colleague in the car, and as Rob continued to watch, they had then slowly drove off down the street. Feeling instantly relieved, he had slumped down on the couch, and with shaking hands, pulled his cigarette pack from his pocket. With some difficulty, he had managed to light one, and then drawing the smoke deep into his lungs, had blown a long column into the darkness. He had felt suddenly cold, and his whole body trembled.

In the dim light of his cigarette, his eye had fallen on his grandmother's cocktail cabinet. Rising from the couch, he had gone over to check if, by some stroke of luck, it was unlocked, and to his surprise, it was. And so, picking out a nearly full bottle of Johnny Walker, he had then flopped back on the couch, and unscrewed the cap.

The spirit burned his throat on the way down, but had also settled and warmed him, and he sat in the silent darkness for quite some time, smoking and sipping from the bottle, until he fell into a kind of soporific dream. When he finally became conscious of time passing, he had shaken his head and decided he had better make a move, and the sooner the better. Still clutching the bottle, he had then left the living room, and climbed, somewhat unsteadily, up the stairs to his room.

It had taken only minutes to stuff his few belongings into his scruffy old backpack, and then, as an afterthought, the whisky. He had then pulled from behind the wardrobe, the hidden stash of drugs he had brought with him from London; luckily he had hardly touched anything in the last few weeks, and still had more than a few days supply. After snorting some amphetamine sulphate, he had put the rest of the stash in one of the pockets of the backpack, and slung it over his shoulder.

Thinking it best to leave by the back door, he had then moved slowly and carefully down the garden, until he came to the fence adjoining the neighbouring house. And then, with the aid of the garden bench, had clambered over, and dropped silently into the next garden.

He had waited in the darkness for a minute or so, to gauge the situation, and then, seeing there was no lights on in the house whose garden he had just entered, he had felt safe enough to edge his way down the side of the house, and check the street.

Getting to London was his goal; this decision had been made as soon as he had got the call from his mum. The problem was he didn't have enough money to cover the train or bus fare. He also didn't want to be spotted by the police trying to hitch a lift, and had reckoned his only option was to steal a car. He was a passable driver at best, having had a few basic lessons from his dad, but as he plainly didn't have any other choice, this fact hadn't even entered his head; it just had to be done.

Car theft, however, wasn't that easy; what with alarms, steering locks and such, it was now nigh on impossible to achieve. He had been mulling this over, when the sound of a car coming up the street had made him draw back into the darkness. Afraid it was the squad car returning, he had been relieved to see a dark blue Vauxhall come into view and stop right outside the house.

As he continued to watch, a tall, slightly stooped, elderly man had got out of the car, and stretching his arms in the air, had groaned, as if in relief. Without bothering to remove the keys from the ignition, or close the car door, the man had then gone to the back of the car, and opened the boot. When Rob had seen the old man stoop down and begin to search inside, he had grabbed his chance. Before the old man knew what was happening, he had been knocked to the ground, his head making a dull thud as it hit the road. As he lay there stunned, he had been, as he later told the police, vaguely aware of a hooded figure slamming the boot shut, jumping into the driver's sear, and speeding off.

Rob had then managed, after carefully negotiating the quiet suburban streets, to drive directly up the motorway, and finally arrive in London in the early hours. It had been necessary to put some fuel in the tank at an all-night petrol station, as he wanted to be certain that he could drive around until he could find a suitable place to park, and perhaps get some rest. But even after finding sanctuary in a Sainsbury's car park, he found it impossible to get to sleep, and had instead, downed more speed, and drank more whisky.

At daylight he had driven past his mum's estate, but felt apprehensive about stopping, and perhaps being recognised, and so had found a quiet street in which to leave the car. He had spent the rest of the day wandering round the west-end, stopping every now and then to top up his drug and alcohol intake. As evening fell, he had again picked up the car, and driven around, until it got dark enough that he felt safe to stop.

He had been fortunate in the respect that he had only been parked in sight of his mum's block for half an hour or so, when he saw Nazz enter the building. He was, however, unsure what to do next; he obviously wanted to see his mother, but did not, if possible, want to confront Nazz.

After waiting for a further hour he began to think that Nazz would now perhaps be there for the night, and decided it would probably be better to come back tomorrow. But just as he was about to drive off, a cab passed by where he was parked, and stopped outside his mother's block. Curious now, he decided to wait, and minutes later, he saw Nazz come striding out the main door, followed by a stocky looking youth. Both men entered the cab, which then made a u-turn, and came back toward where Rob was parked. Seeing this, he quickly slid down out of sight, and waited until the cab was well gone before stepping out of the car and making his way towards the flats.

Chapter 22 (5th Sunday)

Mickie reached over and checked the time on his phone: it was just after seven o'clock. He laid his head back on the pillow, and stared up at the ceiling. Recent events had caused him a sleepless night, and were still foremost in his mind: his daughter was going home tomorrow, he had managed to alienate both Laura and Billy, and as usual, his ex-wife was doing her best to wind him up. *Well done, Mickie,* he thought. *Fucked it up yet again.*

After what happened with Laura and Billy on Friday, he hadn't felt like talking to anyone. And even when dropping Mona off at Sadie's that evening, he had refused her offer of dinner, not savouring the prospect of again being the target for Sharon's hatchet tongue. He had stayed only long enough to give Mona a goodbye hug and say he couldn't wait to see her again tomorrow. He still wasn't sure why she couldn't have stayed with him one more night, but Sharon hadn't given a reason, and he wasn't in the mood to push for one; but at least he was grateful that he would be spending one more day alone with his daughter.

It had been his intention to go straight home, but instead his mood had taken him into the first Ealing pub he came across, and in which he sat, cocooned in solitary self-pity, until closing time.

The arrangement for Saturday had been that he would pick Mona up from Sharon at Queensway Station, and then he and

Mona would visit Buckingham Palace. When he met them outside the station, he could tell that Sharon knew immediately that he was hungover, and the look on her face had only increased his sense of guilt.

"Feelin a wee bit under the weather are we, Mickie?" she had said with a smirk. Mickie knew he probably deserved some stick, but did she have to say things like that in front of Mona. He pretended to ignore the comment, and picked the pensive little girl up in his arms, and hugged her.

"We're gonny have a great day, aren't we, darlin?" he had said, grinning through his hangover. Mona had responded with a smile, and a kiss on his cheek, which made Mickie's face crease with emotion.

"Ah'm meetin Margaret's sister, Sheila," Sharon had said. "We're goin shoppin, and then for something to eat, and then maybe a movie. So ah probably won't be there when you get back."

Mickie, took this as good news, as he'd had enough of feeling bad.

In the end, he and Mona spent a wonderful day together; the ease, with which they made each other laugh, had so brightened Mickie's spirits that he even managed to forget his troubles for a while. He had bought food for an impromptu picnic from a Marks & Spencers next to Green Park Station, and then they had crossed over and strolled down through St James's Park, and sat in the shade of a big oak tree, before going on to the Queen's house, as Mona like to refer to it.

To his surprise, Mickie had found the tour of the Palace more interesting than he would have imagined, perhaps because of Mona's enthusiasm and wonderment at the splendour of it all. Afterwards, It had been arranged that they would go back to Mrs. McIntyre's for dinner, and then Mona could say her goodbyes to Lucy and Sammie.

It was while they were having dinner, that Lucy had mentioned that Billy had called round earlier, looking for him. Mickie had responded with a brief, embarrassed smile, and said he would give him a call. He had begun to feel guilty about how he had left things with Billy and Mary, but was finding it hard to control his emotions at present.

After dinner, Mickie watched as his daughter hugged Lucy and Sammie goodbye; this affectionate farewell, however, had again made Mickie's emotions rise, as he knew it would soon be his turn to say goodbye.

Waking from his bittersweet reverie, Mickie groaned, stretched his arms in the air, and then reached out for his phone. Billy had left another couple of messages after calling round on Saturday, but receiving no response, he had obviously given up. Mickie decided it was time to stop being a fool, and return his calls, but then realising it was a bit too early to phone, he sent a text:

Hiya, Billy. I'm sorry about the other day; I know I behaved like a tosser. I'm leaving to see Mona in Ealing round about two o'clock today, as she goes home tomorrow. But maybe we could grab a pint before I go. We need to talk.

He placed the phone back on the table, and gazed out the window for a while, not thinking of anything in particular. He heard movement in the house, and considered getting up, but then, turned on his side, and closed his eyes. *Another couple of hours, and I might feel better.* He thought.

* * *

In the silence of the living room, Rob sat hunched over the table by the window. It had now been over forty-eight hours since he had slept. That, combined with the various stimulants he had been feeding into his system, had only exacerbated the horror of the situation he now found himself. He felt utterly desolate, and alone.

He had finished the whisky, and his stash of speed some hours ago, and was now slugging from what remained of the bottle of vodka that Shank had left in the kitchen. With a trembling hand, he drew a cigarette from the pack he had earlier found on the floor of his mother's bedroom. For a brief, pensive moment, he scanned the pack, almost as if it was some sort of strange heirloom, but then with a scowl he dropped it back on the table, and lit the cigarette.

The morning light streaming in the window, made his face appear ghost-like. He looked hollow-eyed, and white as the papers he now pulled from the nearly empty Rizla pack. He tipped the last of his grass from the plastic bag onto the table, and began to roll a spliff.

Last night, after he had seen Nazz and his accomplice leave in the cab, he had walked over to the block, and climbing up to the second floor landing, had let himself into the gloomy, unlit flat, closing the door behind him.

On entering, he had called out to his mother, but when no answer came, he had, with a mounting sense of foreboding, pushed open the door to her bedroom, and switched on the light. The sad, grotesque spectacle of her lifeless body, so stark in the glare of the single bare light bulb, had so paralysed him with shock that he had been unable even to cry, and could only stand transfixed, gazing like some perverted voyeur at the sad, pathetic figure that had once been his mother.

It was only after the reality of what he was actually looking at had sunk in, that a searing bitter anger had raged through him, and as the tears had begun to fall, he had collapsed in hopeless, heartbreaking despair. All the burning hatred that had festered in him for so long, resurfaced, and all he could think of was revenge. *These bastards have to pay for this,* he thought. *Somebody has to pay for this.*

He stubbed out his cigarette, and lit the misshapen, badly made spliff. The bitter weed, instantly made him cough, causing him to send a thick column of smoke out into the airless room.

The fact that he couldn't sit here forever, and would soon have to take some sort of action, had been slowly seeping through to his addled brain. But not surprisingly, he still couldn't seem to get his mind to function in any logical way. *What am I supposed to do? I can't just walk out,* he thought. *My mum has to be taken care of.* But even in his present state of mind, he was aware enough to know that this would inevitably involve the police.

The sudden, loud, harsh sound of Rap cut through his jumbled thoughts and made his whole body jerk in fright.

"Fuck!" he cried, and pulled his phone from his pocket.

When he didn't recognise the number, he immediately became paranoid, and stared blankly at the phone until the noise stopped. His mouth was dry, and he found it difficult to swallow. He took another gulp of vodka.

A moment later, his paranoia was further heightened, when he looked out the window, and saw a police car come to a stop outside the block. A squad car cruising this estate wasn't unheard of, it did in fact happen several times a day. But when Rob saw two officers get out of the car and walk straight towards the front door, he immediately knew where they were heading.

Panic seemed to clear his befuddled brain enough to startle him into action. He threw down the joint, and grabbing his rucksack from the floor, leapt up from the table. He stuffed the vodka bottle and the pack of cigarettes into the bag, and then hurried towards the front door. When passing the kitchen, however, he caught sight of a small, stained carving knife lying on the worktop, and something made him stop, pick up the blade, and slip it into the inside pocket of his jacket.

With his heart now banging hard against his chest, he was just about to open the front door when he suddenly realised there was no way out of the block without confronting the police. Fear froze him to the spot.

Unable to move or think, it seemed like everything was lost, until his eyes fell on the hall closet. Without wasting another second, he opened the door, stepped inside, and closed it behind him.

Aw, fuck, he thought *the front door.* It suddenly occurred to him that it would be easier, and save precious time, if the police could walk in unhindered. He quickly reached out from the closet, opened the front door, and pulled it slightly ajar, and then just had enough time to conceal himself again, before the police reached the flat. The front door being open, however, made them wary, and they hesitated before entering. But seconds later, Rob heard the creak of the door as it was slowly pushed open.

"Hello," cried one of the officers. "Anybody there?"

Rob held his breath as both officers then edged their way down the hallway. A moment later, he heard the same voice as before, cry out:

"Oh, Jesus, in here, Brian"

Rob then heard the other policeman, who must have been in the living room, walk through and join his colleague.

"Tch! What the fuck is wrong with these people?" said the second officer, without emotion.

Realising that both policemen were now in the bedroom, Rob grabbed his chance and pushed open the closet door. But to his horror, it came into loud contact with the front door, which had been left open. Alerted by the sound, one of the officers immediately appeared in the hall, and catching sight of the fleeing Rob, called out:

"Hey you, stop! Police, stop!"

With his heart pounding, Rob leapt out onto the landing, and pulling his hood over his head, ran full speed towards the stairwell. He flew down the stairs, and ran out the rear entrance of the block into the maze of back streets. He didn't have to look back to know the police were close behind, he could hear the thud of their boots on the ground. He felt sick, and didn't think he could keep up this pace for much longer; he had to find a way to lose them.

In desperation, he turned into a street that he knew would lead him in a u-turn to the front of his block, and was hoping upon hope that he could reach the Vauxhall before they caught up with him. *Why didn't you do that in the first place, ya wanker,* he couldn't help thinking.

He was burning up with sweat and fear, and his legs felt numb, like they were no longer his own. As he approached the car, he aimed the fob at the doors and pushed the button, and to his relief he heard them unlock. He scrambled into the driver's seat, and locking the doors behind him, started the engine.

He had somehow managed to put enough distance between him and the police to be able to drive off before they reached him, and glancing round he saw them standing in the road, somewhat bemused by the sight of him in a car. Seconds later, however, he again caught sight of them in the rear-view mirror, running towards the squad car. He knew they would be calling for back up, and giving the number and description of the Vauxhall.

Realising his only hope of escape was to lose them long enough to abandon the car, and disappear, he gunned the engine. But due to his wasted state, his initial control of the vehicle was erratic, and he zig-zagged all over the road. Fear and adrenalin, however, soon sobered him enough to overcome this. His face then became a blinkered, wide-eyed mask, and clinging desperately to the steering wheel, he aimed the car at what he hoped would be freedom.

* * *

"Yuh want anyting, darlin?" said Sammie, setting his old pork-pie hat at a jaunty angle on his head.

"Not right now, Sammie," said Lucy over her shoulder. "Mi goin down later to get some tings. Mi tink mi gonna make some ribs."

Sammie inadvertently licked his lips at this information.

"Mmmm," he said, grinning at the thought. "Well, mi suppose mi better get someting to wash them down."

Lucy, who had turned from rinsing some dishes at the sink, rolled her eyes, and smiled back at him.

"Well, don't be too long, mi want yuh to fix that cupboard door. Mi been wantin yuh to get to it all week, yuh know."

Sammie gave her a wry smile, and nodded his big head, and then lighting a freshly rolled cigarette, strolled out of the kitchen towards the front door.

Lucy dried her hands, and went over to open the back door to check the weather and let in some morning air. She had only got it halfway open, when the fleeting figure of Dizzy darted through her legs and went directly to his bowl.

"Oh, here yuh come now, Mr Midnight," she said looking down at the little cat. "What yuh been up to all this time, huh?"

Dizzy ignored her, and carried on eating. Lucy made a face, and kissed her teeth at his lack of respect, and then picking up her laundry basket, went into the yard to fetch her washing. She looked up at the sun struggling to peep through some dark clouds, and knew rain wasn't far away. It was darker still, when a few minutes later she made her way back to the kitchen with her full basket. She had just placed it on the table, when she heard the slow soft tread of Mickie's feet on the stairs.

"Mornin, Mrs McIntyre," he said, entering the kitchen, carrying his boots in his hand.

"Mornin?" she replied, looking over her glasses at the kitchen clock. She could tell by the look on his face that he wasn't in the best frame of mind.

"Yuh lookin rough, bwoy."

Mickie gave her a brief smile.

"Yuh want someting to eat? Breakfast already gone, but mi could fix yuh someting. Sammie just gone down to Jamal's to get some tobacco."

Mickie seemed to consider this a difficult question, as he took his time in answering. As Lucy continued to look at him, her face began to crease in a frown.

"Eh, maybe just some coffee, thanks," he said at last. "But first ah need to go down and get some cigarettes."

Yuh okay, bwoy?" Lucy said, taking clothes from the basket, and folding them onto the table.

Mickie tilted his head, and gave her another half-hearted little smile.

"Och, ye know. What can ah say? My daughter's goin back tomorrow, Laura's not speakin to me, and Billy thinks ah'm a fool. So, same old, same old, ah'm afraid."

"Billy is a good friend, yuh know. Mi hope yuh realise it."

"Oh, ah know, ah sent him a text earlier to apologise, so hopefully he'll come round shortly, and we can go for a couple of beers before ah go to Ealing."

Lucy didn't comment, but watched him go into the hall and sit on the stairs to pull on his boots. He clumsily threaded the laces through the holes, and then yanked the ends hard before tying them.

"Okay, Mrs. McIntyre ah won't be long."

He got as far as the door, but then turned, and frowning at her, rolled his eyes in frustration.

"Tch, ah've left my money in my jacket," he sighed, making for the stairs.

Lucy shook her head as she watched him plod slowly back upstairs to his room. She then continued to concentrate on folding her washing, but then something made her stop, and clutching one of Sammie's shirts to her breast, she turned and gazed out the window at the ever-darkening sky.

* * *

Sammie, engrossed in the racing section of the paper, was taking his time sauntering back up the street towards the house. He was unaware of the change in the weather, until a raindrop splashed onto the page, followed quickly by another. This instinctively made him lift his head with the intention of checking the sky. When he did, however, his eyes widened in disbelief, for standing a few feet in front of him was the disheveled figure of Rob.

Sammie was instantly alarmed by the wild glazed look in the boy's eyes, and the agitated way he kept swaying his head from side to side, while bouncing from one foot to the other. For a long minute, they stood in the rain staring at each other, until Sammie felt he should say something, anything, in an effort to diffuse the situation.

"Yuh okay bwoy? Yuh don't look so good."

"I aint yer fuckin boy," replied Rob, his voice cold, and raw with emotion.

Sammie stood motionless, frantically trying to think of what to do next. In his panic, his brain latched onto something that had been troubling him ever since he saw Patsy in the Bulldog. The sudden realisation of who she was, had shaken him, but he now decided he had no choice; it was time to take a desperate gamble.

"Okay, son, mi don't want no trouble, now. But mi got to tell yuh someting important, that mi tink yuh should know."

Rob eyed him suspiciously.

"Mi knew your daddy, son," said Sammie, with as much sincerity as he could muster. "He was my best friend, and his name was Harry McIntyre."

Rob thought he was hearing things, he looked at the big man with contempt, and then taking a step forward, snarled:

"Arry? Fuck off! My dad weren't called Arry. And I know for sure he would have fuck all to do wiv you."

Sammie gently laid down the bag of beer he had been holding, and offered his right hand as a sign of friendship.

"Believe me, son, it's true. Ask your momma. Mi knew her too, before yuh were born."

At this last statement, Rob's face twisted into a scowling mask of hate, and before Sammie knew what was happening, the boy had pulled the knife and slashed the blade across the old man's outstretched hand. Sammie gasped, dropped his paper, and clasping his wounded hand, instantly drew away from the boy. Standing there in shocked disbelief, he suddenly became aware of Mickie pounding up the street behind Rob, yelling:

"Hey, you! What the fuck are ye doin?"

On seeing Sammie's eyes widen, and someone cry out, Rob instinctively spun round, and as Sammie looked on horror-struck, Mickie ran straight into the blade Rob was still holding in his hand.

Rob stepped back, and watched, stunned as Mickie, his face a mask of shock and surprise, looked down at the blood beginning to seep through his shirt.

As Rob continued to watch, Mickie put both his hands over the wound in a feeble attempt to stem the flow. But then, almost in slow motion, he dropped to his knees and fell into the foetal position on the sodden street.

Still holding the blooded blade, Rob looked down open-mouthed at the fallen figure, and then, turning to Sammie with the same glazed look, he dropped the knife as if it had suddenly become red hot. Sammie could see the terror in the boy's eyes at the realisation of what had just happened.

It was then, out of nowhere it seemed to Sammie, that Billy suddenly leapt from behind him and grabbed Rob by the throat. The bewildered boy made no attempt to defend himself as Billy savagely struck the boy repeatedly in the face. Under this sustained assault, it didn't take long before Rob's knees began to buckle, only then did Billy release his grip, and let him fall sobbing onto the sodden street.

The minute Mickie had left, Lucy, suddenly feeling a sense of foreboding, had walked through to the sitting room, and looked out the window.

On seeing Mickie start to run, she had immediately followed him onto the street, and now stood stunned at the sight she was witnessing. Billy was kneeling over the fallen Mickie, talking into his phone; Sammie was sitting on the wall with his head down, cradling his bleeding hand inside his old hat. She took in the other figure lying in the street, but did not yet register it as Rob. She continued to stand in the rain, as if frozen to the spot, until the wail of a siren seemed to jolt her into action, and she then ran towards the tragic scene.

A squad car squealed to a halt just as Lucy reached the group. The two policemen, who leapt from the car, were the same officers who had been pursuing Rob earlier, and still being in the vicinity, were the first to arrive, and immediately recognised the sobbing figure on the wet street from his clothing.

"What's been occurring here, then?" said the taller of the two policemen, addressing no one in particular. Billy, who was still kneeling over Mickie, ignored him, and the officer, spotting the blooded knife lying on the pavement, was obliged to speak again:

"I'll have to ask you to step away, sir."

Billy's only movement was to slowly turn and give the officer a hard look.

"This is my friend, and this fucker," said Billy, motioning with his chin to the still sobbing figure of Rob, "has just stabbed him."

"I sympathise, sir, but I still must ask you to step away until we get this cleared up."

Billy stood up, but continued to look hard at the policeman. The officer held his gaze, and then, noting Billy was holding a phone, he asked:

"Were you the one who made the call?"

"Aye,"

The second officer, who had also caught sight of the knife, walked over and stood guard over it.

"I assume you've also called an ambulance?" continued the first policeman.

"Oh, what do you think?" replied Billy, trying hard to keep his emotions in check.

"Look, sir, I'm only trying to do my job, and I need to ask these questions. The Serious Crime Squad, and paramedics will be here shortly, but until then . . . "

His voice was suddenly drowned out by the deafening howl of sirens again filling the air, and seconds later, a large dark blue car drew up at the kerb, followed by an ambulance.

Until now, Lucy had been standing, silent and wide-eyed, still trying to make sense of the horror of the scene before her. With the arrival of the ambulance, however, she suddenly seemed to be struck by the reality of the situation, and started wailing, and flapping her hands the air.

"Oh God, oh, God, what appenin? Mi got to take this bwoy home."

She then got down on her knees on the wet pavement, and started stroking Mickie's head. On seeing this, one of the paramedics approached and gently tried to ease her away from Mickie, but she strongly resisted, until she heard Billy's voice.

"Come on, Mrs McIntyre," he said softly. "We need to let these people do their job."

Billy removed his jacket and placed it over Lucy's shoulders, and then taking her gently by the arm, guided her over and sat her on the wall next to Sammie.

Billy then watched grim-faced, as a police photographer started rapidly taking shots all over the crime scene. To Billy, however, it seemed that their priorities were all wrong, and the paramedics, who were standing by, were taking too long to attend to Mickie.

"Why don't ye fuckin help him, he could be bleedin to death, lyin there."

One of the recently arrived Serious Crime Squad officers approached Billy.

"I'm sorry, sir, but we do have to follow certain procedures."

Billy ignored him, and continued watching as the photographer left the scene and the paramedics sprung into action. They immediately checked Mickie's air passages weren't blocked, and he could breath, checked there was a pulse, and then cut open Mickie's shirt and put a pressure dressing on the wound. Another member of the team went over to attend to Sammie; she examined the cut, and then cleaning the wound, applied a dressing.

Before Billy knew what was happening, the ambulance crew had strapped Mickie onto a gurney, placed a quilted cover over him, and scooped him up into the ambulance. The female paramedic, who had attended to Sammie, then helped both him and the distraught Lucy on board. The wailing ambulance then sped away leaving Billy gazing after it, with a curious beaten look on his face.

The now handcuffed Rob, who's face was blooded and badly bruised, stood with his head down, next to the squad car. The taller of the two officers who had first arrived on the scene, held him firmly by the arm, while reading him his rights. Tears still shone in the beaten boys eyes.

On a command from one of the detectives, the policeman ushered the boy into the back of the car, and then walking round, opened the other door, and joined him in the adjacent seat. His colleague, holding the now bagged knife, had a few words with one of the Crime Squad officers, and then he too walked over, and slipping into the drivers seat, started the engine.

As Billy watched the squad car leave the scene, he felt utterly weak and confused. The colour began to drain from his face, as he looked down at the blood on the pavement, which the rain was now washing in rivulets into the gutter. He realised that soon there would be no sign that Mickie was ever there.

"I'm going to have to ask you to accompany us down the station, sir," said one of the detectives, placing a hand on Billy's arm. "We need to ask you a few questions."

Billy didn't even look up, but just dumbly nodded his head.

Chapter 23

The A&E waiting area, after being hectic and noisy when Lucy and Sammie first arrived, is for the moment relatively quiet. Lucy sitting alone at the end of a row of seats at the back of the room, looks weary and forlorn. Sammie after a wait of nearly three hours had finally been called to the treatment room to have his wounded hand stitched and dressed. Lucy, however, had wanted to remain in the waiting area, in case there was news of Mickie.

Earlier, on arriving at the hospital, they had watched as Mickie was taken from the ambulance, and wheeled at speed through the already open doors into the hospital. The girl paramedic, who had treated Sammie's hand, had then helped them both from the ambulance, and seeing the look on their faces as they watched Mickie disappear, had tried to ease their distress by explaining that he was being taken to the 'Trauma' area, where he would immediately receive vital, expert care.

She had then shown them to the A&E reception desk, where, after explaining to the nurse the cause of Sammie's injury, and then making sure they both understood the procedure, she had said her goodbye's. The nurse had then went on to ask Sammie for the requisite personal details she needed to complete the form, after which, they were asked to take a seat.

Once seated, however, they had fallen into a lingering ominous silence. Their reluctance to comment being an obvious consequence of the terrible situation in which they now found themselves. It was impossible for them to express the dread they were both feeling.

In her isolation, Lucy now sat with her head down, gazing at the floor, while nervously twisting her wedding ring back and forth on her finger. Hospitals held only bad memories for her. She had spent too many long, sad hours, just like this, while Harry had had undergone intensive treatment for the ever worsening cancer that had eventually taken his life.

Troubling thoughts ran through her mind, and she found herself tortured by unanswerable questions: would Mickie still be lying seriously wounded if she'd had the sense to contact the police the minute Rob had started stalking the house? She knew that thinking like this was a useless, bitter exercise, but she still felt guilty.

The sudden shrill sound of the phone ringing at the reception desk, shook her from her morbid thoughts, and made her look up. She had been instinctively doing this every time it rang, fearing she would be summoned to reception in order to be informed of the one thing she couldn't bring herself to consider.

But, yet again the summons never came, and she glanced around the room searching for some cheer; however, most of the remaining people were sitting like her, with their heads down, lost in their own thoughts.

A few minutes later, the peace, such as it was, was suddenly interrupted by the noisy arrival of two black youths wearing the seemingly obligatory gang uniform of gleaming white trainers, low-slung jeans, and hooded tops. Lucy watched with growing irritation, as they strode up to the reception desk, and rudely demanded immediate attention.

One of them, who in Lucy's estimation, could only have been in his early teens, had obviously been in a fight: his face was cut and bruised, but still he strutted into the room in an ignorant, arrogant way.

"Look, just calm down," said the nurse, from behind the desk. "You'll be seen as soon as possible. But in the meantime, you'll have to take a seat and wait like everyone else; that is, after you've given me your details."

At this, they became even more agitated, loudly sucking their teeth, and sneering at the nurse.

"We aint waitin in no queue, bitch," bawled the uninjured youth, inches from the woman's face.

Before the nurse could respond, Lucy was out of her seat, and striding towards the desk in a blind rage, her fury rising with every step.

"Hey, fool," she yelled, on reaching the surprised youths. "Why yuh come in here causin trouble? Don't yuh tink we got enough trouble? Yuh tink we here for fun, bwoy?"

The two boys stood dumbstruck. Lucy was now seriously in their faces, and they could see she wasn't in the least intimidated by their arrogance.

"What give yuh the right to come in here demandin shit? Mi seen more misery in mi life than yuh'll ever know. Right now, because of some fool like you, mi waitin to hear if someone mi care about is gonna die, and yuh . . . "

Lucy couldn't finish; tears shone in her eyes. The realisation of what she had just said, had struck her dumb; she hadn't wanted to think of Mickie that way.

The two youths now stood silent, their heads bowed with shame. They both had grandmothers Lucy's age, and that somehow had struck home.

The nurse, who in the meantime had called security, stood up and came from behind the desk to comfort Lucy, who still stood, unyielding staring at the youths, her fists clenched in anger.

"It's okay, it's okay," said the nurse, in a soothing tone.

She had just put her arm around the still rigid Lucy, when Sammie appeared out of the treatment room, and sensing immediately that something was wrong, he made straight for the group.

"What happenin here?" He demanded, glaring at the two boys.

On hearing his voice, Lucy turned, and feeling her strength finally weaken, fell sobbing into his arms.

* * *

Billy's anxiety over Mickie's condition, compounded by the fact that he didn't know, if or when he would get to the hospital, had made the police procedure seem achingly slow.

On his arrival at the station, he was asked his name, address, and date of birth, all of which were duly noted on his charge sheet. He was then asked to hand over all personal items: his mobile phone, wallet, watch, belt, etc. These he was told would be held secure until his release. After these initial formalities, he had then been escorted to one of the cells, to be held there until such times, as the detectives felt ready to interview him.

This cell-time in particular, had felt like an eternity, for without the aid of a watch or phone, he had no means of telling how fast or slow time was passing.

On finally being released from the cell, his first thought had been to ask if there had been any news from the hospital on Mickie's condition. But to his mounting frustration his question was met with blank faces, and shaking heads.

After being cautioned, he had then been taken into an interview room where he had been endlessly questioned, mostly about his relationship to the other people at the crime scene.

The officers seemed particularly interested to know if he had been acquainted with Rob's mother, whom one detective had bluntly informed him had died of a drug overdose the previous evening, and that Rob had been present at the scene. On hearing this news, Billy thought it best to deny he had ever seen Patsy. He did, however, knowing that Lucy and Sammie would eventually be questioned, relate at length how Sammie had initially got on the wrong side of Rob, who as a result, had begun to harass them by stalking Lucy's house.

At one point, because the questions kept being repeated, and seemed never-ending, Billy had struggled to stop his frustration from spilling over into anger. He had, however, been aware enough to realise that this would have only further delayed any hope of a quick release. With this aim in mind, he had made an effort to placate his interrogators, and endeavoured to answer even repeated questions with patience and clarity; Billy knew this game well, it wasn't the first time he had been questioned by the police.

His patience had eventually paid off; they seemed to conclude, that although no innocent bystander, his actions had been to a certain extent justified, in that he had prevented further harm being inflicted on the others at the scene. He was at last released on conditional bail on the understanding that he would report to the station when requested.

On receiving back his phone, Billy had immediately called a cab to take him to the St Charles hospital, where he was told Mickie had been taken. His second call wasn't so easy.

"Hello, Mary . . . Aye ah know yer just about to start yer shift . . . Look . . . Mary, gonny just listen? Ah don't know how to say this any other way than just to say it: Mickie's been stabbed . . . Ah don't know, Mary . . . Darlin, ah need ye to stay calm and help me here, as ah don't have time to go into details, but it happened about, oh, ah don't know, half eleven, twelve . . . Mary, will ye just fuckin listen to me. Mickie was taken to St Charles, along with Mrs McIntyre and Sammie . . . Aye, ah would think they would still be in A&E. If ye could find out how Mickie's doin, and then check on Mrs . . . Oh, here's my cab, ah have to go. Look, Sammie will fill ye in on what happened, and ah'll be there shortly."

* * *

Owing to heavy traffic, Billy's taxi journey had been frustratingly slow, and this on top of everything else had only further heightened his anxiety. As he pushed open the main door of St Charles, he was trying his best to maintain control over his emotions, but it had been a long day, and it wasn't over yet.

The A&E waiting area had again become so crowded, that Billy had to scan the sea of faces two or three times before he caught sight of Mary and Lucy sitting near the back of the room. As he walked over to join them, Mary happened to turn, and on seeing him, her face instantly mirrored all the worry and fear she had been feelin since hearing the tragic details from Sammie.

"Oh, Billy, darlin," she said, rising to embrace him. "Are ye all right?"

"Aye, ah'm fine, ah'm fine, " Billy said almost curtly, and then realising this, he added:

'Och, Mary, ah'm sorry. Ah'm just a wee bit on edge."

Mary shook her head, and gave him a tender look.

"Oh, Billy, what a thing to happen."

With a subtle sideways glance, she then drew Billy's attention to Lucy, who sat slumped in her seat with her head down, looking at the floor.

"Are you okay, Mrs McIntyre?" asked Billy.

Lucy didn't seem to hear the question, and so Billy looked enquiringly at Mary.

"Where's Sammie?"

"He's just gone to get some coffee."

Billy acknowledged this with a barely visible nod of his head. He was almost afraid to ask the next question:

"So, what's happenin with Mickie?"

He had addressed the question to Mary, but kept his eyes on Lucy, who again didn't look up or acknowledge that he was even there. Billy was starting to feel this was a bad sign. He again looked at Mary, who frowned and seemed reluctant to answer.

"It's difficult to say right at this minute, Billy," she said, looking ill at ease. "They're still . . . "

To Mary's obvious relief, Sammie's voice cut her off mid-sentence:

"Billy man. How yuh doin, yuh okay?"

Billy turned to greet the old man, and was startled to see how completely worn out he looked. He was standing with his shoulders hunched, trying to hold on to two flimsy plastic containers of coffee, one of which had stained the dressing on his injured hand.

"Can mi get yuh a drink, son?" he said, attempting a smile. Billy felt for the big man; it was so obvious he was trying to stay strong for Lucy, but Billy could see the whole ordeal had taken a toll on him. Billy shook his head.

"Naw, ah'm all right, Sammie. You sit down and have yer coffee. Ah'm just gonny have wee word with Mary."

He then took Mary by the arm, and led her out of earshot of the old couple.

"What the fuck is happenin, Mary?" Ah'm goin out of my mind here."

"I know, Billy, I'm sorry," she said, looking him straight in the eye. "But I didn't want to upset Mrs McIntyre anymore than she obviously already is. She blames herself for all this."

Billy sighed, and shot a quick glance at Lucy.

"Well, ah'm sorry to hear that, but ah still need to know. What the fuck is happenin with Mickie?"

"It's serious, Billy," Mary said, still holding Billy's gaze. "If an abdominal artery was severed, there may be internal bleeding. As far as I can tell they're still operating, and I'm afraid that's all I know right now. I'm sorry."

Sorrow clouded Billy's face. Mary could see in his eyes that his worst fears were in danger of being realised. He let out an audible sigh, and his head suddenly dropped to his chest.

"Look, Billy," continued Mary, almost sternly. "These doctors are dedicated people and will do everything they can to help Mickie. I don't want you giving up."

Billy didn't answer, but kept his head down. Mary quickly became aware that what her husband needed was a sense of purpose. She knew he was a strong man, but she also knew he was at his strongest when being relied upon by someone in need.

"Billy, I know this whole thing is like a nightmare, particularly for you, but you can see how busy we are, and if I don't get back to my own duties, I'll be in trouble. Lucy and Sammie are both exhausted, and emotionally vulnerable, especially Lucy, so you have to be strong for them. I tried to persuade them to go home for while, and get some rest, but Lucy won't have it. I thought maybe you could try and make her see it's for the best."

Billy looked up, and breathed a resigned sigh.

"Yer right darlin. You go. Ah'll be fine."

Mary put her hand in her uniform pocket, and her face creased in a frown.

"What?"

"Oh, Billy, I almost forgot. I thought you would want to take care of this," said Mary, holding out Mickie's mobile phone. "But I'm not so sure now."

Billy looked down at the phone; small traces of blood were visible on some of the keys.

"Ah have to phone Sharon," Billy muttered this so softly that Mary didn't quite catch what he said.

"I'm sorry, darlin?"

"Sharon, ah have to phone Sharon," he again said it so quietly, it was almost as if he didn't want it to be true.

"Aw, fuck. What is she gonny say to Mona?" he added, louder this time, his face almost crumpling in despair.

"Oh, Billy," said Mary, holding back her own tears. "You don't have to deal with this, there are trained people here who's job it is to contact relatives."

"Naw," said Billy, swallowing hard. "Ah have to do this."

He took the phone from Mary's hand, and slipped it into his pocket.

Mary hugged him, and then hurried away without looking back; Billy watched her until she disappeared through the swing doors into another ward. He took a deep breath, puffed up his cheeks, and let the air out slowly, and then turned his attention back to the old couple. He saw they were still sitting in silence, each in their own world, but as he approached, Sammie got up to meet him.

"Mi need a word, Billy," he said, guiding Billy away from Lucy's hearing.

"What's up?" Billy sensed the old man's anxiety.

Sammie appeared to look at something in the distance, and then sighed deeply.

"That bwoy, he's Harry's son," he said, still not looking at Billy.

"Boy? What boy?"asked Billy, and then his eyes widened in disbelief.

"Wait a minute here. Are you trying to tell me that scumbag is Harry's son?"

The old man looked into Billy eyes, and then slowly nodded his head.

"Fuckin hell," said Billy raising his eyes to the ceiling. "This just gets worse and worse."

In his confusion, Billy couldn't think straight, and for a few seconds he seemed dumbstruck, but then something occurred to him, and he stared hard at Sammie.

"How long have ye known about this?" he asked, his voice raw with ill concealed anger.

Sammie looked sheepish, then staring down at the floor, tried to explain:

"The day before mi come to see you at the garage, when mi went to the Bulldog. It was then that mi recognised the junkie woman, and realised who she was. Mi didn't tell you then because mi didn't know what to do. Mi didn't want Lucy to get hurt, and mi just hoped the bwoy had gone for good."

At this, Billy's anger receded somewhat, and he stood lost in thought for a moment.

"Does he know about this?"

"He does now," said Sammie, still not looking up. "Mi made the mistake of tellin him today on the street. That's why he cut me."

"And Lucy doesn't know?"

Sammie looked as if he had been slapped.

"No, man," he said, staring at Billy in alarm. "But mi so vexed at myself, because it bound to come out now, and mi don't know if Lucy can take anymore."

Billy glanced over to where Lucy sat, and then turned back to Sammie.

"Sammie, whatever happens, happens, and there's nothing we can do to stop it now. All ye can do is be there for her, because who the fuck knows how Rob reacted to being questioned."

Billy waited a heartbeat, and then added:

"There's something else, Sammie. While ah was at the station, they told me that Rob's mother died yesterday from an overdose, and it looks like he was the one who found her."

Sammie shook his big head, and gave a joyless grunt of a laugh.

"Oh man! No wonder he cut me. When mi said mi knew his mother, he must have thought mi was just another black man that mess her up."

"It's not your fault he's fucked up, Sammie."

Billy let this statement hang in the air for a moment, but when there was no reaction from Sammie, he put a comforting hand on the old man's arm.

"Look, Sammie, ye didn't do anything wrong, so stop blamin yerself."

The old man's face mirrored his conflicting emotions; he looked over to where Lucy sat and let out a mournful sigh.

"Go on, Sammie, you go back and look after Mrs McIntyre. Ah need to make a phone call."

Billy watched as the big man walked over, sat down next to Lucy, and put his arm around her shoulder; Billy then turned away, and taking Mickie's phone from his pocket, searched for Sharon's number.

"Ah fuckin hate this," he said, loud enough to attract the stare of one of the two black youths sitting nearby; but when Billy glared hard back at him, he quickly turned away. Billy then slipped the phone back in his pocket, and went to find a quiet place to make his call.

* * *

It was shortly after midnight when Billy saw the nurse enter the A&E waiting room. He didn't know why, but even before she spoke to her colleague at the desk, he knew she had come looking for them.

For the last few hours, he and Sharon had been resigned to sitting seats apart in awkward silence; the only relief from which was when Sharon went outside for a cigarette, and in the last hour or so, it seemed to Billy that these excursions had become even more frequent.

His earlier call to her had clearly been a tender and difficult one for him to make, and he couldn't stop thinking of Mona the whole time. He had, however, been as sensitive and compassionate as it's possible to be when relaying such shocking news. But much to Sharon's irritation, he had insisted she be in a different room from Mona, before he would say why he was calling.

Of all people, Billy was the last person from whom Sharon expected to receive a call. Having earlier left Mickie an irate message, she had initially jumped to the conclusion that he was phoning on behalf of her ex-husband, in order to give some lame excuse as to why he hadn't already arrived in Ealing. Her sarcasm, however, had soon turned to genuine grief when she realised the reality of what Billy was saying.

After receiving the call, she had arrived at the hospital within the hour, and in that short time, her distress had somehow festered into raging anger, and the sole target of her fury, was Billy. On arriving in the A&E waiting room, it had taken her some minutes to locate him in the busy throng. But when she caught sight of him sitting with Lucy and Sammie, she had wasted no time in marching over to lay bare her rage in a loud torrent of abuse:

"Ah blame you for this, Billy Dunn; you've always been a dodgy wee wanker. Why could ye not mind yer own business, and stop fillin Mickie's head with stupid ideas about London. He was perfectly happy in Glasgow, until you stuck yer neb in . . . "

Billy was initially taken aback, but managed to keep his temper long enough to interrupt her flow by taking her firmly by the arm and marching her, struggling and belligerent, to the back of the room.

"Listen, you," he said, inches from her face. "Ah don't have to take this shite, especially from you. You've been tormentin that man for a fuckin long time now, and you've been cruel enough to use his daughter to do it. Now ah've been through hell today, and it's not over yet, so if yer not here to give support, then fuck off."

Sharon had been speechless with fury, and could only stand glaring back at Billy, her face a strained mask of hatred and confusion. This however, had begun to crumble into grief the longer she looked into Billy's hard unblinking stare. In the end she'd had to look away, and then brushing past him, had headed for the exit.

It was shortly after this confrontation, that Lucy had finally been persuaded, that if she didn't allow Sammie to take her home for some rest, she was going to make herself ill. It hadn't been an easy task, as she had become stubbornly convinced that she had to be there for Mickie, and if she left, she would be abandoning all hope.

The deciding factor had been when Billy, who had been walking back to join them, saw Lucy rush past him with her hands over her mouth. An anxious Sammie had explained that she had suddenly felt nauseous, like she was going to throw up, and was making a dash to the toilet.

She had remained in there long enough to cause concern, and so Billy had requested help from a passing nurse. The nurse had then entered the toilet and found Lucy in a near faint, slumped over a sink into which she had obviously been sick. On learning of Lucy's condition, Billy hadn't wasted anymore time, and had immediately called a cab. After the nurse had attended to Lucy, Billy had then helped Sammie to escort the still weak Lucy to the front entrance, and safely into the taxi.

He had just been about to enter back through the main door, when he saw Sharon standing a few feet away in the semi-darkness, smoking a cigarette. Much as it pained him to do so, he felt he should, under the circumstances, try and make some sort of compromise with her, and so, taking a deep breath, he had walked over to where she stood.

"Look, Sharon, we both know we're never gonny be friends, but don't ye think we should make an effort to be a united front for Mickie. Ah know yer hurtin and want to lash out, but ah'm too tired and troubled to stomach any more of this bitterness. Why don't ye come back inside, ah'll get us some coffee, and we can at least try and be civil with each other."

Sharon hadn't replied, but had simply dropped her cigarette butt at her feet, and then proceeded to grind it into the pavement with her shoe, all the while, scowling at Billy. She had then turned, and strode off through the main entrance, leaving Billy shaking his head at her arrogant stupidity. Billy followed her back into A&E, and had just taken a seat when he heard a nurse call his name.

"Mr Dunn?"

Billy saw the nurse coming, and felt himself tense up.

"Yeah, that's me," he said, rising from his seat.

"Mr Dunn, could you follow me please, Dr Singh would like a word with you."

Sharon saw Billy follow the nurse through the waiting room door, and the sight froze her to the spot; in that instant she imagined the worse.

Chapter 24 (6th Monday)

It was still dark when Laura finally gave up, and opened her eyes. For more than an hour, she had been trying in vain to get back to sleep after thirst had driven her to leave her bed in order to fetch a glass of water.

On returning to bed, she had then found it difficult to stop her thoughts from straying into that troubling zone, when, especially at night, lying alone in the dark, your worries seem amplified and insurmountable. Turning on her side, she curled into the foetal position, and lay staring up at the fading moon through half-closed eyes, and tried not to think of Mickie.

Last night, shortly after nine, she had got back from another long day the studio. Her intention had been to put everything out of her mind for the rest of the evening, and relax with a couple of glasses of wine, but for some reason she couldn't settle. Her quandary was, that even though the job, at least for the moment, was going well and was now ahead of schedule, it gave her no satisfaction, as she still felt bad about Mickie.

She had entered her flat, and then without bothering to switch on the light, had walked through to the dark living room. She had sat there, in the dim light of the street lamps, considering whether or not to call Mickie, but then reasoning he would be with his ex-wife and daughter had decided against it. The rest of the evening was spent sipping her way through a whole bottle of wine, while gazing at the television; but if questioned about what she had viewed, she would have had no answers.

The moon had now almost faded to nothing, and she decided she might as well get up and make some tea. *Chamomile,* she thought: *That might do the trick.* But she wasn't overly confident. While waiting for the kettle to boil, she looked out the kitchen window at the dawn breaking over the rooftops opposite. Catching her reflection in the glass, she thought she looked tired and sad. She turned away; it seemed she couldn't escape this feeling of despair.

* * *

Tears clouded Mary's vision, as she stood in the dim light of the still curtained living room gazing down at the unkempt figure asleep on the couch. Billy lay on his side with his arms crossed over his face. Scattered across the coffee table, were various crushed beer cans, and a bottle of whisky, more than a third of which had been consumed.

At the hospital earlier that morning, it had been getting on for 2am, before a colleague had managed to find her and tell her they had finished operating on Mickie, and that his condition was stable. It was a term she knew well, but hoping for the best, she had then rushed immediately to the A&E waiting area to tell Billy, but he was nowhere to be seen. She had then called his mobile number, but it rang out and went to voice-mail, and so she had left a message asking him to call her, but he never did.

For the rest of her shift time seemed to stand still, and she had trouble concentrating on the simplest task. And even when her shift eventually ended, she had been torn with heartbreaking anxiety all the way home.

She now took a deep breath, slowly released it, and then taking a tissue from the pocket of her uniform, wiped her eyes. The air in the room was warm and heavy with alcohol and body-odour. Without drawing the curtains fully back, she slid open the windows, and felt the morning air flow into the room. She glanced back to check on Billy, and then removing her jacket, she placed that and her bag on a chair, and went into the kitchen.

Coffee, that's what we need. She used this simple thought to try and block out her overwhelming sadness. She busied herself filling the kettle, and then after flicking the switch, spooned sugar and coffee into two cups. She had, however, to wipe her eyes again, before fetching the boiling kettle, and preparing the coffee.

On returning to the living room with the tray, she saw that Billy had moved, and now lay on his back. She managed to place the tray on the end of the table, and then picking an off-licence bag from the floor, started to clear away the empty cans.

Billy jerked awake with a groan, removed his arm from his face and opened his eyes, but then instantly shut them again.

"Oh, Mary," his voice sounded like it was coming from far away. "Ah feel like shite."

It was on the tip of her tongue to say: "I wonder why?" But she thought better of it, and simply said:

"I know, darlin."

She took the bag of empty cans, and what was left of the whisky into the kitchen, and when she returned Billy was sitting up, but he looked decidedly bleary.

"Here drink your coffee," she said, placing the cup in front of him.

He put the cup to his lips and took a sip, and his face twisted into a frown.

"Aw man, what's goin on with my taste buds; it feels like somethin shit in my mouth."

Mary smiled a weak tight-lipped smile, and then fetching her cigarettes from her bag, lit one, and sat down opposite Billy. She had no idea what to say; in her profession, she had to deal with situations like this everyday, but this was different, this was too close. Billy tried another sip of coffee, but then placed the cup back on the table, and gazed out the window. They both remained silent for a time, lost in thought until Mary felt she should a least try and give Billy some hope.

"They've done all they could for Mickie, and his condition is stable. I know that's a relatively obscure term, but their hopeful; he's a strong boy…"

She couldn't finish; she sighed, looked down at her hands, and then took a long pull from her cigarette.

Without turning his gaze from the window, Billy sighed deeply and said:

"Ah need to tell Laura. But ah can't do it with a phone call; that would just feel too cold."

Mary's heart went out to him, and she felt the tears well up again. Since this whole tragic mess had happened, he had been taking the weight of it all on his shoulders. She knew it was his nature to make sure everybody else was taken care of, but she also knew that right now, he must be feeling so bad, and she felt guilty for struggling to think of anything to say to ease his hurt.

"Do ye want me to come with ye?"

Billy turned and gave her a wan smile.

"Naw, it's alright, ah think ah'll be able to handle it better on my own. But it's gonny be strange, havin never even met the girl."

He turned away and again gazed out the window.

"Martin & McLean," he said, almost to himself.

"What?" asked Mary, dabbing her eyes with a fresh tissue.

"Martin &McLean, that's where she works; ah better find out where it is."

"I'll do that after we've had our coffee. But do ye not think ye should have a wee rest first?"

"Naw, ah need to get this done," Billy replied almost sternly. "It feels really weird that she doesn't even know yet."

He rose suddenly, and went into the kitchen. Returning with the whisky bottle, he poured a generous shot into his coffee, and then offered the same to Mary, who accepted with a single nod of her head.

When ah've had this and a shower, ah'll feel better," said Billy.

Mary inhaled the last of her cigarette, stubbed it in the ashtray, and then looked tenderly at Billy.

"What about Sharon?" she said, softly. "Her and Mona were supposed to be goin home today."

At the mention of Mickie's daughter, Mary saw a grimace of pain pass over Billy face. He then looked at the floor, and shook his head.

"Ah've no idea. She seems to blame me for this. She really laid into me when she arrived at the hospital, and then refused to talk to me for the rest of the time we were there. The last ah saw of her was when ah came out the doctor's office after being told about Mickie. She must have guessed it was serious by the look on my face, because she barged past me without sayin a word, and went straight in to see the doctor. Ah'd had it by then, and ah just wanted to get out of there."

Mary's heart sank, as she saw Billy's face crease in anguish, and tears fill his eyes. He covered his face with his hands.

"Oh, Mary, what a mess, what a fuckin mess."

* * *

It may have been Billy's unconsciously gruff manner, or his grave, hung-over appearance that caused concern, but for some reason the receptionist at Martin & McLean, seemed reluctant to give Billy information about Laura. She claimed it was a policy of the firm not to divulge personal details to strangers unless in certain significant circumstances.

This sounded like bullshit to Billy, and he continued to insist that his request to see Laura was important. His quandary, however, was that he didn't want to reveal the reason for his visit, unless it was to Laura herself.

In the end, something in his eyes must have convinced the girl that he was genuine, for she held up her hand to stop him midflow.

"Okay, Mr Dunn, I'll see what I can do."

As she had done with Mickie, she then made a call to John, who luckily remembered he had heard Laura speak of Mickie's friend, Billy.

A few minutes later, John came tripping down the stairs, and with some trepidation, introduced himself to the stocky, tough looking man sitting in reception.

"Hi, my name is John Light, can I help?"

"Ah have to speak to Laura Taylor," said Billy. "It's very important."

"Oh, well I'm afraid she's not here at the moment."

Billy gave John a hard stare; he was becoming increasingly irritated that for some stupid reason, he was being prevented from seeing Laura. However, he managed to hold his anger in check, and under the circumstances, decided he had no choice but to tell John the reason for his visit.

Now the moment had come, however, he found it hard to speak the words. All the way there he had been steeling himself to say them to Laura. But in the end he knew there was no way past this, other than to say it:

"Mickie got stabbed yesterday."

A stupid look came over John's face, and he looked at Billy as if he had mis-heard what he had said.

"What?"

"Mickie got stabbed yesterday. He's in intensive care."

The reality of Billy's blunt statement took a minute to register in John's face, but then he let out a sudden involuntary gasp, and buried his face in his hands.

"Oh, my God, poor Mickie," he said through his hands. "Oh, God, this is so awful."

Billy swallowed hard and looked over at the receptionist, but luckily, she had her head down and was talking on the phone.

After a minute, John withdrew his hands, and looked at Billy, who could see the glint of tears in his eyes.

"I'm so sorry about your friend," he said quietly, and then all in a rush: "I only met him a couple of times, but he seemed like a lovely guy. Oh, God, I can't bear it. How is Laura going to deal with this, especially as they recently had a bit of a falling out? I know they had only known each other a short time, but I could tell immediately that he was something special to her; she talked about him all the time."

Billy nodded his head.

"It was the same with Mickie. That's why ah felt ah had to come and tell Laura in person; ah'm sure she wouldn't want to hear something like this over the phone."

"Oh God, no," replied John.

They sat in silence, until Billy was compelled to ask, yet again:

Can ah see Laura now?"

"What/" said John, still deep in thought.

"Laura?" Billy repeated. "Ah have to speak to Laura now."

"Oh God, I'm sorry, of course, but as I said, she's not here, she's in the studio, on a shoot."

Billy let out an audible sigh of frustration.

"Aw ah'm sorry, but couldn't that bitch have told me that when ah first arrived, instead of putting me through all this?"

John looked slightly taken aback by Billy's brusque manner, but he also now understood how hard this must be for him.

"I'm so sorry, I do apologise, but she obviously had no idea who you were or why you were here, and was only trying to do her job. But I can assure you she will be devastated when she finds out."

Billy again sighed, and said:

"Where can ah find Laura?"

* * *

Billy came out of Park Royal underground station, turned right onto Western Avenue, and then followed the directions to Black

Island Studios that John had asked the receptionist to print out for him.

Situated in a west London trading estate, Black Island was central London's largest film and television studio complex, and was comprised of six stages; Laura was apparently working on number three stage.

It took him a few minutes to find the actual studio complex, but as he approached the main building, Billy saw there were people standing around in small groups outside the large open shutter door that seemed to be the main entrance to the stages. He guessed it must be lunchtime, and glancing at his watch, saw it had just gone one-thirty.

A sloping driveway led up from the entrance to the various stages, and he could see by a large number stencilled onto the door, that stage three was situated in the right hand corner of the complex. Billy stood for a moment, uncertain of what to do, for even though it was lunchtime, he didn't know whether it was permissible for a stranger just to wander into the studio unannounced.

He looked around for what he thought would be a suitable person to ask for information. It was then his eye was drawn to a man sitting on a canvas chair just inside the main shutter door. He was engrossed in a laptop he had balanced on his knee.

The man was hard to miss; he was wearing a banana yellow shirt, faded pink, calf-length, baggy shorts, tan Timberland boots, and a baseball cap worn back to front. Now this colourful ensemble would be striking enough if worn by a skinny teenager, but Billy guessed this guy was in his late thirties, and he more than filled out his attire.

He didn't know why, but Billy felt that somehow this was the man to ask.

"Excuse me, ah wonder if ye could tell me where ah could find Laura Taylor?"

The man continued to gaze down at the computer screen for a good few of Billy's heartbeats, but then, slowly lifted his head and looked over his glasses at Billy.

"Sorry?"

"Could you ye possibly tell me where ah can find Laura Taylor?"

On hearing the Scottish accent, the man gave Billy a quizzical look, but then his face broke into a beaming smile.

"Mickie?"

"Naw," Billy replied rather sharply. "My name's Billy Dunn; ah'm a friend of Mickie's"

"Oh, right," replied the man, holding out his hand. "I'm Tim Farrell; I work with Laura."

Billy grasped the outstretched hand firmly.

"Laura's just having a spot of lunch right now, but she'll be back down from the canteen shortly. Is there anything I can help you with?"

"Naw, not really."

Tim Farrell may have appeared somewhat eccentric in appearance, but in reality he was a sensitive, wise man, and he immediately sensed there was something troubling Billy Dunn.

"Well, at least let me get you a drink of something," he said, snapping shut his laptop. "Let's go into the studio, it's a bit quieter in there."

Billy followed Tim through a small door in the large shutter, and entered stage number three.

While Billy stood looking around, Tim placed his laptop on a chair, and then walked over to a trestle table, on which there was a large stainless steel urn, stacks of plastic cups, and cakes and sandwiches laid out on paper plates covered in clingfilm.

"Tea or coffee?"

"Eh, coffee please," said Billy walking over to join Tim, who after preparing the coffee, handed it to Billy.

"Help yourself to sugar, and whatever," he said, taking his phone from his pocket.

"I'll just give Laura a quick call, in case she wanders off somewhere."

Before he had time to dial the number, the studio door opened, and through it came the slight figure of Laura. She appeared to be deep in thought, and initially didn't seem to notice Tim and Billy standing in the corner of the studio.

"Ah, the very woman," cried Tim.

Laura looked round in surprise, and hesitated for a moment, before walking over to join the two men.

Billy laid his coffee back on the table, and felt his chest tighten with apprehension. He could see that Laura was everything Mickie said she was, but to his further dismay, he could also see how sad and weary she looked. She glanced at Tim, and then acknowledged Billy with a brief smile.

Billy took in a deep, audible breath, and held out his hand.

"Hello Laura, we've never met, but ah feel as if ah already know ye, because of Mickie; my name's Billy, Billy Dunn."

Laura looked bemused for a second or two, but then smiled warmly at Billy, and took his hand.

"Of course, Billy; Mickie talks about you all the time. How nice to meet you at last."

Looking into Laura's lovely sad eyes, Billy felt his courage falter.

"Aw fuck, this is so hard," he said, closing his eyes, but still holding on to Laura's hand.

Laura looked somewhat startled by this statement, and had an instant feeling of foreboding, but before she could ask for an explanation, Billy opened his eyes, and looking straight at her, uttered the inevitable:

"Ah'm so sorry to have to tell you this, but Mickie's in hospital; he's in intensive care, in fact."

Tim Farrell, who had been standing quietly observing the scene, now turned and looked open-mouthed at Billy. Laura also stood gazing at Billy as if he were mad, and then abruptly withdrew her hand.

"I don't understand," she said, frowning and shaking her head. "What do you mean? Wha . . . What happened?"

Billy blew a long, audible column of air out through his mouth.

"It's a long story, but he was stabbed yesterday . . . It was bad . . . We, we don't know if . . . "

Billy's emotions got the better of him, and he had to stop and turn away.

Tim Farrell noticed that Laura had started to shake; her whole body was trembling, and her pale drawn face mirrored the jumble of terrible, unbearable thoughts that were running through her mind. He put his arm around her, and gently led her to one of the studio chairs, and tried to comfort her as best he could. After a few minutes, he came back over to where Billy stood.

"I have to take Laura home, she's in no condition to face any of this here. What the hell happened?"

Billy took a deep breath, slowly let it out, and proceeded to give Tim as concise an account as he could under the circumstances:

"It happened yesterday mornin. Mickie had apparently just left the house to go and get some cigarettes, when he spotted Sammie, an elderly friend of ours, bein hassled in the street by this fucked-up hoodie. Mickie had immediately started shouting out to the guy, and ran up the street to help Sammie. But just as he was nearly on him, the guy turned to see who was shouting, and Mickie ran straight into a blade the fucker was holdin. Ah got there just as it happ . . ."

Billy couldn't continue; his face creased in distress, and he had to swallow hard to stop from breaking down. Tim Farrell had listened with mounting dread, and now reached out and tenderly placed a hand on Billy's shoulder.

"I'm so sorry, Billy. That's fucking awful," he said, softly. "I can only guess how hard this must be for you; however, I have to ask you big favour, could you look after Laura while I make a phone call?"

Billy nodded, and then walked over to where Laura sat staring at the floor, and hugging herself, as if suddenly cold.

Tim took out his phone, and hit a number.

"Hi Rita, it's Tim, is John Light in the building? . . . Good, let me have a word . . . Hi John, I need you to do something for me. I'm just about to take Laura home from the studio, as she's had a . . . Oh, you already know . . . Okay, I see. Well, as you can imagine, she's in bits, and I don't want her to be on her own . . . Exactly, so can you be at her flat in about forty minutes or so . . . That's all right, I'll sort things out here, and clear it with Andrew . . . Okay John, thanks, I'll see you soon. "

Tim replaced his phone, and then stood lost in thought, until the sound of the door opening, and the chatter of the crew coming back from lunch brought him back to reality. He immediately walked over to have a word withMark Shaw.

Billy was at a loss as to what to say to comfort Laura. He had sat down next to her, but she didn't seem to even notice he was there. He put his head in hands in an attempt to escape all this overwhelming grief, but then he felt the touch of another hand on his; he looked round into the tear-stained face of Laura, who then gripped his hand tightly.

Chapter 25 (Autumn)

The prison visitors centre was crowded, but Sammie, lost in thought, was only partially aware of the other people in the room. In the three and a half months since Rob had been sent down, this was Sammie's third visit.

He had thought long and hard about it before he finally made up his mind to contact the boy. His reasons for doing so were complex, and because, under the circumstances, it would obviously be seen by others as a volatile move, he had decided, for the present, not to tell anyone about the visits. Lucy especially wouldn't understand; she had refused to attend Rob's trial or hear any mention of his name, or indeed, anything related to that tragic day.

Sammie already felt like a man caught in the middle of something he didn't really understand; he was running on instinct, but knew in his heart that he would eventually have to deal with the consequences of his actions.

What had finally spurred his decision was when he found out at Rob's trial, that the boy had been on suicide watch since being arrested, and there was no guarantee this would continue after he was sent to Wandsworth. He had been allowed to attend his mother's funeral, but this had in no way eased Rob's depression, on the contrary, it had instead had brought home to him how desolate his life had become.

Sammie had made enquiries regarding the procedure for making prison visits, but was thwarted by the fact that the prisoner was the one who had to sanction any visitors before any further action could be taken, and Rob had not been in any frame of mind to do this.

But the old man had persevered, and began writing short weekly letters. In these he restated that he had indeed known Rob's real father, and also made it clear that he would in no way be judgemental; he only wanted to try and help the boy come to terms with all that had happened to him. And so, whether out of curiosity or loneliness, Rob had finally agreed to a visit.

That first time had been, not too surprisingly, strained and difficult; Rob had been morose, suspicious, and mostly silent. Sammie had come away from the meeting thinking that this would be his one and only visit. But to his surprise, he was allowed a second chance, and as he later found out, the reason for this was that Rob's grandmother had finally confessed that Rob's real father had not been the man he thought had abandoned him, and gone to America.

The sound of one of the visitors centre staff announcing it was time to proceed to the visits hall roused Sammie from his thoughts, and he rose to join the queue.

On entering the visits area, he stopped at the snack bar to fetch two coffees, and a sandwich. And then, searching out Rob, he walked over and smiled nervously at the boy, who responded with a slight lift of his chin. *He looks better,* thought Sammie. *Not quite as grim and dejected as before.*

"Mi hope yuh like cheese," he said taking a seat. "They don't have much of a choice."

Rob nodded, and then tearing open the sandwich, took two greedy bites, and then washed the food down with a noisy slug of coffee. *This bwoy is hungry,* thought Sammie, but he remained silent, quietly sipping at his own cup, until the boy had finished eating.

"Yuh need anyting?" he then asked. What about music; yuh get to listen to music?"

Rob, ignoring the question, drained his coffee, and then looked at Sammie.

"Why do you come ere?"

Sammie was a little taken aback by the question, and thought for a few heartbeats before answering; but then, shaking his head, he said:

"Mi not sure. It's complicated, and mi haven't really figured it out yet. But your daddy was my best friend, and mi somehow feel he would have wanted me to try and help yuh."

"Even after what I did?"

"Mi only now understandin what your life was like, and mi would like to try and help yuh get through this. But yuh have to be strong, and want to change."

Rob looked away, and stayed silent for a long minute.

"How come he didn't want to know me?"

Sammie looked straight into the boy's eyes.

"Listen, the whole ting broke the man's heart; mi tink it killed him in the end. His wife, Lucy, couldn't have babies, and so when he had to tell her about you and your momma, it hurt the woman so bad, he couldn't face bringing any more misery to her door. And anyway, your momma took yuh and disappeared shortly after yuh were born, and he didn't know where yuh were. But mi know he made sure money went into an account for you and your momma every month."

"He could have stopped her takin smack."

Sammie again shook his head.

"He didn't know, because she wasn't takin it then, and anyway, nobody can do that. But your daddy felt the weight of his mistake until he died."

"Oh, so I was a mistake?"

Sammie looked away and sighed. He knew the boy had enough misery and pain in his life, but nevertheless, he had to try and straighten him out, and he wasn't going to lie.

"Listen, son, mi can't speak for Harry, and he can't speak for himself, but mi know this: yuh gonna have to grow up and except the way tings are now, because if yuh don't, yuh gonna be lost in shit like this forever."

They stayed silent for a time, and Rob looked down into his coffee cup.

"I like music," he said, suddenly looking up at Sammie. "I don't know why, but I always wanted to play an instrument. But we moved around so much, I never got around to it."

A light came into Sammie's eyes; he smiled at the boy, and then held out his hand.

"Well, mi gonna have to do something about that."

Rob hesitated, but then gave a slight lift of his chin, and grasped Sammie's hand.

* * *

Toto gazed up at the already darkening sky and drew nervously on his cigarette. Beside him, erect and silent, stood a huge olive skinned man. The man, with his big hands held loosely in front of him, and an unwavering look in his narrow dark eyes, had the daunting presence of a primeval sentinel, which in a bizarre way, he was.

Toto blew smoke into the air, and gave the big man a brief, furtive glance. He couldn't help wondering how it had come to be, that he was standing outside a back street Liverpool pub in the company of a giant; and how once again, he had managed to get himself in the frame.

He thought back to the day he had fled from Patsy's flat after lashing out at her, and how the realisation of what he had done, had caused him to spend the rest of that day being sick with worry at his stupidity. He at least knew the big man well enough by now, to be certain that he would never let something that could jeopardise his business, go without payback. And so, by early evening, he had realised his only option was to get away from London, and as soon as possible.

In his desperation, he had even made a long overdue call to his older half-sister, Janine. That they had never been close had been more than evident in the suspicious tone in her voice when she had taken the call. Her suspicion had been even more apparent, when he had asked if he could come up and stay for a while.

She knew him enough, however, not to ask why, as long as it was understood he had to pay his way. As a single mother with two teenage sons, she was by no means an easy touch.

Up until standing in the gathering dark with a giant, Toto's time in Liverpool had been uneventful. For the first week or so, he had kept things to himself and tried to avoid answering too many questions from his two young nephews. But the more he began to relax, the more his former exaggerated sense of his own importance had once again come to the fore. It didn't take too long before he was openly boasting to the youths about his exploits as a London gangster. And when it became apparent that the two boys were themselves active in the Toxteth drug trade, he began hanging out with them on a more regular basis, basking in his self-made reputation as a big city drug man.

They always frequented the same local pub, where the more Toto had to drink, the more he had regaled his nephews with his legend. They, however, had not been the only ones who found his exploits of interest. A severe looking man, who always sat quietly at the corner table, had been more than keen to listen in on the sly to these wild tales.

Toto had noticed that his nephews always acknowledged the silent man on entering the pub, and when he asked why, all they said was that he was a local businessman. Toto had not thought much more about this, until one of the boys informed him some time later, that the man had inquired after him, and wondered if he could possibly have a quiet word.

At first Toto's suspicious nature was aroused as to why this man would want to speak to him, and what the topic of that conversation might be. But when the nephews informed him that the man was known on the street as, Ari the Gun, and explained to what type of business the name referred, Toto was intrigued.

His curiosity and greed were further aroused when he was told that Ari had money, some of which he would be willing to hand over, if Toto could supply him with certain type of information.

With money on his mind, Toto hadn't thought too deeply of the consequences; he had naively convinced himself that the man was obviously seeking some of his expert advice, and therefore assumed that dealing with this older, balding man would be easy.

That plan, however, had been instantly foiled. For when he had turned up alone at the pub for the meeting, he had found Ari in the company of two heavy looking younger men. Disconcerted as he may have been by the cold stares of Ari's muscled associates, his greed, as always, had overruled his caution, and he had taken a seat opposite the three men.

"I took the liberty," Ari had said, in a surprisingly refined, soft voice, while gesturing to a large Scotch on the table in front of Toto.

While Toto had begun to wonder why somebody with money would be seen in such a cheap suit, Ari had continued in his smooth honey-like tone, to get straight to the point:

"Now, what I believe I have gleaned from casually overhearing your entertaining anecdotes, is that we may have a friend in common; in short, a large black gentleman, with a rather damaged nose."

Toto had been instantly unnerved, not only by the man's articulate language, but also by his direct reference to Nazz, and as a result, had swiftly reverted to his customary, cagey self.

"What makes ya fink I know somebody like that?" he said, pretending to check his watch.

Ari had given him a bemused look, and then with a sigh, had looked up at the ceiling, bringing into focus a long white scar under his chin.

"Look, Mr, er, Toto, I'm a busy man. It may look like I live the life of a bon-viveur, but I can assure you my business takes up most of my time, and you're wasting it."

Once again, this strange man had unsettled Toto with this subtly voiced, but not too thinly veiled threat, causing him to unwisely continue to be evasive.

"What if I do know this geezer?"

Ari had then looked at Toto as you would a dim-witted child.

"My little friend, I don't think you quite understand the rules of this, er, get-together. In a nutshell, I ask the questions, and you give the answers."

Toto had felt a stream of sweat run down his back at the realisation that he may have badly misjudged this scenario.

"Look," he'd continued, his voice taking on a more anxious tone. "Before I say anyfing else, I need to know what the deal is wiv you and this bro."

Ari had almost scowled, but had then quickly regained his composure.

"Let's just say he took something that didn't belong to him, and I would be grateful for the opportunity to discuss it with him."

Toto had looked down into his whisky and let this statement sink in, and then said, almost in a whisper:

"Ow much?"

"Sorry?"

"Ow much for the information?"

"Are you offering information?" Ari had said, giving Toto a scary tight-lipped smile.

Toto had found this smile all the more alarming, given that the suppleness of the man's face seemed to be badly diminished; no doubt due to the fact that it looked like somebody had been jumping on it. And so, in a pathetic effort to appear nonchalant, Toto had merely shrugged.

"I just wanna try and elp, innit."

At this comment, Ari had been unable to resist displaying a sly smirk.

"Yes, well, we will discuss payment in due course, but first of all, why exactly would you want to divulge this information?"

Toto had hesitated, but then after a few seconds, his face had contorted with venom.

"Because I hate that fucker."

Ari had then given another one of his fleeting, scary smiles.

"Well, now, could it be we're starting to get somewhere; assuming of course you know where this, fucker" Ari mimicked the word exactly like Toto, "is to be located?"

"I fink e's holed up in Brixton."

"You fink e's holed up in Brixton." Again, the mimicry had been uncanny.

Ari gave Toto a wry look, and after taking a sip of his drink, had again displayed his chilling smile.

"Well, Mr Toto," he pronounced the name as if he had a bad taste in his mouth. "I'll tell you what my instincts are telling me, and please do correct me if I'm wrong. My instincts are telling me that you two old chums have had a bit of a tiff, and you are in Liverpool only because you don't wish to meet up with our mutual friend anytime soon, as it may be detrimental to your well being."

It was at this point that Toto had felt a real need to take some time out to soothe his jangling nerves. He felt confused and trapped, and knew he needed to try and come up with some sort of plan to ensure he came away from this deal intact.

"I need a cigarette."

Ari had looked hard at Toto, and then with a slight movement of his chin, had gestured to his hulking younger cousin, Yannis, to escort the little man out of the pub.

A short time later, while taking a final drag of his cigarette, Toto had to concede that unfortunately no magic solution to his predicament had presented itself. His brain seemed to be exclusively jammed with past failures of logic; he sighed and flicked the butt into the gutter. He had earlier realised it was useless to attempt to converse with his new large friend, and seeing no reason to start now, he ignored the hulking Greek, and re-entered the pub.

Resigned, he again took his seat at the table, and sucking in a deep breath, he slowly released it; the cigarette hadn't really helped.

Seeing another large whisky in front of him on the table, he drained the first, and waited. Ari eyed him for a few seconds, and then took a sip from his own glass and placed it back on the table.

"So, what makes you think our friend is residing in Brixton?" he asked, again getting straight to the point.

Toto no longer saw any sense in trying to be evasive, or clever.

"I got word from London that the bitch who's flat we'd been using, had OD, and that had brought the old bill sniffin around, and Nazz had to do a rapid disappearing act. It seems the night it appened, er son ad been watchin the flat, and told the old bill e ad seen Nazz and anuvver bro goin into the buildin around that time. So you aint the only one wantin to discuss fings wiv im."

Ari slowly nodded his head.

"And would you happen to know where exactly in Brixton Mr Nazz would be, as it were, holed up?"

"I drove im to a woman's place there once, and I reckon that's where e'll be."

Ari again lifted his glass to his lips and sipped his whisky, but never took his eyes off Toto.

"Well," he said, placing his glass back on the table. "Brixton it is then. Demetrius, bring the car round, I'm sure Mr Toto will have finished his drink by then."

Toto looked confused.

Ari favoured him with another grim smile.

"Were all going on a trip to the Capital, my little friend, and you're going to be the bait that will lure our man from his hole."

Toto now looked confused, and alarmed.

"Oh, wait a minute, man, I can show you where I fink e's stayin, but I aint gonna be no bai . . . "

Toto didn't get to finish the sentence; Yannis, surprisingly swiftly for a big man, had reached over and clamped a huge hand tightly around the startled man's throat.

Without any undue haste, Ari lifted his glass and took another sip of whisky, and then, looking hard into Toto's bulging, terrified eyes, he said:

"I think you'll find that what my colleague is attempting to convey in his own inimitable fashion, is that refusal is not an option."

Chapter 26 (Monday)

From the bed, Nazz looked out at the dismal weather; time was beginning to hang heavy on him, and the pale morning light seeping into the room did little to lift his spirits. Reaching over, he slid a cigarette from the pack on the bedside cabinet, lit it, and inhaling deeply, blew a perfect smoke-ring into the air. He watched as it sailed lazily across the room, and then, moments later, dissolved against the rain-splattered bedroom window.

He had been awake for some time, and had earlier heard Alisha leave to open up her Beauty Salon. He took another long pull on his cigarette, and then, laying his head back on the pillow, thought about how long they had known each other.

He had been fifteen years old when they had first met, and for a while at least, he had virtually become part of her family. By then, however, he had been transformed from a normal easy-going kid, into a brutal, fearless feral boy with a vendetta against everyone outside of this adopted family.

There had been various reasons for this change, paramount, however, was when, two years earlier on his thirteenth birthday his father had been killed in an argument over a woman. His father, Benjamin, had been extremely drunk at the time, having on that particular afternoon, enjoyed an unusually good result at the bookmakers. After collecting his winnings, and actually holding the proof of his good fortune in his hands, Benjamin had easily convinced himself that this was more than enough reason to go straight to the pub for a celebratory drink.

After the first few drinks, time had seemed to stand still, and the more he drank, the more he wanted. Everybody was suddenly a friend, and he felt elated to be in such good company. With every drink, his family responsibilities had melted away, until even his son's birthday had been completely forgotten.

At closing time, many hours later, two of the regulars who had benefited from Benjamin's drunken generosity, had gently, but firmly escorted the now hopelessly inebriated man out of the pub. Once outside, they had managed to lean him against the wall, where for a few minutes he had stood comically puffing out gasps of air. After giving two men a final glazed look, he had launched himself off the wall, and started lurching his way along the street.

As the two men had continued to watch, Benjamin, full of rum and drunken bravado, and obviously thinking his luck still held, had come on to a blonde woman standing in the street. The woman, however, had turned out to be a prostitute, and when she had tried to negotiate her terms, Benjamin had evidently taken offence, and had started waving his arms in the air, while shouting in outrage at her brazenness.

These drunken gestures of protest had unfortunately caused him to lose his balance, and in an effort to keep from falling over, he had grabbed hold of the woman. The woman, who didn't take kindly to being manhandled, especially for free, had forcefully retaliated, which in turn had attracted the attention of her pimp.

The pimp, a tough Ukrainian ex-soldier, who had been watching the pantomime from a car parked across the street, had immediately stepped in, and pulling the drunken man off, had then viciously thrown him against the wall. Benjamin, whose survival instincts had been severely dulled by his befuddled state, had been unable to prevent his head from hitting the brick wall with a sickening crack. As the woman and her pimp watched, he had slid slowly down onto the pavement, leaving a trail of blood on the wall.

At first, the sight of Benjamin being harassed by a woman, who to them was obviously a prostitute, had greatly amused the two regulars. But they soon realised the seriousness of the situation when they had seen the pimp appear and push Benjamin hard against the wall. Horror struck, they had immediately started to call out, but then had to stand by helpless, as the couple, ignoring their pleas, had run to the car and sped off into the night.

In panic, one of the men had begun banging on the door of the pub, and calling out to the landlord to call an ambulance, while the other had rushed over to be with the now unconscious Benjamin.

The ambulance had got to the scene within twenty minutes, and then, on arriving at the hospital, Benjamin had been immediately rushed to the emergency room, where despite the dedication of the medical staff, he never regained consciousness, and died shortly afterwards.

The prostitute and her guardian were eventually caught and brought to trial. However, when the woman had been called to the stand, she had strenuously denied being a hooker, and had been extremely convincing in stating that it was in fact, she, who had been attacked first, and that her boyfriend had merely come to her aid. She had continued in this confident manner, adding that her boyfriend had merely pulled her attacker off her, and that Benjamin had then fell against the wall because he was so drunk.

Nazz and his mother had sat stunned when the jury, having obviously believed this bogus testimony, had returned a verdict of accidental death, which resulted in the pair receiving considerably lighter sentences.

This verdict had started a slow burn of rage in Nazz, and due to the testimony of the prostitute, a deep seated loathing of blonde white women, especially those he perceived to be users. This feeling intensified in the years that followed, as he watched his mother deteriorate into a hopeless embittered alcoholic, who showed little interest in anything but her next drink.

No matter how hard he tried to help her recover her former strength and dignity, she seemed intent on destroying herself. After a while, he couldn't stand to watch this slow deliberate suicide, and began to spend most of his time on the streets. He soon built a reputation as a dealer, and someone only a fool would mess with; he became a loner, who kept things close, and trusted no one.

Alisha had lived on the same estate, and he had initially only known her by sight. Their lives, however, would soon be forever linked, when one evening he happened to visit one of the blocks on a bit of business. On entering, he had noticed that the lights inside the entrance appeared to be dimmer than usual, and assuming them to be faulty or broken, hadn't thought too much about it. It was when he had started to climb the stairs that he heard the muffled sound of what seemed to be a girl in some distress.

The noise seemed to be coming from under the stairwell, and for some inexplicable reason, he found himself going to investigate. He followed the sound, and came across a terrified Alisha in the process of being sexually assaulted by three older youths.

He recognised the youths, who were also from the estate, and although by this time he put himself out for no one, something spurred him to take Alisha's side. He knew these guys to be flash no-account bullies, and perhaps just because of that, he had felt like tearing them up a little.

Without any loud show of bravado, he had then simply walked up to the group, and quietly told the youths to stop what they were doing and leave the girl alone. The youths had looked at each other in mock fear, and then laughing in Nazz's face, had brazenly continued molesting the frightened girl.

That had been their big mistake; Nazz had then moved with the speed and instinct of an animal. He grabbed the one he knew to be the mouthy leader by the neck, and smashed his face hard against the wall. Before the other two realised what was happening, one of them had a gaping knife wound on his thigh, which caused him to wail, and slink away from the girl, while trying to stem the flow of blood from his leg. On seeing this, the third youth had tried to make a run for the back door, but wasn't quick enough, Nazz had swept his legs from under him, and then systematically kicked him until he lay helpless and groaning on the floor. He then again turned his attention to the stunned leader, and finished the job by giving him a crippling boot to the groin, and then punching him repeatedly, until he too, lay in a heap on the floor.

Alisha had watched all this happen as if in a dream, seconds before, she had been certain she was going to be raped, and now, her attackers were beaten and blooded on the ground. She had been further amazed that her saviour had taken the time to quietly comfort her, and then with her permission, had offered to escort her home.

From that point on, Alisha had been like his younger sister; they looked out for each other. When a year or so ago, she had confided to him her ambition to start her own hairdressing and beauty business, he had, after what he had only referred to as a lucrative bit of business in Liverpool, put up the money for her to open her salon.

She was a smart, true woman, and one of the few people he ever trusted. She was also, however, her own woman, with her own life, and had paid him back in full as soon as she was able. And although she would never actually say it, he knew what she was thinking: that after three months, he had somewhat overstayed his welcome. She was right, he knew he had been holed up long enough, and it was time to get back out there and take care of business.

After Patsy died, and things had gotten a little complicated, he had considered leaving town for a while, but soon decided against it, as it would seem to rivals that he had been weakened by the stupidity of a fool. As the final verdict on Patsy had been accidental death: Rob's evidence hadn't been taken too seriously, as people died of drugs everyday in London, and Nazz knew the police would eventually get bored, and things would again smooth out a little.

As for the fool, Shank had asked around, and searched all the usual places he was likely to be found, but there had been no sign of Toto since the day he had disappeared after cutting Patsy. Nazz knew the man was a no-account, but the fool had cost him dearly, in respect and money, and when he eventually crawled out of his hole, Nazz would be waiting.

He stubbed out his cigarette and checking his phone was surprised to see he had missed a call from Shank. He wondered why he hadn't heard it ring, and then remembered he had put it on silent while watching a movie with Alisha last night.

It had been a while since he had talked to the boy. There hadn't been much point, as Shank had been so shaken up after finding Patsy dead, that he had soon after said he wanted out. That was okay, Nazz had understood; the youth had always been straight with him, and as the boy was never really in the frame, he would keep his mouth shut. And of course, Nazz knew there would always be somebody else greedy enough to want to make good money fast.

He punched in Shank's number.

" . . . Hey, bro, wha appenin? . . . Oh yeah? . . . No, man, I'm still takin time out, but I need to get somethin appenin soon . . ."

All of a sudden, he sat bolt upright.

"You're fuckin kiddin me. The slimy little fuck . . . You sure about this? . . So the bro who eyeballed him, definitely said it was him?"

Nazz plucked another cigarette from the pack, and lit it.

"Listen if he's there again tonight, I want to know immediately, man, I mean immediately . . . Okay, man, I owe you."

He dropped the phone onto the bed, and finished his cigarette while gazing out the window; all of a sudden, he felt hungry

* * *

The pale autumn sun, partly hidden by the gathering clouds, was trying its best to warm the day, but the chill of winter was in the air.

Billy, sitting in his usual spot just outside the shutter door of the garage, zipped up his jacket, and then leaning back on his greasy old chair, gazed up at the sky.

In the last few months, his work-mates had noticed that he had drawn more into himself, and become quieter, more subdued.

Earlier, while washing up before lunch, both BeeJay and Pete had tried to persuade him to join them in the café, but he had declined, and they knew better than to push it.

Fate and the passing of time had recently been much on his mind. He had been pondering on the fact that no matter how much you would sometimes otherwise wish, time just kept on ticking away.

He continued to gaze at the clouds for a few minutes more, and then shaking his head as if clearing it of dark thoughts, drained off the last of his coffee. He was just about to reach down for his lunch container and return to work, when he saw a figure walk into the yard; Billy immediately recognised Shank. He hadn't seen the boy since the day they had spoken in the Bulldog. He remained seated and watched him approach.

"Hey, bro, is Bee-jay around?"

Billy shook his head.

"No, he's in the café."

Shank acknowledged this with a slight lift of his chin, and then hesitated. Billy said nothing more, for he sensed the boy had something on his mind, but then Shank seemingly thought better of it.

"Okay, man, I'll go meet him," he said, and then turned and walked out of the yard.

Billy watched him go, and thought it a coincidence, for only the other day he had asked Bee-Jay if he had seen Shank recently. The boy had said that he hadn't seen or talked to him since the day he had come to the garage, and according to some of his other friends, Shank had simply disappeared from the street.

Billy was obviously aware of Shank's involvement with Nazz, but at Rob's trial, only Nazz was mentioned by name, and he too had apparently disappeared. Rob had informed the police that he had seen Nazz and another man leave his mother's building shortly before he himself had entered, and found her dead from an overdose. His testimony, however, had little effect, as there was no real evidence to link Nazz to his Mother's death, as she was a well known junkie, and her demise was seen as an occupational hazard.

Since then, Billy had wondered if the other man had been Shank, or the arrogant, flash little fucker he had confronted that day in the Bulldog. In Billy's opinion, the overriding consequence of Rob finding his mother dead had been that Mickie had got stabbed, accidentally as it turned out, but nevertheless, Billy had questions, and now maybe Bee-jay would have answers.

* * *

By late afternoon, the dark clouds that had earlier been threatening, had finally obscured the sun, leaving the day cold and grey, and now as night fell, it had become colder still. The light from the windows of The Raven pub, threw a dull yellow hue onto the damp pavement.

From the warmth of a large BMW parked on a side street opposite, three men watched as the slight, hunched figure of Toto, crossed the street and entered the pub. Ari had earlier decided, when considering his next plan of action, that a local Brixton pub would be the obvious location to plant his bait; however, when he had informed the little man of this, Toto had said nothing in reply.

"Okay, Yannis, same as yesterday," said Ari, from the front passenger seat. "Give him five minutes, and then follow him in. He gets one more chance to deliver our prey, and if he is playing games, which I am beginning to suspect is the case, we will have to think again, and perhaps be a little more forceful. On the other hand, it could be that our friend, Nazz is merely being extra cautious, and we should be patient a little longer."

With an audible groan from the suspension, the big Greek slid from the back seat, and after closing the door behind him, lit a cigarette. He walked a short distance from the car, and then stopped, all the time keeping his eyes focused on the pub entrance. After looking at his watch to check the allotted five minutes was up, he took a final pull of his cigarette, flicked the butt into the gutter, and made his way towards the pub.

Being a Monday evening, the Raven's bright spacious, somewhat shabby lounge, held only a scattering of local punters. Toto had ordered himself a large rum, and was now sitting at a table in the corner, trying his best to look inconspicuous, although being clearly visible was meant to be the whole point of him being here

On entering Brixton yesterday evening, after the drive from Liverpool, Toto had spotted the pub as they sat in traffic on a main road. All the way down he had been desperately trying to devise some plan of escape, but again had come up with nothing; and so, frantically grasping at anything that might garner him more time, he had pointed out the pub with all the fake enthusiasm he could muster.

"Hey, man, this is the place. This is the place you should use. Nazz and me used to drink in this boozer all the time."

For a long few minutes his remark was met with total silence. But then Ari turning in his seat, and looking quizzically at Toto, had said:

"Demetrius, pull into that side street."

When the car had come to a stop, Ari had continued to look long and hard at the nervous little man, as if searching for some sign of treachery, but somehow, Toto had managed to keep his nerve.

"How can I be sure that our man will be informed that his favourite former associate is back in town?" said Ari.

"Oh, trust me, man he'll know," Toto had answered eagerly.

This remark had caused Ari to emit a dry brittle laugh.

"Trust you? Do you think me a fool?"

He had again looked silently at Toto for quite a few of the little man's almost audible heartbeats.

"Okay, we will try it your way, but only because you will always be in our sight, and more importantly, within Yannis's reach."

Toto was of course lying. In his desperation to somehow foil their plan to use him to lure Nazz, he had failed to inform the Greeks that he wasn't a Brixton boy, and had in fact gone on to brazenly assure them that he was a well known face in this part of town.

This delaying tactic had worked so far, only in as much as he had sat at this very table the whole of the previous evening without one person, apart from Yannis, even looking his way. By the time the final bell had sounded, however, he had been too drunk to care whether Ari had guessed his ruse or not. It was then, when there had been a scramble for last orders, that Yannis had taken him by the arm, and subtly escorted him through the Sunday night crowd, and out the door.

On waking, sometime this afternoon, he had found himself in a small, dull room, lying fully clothed on a spindly fold-down bed. His aching body had made him feel like he had been bounced off a few walls. His throat was parched, and his mouth was sour with the acrid taste of rum. He had looked out at the already darkening grey sky with a feeling of hopelessness; he had no idea where he was, and dreaded what was coming next.

His memory of the previous night was to say the least, patchy, but he had a vague recollection of being steered forcefully from the pub at closing time, and then bundled into the back of the car. He must have fallen asleep, because he remembered at one point being shaken and slapped awake by Yannis, and then taken through the door of a seedy flat, and thrown into the room he now found himself.

He had continued to gaze out at the darkening sky, but hadn't been able to gauge for how long, for when he had looked to check the time, he found he no longer had a watch or phone. It was then, just to add to his troubles, that he had felt the urgent need of a toilet.

Leaping out of the bed, he had tried to open the door, only to find it had been locked. In his panic at his need becoming increasingly imminent, he had begun shouting and banging incessantly on the door, until, to his great relief, it had been opened by the imposing figure of Yannis.

Wide-eyed, Toto had pushed past the big man and started pacing frantically up and down the hallway, and shouting:

"Where's the fuckin toilet?"

With a jerk of his head, the big Greek had motioned to a blue door, which then Toto had almost fell through, leaving Yannis in the hall, wearing a very seldom seen wry grin.

An hour or so later, after being given some breakfast, and allowed, after a fashion, to freshen up, he had been led to the car, and again found himself being driven though the streets of London.

And now, after a forty-five minute, stone-silent drive, here he was, once more seated at the corner table of the Raven. His thoughts were far from confident; he knew he was running out of time. Ari was no fool, and continually looked at him as if he already suspected deceit, and no matter how hard he tried, Toto could see no way out.

He pretended not to notice when the Yannis entered through the door, but then took a quick glance when the big man turned his back to take a seat at the bar. Toto was convinced he saw the bar stool strain under the weight, and began praying for it to give way entirely, and then perhaps with Yannis sprawling around on the floor, he would have a chance to run before the Greeks knew what was happening. But the big man, almost as if he knew what Toto was thinking, looked over and gave him a brief scornful look.

Toto sighed, took a sip of rum, and then, in an effort to relieve his paranoia, he had a quick furtive look around the room to double check there was no one in the place he knew; unfortunately for Toto, however, someone certainly knew him.

The young barman, who's presence Toto had, both the previous evening, and again minutes ago, hardly acknowledged, had recognised him the minute he had walked through the door yesterday evening. Toto had, without even looking at the youth, rudely grunted his order, and then, as if to further demean the boy, had on receiving his drink and change, turned and walked away without offering thanks.

Watching the little man walk away, the boy had scowled, and kissed his teeth in irritation. But then, giving Toto a defiant look, he had turned and slipping his phone from the back pocket of his low-slung jeans, disappeared through a door at the back of the bar.

It was unfortunate for Toto, that the barman, who's name was Darryl, had known Shank since school. Although he was a year younger, he, like BeeJay, had been lucky enough to have Shank look out for him, which meant he didn't get heat from any older youths.

After leaving school, Darryl had managed to get enrolled as an apprentice carpenter at Lambeth College, and for convenience had taken up lodgings with his aunt in Brixton. He had then found work in the Raven to supplement his meagre student grant, and help pay his way, but he still occasionally bumped into Shank when he visited his mum on the estate.

It was on one particular visit, when he happened to be sitting in a local café, that he saw Shank pass the window in the company of a small man whose flash appearance had been hard to miss. He vaguely knew who Toto was, and had heard that he and Shank had something going with a big scary looking bro, who Darryl had never seen. Word was also out, however, that Toto had been making a name for himself as a jumped up fool.

Darryl liked and respected Shank, but he himself had always tried to maintain a low profile, and had never, apart from the odd spliff, ever been tempted by drugs, and certainly had wanted nothing to do with dealing; it was just too scary. Because of this, he thought that little man Toto would consider himself way too cool to ever take notice of someone like him, and that was fine with Darryl.

Shank on the other hand, had caught sight of Darryl through the café window, and had taken the time to come in to say hello. After the initial greeting, they had both watched with squirming amusement, the pretentious antics of the ridiculous shell-suited little man outside. He strutted about, puffing on a cigarette, flashing his gold, and trying in vain to impress any girls that walked by.

Not long after this meeting, Darryl had again run into Shank, but this time, although friendly enough, Shank had seemed tense and distracted.

"Hey bro, wha appenin?" Darryl had asked, bumping fists with his friend.

"Oh same old, same old," Shank had replied, and then thinking on, had asked:

"Hey, you remember the little blood-claat I was wiv the last time I saw you.

"Wha, Mr Flash? Yeah, a bit ard to miss im, bro."

Shank had given a brief dry laugh, and nodded in agreement.

"You aint seen im around ave ya?"

Darryl had shaken his head.

"Naw man, why?"

"Long story, but listen," Shank had said, taking his phone from his pocket. "I'll give you my number, and if you ever see im, let me know; and I mean right away, bro."

They had exchanged numbers and Darryl had thought no more about it; that is, until yesterday evening, when to his amazement an anxious looking Toto had come skulking into the pub.

After serving the rude, gruff little man, Darryl, as instructed, had immediately called Shank and informed him that Toto had just walked into the very bar where he worked. Shank had seemed equally as surprised, but thanked Darryl and said he would be in touch again soon.

It was, however, a frustrated sounding Shank that had called back thirty minutes later, saying he would have to get back to him again tomorrow, but in the meantime could he try and keep an eye on Toto. This, Darryl had attempted to do, but in the end, the pub had been so busy, he hadn't even seen Toto being steered out the bar by the huge Greek.

This morning, however, a more positive Shank had again called when Darryl was walking to college, and enquired if his friend was again going to be working a shift at the Raven that evening. Darryl had confirmed he was, and said he would be sure to call if, and when, Toto again came into the bar.

When Darryl had re-entered the bar from making that very call, he briefly glanced over to check that Toto was still on the premises, and then served the huge swarthy looking guy, who was now sitting at the bar. Moments later, while washing some glasses, he found himself becoming intrigued as to why Shank was so interested in the whereabouts of this ridiculous little man.

* * *

After the frenetic hustle and bustle of a typical Martin & Maclean Monday, Laura was more than happy to be ensconced in the warmth and quiet of the library.

She was sitting at one of the communal study tables engrossed in a large book of Rembrandt's paintings. As she gazed down on one richly coloured reproduction after another, she found herself being drawn back to the raw beauty of his later work, especially the self-portraits: that big soulful face gazing out at a world that he thought had long forgotten him. But even in his poverty stricken old age, she thought he had a majestic dignity.

Her interest in painters had lately been renewed. She had always been able to draw, but all through Art College, she had never been convinced that she had a talent for the physical act of painting, and therefore had never considered becoming what she thought of as a proper artist.

Apart from deciding that her talents should be employed elsewhere, she also felt that particular path seemed too lonely a life, too fraught with soul-searching, and frustration; and now, looking into Rembrandt's sad, weary eyes, she felt, that for her, she had made the right decision.

Her part in the last Martin & McLean commercial had reinforced this theory, for even though that project had had its share of frustrations, it had been a team effort. Although Laura was well aware she didn't have what it took to be a painter, she was, however, in love with one.

She lifted her eyes from the book and gazed across the room at the table by the window where she had first laid eyes on Mickie, and a shy smile of remembrance lit up her face. After a minute or so, realising that she had been lost in a sort of smiling dream, she felt a little embarrassed, and wrinkled up her nose at what she considered a moment of silliness. She was just about to continue studying Rembrandt, when a small, elderly man, who was sitting a few seats along, on the other side of the table, spoke:

"Ye have the look of love about ye, darlin."

At first, Laura didn't know if she was hearing things, or if indeed, the man was speaking to her, but as he was the only other person at the table, she felt she had to respond.

"I'm sorry?" she said, looking into the old man's gentle smiling face.

"Ah said, you have the look of love about ye, darlin," he repeated, softly."

Laura felt the colour rise in her cheeks, as he continued to smile at her. She couldn't help noticing that he had the bluest eyes, and that their glow seemed hardly diminished by age. While she tried to think of something to say in response to his intriguing comment, the old man came to her rescue.

"Ah'm sorry, darlin, ah've embarrassed ye. It's just ah know that look so well, and it always gladdens my heart to see it."

"Oh no, that's okay," said Laura, finally finding her voice. "You just took me by surprise."

They were silent for a few heartbeats, until Laura felt she should say something.

"I know this is going to sound silly, but by your accent, I would say that you're Scottish."

"Aye, man and boy," said the little man, puffing out his chest, and flashing a comical grin."

Laura giggled.

"Well, at least ah've made ye laugh," continued the man, now feigning an insulted look, which made Laura giggle even more.

"When yer quite finished," he said, again feigning insult, but he couldn't keep up the pretence, and began laughing.

"I love the Scottish accent," said Laura. "Where are you from in Scotland?"

"Glesga," said the little man, proudly, and then added: "but ah've been a Sassenach for over forty years now."

Laura was about to comment further, when a voice she instantly recognised, spoke up behind her, and addressed the old man:

"Hey, Jimmy, are you tryin to chat up ma burd?"

The old man's face immediately lit up, and creased in laughter.

Mickie caressed Laura's cheek, kissed the top of her head, and then walked round to the old man and shook his hand.

"Howye Joe, sorry ah haven't seen ye for a while. How ye keepin?"

"Och, ah'm fine, son. How's yerself? Yer lookin a wee bit peely-wally. Have ye been ill?"

"Naw, naw, ah'm hunky dory, Joe, hunky dory. How about Ella, is she all right?"

A cloud of grief seemed to pass over the old man's face.

"Och, not so good, son. Ah'm just killin time before ah go and see her in the hospital."

"Och, Joe, ah'm so sorry to hear that. Ah hope she gets better soon; and you be sure to tell her ah was asking after her."

The old man just smiled sadly, and slowly nodded his head.

"Will ye be in here tomorrow, Joe?" said Mickie, noting the sadness in the old man's eyes. "Because ah could pop in, and we could have a good auld catch-up, and then, if it's okay, ah could come and visit Ella with ye, eh?"

The old man smiled.

"Aye, that would be great, son. She would like that."

Mickie laid a tender hand on the old man's shoulder.

"Well, that's a date for tomorrow, Joe, awright? But right now, ah'm afraid ah've got to shoot off, and drag this lassie wi me."

He then turned and grinned at Laura, who had been sitting captivated by this encounter, but because of the broad Glasgow patios, and the speed of the delivery, she had little or no idea what had actually been said.

"Hello, darlin, sorry ah'm a wee bit late, but Mrs McIntyre kept me talkin. You want to see what she's cookin up for us tonight."

"Oh, that's okay, Mr, er . . . I'm sorry," she said, turning to address the old man. "But I don't know your surname."

"Aw, you can call me Joe, darlin," he replied.

"See what ah mean," said Mickie interjecting. "These Glesga punters don't miss a trick, eh?"

This, as Mickie hoped it would, set Joe off laughing again.

"Well," said Laura. "Joe here has been keeping me well entertained." And then, smiling over at the old man, she added: "It was lovely to meet you, Joe. And I hope to see you again soon."

"The pleasure will be all mine, darlin," said Joe, looking tenderly at Laura. And then he winked, and added: "And ah was right, wasn't ah?"

Laura looked into his sparkling blue eyes, and then, attempting her best Scottish accent, she replied:

"Aye, Joe, ye were."

"Awright, awright, that's enough of that," said Mickie, "Ah'm getting jealous here."

Again, Joe's face creased in laughter.

Laura smiled, and got up, replaced the Rembrandt book on the shelf, and then winking at Joe, gave Mickie a peck on the cheek. Mickie grinned, and put his arm around her.

"Ah'll see ye tomorrow, Joe. Take easy."

Laura gave the old man a goodbye smile, and then she and Mickie turned and walked away, hand in hand. With a tender, poignant look on his face, the old man watched them go through the main door of the library, and out into the night.

* * *

Sammie sat at the kitchen table sipping a beer. He had a soft, gentle smile on his face, as he watched Lucy, who was standing at the stove, lazily sway her hips in time to the music coming from the radio.

He was relieved and happy to see that she had almost become her old self; she had even started going to the market on her own, which Sammie hoped was a sign that perhaps she was finally overcoming her depression.

The aftermath of Mickie being rushed to hospital in such a life threatening condition, had been a dreadful time for everyone, but it had seemed to hit Lucy especially hard. For a worrying period of time, nothing Sammie, or anyone else said, or did to try and ease her pain, seemed to make any difference to her frame of mind; the world for her had become a terrible cruel place. For a woman who had always endured adversity with such strength and humour, it had been heartbreaking for those who cared for her, to see her so broken.

For Sammie, it had been like torture; the burden of his guilty secret weighed heavy on him, especially after his decision to visit Rob in prison. He would come back from Wandsworth to find Lucy sitting motionless in the dull, unlit kitchen, staring out at the darkening sky, seemingly unmoved by her beloved cat's pathetic pleas for attention, and food. He would look down at the empty bowl on the floor, and perceive it as sad, tangible proof of how low Lucy had fallen; even poor Dizzy's cries of hunger seemed unable to lift her from her gloom.

In these last months, in a vain attempt to ease his guilty conscience, he had begun to drink more, but even this brought no response from Lucy, if indeed she noticed at all. Yet, through all of this, he had loved and cared for her as best he could: cooked the food, of which she ate little, and made sure she felt safe. But no matter how much he drank, he could never see a time when he could unburden himself and confess Rob's real identity to Lucy; it just didn't seem possible.

Just as he was thinking this misery was going be forever, Mickie finally came home from the hospital, and to his delight, Sammie saw things immediately change for the better. For Lucy, the clouds seemed to lift with every day that Mickie got stronger; she lost herself in caring for the boy, and in turn, her own strength and fight seemed to echo Mickie's return to health.

It was only then that Sammie allowed himself to feel a little more hopeful, like the sun had got a little brighter. And when, to his further delight, Lucy had begun to gently scold him again, he dared to feel that the woman he loved was perhaps no longer lost to him.

At that very moment, as if on cue, Lucy turned and looked over her glasses at him.

"Sammie Turner, you gonna sit there drinkin and dreamin all evenin, while mi over here slavin away, dry as a bone, and cravin a drop of Guinness?"

Sammie grinned, and instantly got up and went to the cupboard to fetch a bottle of stout. He flicked off the cap, and then after carefully and gently pouring the foaming black liquid into a glass, he brought it to Lucy. She took a long, slow mouthful, savouring every drop, and then placed the glass on the worktop.

"Thank you, darlin," she said, smiling at him.

Sammie again flashed a wide grin, and wrapped his big arms around her.

"Steady, bwoy," she said. "You gonna have all my hard work on the floor."

But he continued to embrace her and nuzzle into her neck, until she responded to his affection by taking his face in her hands, and kissing him tenderly on the mouth.

"Now, let me be bwoy," she said, turning back to her cooking. "Mi don't want tings to spoil." And then, as an afterthought, she added:

"You tink we should get some more beer?"

"Sure, darlin, mi goin down to get some tobacco, anyway."

Still smiling, Sammie left the house and strolled down the street towards the corner shop. But as he approached the spot, where on that fateful day everything became a nightmare, his smile began to fade, and he couldn't help feeling a stab of guilt.

He knew in his heart that none of this was his fault, but he couldn't seem to rid himself of the feeling that his deceit would be his undoing. Everyday he considered whether he was being a fool in caring what happened to Rob, and how long he could continue without everything he loved falling apart.

He was still brooding over his dilemma when he reached the shop and pushed open the door. To his surprise, he saw Billy waiting at the counter, laden down with two four-packs of Stella lager. Billy, however, was too interested in what was going on with the customer currently being served to notice anybody coming in. Sammie went and picked four bottles of Guinness from the shelf, and then stood silently watching the little scenario being played out at the counter.

Standing in front of Billy was an elderly man who was apparently attempting to buy cigarettes; however, he seemed to be somewhat confused about where on his person he had secreted his money, and was becoming a little anxious.

"I'm sorry, son," he said to the young Asian shopkeeper. "I'm sure I ad it when I left the ouse. It's got to be ere somewhere."

"Och, yer not pullin that one again, are ye Ron?" said Billy, putting his beer on the counter. "Tch, honestly, what are ye like?"

The old man looked open-mouthed, from Billy to the Asian man, obviously aghast at the accusation.

"No, no, I've got money, I can pay, it's just . . . "

Billy rolled his eyes, and laughed.

"Ah'm kiddin, Ron, ah'm kiddin," he said, and then turned to the Asian boy, who was biting his lip, and trying not to laugh.

"Put the fags on my bill, and Ron can sort me out later."

"Aw, son that's very good of you," said Ron, and then giving the Asian boy a mischievous look, he added:

"And im a Jock an all."

"Hey don't push yer luck, pal," said Billy, slipping the cigarettes into the old man's pocket. "And remember, ah know where ye live."

The little man gave Billy a big crooked grin, said his goodbyes, and then shuffled towards the door. It was when he turned to watch the old man leave, that Billy became aware of Sammie.

"Oh, hiya, Sammie. How ye doin? Ah didn't see ye come in."

"Oh mi just pickin up some Guinness for Luce."

Billy acknowledged this with a nod of his head, but said nothing more.

Sammie then walked over to the counter, where without further comment, the two men paid for their goods and left the shop.

As they walked slowly back to the house, Billy sensed that Sammie was uneasy about something.

"You okay, Sammie?"

"Yeah, man," replied the big man not too convincingly.

Billy gave him a sideways glance.

Lucy okay?"

"Yeah, yeah, man."

Billy again gave him a look, and then stopped, and to Sammie's surprise, sat down on the low wall in front of one of the houses.

"Okay, Sammie," he said, looking directly up into the old man's eyes, "let's have it."

Sammie made a face, shrugged his shoulders, and pretended to be confused by Billy's statement. But as Billy continued to stare silently up at him, he somehow knew that here and now was the time to speak; and if there was anybody he thought would be the right person to open his heart to, it was Billy. Sammie knew him to be tough, and nobody's fool, but he had also proven time and again that he had a heart, as was evident in the kindness he had just shown to the old man.

Sammie sat on the wall beside Billy, and placing his carrier bag on the ground, took out his tobacco and papers, and began to roll a cigarette. He lit the cigarette, and with a deep sigh, blew a column of smoke into the cool night air.

"Mi been visitin the bwoy in prison," the words seemed to hang in the air for a time, before Billy responded.

"Ah know," said Billy, looking at the ground.

The big man's head swivelled slowly round; he wasn't sure he had heard clearly what Billy had just said.

"What?"

"Ah know," repeated Billy, looking into Sammie's puzzled face. "Yer man Shank came into the garage today lookin for Bee-Jay, and ah got the feelin he wanted to tell me somethin, but then he seemed to change his mind at the last minute. Anyway, when ah told him Bee-jay was in the café, he left, sayin he would go and find him. But when BeeJay came back from lunch, he told me Shank had asked him to fill me in on what it was he wanted to say. It seems he has a mate whose young brother is also doin a stretch in Wandsworth, and Shank had made a point of askin this mate if his brother would check out how Rob was doin."

"Shank apparently feels bad about what happened to Rob's mother; ah don't know why, as Bee-jay didn't say, and ah didn't ask. But this mate must owe Shank big time, because Shank more than insisted that this brother keep a friendly eye on Rob. It seems he feels partly responsible for how Rob was behavin on the day it all kicked off. Ah think that's why he couldn't tell me personally, but still wanted me to know."

Billy hesitated for a few heartbeats, to try and gauge Sammie's reaction to this information, but the big man had his head down, looking at the ground.

"Anyway," Billy continued. "It was during one of his conversations with this mate, that Shank happened to ask if Rob got any visitors, and the guy told him he only has two: his granny, who apparently comes every two weeks, and a big old black guy, who had begun to visit him regularly. Well, Sammie, after what ye told me about Harry and the boy, it didn't take a lot of workin out."

Sammie took a pull of his cigarette, but remained silent.

"Look Sammie," continued Billy. Ah'm no judge, and ye've obviously got yer own reasons for doin this, but ah . . . "

"He's Harry's son," interrupted Sammie, suddenly looking up. "That's the only reason mi have; and mi don't know if even that's good enough, but mi doin it anyway."

Billy sighed, and looked at the despair in the old man's eyes.

"Ah'm guessin ye haven't told Mrs McIntyre about this?"

Sammie frowned, and shook his big head.

"No, and it's tearin me up tinkin what might happen if mi try to explain."

They sat in silence for a time, and then Sammie took a final pull of his cigarette, and then threw the butt into the street.

"Mi cain't do it Billy, man," he said, suddenly standing up. "Mi cain't take the chance. How can mi tell Lucy and Mickie after all they been through. They wouldn't understand; mi don't even understand why mi doin it."

"Ah feel for ye, Sammie, ah really do," said Billy, looking up tenderly at the big man. But it's got to be your decision, and ah certainly won't say anythin; but ah really think ye might be underestimatin Mrs McIntyre, and Mickie. And remember, there's no rush; Rob's not goin anywhere, so ye've got plenty of time to decide. And now that everybody knows what a shit life the poor fucker had been dealt, maybe they'll think differently. Fuck, even ah feel for the boy, and ah wanted to kick him fuckin senseless."

Sammie stood silent, for a moment - Billy thought he resembled a bewildered Buddha - but then he sighed, and looked down at Billy, and said:

"Thanks, Billy; thanks for listenin, man."

"No worries, mate," said Billy, rising to his feet and placing a reassuring hand on the old man's arm. "Time, Sammie, ye've got to give it time. Come on, ah don't know about you, but ah could do with a drink."

They heard the laughter as soon as they came through the front door, and on entering the warmth of the kitchen, they found Lucy, Laura and Mickie, seated round the table.

"Oh, there ye are," said Mickie, rising from the table to shake Billy and Sammie by the hand. "Just in time for the bevvy as usual."

"Talkin about drink," said Billy, handing Mickie the bag of lager. "Stick these in the fridge, will ye, pal."

"Aye, right away, yer Majesty," said Mickie, bowing, and touching his forelock.

"Aw, gie me peace, and get on with it," replied Billy, grinning.

"Mi startin to tink you got lost," said Lucy, looking over her glasses at Sammie, whom she thought looked a little preoccupied.

"Oh, that was my fault, Mrs McIntyre," said Billy, "Ah was yakkin to somebody in the shop as usual. Oh, by the way, Mary will be another half an hour or so getting back from work, if that's all right."

Lucy smiled, and dismissed his concern with a wave of her hand. Billy gave her a hug, and then turning to Laura, he said in his best posh voice:

"So, Miss Taylor, I hear you're soon to have a lodger, eh, what?"

Laura stuck her nose in the air, and replied in equally crisp vowels:

"I certainly am, Mr Dunn, and looking forward to it immensely."

Billy laughed, and hugged her tight.

"That's great, darlin, ah'm so happy for ye both."

Mickie then returned from the fridge with a bottle of Champagne.

"Oh, aye," said Billy. "What's this in aid of, then?"

"Oh, quite a few things, actually," replied Mickie, starting to open the bottle.

Mary will be sorry she missed this," said Billy. "She loves a drop of fizzy." And then added with a grin: "Actually, she loves a drop of anythin."

Oh, don't worry," replied Mickie. "Ah wouldn't forget Mary, there's another bottle in the fridge."

The cork popped, and Mickie filled five glasses.

"Well," he said, holding up his glass. "This is just to say; ah'm a happy man, and the people standin round this table are the reason why. Ah want to thank all of ye for yer love and support durin the last few months. And ah want to give a special thanks to Mrs. McIntyre for helpin me organise this thank-you dinner, and for, as usual, cookin up a storm. Ah've had a lot of time recently to think about things, and . . . "

"Aw, naw! Are we ever goin to get to drink this?" Billy cut in, looking comically at his glass.

"Aye, very good," said Mickie, laughing. "Thanks, Billy, on the button as usual. But yer probably right ah was nearly getting maudlin there. But, apart from that, ah really have reasons to be happy. First of all, as ye all know, ah'm movin in with Laura, which is fantastic enough, but also, as ah've just found out, Laura's friend, Tim, has got a gallery interested in my paintings; which obviously ah'm very excited about, but also a wee bit nervous, as . . . "

"Still got a thirst here, pal," Billy again cut in, making everybody laugh.

"Awright, awright," said Mickie, grinning, "This really is the last bit, and ah like to think the icing on the cake; Sharon is bringing Mona down from Glasgow on Saturday, and she'll be staying with me and Laura for two whole weeks; and ah'm delighted."

At this point Laura gave him a questioning look, causing Mickie to quickly add:

"Obviously, what ah meant to say was, were both delighted. Sorry, darlin, just a wee bit nervous. And so, before my auld pal collapses through alcohol deficiency, ah'd just like to repeat; ah'm a happy man, and ah want to wish the same to all my friends, cheers."

Everyone lifted their glasses in a toast to Mickie, and happiness. And in the laughter and chatter that followed, and while Mickie hugged Laura, and then Lucy, Billy smiled, offered his hand to Sammie, and with a sly wink, said softly: "Time, Sammie, time."

Chapter 27

Situated in the middle of a short parade of shops on the opposite side of the street from the Raven, there was a dark, narrow alleyway which led back, the width of the building, to a lane that ran parallel to the street. The main daytime use of this alley was to give access to people delivering replacement stock to the shops storerooms, via the lane. At night, however, most people deemed both alley and lane too dark and forbidding to ever consider using them.

But for the bulky figure now lurking in the shadows a short distance in from the alley's entrance, it offered the ideal vantage point. For the short time Nazz had been keeping close watch on The Raven, the only visible sign of his presence was the occasional burning glow of his cigarette.

He had wanted to check things out before venturing towards the pub, and being ever cautious, he had approached the alley from the back using the lane. But after considering the situation for a few minutes more, he now decided the only way to do this, was to do it; and so, crushing his cigarette under the heel of his boot, he left the alley, and crossed the street.

On entering the pub, he stood briefly by the door, and thoroughly scanned the room. It didn't take him long, however, to ascertain his flash former associate was nowhere to be seen. Guessing the obvious reason for this, he checked out the sign for the gent's toilet, and then walked over to the bar and ordered a large Scotch.

As he waited for his drink to be served, he made use of the large mirror on the wall to subtly check out the big swarthy guy sitting next to him at the bar. While scanning the room, minutes before, Nazz had instantly taken notice of this man, mainly because of his size. But now, as he continued to gaze at him sitting hunched over his drink, seemingly deep in thought, he sensed there was something else about the big man that felt wrong; for the moment, however, he couldn't quite figure out why.

The young barman returned with his whiskey, and to Nazz's continuing bewilderment, again started grinning and nodding at him like they were long lost buddies. Nazz had noticed this when first ordering his drink, but hadn't thought too much about it, but now it was becoming weird. He kissed his teeth in irritation and scowled at the boy while thinking: *What the fuck is wrong with this fool?* But then the reason suddenly struck him: this must be Darryl, the youth who had given Shank the word about Toto.

This was indeed the reason. Although Darryl had never laid eyes on Nazz before, he had heard enough through the grapevine about Shank and the big scary looking bro with re-arranged nose, to realise that this had to be the man. And when Nazz had walked over to the bar, and Darryl had to look into that cold, scary face, it all became clear: this was the reason Shank had wanted him to call, if and when, he ever saw Toto again.

Guessing that something might be about to go down, Darryl had foolishly thought that he should make plain his allegiance, and when the big man had ordered his drink, Darryl had put on what he thought was his best street-bro act.

While Nazz was grateful for the information, the last thing he wanted right now was some delusional kid acting weird, and making some careless remark. To drive this point home, he placed a ten-pound note on the bar, and then glared, silent and stone-faced at the boy until his grin melted, and he quickly turned and went to the till to get the big man's change.

The boy had just sheepishly put the change back on the bar, when the door leading to the toilets opened, and through it came the hunched figure of Toto. As he walked slowly back to the table in the corner, Nazz watched him in the mirror, and was mildly amused to see that the little man seemed so solemn and preoccupied that he hadn't even noticed his nemesis standing at the bar.

Nazz coolly picked up his whiskey and change, and walking over to where Toto sat staring into his drink, he stood towering over him, his bulky frame casting a dark shadow across the table.

"Watcha!" he said, in a bright sarcastic tone.

Awakened from his gloom, Toto looked up, wide-eyed, to see Nazz smiling down at him with chilling intensity. He tried to speak, but his mouth only flapped wordlessly up and down. He could only gaze up in bewildered shock as Nazz continued to speak.

"We need to ave a word," he said, in the same, almost jolly tone. "So, drink up, asshole, were goin for a little walk."

With this, Nazz drained his glass, and placed it on the table. Toto, seemingly still frozen with fear, remained seated, his face an open-mouthed mask. He seemed unable to make his body respond to Nazz's demands, but the big man didn't fail to notice that Toto's eyes kept flicking towards something at the bar. Without turning round, Nazz sensed the recipient of this attention was the silent giant.

Nazz, not wasting anymore time, firmly gripped Toto by the arm and pulled him from his seat. The little man, now almost like a broken doll, gave no resistance and allowed Nazz to walk him towards the door.

Yannis, still sitting at the bar, never moved, and although Nazz still wasn't sure what the connection was, he was certain the big Greek was checking the action through the mirror.

Once outside, he marched the limp little man across the street and into the alley. Toto remained frozen silent, as Nazz, still with a firm grip on his arm, guided him to the far end of the alley, and into the moonlit lane.

"Don't kill me, man," Toto suddenly pleaded, finally finding his voice. "I can get money, man. I can pay you back."

Nazz clamped his hand around Toto's clammy neck.

"I aint gonna kiil ya. Do you seriously think I would risk gettin sent down for a fuckin weasel like you? You aint worth killin, but by the time I'm done, you're gonna wish I fuckin ad."

"Help me ya fuckers," cried Toto suddenly. "Where the fuck are ya?"

The little man's sudden, loud yelping cries alerted Nazz just in time, as the huge form of Yannis now appeared round the corner of the alley. He made a lunge at Nazz, but wasn't quite quick enough, for Nazz, who's instincts were always sharper than any opponent he had ever encountered, swung the limp Toto round, and pushed him into the path of the big Greek. This confused Yannis long enough for Nazz to land three lightning-fast, solid punches to the big Greeks throat. He then swept the wide-eyed Toto out of the way and proceeded to finish the job on Yannis, who was now gurgling like a baby, and holding his throat. Nazz head-butted the big Greek so hard, that the man's nose burst open like a geyser. And while the terrified Toto looked on, Nazz then took time to step back and deliver the already beaten Yannis, two sickening kicks to the groin. The big Greek sank to his knees, and Nazz gave him a final boot in the face, which sent him flat on his back.

Realising he had been set up, Nazz, now with renewed vengeance, once again turned his attention back to the trembling, terrified Toto. He slapped him a hard backhand slap across the face, and was about to add to the little man's pain, when he heard heavy footsteps running down the alley.

For what seemed like a long few seconds, Nazz dumbly gazed into the sneering faces of Ari the Gun, and his brute of a nephew, Demetri. He then turned back in astonishment to Toto, but before he had time to figure out what was going on, he heard a click, and then saw a blade flash in the moonlight. Demetri let out a roar, and stepping forward, swung the blade viciously at Nazz, but the big man instinctively swerved away from the curving arc of the blade, and brought a heavy boot down on Demetri's outstretched leg, just above the knee. There was an audible crack, and with a squeal of pain, the big Greek collapsed sideways onto the damp surface of the lane. Nazz then stamped on the hand holding the knife, causing it to skid against the wall, and then kicked Demetri repeatedly about the head, until he too lay blooded and still. Nazz's breathing was now heavy and rasping with effort and adrenaline, but he looked at Ari the Gun, and a wicked grin creased his face.

"Well, well, look who it is. How the fuck did you two weasels ever get together? It don't matter, really, cause this is where it ends. When I finish wiv you, shithead here is . . . "

Nazz didn't get to finish, for Toto, in a state of terrified lunacy, had grabbed the knife, leapt onto Nazz's back, and drew it lethally across the big man's throat.

Ari, astounded, watched as the big man, wide-eyed with confusion, and bleeding to death, sank to the ground with Toto still clinging to him like some deadly little animal. Blood was already soaking the little man's clothing, and forming a dark pool on the surface of the lane.

It took Ari a few minutes to get his head round what had just happened; he stood gaping at the scene, trying to get his brain to work. But then, ignoring Toto, he walked over and started to try and rouse his two minders into action. They were still in a badly dazed and confused state, but at Ari's urgent pleading, they eventually managed to struggle to their feet.

"Come on, come on," he hissed. "We've got to get out of here, now."

Yannis had to help the hobbling Demetri to walk, but within minutes, the three men had gone, leaving the pathetic stunned figure of Toto sitting on the dark cobbles of the lane.

With the knife still in his hand, and the big man's head on his blood drenched lap, he sat for some time gazing wide-eyed into the darkness. But then, suddenly realising what he had done, his face distorted in despair, and lowering his head to his chest, he began to silently weep.

The end

Blue Like Monday

Ian MacCabe is a Glasgow born artist and author, who's paintings are in private collections throughout the world. He lives in London, and this is his first novel.

Printed in Poland
by Amazon Fulfillment
Poland Sp. z o.o., Wrocław